Y0-BGW-134

SAPPHIRE STORM

Also from Christopher Rice and C. Travis Rice

C. Travis Rice
SAPPHIRE SUNSET: A Sapphire Cove Novel
SAPPHIRE SPRING: A Sapphire Cove Novel

Thrillers
A DENSITY OF SOULS
THE SNOW GARDEN
LIGHT BEFORE DAY
BLIND FALL
THE MOONLIT EARTH

Supernatural Thrillers
THE HEAVENS RISE
THE VINES
BONE MUSIC: A Burning Grill Thriller
BLOOD ECHO: A Burning Girl Thriller
BLOOD VICTORY: A Burning Girl Thriller
DECIMATE

Paranormal Romance
THE FLAME: A Desire Exchange Novella
THE SURRENDER GATE: A Desire Exchange Novel
KISS THE FLAME: A Desire Exchange Novella

Contemporary Romance
DANCE OF DESIRE
DESIRE & ICE: A MacKenzie Family Novella

With Anne Rice
RAMSES THE DAMNED: THE PASSION OF CLEOPATRA
RAMSES THE DAMNED: THE REIGN OF OSIRIS

SAPPHIRE STORM

Sapphire Cove, Book 3

Christopher Rice
Writing As
C. Travis Rice

Sapphire Storm
By Christopher Rice writing as C. Travis Rice

Copyright 2023 Christopher Rice
ISBN: 978-1-957568-25-6

Published by Blue Box Press, an imprint of Evil Eye Concepts, Incorporated

All rights reserved. No part of this book may be reproduced, scanned, or distributed in any printed or electronic form without permission. Please do not participate in or encourage piracy of copyrighted materials in violation of the author's rights.

This is a work of fiction. Names, places, characters and incidents are the product of the author's imagination and are fictitious. Any resemblance to actual persons, living or dead, events or establishments is solely coincidental.

Acknowledgments from the Author

A huge thank you, as always, to the amazing team at Blue Box Press for being the perfect home for this series. Liz Berry, Jillian Stein, and M.J. Rose, along with the amazing Kim Guidroz, Kasi Alexander, Stacey Tardif and Asha Hossain. A big shout out to Ann-Marie Nieves and Tanaka Kangara.

A big thank you to Jenna Jiampietro, the guest relations manager at Montage Laguna Beach, for giving me an amazing backstage tour and for introducing me to the incredibly talented Lee Smith, their executive pastry chef. Lee helped design "Point Loma"—the dessert, not the landmass—and assisted me in giving reality and depth to Ethan's background as a pastry chef with an international résumé.

One of the many perks of being best friends with the amazingly talented writer Eric Shaw Quinn is that he is also a genius at plotting and story development. He gave this one a transformative read, and I'll be forever grateful for it. A reminder that we have a weekly podcast called "TDPS Presents CHRISTOPHER & ERIC" which you can find on your podcast platform of choice or at:

www.TheDinnerPartyShow.com.

You should also read his *Write Murder* mystery series because it's as funny as he is.

Author's Note

Dear Reader,

This is my third visit to Sapphire Cove. If it's your first, it's the perfect place to start. In these pages, readers will meet Ethan Blake and Roman Walker for the first time. My hope is that every entry in the series transports you to the same sparkling, beautiful coastal paradise where men find the courage to release the shame that blocks their hearts' desires.

Shortly before I began writing this book, I experienced a profound loss. My mother, one of my best friends, as well as a brilliant colleague and business partner, died suddenly at the age of eighty due to complications from a stroke. And so it should surprise no one that while SAPPHIRE STORM is very much a romance novel, some of the characters within its pages are dealing with grief in its many forms, specifically grief caused by the sudden loss of a loved one. Readers with sensitivities to those themes should be advised.

If this is a return trip for you, I want to thank you for making the journey with me this far, and I promise you many more Sapphire Cove stories to come. If it's your first visit, welcome to Sapphire Cove. As I always tell guests, you can check in at any time.

xo,

C. Travis Rice

1

Someone was crying in Ethan's pastry kitchen.

He'd lived all over the world, trained in some of the finest restaurants and hotels on the planet. At forty-three, he'd finally landed his dream job, head pastry chef at an exclusive resort. He knew full well that most professional kitchens were nonstop hives of frenzied activity, places of frequent injuries and near infernos.

Still, it was out of the ordinary to discover one of your team members rocking back and forth on her knees in front of the oven as if the Virgin Mary had just appeared to her in the window. And insulted her cooking.

But that was exactly the sight that greeted Ethan when he arrived at Sapphire Cove on Saturday morning.

He noted the sharp scent of burning sugar and diagnosed the scene instantly. Carefully, he crouched down beside his distraught junior chef.

"I'm an idiot and I should die!" Stephanie Powell wailed.

The young woman weighed almost nothing soaking wet, but his attempts to bring her to her feet with several gentle tugs on her forearm all failed. "You're not an idiot," he said, "and I'd very much appreciate it if you lived as I enjoy working with you."

"Oh my God. It stinks. Everyone's going to *hate* me."

Indeed, she'd made a rookie mistake, but he saw no point in pouring salt on the wound. Once she'd stood of her own volition, he said, "We'll call engineering and see if there's a side panel they can remove it through. Now please. Let's not descend into a shame spiral over this."

Stephanie sniffled, then wiped her nose with the tissue Ethan had yanked from a nearby box. "I just wanted to make everybody some pudding, and I thought if I put it in the oven for a bit, I could finish it off with a nice crust."

"Yes, well, it sounds like you *jammed* it in the oven, and so word to the wise, if the pan doesn't quite fit at first, don't risk it. There's a good chance it'll expand during the cook cycle and be impossible to get out. Also, while I do realize we work in a bit of a bubble here in the pastry kitchen, most grown-ups don't have pudding for breakfast."

Stephanie grabbed him by his shoulders. "Please fire me, Chef. If you don't, everyone'll give me a terrible nickname over this. Like Puddin'. Or Bernie. Or Crusty."

"No one's going to give you a nickname. We don't do nicknames here."

"Morning, Puff Pastry!" Chloe Simmons bellowed as she threw open the door to the pastry kitchen. The head chef's work on the breakfast buffet had left her with a sweaty brow and cheeks so flushed they almost matched the flame red curls spilling out from under the black handkerchief she was using as a headband.

"She's main kitchen," Ethan whispered to Stephanie. "She doesn't count."

Chloe barged her way in. "Jonas is looking for you, Ethan. *Woah.* Stinks in here! You guys puttin' crude oil in the profiteroles now?" Dramatically waving one arm in front of her face, she zeroed in on the offending oven. "Jammed it in, did yah? Smart! This should only set you guys back like, what, a day?"

Leaving Stephanie with instructions to call engineering and several more assurances that her career wasn't over, he stepped out into the main kitchen, where breakfast buffet items were being busily prepared on all sides of him.

A summons to the office of the resort's special events director was usually serious business, and he intended to make haste.

Matching him step for step, Chloe quietly said, "You need to fire her. Kitchens are all stress all the time. She's not up to it."

"A correction, my dear Chloe. *Your* kitchen is all stress all the time. My little corner of Sapphire Cove is a place of artistry and wonder, where dazzling creations are assembled over a period of days while your staff tears each other apart over who's going to haul six hundred pounds of scrambled eggs up to the breakfast buffet."

"She doesn't know how an oven works, Ethan. And she's crying at ten a.m. Give her the boot or you'll pay for it, promise."

"Nonsense. Her problem was one of scale and mathematics. I made a similar mistake when I was her age, only the hotel where I was working was an old Scottish castle and the ovens were wood fired from the cellar. It took seventy-two hours to get them back on. Nobody fired me."

"Probably because you were the cutest one there."

Ethan stopped and turned to face her. "A question, Chloe. Are you following me right now because you know I'm a better chef and you're desperate to learn from my brilliance?"

She grinned and pinched him on the cheek. She loved their regular sparring as much as he did. Like so many people who made professional cuisine their profession, adrenaline and edge drove her.

"A word of warning, brother," she said. "Whatever Jonas wants to talk to you about, it's the Peyton wedding, so expect everyone to be out of their minds because that event's already making people..." She finished off the sentence by twirling a finger through the air next to her ear.

"I appreciate it," he answered sincerely.

And he did.

Diana Peyton, one of the most famous actresses in the world, had booked two of the hotel's ballrooms for her daughter Rachel's wedding in a little over a month. Not only would it be the biggest event on the calendar that year, it would be one of the biggest in the hotel's history. Two celebrities were involved, and while the mother was considerably more famous than the daughter, the daughter had won a Tony a few months before and was widely considered the better actress of the two. Three different entertainment shows were scheduled to cover the event, and so many celebrities were expected to attend there were plans to set up a red carpet in the hotel's motor court.

In the marble-floored lobby, beneath its three-tiered crystal chandelier, Ethan wound his way through guests departing the breakfast buffet. Families redolent of freshly applied sunscreen made their way toward the hotel's sparkling pool or the cliff-hugging staircase leading to the resort's little crescent of private beach. The brassy, sun-filled energy of Sapphire Cove's lobby made for a welcome change of pace from the resorts he'd worked at over the past few years, five-starred affairs where the guests and staff rarely spoke above an aristocratic whisper.

When his phone vibrated in his pants pocket, he saw the caller was Donnie Bascombe, the good friend he'd been putting off with curt text messages all morning. Fifteen years of friendship had taught him there was no deflecting Donnie when he'd scented a bone. Worse, management and staff used their personal cell phones too often for Ethan to silence his during work.

"I told you I'd call you later," Ethan said by way of answering.

"Which is total BS, so give me the update, dude. Come on. You've been on the apps three weeks. You've gotta have something cooking. What's happening with the kid who—"

"Three weeks," Ethan cut him off, "in which all of my worst suspicions about them have been confirmed. Actually, make that *re*confirmed. They remain a soul-killing place where all other metrics of success fall before the sword of body fat percentages, creating a suffocating meat market in which the facts of who you are matter far less than how you look in a bathroom mirror."

"So the Beach Boy kid shot you down?"

Ethan turned to the nearest wall and lowered his voice to an angry whisper. "Try wasted my time. BeachBoy24 and I chatted for a week, and when I tried to get him to agree to an actual coffee date, he demanded to see a shirtless selfie. I refused at first, and when I finally caved his response was—and I'm quoting now—'Yikes. No thanks, Gramps. Over and out.'"

After a brief, tense silence, Donnie said, "Well, did you lie about your age?"

"Oh, for Christ's sake," Ethan barked. "I'm one of the only men out there who *isn't* lying about his age." Shooting glances in every direction to make sure his outburst hadn't earned him any lingering stares from guests, Ethan managed a deep breath. "Donnie, you know I love you more than baked Alaska, but do not—I repeat, do *not*—pressure me to get on the apps again. This was little more than a degrading exercise that insulted both my intelligence and my integrity."

His friend's exhale whistled through his teeth. "Man, I wish I was a bottom 'cause I'd probably be so turned on by your anger right now."

"I'm serious. Stay out of my dating life. Please."

"You don't *have* a dating life, Blake. That was the point. I just wanted you to get out of that apartment sometime. All you do is work."

"Exactly. I love what I do, and I've worked my entire life to get to a place where I can do nothing but work."

"Hey, I love what I do too, but I don't need to do it all the time."

"You make porn. You *can't* do it all the time because half of your models don't show."

"All right, easy, Chef Boyardee. I'll have you know Parker Hunter's one of the most professional studios in the business."

"Please stop deflecting. I need you to hear me on this. Do not pressure me to get on the apps again. I only did this to shut you up and look how it played out."

A chair squeaked on Donnie's end of the line, probably because he'd pushed himself back from his desk so he could make the big hand gestures he always did when he was worked up. "Look, I didn't say anything about *dating*. I said have fun. Do what I do. Book a guest appearance for some married couple who both want to throw their legs in the air at the same time. Find a hot little number at the hotel next door and meet him in a public restroom or something."

Ethan groaned. "Because all of that sounds like my style, Sex Monster."

"Fine. Hook up in your car then. But it's new, so, you know, be careful of the seats."

"I'm ten years older than you. I have had my fun. If I'm going to spend time on this area of my life, I want it to be for something serious. Not deranged role-play with a two-dimensional square on a dating app who's probably some broken basement dweller with a row of trophy skulls above his desk."

"All right, well I think you're giving up too soon. On the apps, not ButtBoy69 or whatever his fake name was."

Ethan said, "We have exhausted this conversation's potential. Let us move on now to the subject of my visit this week. Have you decided where you want me to take you to dinner yet?"

"Someplace really expensive. And you'll be nicer to me while you're here, right? 'Cause isn't the whole point of this trip to pay me back for getting you your dream job?"

"You got me a meeting with the hotel's general manager. Not quite the same thing as getting me the job. But to answer your question, yes, the spirit of the trip will be one of enormous gratitude."

"Excellent," Donnie said, tone dripping with self-satisfaction. "'Cause it's about time."

"*Provided* you leave me alone about dating apps from now until the end of humanity."

"Deal."

When the call ended, Ethan found himself staring down at his phone, wondering if he should be more charitable in his description of Donnie's contributions to his recent career developments.

His good friend was close with Sapphire Cove's general manager and director of security, who were also a happily engaged couple, and so he'd strongly encouraged both men to sample Ethan's work during a visit to London earlier that year, back when he was still working under the executive pastry chef at the Mandarin Oriental Hyde Park. There, he'd wowed them with a French wedding cake so tall Connor Harcourt and Logan Murdoch had struggled to see each other over the pyramid of profiteroles he'd proudly set between them. They'd walked away fans, which had nicely set the stage for an interview once Ethan started looking for a new gig back in the US. That the interview would also yield the biggest promotion of Ethan's career was not something he'd been expecting when he first sat down with Connor over Zoom.

And maybe he'd been too hard on Donnie in general, but reliving the sting of BeachBoy24's rejection had brought unwelcome blood rushing to his face.

He was no stranger to the shallow cruelty queer men could show each other on the Internet. But the young man's rebuff had been startlingly decisive and swift. A few days of messages followed by longer and more intimate texts, all down the drain in an instant thanks to a single photograph that didn't make the cut. A picture in which he hadn't used clever tricks or computer-generated effects to hide new truths about his body.

There'd been a time in his life when he could stop a room just by entering it, when he'd had every muscle that might have sealed the deal with BeachBoy24. He'd also been BeachBoy24's age at the time. And considerably less focused on the career that eventually brought him happiness and fulfillment.

He'd prepared to get older. He hadn't been prepared to be erased. In certain circles, largely populated by adolescent nincompoops, they seemed to go hand in hand, and so he preferred to stick to worlds where his enduring talents and attributes were valued above all others—worlds like Sapphire Cove.

2

A few minutes later, Ethan was knocking on the door of the special events director's office, which sat in a little corridor of the hotel next to the conference center, separate from the other management offices.

"Come in," Jonas Jacobs answered.

When he peered around the door, he saw his direct supervisor sitting behind the desk, staring wide-eyed at his laptop. Standing next to him, also riveted by whatever was on screen, was Connor Harcourt, the hotel's general manager. The two men made for a study in contrasts. Jonas was Ethan's age, his head a dark bald dome, with wire-rimmed glasses that gave him a studious air. As always, his pocket square matched his tie; today they were both purple. The hotel's GM, on the other hand, was about five foot four with a shock of bright blond hair and round blue eyes and Casper the Ghost skin. It amused Ethan to no end that the most powerful person on the property was also one of the shortest on staff, a *sparkly little ass kicker*, as Chloe often referred to him with an admiring smile.

"Forgive me. I hope I didn't interrupt," Ethan asked.

Connor stood up like a gun had gone off. Jonas snapped the laptop shut with one hand.

Had they been looking at porn? Doubtful given what professionals both men were.

"No, please. Have a seat," Connor said with a big, forced smile.

Ethan complied. To hear others tell it, Jonas's office resembled what most of the hotel looked like before its big renovation a few years back. Puddling drapes and Louis XIV furniture. None of the clean white surfaces and modern sculpture pieces that filled the corridors beyond.

"We know you already have a really busy day ahead. But we have to add something to your schedule, I'm afraid."

"About the Peyton wedding," Ethan said. "Of course."

Connor nodded and gestured for Jonas to fill in the rest. The event director's voice was a bass counterpoint to Connor Harcourt's high-pitched one. "We've had some concerns from their team about the wedding cake, apparently. They'd like to try some new samples."

Ethan nodded. He'd seen this coming, but it wasn't his place to object. One challenge of celebrity weddings was how detached the bride and groom were from the actual planning, which meant they often brought things to a halt—sometimes at the last minute—over choices their underlings had made weeks before. Thank God they still had a month to go.

"So is the tasting with Diana Peyton or her daughter?" Ethan asked.

He rarely got starstruck, but Diana Peyton was a household name. When he was a little boy, his mother had never missed an episode of *Santa Monica*, the trashy nighttime soap that had turned the woman into a world-famous celebrity. For multiple seasons, she'd played the head of a powerful advertising firm whose workdays consisted of storming into conference rooms in dazzling sequined dresses and firing people, a fact that had once prompted young Ethan to ask his mother how the advertising firm could stay so successful when a senior employee was dramatically shown the door every week and for infractions like attempted murder or kidnapping babies out of their cradles. She'd been beautiful, for sure, the kind of TV star whose hairstyles influenced young women all over the country, but she'd never been very good.

Connor and Jonas exchanged a look. "Neither, I'm afraid," Jonas finally said. "You'll be meeting someone they're calling…a nutrition and diet expert."

"Of course. Not to complicate this further," Ethan said, "but if the issue is that the bride and groom aren't happy with the selection, we should make every effort to get samples to them directly. Would you like me to conduct a tasting at their home? Or we could package something and have it sent over."

"They're pretty insistent on this meeting," Jonas said, then exchanged another look with their boss.

"And," Ethan said after a tense silence, "if I may say so myself, you both seem pretty uncomfortable about it. So, please, share your concerns."

"He's a trainer!" Connor blurted out. "Their big, fancy nutrition expert was a *trainer* up until, like, five minutes ago."

Smirking, Jonas added, "Now, he worked at Apex in West Hollywood less than a year ago, which is a pretty nice gym. And probably where he hooked up with the Peytons. But still, Connor's point remains the same."

Jonas's guess sounded correct. Apex was one of the most exclusive gym chains in the world. Ethan had pumped iron at a couple of its locations in London and New York, but always as the guest of a friend who could afford it. Over the years, he'd read a few magazine write-ups of the West Hollywood location, a two-story glass and chrome palace on the Sunset Strip, depicting the place as a see-and-be-seen magnet for A-list celebrities looking to tone up before their next big role.

"Does he have any kind of background in nutrition?" Ethan asked. "Any degrees?"

Jonas said, "I did some digging and found a former website he had for personal training services. It mentioned some time studying kinesiology at Cal Poly San Luis Obispo. But there wasn't even a degree for *that* listed."

Ethan smiled. "I see. So you're afraid I'm going to be lectured on how to make a wedding cake by someone who might not know what he's talking about and you're concerned my response might be less than professional."

Connor nodded. "You've been an absolute prince since you started working here, Ethan. Truly. But the reason you got this job is because your predecessor rammed a room service cart into a wall five times in a row because someone told him his lemon meringue pie was too tart."

Ethan laughed. "Mine is a business of big egos, for sure. But trust me when I say I'd never act in an intemperate manner in any professional situation. Much less around an event of this importance. And with this many strong personalities already in play."

Beaming with gratitude, Connor bowed his head in silent thanks.

"Good," Jonas said, "because we think the guy's sleeping with

Diana Peyton."

Connor raised one hand at his events director. "Jonas, come on now. We don't know that for sure."

Eyes locked on Ethan, Jonas said, "Roman Walker is hot as a desert wildfire. Almost eight hundred thousand Instagram followers and over a million on TikTok, with views through the roof. And apparently he lives in her big mansion down in Laguna, the Castle by the Sea. I had the concierge make some calls around town, and it seems this *trainer* drives everywhere in a four-door Bentley that's the cost of a house in any state that's not California. Make of that information what you will, but my verdict is boy toy."

"I see," Ethan said, trying to contain his laughter. "And would his social media profiles be what you gentlemen were looking at on the computer when I came in?"

Jonas and Connor both bowed their heads and then muttered, "Yes" in unison.

There was a brief silence before Jonas popped open the laptop again. Connor and Ethan both sprang behind his desk like horny teenagers.

He wanted to be unimpressed by what he saw. In Ethan's opinion, most people mistook the genetic advantages of youth for physical beauty. Baby smooth skin, bodies kept slender by youthful, humming metabolisms—these were not the same things as a facial structure that looked composed by the gods or a V-shaped torso that suggested hours of strenuous gym time. Roman Walker had both of these things.

Composed by the gods. It was a perfect description of the images Jonas was scrolling through.

At first Ethan blamed the preponderance of Speedo-encased butt shots for the electric tension in the sides of his neck. He was a hopeless ass man and always had been. And while he figured they were being treated to a fair amount of Facetune and Photoshop, what leapt out from the screen was flawless skin and perfectly proportioned muscles and penetrating hazel eyes that looked incapable of hiding emotion. The young man had to be about six foot three, olive skinned, his black hair styled in a long, layered fringe with a low fade that highlighted his muscular neck. In many of the images, the social media star and trainer to one of the most famous actresses in the world flashed a perfect smile that could have sold everything from tooth whitener to car insurance.

"Well," Connor finally said, "at least he'll be something to look at if he turns out to be a condescending poseur."

Before he could memorize the image of Roman Walker gazing into the cameras as shower water sluiced down the back of his neck and across his perfect chest, Ethan walked out from behind Jonas's desk.

"Gentlemen," he said firmly, standing at attention, "rest assured, I will handle this meeting with absolute professionalism. And I must say I appreciate your cautions here. Truly. But I suffered the mean streets of New York City with barely a penny to my name without ever losing my cool, and my reward is that today I'm senior staff at one of the *finest* and most well-run resorts on the face of this great planet where I'm honored to spend my days working alongside extraordinary men like the two of you." Connor blushed. Jonas nodded deeply and smiled. "In other words, I can handle some arrogant little *fitfluencer* who thinks he's hot shit 'cause he's got a rich sugar momma."

"All right," Connor said. "If you charm Roman Walker the way you charm everyone else, things should be okay."

Ethan rose, gave them both a deep bow, then headed for the door, a skip in his step. Maybe it was the scandals the hotel had survived, or maybe it was the fact that queer men occupied positions of power throughout the resort, but there was a sense of camaraderie at Sapphire Cove that hadn't existed in any of his other places of employment. He'd had mentors during his career, but those relationships were usually one-on-one, little islands of refuge in environments of relentless competition and stress.

At Sapphire Cove, it felt like everyone had his back. A refreshing change of pace.

3

At 7:30 p.m. on the dot, Ethan knocked on the door to Sapphire Cove's penthouse suite.

"It's open," boomed a youthful voice in response.

Ethan entered.

On the other side of a black lacquer dining table, Roman Walker turned from the open deck door. In response to Ethan's solicitous smile, he raised one dark eyebrow and wet his full lips with the tip of his tongue.

Night was minutes away from taking hold of the horizon outside, and the two-room suite was filled with pillar candles inside cylinder vases. In their flickering light, the cake slices spread across the table on bone china plates looked like they were melting.

When the young man took a step away from the taffeta drape fluttering in the ocean breezes, the light from the chandelier over the dining table revealed subtle gold highlights in his brushed-forward hair that matched the stud in his left ear. The thick choker around his throat looked like a bronzed collection of little finger bones.

He wore some designer's lusty take on a varsity letterman's jacket, snugger than any high school would allow. Despite its shiny leather, the black and white team number patches on the sleeves triggered years of frustrated adolescent fantasies Ethan had cultivated while repressing his sexuality at a conservative Southern high school where football was king. His black jeans looked poured on, and Ethan knew if he let his eyes drop below the guy's waistline, he'd encounter a well-highlighted bulge. But when he stopped himself short, he ended up staring at a band of flat, tan stomach visible above the man's shining belt buckle. He was either shirtless underneath the jacket or wearing a midriff shirt.

There was one other fact about the scene before him that was far more significant than the details of his body—Roman Walker was alone.

No sign of the wedding planner Ethan had met with several times; no gaggle of friends and assorted hangers-on whose presence would justify the champagne bucket at one end of the dining table.

A champagne bucket accompanied by two flutes.

Danger, Will Robinson, Ethan thought instantly.

There had been a time in his life when he'd regularly entered hotel rooms with strange—sometimes threatening—men, and it had left him with a set of spidey senses for the presence of an agenda that went beyond even the cautions his boss and supervisor had given him earlier that day. He sensed one now, straightened, and left the door open behind him as he entered the room.

Strengthening his smile, he stepped forward firmly and extended his hand. "Good evening, Mr. Walker. I'm Ethan Blake, the hotel's executive pastry chef. I'm so grateful you were able to come out this evening, and I'm so very sorry if some of our earlier samples weren't to the liking of our bride and groom. I'm sure we'll come up with something they'll just adore."

Gazing into his eyes with unnerving intensity, shaking his hand as if their joined arms were stuck in molasses, Roman Walker said, "Oh, yeah, this isn't about them. I wanted to meet you in person. You know, get a sense of the man behind the cake." His voice sounded breathy but distant. Like an attempt at seduction mired in distraction.

"Apologies if I misunderstood."

"I mean, don't get me wrong. I want to make sure you're working your absolute hardest." Roman's eyes scanned Ethan's body, traveling low enough to make clear that yes, this had been some attempt at bad porn dialogue.

Ethan smiled. "Rest assured, this will be one of the finest wedding cakes I've ever made."

"Close that." The young man jerked his head in the direction from which Ethan had just come, then wet his lips with the tip of his tongue.

The order was both brusque and inappropriate, but Roman Walker's tone and drowsy half smile suggested Ethan would be happy with the end result once he complied; Ethan felt otherwise.

"Perhaps we leave it open a little, if you don't mind. The room tends to get a bit warm, especially if it's been unoccupied all day. And sugar heats up the blood, as I'm sure you well know."

"Sugar is poison," he said. "But sometimes poison can be addictive, right?"

"One way of putting it. Have you had a chance to try any of the samples?"

Was Roman's sudden glare meant to be seductive? Even if it wasn't, Ethan thought it best to swiftly put some distance between it and him by walking along the edge of the table and taking up a position a few paces away.

"No," Roman finally said. "I was waiting for you to lay it all out for me, big man." The fitfluencer leaned against the edge of the table and looked from Ethan to the cake slices. *Big man. Sugar is poison.* Flirting, or making a dig about Ethan's weight? Ethan was pretty regular with his gym time, but his abdomen had developed a mind of its own when he turned thirty-five, and no amount of sit-ups had been able to restore the washboard stomach of his youth. When he saw Ethan's blank expression, Roman laughed, an awkward, nasally sound that didn't match the poised perfection of the rest of him. "Sorry," he said quickly, "you just, uh. I'm a little nervous."

"Oh, you shouldn't be, Mr. Walker. Rest assured, all the resources of this hotel are at your disposal. We'll make sure your employers are nothing but pleased, I guarantee it."

"No, I mean about you, Mr. Blake. You look as good as you do on TV."

"Oh, I see," he said, realization dawning. "*Cake Face*, I take it."

Roman nodded, resting his hip against the edge of the table. "You were too hard on that girl from Minnesota, though. Her cake totally looked like Eleanor Roosevelt."

"Eleanor Roosevelt in a tornado, perhaps."

"Whatever. I was really into it."

"The cake or the show?" he asked.

"You," Roman said.

Ethan swallowed. "Thank you. I did it as a favor for a friend I used to work with. It was supposed to be a web series. I never expected Netflix to pick it up."

Roman took several steps toward him. "Hey, now. It was educational. For some of us, at least. I mean, I know way more about a bunch of our old presidents than I did before."

The show had required its contestants to make cakes that looked like famous dead people while baking and bickering and getting obnoxiously drunk inside a warehouse decked out like a cheap spaceship. Ethan had been a judge for the "Grand Old Pavlovas" episode, in which the players were required to capture the visages of famous pre-Eisenhower-era political figures, and the season finale in which the winner had been declared. If Roman thought *Cake Face* was designed to inform, he'd probably skipped the "It's Buttercream, Bitch" episode, in which the entries had to be fashioned after '90s pop stars. Although, given his age, maybe that would have been an education for him too.

"I never thought about it that way."

"Also, you look good on TV." Roman ran his finger through one of the slices, scooping up a dollop of icing on one finger. "But you'd look good anywhere." He sucked the icing off gently.

Is this kid for real? Ethan thought, even as he felt an involuntary stirring down below.

Was it remotely possible a fitfluencer drowning in sexual attention had become so smitten with him after his brief appearance on a lousy reality baking show that he'd staged this meeting just to get him alone in a hotel room? The notion was absurd, but for some reason, Roman Walker expected him to believe it. It didn't matter. The man was entirely too young and directly associated with one of Ethan's biggest jobs that year, which rendered him epically off-limits. What the meeting needed was a quick change of tone. As a seasoned hotel employee, he'd long ago learned the best method for deflecting an unwanted advance—change the subject to a nonsexual topic that made the guest feel important.

"You know, I could use your help with something, Mr. Walker," Ethan proclaimed.

"Call me Roman," he said.

"Roman, then. I'm not sure if anyone's told you this, but I have a specialty for weddings. Other than the cake, of course. It's a customized dessert I make out of one of the couple's favorite memories."

Roman shook his head gently. "A dessert made of *memories*? I don't get it."

"I assemble something unique using a bouquet of flavors that reminds them of the moment they fell in love or got engaged, or whatever moment they choose. But I can't do it without a meeting or a call. We've had trouble getting either of them on the books. Maybe you could help."

"Rachel won't be home from New York until Monday. And she'll only be here for a few days before she heads back."

"Perhaps she could come in then? Or the groom, if she's too busy? Scott Bryant, I believe, is his name."

Studying the cake slices next to them, Roman nodded and rolled his eyes. Did the topic of the wedding they were allegedly there to plan bore him? Or did the groom's name leave a bad taste in his mouth? "I'll see what I can do," he said, then, more aggressively this time, he stuck his finger in another slice and popped a dollop of icing into his mouth with none of the seductiveness of before.

Ethan turned to the table. "All right. Why don't I take us through the samples one by one? It looks like we've got a bunch of forks here if you'd rather not use the same one. Although, if I've done my job, you won't leave any bite behind. Okay, so right here we have—"

There was a loud thud behind him.

Ethan turned.

Roman had moved to the room's door and closed it firmly. Now he was leaning his back against it. "Sorry," he said, "I was listening. Promise. Just...open doors make me nervous."

Well, sexual harassment makes me angry, Ethan thought but didn't say.

Instead, he went very still. A polite, dashed-off response—even a nod—might send the incorrect message that what Roman had just done was okay. So Ethan studied the man closely, coolly, waiting for him to realize his mistake and open it again.

"This is a really nice room," he said instead, slowly scanning the suite. Upon completing his sweep, Roman's attention focused on the king-sized bed visible beyond a set of double sliding doors that had been pushed open. By Roman? Or the staff? Ethan couldn't be sure.

"Yes, well," Ethan said, "with an event this important to the hotel, we really do try to pull out all the stops."

Dammit. He'd meant to reorient things around the professional, but instead he'd made it sound like he was willing to hit his knees to keep Roman Walker happy.

Roman reached behind him and threw the deadbolt on the door. "With a king-sized bed," he said with a leering grin.

"Mr. Walker, I don't want to waste your time. Perhaps we should focus on the cake."

Roman started toward Ethan, shifting his hips as he went. Was he trying to saunter? Maybe his legs were just sore from a tough workout.

"You a big cake fan, Mr. Blake?" he asked huskily.

At some point during the twenty years since Ethan had come out of the closet, the word *cake* had become a euphemism for a queer man's ass. He wasn't sure when. But he was sure this had always been the case in young Roman's world, and that's why the man was throwing the word around now. When he was only a few feet away, Ethan was hit with a blast of the guy's cologne, some pricey, complex Tom Ford scent he'd last smelled while walking through a department store at South Coast Plaza.

Slowly, Roman Walker began to unzip his jacket. When it fell to the carpet at their feet with a soft *woosh*, Ethan discovered there was little to no Photoshop at work in the young man's social media photos.

The fitfluencer and alleged baking show fan stabbed another one of the slices with one finger. "See, I've got a lot of questions, Mr. Blake. Like you said, it's a super important event, and so I need to know how things will taste in a bunch of different circumstances." Roman's dark brown nipples already looked delicious. When he dabbed them both with cake icing, Ethan willed his gaze to remain locked on the man's gorgeous face.

He failed.

Roman smiled.

Ethan straightened. "Perhaps it would be better for both of us if you kept your jacket on, Mr. Walker."

"But I'm hot," he whined, pouting.

Ethan moved to the room's door and opened it by several feet. "We should let some air in then," he said with a smile. He pointed to the open deck door behind Roman. "Cross breezes. They work wonders."

Spectacularly shirtless, resting his butt against the edge of the table behind him, there was anger in the man's expression for the first time since Ethan had entered the suite. It widened his eyes, making them look strangely familiar. He told himself it was just the residual effect of quietly thirsting for the young man in Jonas's office earlier.

"Now I'll get cold." This time, the young man's pouty whine had an edge to it, as if he could sense the imminent collapse of this seduction.

"If the prospect of putting your jacket back on seems impossible, I'll have staff bring up a hotel branded T-shirt for you." Ethan smiled as politely as he could. "It'll keep you much warmer than that icing."

The man was clearly fighting a snarl. Ethan knew that look—the split-second anger of someone young and entitled and achingly beautiful, someone who was so used to men and women throwing themselves at him he regarded any form of sexual rejection as a personal attack.

Eyes locked on Ethan's, Roman Walker unsnapped the front button of his jeans.

"Mr. Walker." The clear forcefulness in Ethan's tone caused the fitfluencer's hands to freeze. Ethan spoke quickly, before he could be seized by thoughts of pushing the man to the bed in the adjacent room and finding out if he went rigid or pliant under the force of Ethan's thrusts. "We're going to reset here. I'll have the staff bring the slices down to one of our conference rooms, and then our events director Jonas Jacobs can join us. That way we'll be sure that you and the Peyton family are getting everything you're entitled to under your contract for this event."

Roman Walker didn't move. His jaw was tense with anger. There was a firm set to his brow that hadn't been there before.

"Okay," he said softly, "but then after will you fuck me in that bed?"

"I'm very flattered, but no. I will not."

I'll just jerk off to the fantasy of doing so for an hour later tonight while scrolling through your socials, Ethan thought as he stepped from the room.

"Gotcha," came the young man's voice behind him. The softness was gone, replaced by cold, hard anger. "I guess you only fuck married men with kids, *Michael*."

His spine became a steel rod. The one leg he'd stepped out into the hallway froze. When he turned, he saw what a thin veneer of seduction had lain across Roman Walker's anger. The young man's eyes were ablaze, and his nostrils were flaring. As Ethan stepped back inside the suite, closing the door all the way behind him this time, he realized with a racing heart and sweaty palms why the guy looked familiar—the reason had nothing to do with his social media profiles.

All of it came together in a single instant that left him briefly dizzy and breathless before he managed to compose himself.

"That's not my name, *Ronnie Burton,*" Ethan said quietly.

Roman's nostrils flared. "I figured you changed it at some point when I saw you on that stupid fucking show."

"It was never my name. Just like Roman's not yours."

"Whatever. Everyone in California changes their name."

Ethan tried for levity. "Everyone in *Southern* California changes their name."

"Nor Cal too. They just change it to something like Starshine or Rainforest. Whatever. It's Roman now. Legally. Don't call me Ronnie or I'll..."

The fact that he couldn't finish the statement with a threat was a good thing, Ethan thought.

Figuring it was the only way to be a gentleman in this scenario, he sank to one knee and picked up the man's designer jacket. When he went to hand it to him, Roman took it with one hand and hurled it to the floor. "No thanks, *Gramps.* Over and out!"

Ethan couldn't suppress his surprised laugh. "Wow. Okay. So *you* were BeachBoy24?"

Roman nodded angrily and looked to the carpet.

"A two-pronged attack. I see. Knock me down online and I'm more vulnerable to the charms of a young man like you when you get me alone. Clever boy. So is this why the Peytons are having their wedding here? Because you recognized me on Netflix?"

"Don't flatter yourself. They don't know who you are."

"So this is just a coincidence?" Ethan asked.

The young man swallowed. "Sapphire Cove was on Diana's short list. Rachel was leaning toward Montage in Laguna. I convinced her to have it here after I saw you on that stupid-ass show and Googled you."

"So you could...what exactly?"

Roman's anger seemed shot through suddenly with a lightning bolt of shame. He chewed his bottom lip. His chesty grunts made it sound like he was trying for words that were dying somewhere around his heart.

"Get me to try something with you and then accuse me of forcing myself on you?" Roman didn't answer. "Get me fired?"

"Something like that," the young man whispered, eyes on the carpet.

"Seems extreme. Why don't we just talk?" Ethan asked.

"Okay." It sounded like there was a frog in Roman's throat. "I'll go first. You ruined my parents' marriage, and you ruined my fucking life." The guy was breathing fast and hard now, his perfectly sculpted chest rising and falling with a rhythm that looked close to panic.

Most people wouldn't call residency in a major celebrity's multimillion-dollar beach house and a Bentley a "ruined life," but it wasn't Ethan's place to judge. Besides, in Roman's outburst, he'd heard more grief and pain than aggression and hate.

When Roman started crying, Ethan's suspicions were confirmed.

Then, in the blink of an eye, he was speeding away from Ethan and toward one of the nightstands in the adjacent room. With one hand, he opened the top drawer. With the other, he grabbed a tissue to wipe the icing off his finger and chest. The tank top he pulled from the nightstand was so skintight it was like he'd dressed by wrapping himself in a strand of toilet paper. In any other context, Ethan would have chuckled at the meaningless transition.

Slightly less shirtless now, the young man whose life he'd apparently ruined started for him across the plush carpet. "She was crying for a month every night before bed. I didn't know why. I thought she was sick. Or *he* was sick, and that's why he was never home. It turned out she had a file. She'd hired a private investigator to follow you two and take a bunch of pictures. It was her bedtime reading.

"Then, one weekend, she knew he'd lied to her again about staying late at work. So she got me dressed and we took the train into the city, and that's where we found you guys making out on a street corner. I was seven years old. And suddenly I've gone from a private school in Scarsdale to a public school in Victorville, California, where the first words I hear are 'What's up with that hair, faggot?' But hey, at least I learned to fight, right? And it was all because you thought you were young and hot enough to steal a married man from his family."

Ethan did his best to look the young man straight in the eye. "That is *not* what I thought," he said quietly. "I didn't know about either of you."

"Then how'd you know I was born Ronnie Burton?"

"He told me your name that night after you and your mom ran off. He had a total meltdown. We never saw each other again."

Roman rolled his eyes. "His choice or yours?"

"It was mutual."

"Oh, bullshit. I mean, you never suspected? He's taking the train in from the 'burbs? He never once brings you back to his place?"

Oh, if only you knew the half of it, kid, he thought. "I assure you, I did not know he was married, and I did not know he had a child."

"Liar," the guy snarled.

"Even so, I owe you an apology and I owe your mother an apology. And I'm sorry that I never—"

"It's too late!" Roman barked. "She's fucking dead, okay? She worked herself to the bone taking care of me after the divorce and now she's gone. I'd give you directions to the cemetery, but I don't think she wants some dumb slut who wrecked her marriage walking back and forth over her grave." His last words were mangled by a sob that had swelled in his throat.

The young man's slurs didn't anger Ethan, and seeing this fact seemed to upset him further. Rather, they made clear the depth of his terrible pain, the pain he'd been in for years after watching his father French kiss another man on a New York City street corner while his mother clutched his little hand and stuttered with sobs.

Seven.

Lord.

He'd always hoped the boy had been younger, too young to understand what he'd seen, and maybe blessed with a mother who'd tried to explain it away. After all, no words had been exchanged during that moment. Just terrible prolonged eye contact followed by a mother and son's sudden flight down the crowded sidewalk.

But seven seemed just old enough, the age at which a tender young mind could be imprinted and forever scarred.

He'd taken plenty of risks in his life. And what he planned to do next might be his most reckless decision of all. But Roman's pitiful sobs made it impossible to stay silent. The young man looked more wounded than he had on that long-ago night. Because now he was old enough to understand what he'd seen.

Or so Roman Walker, formerly Ronnie Burton, thought.

That gave Ethan only one choice—to tell the truth, the whole truth.

Nothing else in this moment would lessen Roman Walker's pain.

"Three times a month, your father would send me an email with instructions on where and when to meet him in the city. We'd have a romantic dinner together, then for a couple hours we'd walk around Chelsea or the West Village hand in hand so he could pretend to be the out and proud gay man he didn't have the courage to be. And yes, we would end the night together in a hotel room in bed. And in exchange for this service, he paid me three hundred dollars an hour. He knew me as Michael because that was the name I used with all of my clients. And that's what your father was. A client. I wasn't his boyfriend, Roman. I was his escort."

Only once the words had left his mouth did the sheer stupidity of what he'd done wash over him. There were only a few people in his life who knew how he'd earned a living during those first four years after his parents cut him off for being gay—if you didn't count his former clients. Now there was another one, and this one hated his guts. But as the confession had left him, he hadn't seen Roman Walker standing before him. He'd seen Ronnie Burton, a heartbroken little boy desperate for relief from the past.

Now, Ronnie's grown-up alter ego was wide-eyed, silent, frozen, as if he'd been emptied of all feeling and left dazed. The narratives he'd composed about that long-ago night had instantly been rewritten in a language he was struggling to understand.

Or maybe he understood the accurate and complete version all too well. He was working as a live-in trainer to a much older woman, after all.

"I'm not telling you this to defend myself," Ethan continued. "I'm telling you this because if you've tortured yourself for years thinking that he and I would lie in bed together talking about how he could get away from you two, I'm telling you right now, it didn't go down that way. Your mother wasn't the problem, and you weren't the problem. The problem was that your father couldn't accept who he really was. And what I gave him was a fantasy of freedom. A fantasy he wrote for us every time we saw each other. A fantasy he paid for. And no part of that fantasy included me asking him to abandon his wife and child."

The silence felt like it might never end.

Finally, Roman looked to the floor between them. "Don't try to be the dad I never had just 'cause you fucked mine," he finally muttered.

Ethan sighed. "I think we should maybe draw this meeting to a close. For now. If you want to talk more, I'm here for you. Just not when I'm at work. This is…not how we should do this."

The guy huffed with laughter and gave Ethan an expression cold as ice. "Oh, no. I'd much rather we talk about it when you're at work. Maybe your bosses would like to hear about it too." The emphasis he placed on the last word vibrated with menace.

An older version of Ethan took over, the version who could instantly grab the wrist of a client who'd made the mistake of taking him by the arm, seizing it with enough strength to let the guy know any attempt to restrain him would end in broken bones. Roman wasn't touching him now, but his words contained a threat all their own.

As Ethan closed the distance between them, the expression on his face chased the cocky swagger from Roman Walker's.

"All right, look, kid. If you think this is step one in your dazzling little revenge plot, let me be very clear about something. I wasn't a thirsty porn star who posted some dick pics on Rentboy and lived off sketchy airport hotel clients for a few months. I was an escort for years in one of the most cutthroat cities on the planet, and I pulled down six figures annually. My clients flew me all over the world. Two of them are senators now. I never had a pimp, and not once was I manhandled or coerced into something I didn't agree to.

"So if you think you're going to take another run at me, Mr. Walker, you better have an excellent plan. Because what you've got right now is a young man who used his rich, famous boss to lure me, an employee of this hotel, into a room alone where you sexually harassed me. And that's not going to play well if I head downstairs and share that story with my boss. And it's going to play even worse on Twitter if Diana Peyton's name gets tied up in it. Got it, *Roman*?"

They were nose to nose now.

"Keep her name out of your mouth," Roman whispered.

"Save it, Will Smith. But if you'd like some professional advice on how to manage your only client, I'd be happy to provide some. It's the least I can do."

Roman gasped and took a step back. "What the hell does that mean?"

"You rolled in here in a Bentley most CEOs can't afford, and you're a *trainer* who lives in an oceanfront mansion in Laguna Beach. What do you think it means, hot stuff?"

"I'm not a whore."

"Yet."

Roman shook his head at the floor, struggling for breath. Diana Peyton, it seemed, was a topic as sensitive as his cheating dad. He grabbed his jacket off the floor, punched his arms through the sleeves, and brushed past Ethan, bound for the door. Then Roman Walker, formerly Ronnie Burton, was gone. And suddenly the flickering candles all around him seemed ridiculous and in danger of setting the vast suite aflame.

4

Yet.

How could one word—one very short word—fill Roman's bones with anger, forcing him to clench his fists as he stormed through Sapphire Cove's marble-floored lobby?

It wasn't the word, he realized as he shoved his ticket at the approaching valet, it was the tone Ethan Blake—aka Michael the hooker—had filled it with.

So dismissive. So damn superior.

Like he knew everything there was to know.

And everything there was to know said Roman was a moron.

He fired out of Sapphire Cove's motor court so fast the valet jumped back to get out of the Bentley's path. *Guess I'm still Restless Ronnie.* It was the nickname his mother had given him after they left the quaint, leafy streets of Scarsdale and his cheating father in their wake, after he took to the desert expanses of their new home like an explorer in search of buried treasure. *More like Raging Ronnie,* he thought and slammed on the gas.

To most Southern Californians, Victorville was a blip of sunbaked strip malls they blew through on the drive to Vegas. But to little Ronnie Burton, uprooted from everything familiar, all that open land combined with the nearby San Bernardino Mountains became a sparkling kingdom of natural wonders and magical secrets. He ran, he biked, he scaled giant rocks. He stayed up past his bedtime making hand-drawn maps of the terrain he explored. It was during those explorations that a love of physical fitness, a hunger for pushing his young body to the limit, was born. Endurance became the key to his only real freedom after his father's betrayal took his old life away.

And even though he wasn't on foot, that's why he decided to take the long way home now, driving east and inland toward the nearest freeway, hoping its lanes would be free of traffic so he could put his pedal to the medal and roam.

Yet, yet, yet. He slammed the steering wheel with the side of one fist, hoping the pain would keep the word from burning a hole in his mind. Hoping to jar his tears back into submission.

The whole thing would have been easier if Ethan Blake had run from the room or denied it, and Roman would have had an excuse to do the things he'd wanted to all the time ever since his mom had died—yell and scream and lose his shit.

Instead, the man had proved the polar opposite of his mom, who in the years after the divorce had turned away from any difficult subject, especially his dad. Sometimes she'd do it physically, sometimes with a change of subject defined by her constant, nagging worries.

Do you ever hear from him, Momma?

You're not smoking weed, are you, Ron? It's not as harmless as they say.

Lucy Russo, the queen of convenient non-sequiturs.

Once she'd been tender and affectionate. After that night on a New York City street corner, she'd emerged tough and full of purpose.

But first, there were the bad days, the days in which she lay in bed for hours on end, caressing his cheek weakly with one hand if he wandered into the room to see how she was doing. Ignoring the desperate calls from his father, who knew better than to return home and try to lay claim to the house he'd paid for, lest his secret life be exposed. Making Ronnie call the local grocery to see what they could get delivered, asking the neighbors to drive him to summer day camp each morning. He'd been on the verge of believing life would be like that forever when suddenly she roused, did her makeup, and started packing up their things. They were moving west to live with his Grandma Nina, she announced. When they got there everything would be California sunshine and bright new beginnings.

Lucy Burton died that day. Lucy Russo came back to life and replaced her after ten years of zombie-walking beside a man she didn't truly know. But her resurrection left her with a colder heart and thicker skin.

In the years that followed, the stress of becoming a single parent made her even tougher.

They moved into his grandmother's spare desert ranch house, a temporary arrangement that grew permanent over time. The above-ground pool, the chain link fence designed to keep out the neighbor's testy Dobermans, even the crazy vault of stars each night. They all seemed like bright, hard-edged evidence that their old tree-shaded life had been a lie. That this sunbaked reality was the only reality. Meanwhile, his mom built a CPA business from scratch as she deposited the child support payments right into his college fund. After his grandma passed, the house and her tiny nest egg became theirs.

Sometimes during those first few years of dislocation and loss, he'd overhear his grandmother chewing out his mom for not taking his dad to the cleaners in the divorce. After all, she'd had that private investigator file documenting his affair. From what he'd been able to overhear—his mother was never a yeller, even when her own mother was close to yelling at her—Lucy Russo had wanted none of the trappings of a fancy life. They'd all been tainted by her husband's betrayal. Not his nice cars, not his quaint, Cape Cod style house shaded by elms, not his rich, martini-swilling friends who'd never felt like hers.

But every now and then, usually after her weekly glass of Merlot, Lucy would make a comment that laid bare the shame that had driven her to separate from Thomas Burton with a hatchet—she was a secretary who'd married one of the bigwigs at the firm, and deep down, she believed she'd been punished for shooting above her station.

Words like these would set Roman's teeth on edge, but if he tried to console her, tried to tell her she was victim-blaming, she'd wave him back into his chair with one hand and change the subject to his grades, which were never very good unless the subject involved running or lifting weights.

And when his frustration with the brick walls inside his mother became too much to bear, he had canyon trails to explore, cliff faces to scale.

And *Men's Fitness* articles to read, where the gorgeous male models accompanying the workout plans filled his young body with an intoxicating blend of ambition, envy, and terrifyingly raw lust. Models who looked like the man they'd caught his dad kissing that night. And somehow in his young, twisted brain he'd thought the only way to overcome that moment—to make up for the fact that he was developing desires similar to the ones his father had almost kept secret—was to become a better, fitter version of the man who'd convinced his father to stray, who'd killed his mother's gentle and affectionate side. But a version who didn't sleep with other people's husbands, who didn't wreck marriages. Who used his magnetic powers for good.

Now he knew that Ethan Blake hadn't convinced his father to stray. Sure, he'd been an accessory to the murder of a marriage, but apparently a clueless one. It was his father who'd made the call, sent the email, sought out Ethan's good looks and charm, probably after seeing his profile on some website. If Ethan's story was true—and the guy had told it with too much conviction and detail for it not to be—the marriage had the same killer Roman had always suspected: his dear old dad.

The 5 North was humming when he merged with it. The Bentley Bentayga's smooth ride focused him the way those long-ago mountain runs had. Whenever he hit a certain speed, a certain level of exertion, there was no past, no future, just a throbbing, electric now in which his mom would live forever in his heart, and he'd never age another day or gain a pound or lose a single follower.

But his mom was gone, and no amount of speed would allow him to escape that fact.

And now he couldn't stop seeing Ethan's face, still classically handsome, with those big brown eyes that always seemed on the verge of a welcoming smile. The trim, manicured mustache was a recent addition since his reality show debut. Roman kept seeing his patient gaze. Like he wasn't just looking at you; like he was *seeing* you.

When when Roman had started to cry, the man had seemed to care.

Or maybe he'd just been afraid of losing his job.

Or maybe he was an expert at making you feel what he wanted you to feel.

That's why he'd been the favored fuck toy of future senators.

Roman merged onto the toll road that would take him north.

This was his new version of his old mountain-cresting hikes, mounting the steep incline that cut through the dry and dusty hills that sat behind Orange County's most famous beaches. Only now, instead of his own aching legs powering him, he was carried along by the Bentley's turbo-charged engine. Dark blue with tinted windows, it drove like a knife through butter, a luxurious four-door attempt at a family car too pricey for most families on earth. It drew eyes wherever he took it, then he'd step from behind the driver's seat and when they saw his age, the gawkers muttered things under their breath like, *Damn. Whose kid is he?* Or worse, *What'd he have to do to earn that?*

It's not my car, he thought. *She lets me use it, but it's not mine. And she lets me live in the house because I'm paid to take care of it when she's in LA. How does that make me a whore?* As angry as the man's final words left him, Roman preferred remembering that version of Ethan Blake to the patient and kind one who'd invited him to barf up years' worth of anger and pain on that penthouse suite's rose-colored carpet. Who invited him to do something he'd done almost none of these last few painful months.

Talk.

Easier to hate the Ethan who'd threatened him.

Threatened him because Roman had threatened him first.

He was tempted to blow past the first sign for Highway 133. But if he kept driving, he wasn't sure where or when he'd stop. So he turned off the toll road, and suddenly he was traveling the narrow, winding canyon road that would take him back to the sparkling sea, only a few hours' drive from the deserts of his youth.

But seemingly a universe away.

5

After a hard left on Pacific Coast Highway and a few serpentine twists, Diana Peyton's famed Castle by the Sea came into view. From street level, Roman could see the sloped, gabled roofs and the brick chimney rising over the wood and concrete wall backed by protective hedges. A few top floor windows were aglow with honey-colored light against the starry night sky. If you were looking up at it from the beach below, it was three stories of impeccably restored French Normandy perfection descending the cliff in a controlled tumble.

In Laguna Beach, giant mansions sat cheek by jowl on any scrap of coast with an ocean view, and the Castle's neighbors were mostly contemporary slabs of concrete and plate glass. But Diana's oceanfront manse had been trading hands between members of Hollywood royalty since the 1950s, back when Laguna was little more than a humble artists' colony boasting great weather and little crescents of beach chopped up by rocky cliff faces. At the height of her TV fame in the mid-eighties, she'd snatched it up, adding bonus rooms and even a lower level to make up for the motor court she carved out of one half of the house's top floor. On the first tour she'd given him shortly before he moved in, she'd proudly explained the work she'd done to preserve the house's original style—low, coffered ceilings, thick Oriental rugs atop pickled hardwood floors, cozy rooms lushly decorated in individual styles, and with none of the trendy open floor plans Diana despised. "If I wanted to live in an airplane hangar, I'd become a pilot," she'd huffed more than once after returning from some engagement at the wall-deprived home of one of her wealthy friends.

After the motor court gate rolled open, Roman hit the gas and almost plowed right into the back of Scott Bryant's parked Range Rover.

What was Scott doing here? He only came down from LA when Rachel was in town, and she wasn't due back for another few days. And Roman, still rattled and raw, had been hoping to escape to his room and shut the door before Diana could see how upset he was.

But just then the front door flew open, and Scott—a former NFL player who'd warmed the bench for a season before a brief career in modeling—bounded toward the Bentley on long, muscled legs before Roman had a chance to kill the engine. He was one of the few men Roman had met who made him feel short. Maybe because he liked to muss Roman's hair like he was a little boy, even though he was only seven years older. When he went to do it this time, Roman jerked his head away.

"'sup, Freestyle? How's your secret boyfriend?" What he'd done to earn the nickname, Roman wasn't sure. He assumed it was Scott's not-so-subtle way of saying he thought Roman slept around a lot. Nothing could be further from the truth.

"I don't have a secret boyfriend. Is Rachel back?"

"Nah, not for another few days. Give me the keys."

"Why?"

"Just give me the keys. I'm driving us."

"Where?" Roman stepped from the Bentley as if his feet weighed a hundred pounds each.

"Dinner. Diana's going to meet us in a bit. She's screaming at her agent 'cause he brought her another cameo in a horror movie. Driver guy's going to bring her over when she's done."

Roman winced. *Driver guy* was named Hank Johnson, and he was more than a chauffeur. He was Diana's chief of staff, which meant he was a bodyguard, part-time handyman, and jack of all trades. The man was both kind and essential, and Scott should have shown him the respect of learning his actual name by now.

But it was the phone call happening inside that dominated Roman's concerns.

Despite being a television icon who regularly presented at the Emmys, his boss hadn't acted in anything other than a commercial for one of her own products in years. But her products sold more than enough to keep her vast empire running. There was her signature perfume, her department store clothing line, and the various pieces of luxury real estate all over the world generating staggering rental income when she wasn't in residence. Smart investments and expert financial management had left Diana Peyton rich in ways that were impossible for most people to comprehend. "Sometimes I just don't know what to *do* with all of it, sugar," she'd once sighed at Roman before sinking back into her sofa cushions wearing a Cheshire cat smile. Still, nothing could change the fact that she yearned to be in front of the cameras again, playing the kind of Oscar-bait roles that had always been denied her.

"Keys, Freestyle." Scott tugged them from his grip. He briefly gripped the back of Roman's neck in his other hand and gave it a little shake that sent unwelcome tingles racing down Roman's spine.

"You know, I'm not really hungry. I was just going to hang in my room tonight."

"Not a chance. Boss Lady's orders. You know how these calls go. She's going to need four courses and a bottle of Merlot to decompress. Apparently, this one's about killer worms, and she was supposed to bite it in the opening scene."

"Worms are, like, the slowest things on earth. How are they going to kill people?"

"From what I could hear, it sounds like they build up under this house in the woods and the victims fall through the floor one after the other or something. So really it's a horror movie about shitty floors, I guess. Anyway! She's not doing it, so who cares? Hop in. I'm so hungry I could eat my own ass."

Gross, Roman thought, but he relented, walking around the back of the car to the passenger side door.

He was starved, too, but he'd hoped to eat alone, and the prospect of spending time with Scott Bryant made him uneasy.

The truth was—and he'd never spoken it aloud to anyone—he didn't like Scott. The guy always played a little too rough for his taste, probably because he was jealous of how close Roman was with his fiancée. But if he was worried Roman knew all the couple's dirty secrets, he was mistaken. Rachel's career had taken off right around the engagement. These days, when she was able to give Roman any time at all, they spent it talking about work.

He'd never told her he thought she could do better.

Much better.

Sure, Scott had piercing blue eyes, a determined jaw, and a chest you could serve a cheese tray on at a crowded party. There were even times when his confident swagger could seem sexy and chivalrous. And apparently Scott was more talented in the bedroom than on the football field because whenever he and Rachel stayed over at the Castle, Roman was forced to jam a pillow over his head to drown out the sounds of their lusty enthusiasm in the room above his.

But Rachel was smart and insanely talented across the board. As an actress, she was Meryl Streep-level good, a chameleon who could disappear into any role. She navigated every conversation like someone whose every word had been scripted by a room full of top comedy writers. She read complicated books on politics and current events and broke them down for Roman in several concise paragraphs he could easily digest. More importantly, once every lunch or phone call, she made Roman laugh so hard he cried. Scott, on the other hand, said mostly the same four things about cryptocurrency over and over again and seemed to think aggressive hand gestures made dumb points sound smarter.

The man sped north on PCH, rapping a Cardi B song—badly—under his breath. Roman fought the urge to turn on the radio and drown the guy out with someone else's voice, but he figured that would be transparently rude. "Where are we going?" he asked instead.

"The Farmhouse at Rogers Garden." He swerved to avoid a blue and gold Laguna Beach Transit Trolley loaded with gawking tourists, then cursed under his breath when he found himself stuck behind a minivan. "Seriously, you can be real with me. You know that, right?"

"Sure. What are we talking about?"

"I mean, if you were out hooking up with someone, you could tell me. Like I want us to be close. You know, like guys close."

"Guys close. Okay. I wasn't hooking up with anyone."

"Well, why not? You're fucking gorgeous, dude."

"Thanks, but, um, to be honest, I'm not really a big fan of, like, casual sex."

"'Course not. You never dress casual. Makes sense you wouldn't *undress* casual either." Scott gave him a look and waggled his eyebrows.

"Watch the road. That was actually kind of funny, though."

"What? Like you're surprised?"

Roman was surprised, but rather than saying so, he just smiled. The more he and Scott chatted casually, the more his actions at Sapphire Cove earlier that night seemed unacceptable. Like some brief trip into a nightmare alternate reality where he'd turned into a character from a rerun of Diana's old show. This was his normal life—being whisked off to a pricey dinner he wouldn't have to pay for, rich people telling him he was hot, speeding up and down PCH with the warm ocean wind blowing through his hair. Everything was fine, amazing even. Why'd he have to go and almost ruin it by confronting his dead dad's side piece?

Escort, he corrected himself. The word felt new and strange inside his head, like the buzz of a crop duster wheeling through the landscape of his past, peppering old truths with something that either concealed them or killed them—he wasn't sure which.

At a red light, Scott turned to him and asked, "So do you like to get fucked?"

"Excuse me?"

"This is what I mean. I want you to be able to talk to me."

"About sex?"

"No, just guy stuff, you know. We're both guys, Roman."

"I might be a guy, but I don't want to hear about your sex life with my best friend."

The light changed. Scott accelerated with a grin. In an instant, they'd roared through Laguna's downtown, a little maze of narrow, tourist-thronged sidewalks that sat level with the beach on a coast dominated by bluffs. As they headed north alongside the dark, hilly expanse of Crystal Cove State Park, Scott said, "You need to relax, Freestyle. You're, like, this hot, young kid whose whole life is being taken care of. You shouldn't be wound so tight. You should be out having fun. Like all the time."

"Diana doesn't take care of my *whole* life."

Scott sputtered with laughter. "She takes care of your house, your car, and your clothes. In California, that's your whole life."

Roman felt his cheeks blaze, heard Ethan Blake's angry parting words.

Yet yet yet yet.

In the beginning, it had felt like a consolation prize. Right around the time his mother died, Rachel had landed the Broadway play that would eventually win her a Tony. He'd figured their trainer/client relationship would end as soon as she flew east. Instead, she'd gracefully passed him off to her mom. Diana, it turned out, had taken a shine to him after their few dinners together and offered to take him on once Rachel left town. First she brought him on for training sessions—so many and at such a good rate he was able to give his notice at Apex West Hollywood—then she gave him a plum gig as live-in caretaker for the Castle by the Sea. It had felt like a fix up, but a chaste and miraculous one, Rachel's way of ensuring Roman was taken care of in her absence. A new family at the very moment the last member of his old one passed away. That's how Diana had described it to him, at least. In the moment, his heart had sung and his eyes had welled up as they embraced.

And despite Ethan Blake's insinuations, it had felt like a chaste embrace.

Not once had he assumed Diana's motives might be sexual. Not once had her hand lingered on his ass or her kisses on the cheek landed uncomfortably close to his lips.

But what did he know?

He was just some dumb kid, while Ethan Blake was older and wiser and had been paid for sex all over the world.

"Aw, shit. Freestyle, come on. I'm sorry. I didn't mean to—"

"I had a weird night, that's all."

"With your secret boyfriend."

"I don't have a secret boyfriend."

Scott nodded, then, after a long silence, he added, "Good."

No, Roman thought, *don't even go there. That's not what this is. That's not what he's doing. There's no way.*

Scott turned into the brightly lit parking lot of Diana's favorite restaurant. The building was a one-story sprawl of blond wood with potted Italian cypresses along the front wall and pin-spot lighting framing the entrance. When the hostess saw them approaching, she got the skip in her step Roman had come to recognize as excitement over a celebrity's imminent arrival. Beaming, she led them to Diana's favorite table, a round top in the far corner of the garden area underneath spindly faux-candle chandeliers.

Heart hammering, his hands shook as he took his menu.

This was all his fault. His crazy behavior at Sapphire Cove had left him seeing dirty motives everywhere he looked. The world was full of normal, boring people who didn't speak in double meanings. Not everyone was Sharon Stone's character from *Basic Instinct*, a movie he and Rachel had watched together many times, howling at its deranged plot twists and rampant queer phobia.

Their server brought a basket of bread, which neither one of them touched. Even though he knew the menu by heart, Roman tried to lose himself in it like it was a good book. Anything to pass the time until Diana showed up. He'd practically memorized all the salads when Scott snapped his menu shut loud enough to make Roman jump.

"Order a drink," Scott said. "I'll drive back."

"Why don't you ride back with Diana and Hank and then you can drink whatever you want?"

Scott studied him with an expression caught somewhere between angry and frustrated.

One of the runners delivered their water with a smile. He was an angel-faced, curly headed blond who looked like he was either still in college or fresh out of it. He gave Roman the kind of long look Roman was used to getting from interested guys. Searching and curious, but also wary. Like they thought Roman might punch them for looking too long. He usually tried to relax them with a smile. The truth was, he liked being looked at. Got off on it, even.

But when he remembered the way Ethan Blake had looked at him earlier that night, with all that sympathy in his eyes, his stomach felt cold and his face felt tight, the same grating sensations that used to afflict him when he was a young boy fighting an unwanted attraction to a male classmate.

The water-bearing cherub departed.

Scott stared after him.

When he got caught looking, he gave Roman a thousand-watt smile. "Your type?"

"Nah, I like 'em older."

"Good. Guys like me can take you to Pound Town way faster than some kid." Scott turned and leaned in to Roman until there was almost no space left between them. "I mean, no offense. When it comes to Pound Town, I hear you like to see the sights on your back."

Roman closed his menu and slammed it to the table. "What the hell are you doing, Scott?"

At first, Roman assumed the pressure on his thigh was the night's cumulative tension finally causing muscle aches. Then the man's powerful, kneading fingers slid up the inside of his thigh. "Here's some advice from someone older, Freestyle," Scott said in a husky whisper. "People can't give you what you want unless you tell them what you like."

Roman shot to his feet. His chair went over backward with a loud clang. The next thing he knew, Scott Bryant was soaked and blinking and holding his hands out in front of him as if he'd tried to block the contents of Roman's water glass a second too late.

"Don't fucking touch me, asshole!" Roman staggered backward away from the table.

A familiar voice cried out behind him. *"Roman!"*

He spun and saw how the terrible confluence of events had played out. Barely a foot separated him from Diana. Most of the other diners had recognized her the second she'd entered the garden, then Roman's outburst had drawn their attention to their near collision. In an instant, he and his famous boss had become the centerpiece of a jarring, ugly little scene. Humiliation replaced his anger.

She was dressed casually in a denim shirt and designer jeans. It was far too warm out for the light pink cashmere sweater she'd tied around her waist. She'd probably added it for color. Her blonde hair was blown out in waves highlighted with platinum gray. It wasn't the mile-high eighties style she'd sported every Thursday night on ABC until 1996, but it was close enough to make her easily recognizable in public to most who'd lived through that era.

"Are you all right, sugar?" Her voice was warm but her eyes were blue steel. She gripped him by his elbows, maybe to hold him in place.

"No, I'm…uh…I'm not feeling well."

"All right, darling, well, why don't you sit and we'll get you something to eat and we'll all calm down and—"

"No, I should go. I'm just going to head back to the house and get some rest if that's okay."

Her expression suggested it wasn't okay, but she would pretend it was—for now. Gently, she rubbed his shoulders, something he'd always found welcomingly maternal before. Now it felt like she was trying to hold him in place.

The awful repercussions of what had just happened were rippling out on all sides of him. Even though it didn't seem possible, he wanted to draw those dangerous waters back to him with the power of speech alone. It was worth a try. "I tried this new supplement, and it's making me really moody. I shouldn't inflict myself on people right now. My bad."

A complete lie, but Diana seemed to buy it.

"Okay, well, whatever it is, let's get you off it because I want my sweet, darling boy back." She patted him gently on the cheek. "Maybe in time for dinner tomorrow night."

Roman nodded, which was a mistake. The simple motion threatened to set loose more of the tears he thought he'd exhausted earlier.

She kissed him on the cheek. Her affection was a comfort, and this relieved him. Now that he'd been exposed to a brazen come-on like Scott's, it was clear no hidden sexual motives lurked inside Diana's gentle affection. His nerves were so raw he was sure he'd be able to feel any desire that might be in her touch.

"You go on ahead. Have Hank drive you back."

Roman nodded.

Scott was staring back at him with a blank, wide-eyed expression.

Diana headed for the table.

Confident she couldn't see him, Roman shot him the bird, then drew one finger across his throat, and shot him the bird again. When the prick smirked in response, Roman mouthed the words *fuck you* and started for the exit, desperately thinking of ways he could keep Rachel from being turned into his mom.

Rachel was probably out with the cast enjoying a celebratory dinner close to the theater. After tomorrow's Sunday matinee, she'd get her second break from her Tony-winning run in *The Burning Days.*

A break that would last three whole days before she returned to begin her final run of performances. After which, she'd have a week to get ready for her biggest performance of all—her wedding.

She probably wouldn't answer a call, but a text she'd respond to within minutes, he was sure. And then maybe he could ask her to talk.

If he didn't throw up first.

Six months ago, on the day that had changed his life forever, he'd been in the middle of a training session with Rachel at Apex West Hollywood when he noticed his manager heading toward them across the crowded workout floor, wearing a pinched and solemn expression.

When she saw his supervisor's slow approach, Rachel had made a soft but startled sound and asked, "Are you getting fired, babe?"

But the news was far worse. His mother had been killed on the way home from the grocery store. An eighteen-wheeler had blown through a red light, and in an instant, she was gone.

Once the words were out, his knees turned to jelly. Then Rachel's arms were around him, steering him through the dense crowd of trust fund babies and famous actors and Beverly Hills housewives who always peopled the gym floors at Apex, as he said "What? *What?*" over and over again, like someone trying to hear a call through a crackling connection. Then they were outside in a blast furnace of Southern California sun, Rachel holding him as he sobbed, ushering him into her car, having her driver chauffeur them all the way out to the Victorville police station—over two hours through soupy LA traffic, and with the two of them still in their sweaty gym clothes, no less—and then the morgue.

It was the worst day of his life, but it was also the day his most famous client became his closest friend. Shouldn't he return the favor by delivering this awful news about her fiancé in person? Then he could put his arms around her if she lost her footing.

After an hour of pacing his room and typing and deleting messages he couldn't bring himself to send, Roman finally curled into a ball on his bed.

His room was a recent addition on the Castle's middle floor, down a narrow hall from the home gym Diana had installed a few years before. There was no ocean view, but a door in his side wall opened onto a landing in a hidden service staircase that ran from the beach below to a side gate next to the motor court one story above. The stairs were steep and concrete. There was too little space between the Castle and its northern neighbor to admit much sunlight by day, but if he opened the door, as he'd done right after getting back to the house, he could fill his room with the sounds of whispering surf and a few strong ocean breezes, something that had always soothed him.

Until now.

Tonight, nothing soothed him.

He was too terrified to leave his room. If Scott and Diana returned home and the man tried to play the whole thing off—or God forbid, lied about it—Roman would lose his shit. He was that close to the edge. And he had been for a while. Ever since…

Ever since...

He saw the morgue's white walls. Felt Rachel's arm holding him up and heard the police officers muttering their inadequate condolences, one of them even telling him how much he'd relied on his mom during tax season every year.

Can't. Stop. Not now, later.

Was subjecting him to a brazen, creepy, unwanted come-on just moments after what he'd done to Ethan Blake the universe's idea of justice?

These thoughts ran crazed circles in his head until he heard the familiar vibrations of the Escalade pulling into the motor court overhead. He braced himself for the barking sound of Scott's voice echoing down the service stairs. But there was only silence before several car doors closed, followed by a sound that allowed him to breathe deeply again—the gentle growl of Scott's Range Rover starting up and turning onto PCH. Headed north up the coast.

Back to LA, please God.

A few seconds later, there was a soft knock against his door.

When he opened it, Diana entered, bearing a sparkling glass of his favorite beverage—Dr Pepper, his not-so-secret indulgence. His mom used to let him have a can on Sundays if he could prove he'd done all his homework by three o'clock. From the moment he'd told Diana the story, she'd started storing pallets of it in the pantry.

"Can I come in, honey?"

"Sure."

She studied the room as if she thought he might have company, which was odd, because he never did.

"We need to get some of your stuff out of storage so you can personalize this place a bit more."

"Yeah, sure."

So you're not throwing me out, he thought with a surge of relief.

There was a bed, matching nightstands, a flat-screen TV, and a blue and white upholstered chair in one corner he figured was a spare from the breakfast nook upstairs. Otherwise, the walls were blank. The only place that looked truly his was his bathroom, where the marble counters were covered with glossy eruptions of beauty and hair products he'd scored through various sponsored posts.

When he accepted the glass from her, he meant to enjoy a tiny sip, but his nerves had him gulping instead. "Thank you," he whispered after he swallowed.

"You must be hungry. I brought your favorite. It's upstairs in the fridge when you want to warm it up."

"Thank you."

Diana took a seat in the room's only chair.

Roman sat on the foot of the bed, heart hammering, feeling like an iron bolt had been driven through his spine. Her thoughtful silence, the way she crossed one slender leg over the other and rested her hands on her knee—these things were all out of character for a woman who always entered the room with polite but firm announcements of what she wanted everyone else in it to start doing now that she'd arrived.

"I understand Scott got a little overzealous tonight."

So Scott hadn't lied and accused Roman of initiating. Another surge of relief powered through him.

But her word choice was strange.

"Overzealous?" he asked.

"Handsy."

Roman nodded. "He told you."

Diana nodded. "We were supposed to discuss it with you first."

Her tone was so casual, the oddness of her response swept past him at first. Then it circled back, knocking the wind out of him on its return. "Discuss what?" he asked.

She raised her eyebrows and sighed. "He's gotten a little reckless. He's been making some mistakes. I thought it would be better for all of us if he kept it in the house."

"Whose house?"

"Mine."

"Which one?"

"This one. The one where you live." When she saw the expression on his face, she made a clucking sound and gave him a piteous expression. "Oh, come on now, honey. Don't look like that. We've worked together long enough for you to know how things play in this business."

"I'm a trainer."

She regarded him with big blue eyes he often had trouble reading. "You're a social media star. And you're on the rise."

"You want me to hook up with Scott so that he doesn't get caught hooking up with random people in LA?"

"He casts his net much wider than LA, I'm afraid." She shook her head. Roman didn't even want to think about what this could mean. Scott had flown to New York several times to visit Rachel during her run. Did this mean he'd cheated on her during their visits? His stomach lurched, and his temples throbbed. "But if that's how you're comfortable phrasing it then…by all means." She twirled a manicured hand through the air and took in a deep breath, as if she thought he'd come around to her way of thinking and was relieved.

He hadn't.

"What about Rachel?" he asked.

"We're protecting Rachel."

"From the truth about her fiancé?"

"From a scandal that will destroy a wedding she needs, Roman. They've already done interviews. They're committed. It's a story. We have to see it through or else it becomes a story she doesn't need."

She got to her feet, brushed invisible lint off the thighs of her jeans with several quick swipes, and closed the distance between them.

"Look, Rachel's at a very sensitive point in her career. I've indulged this theater thing of hers long enough. The Tony only makes it worse, to be frank. Now she's going to start thinking her hobby should be the main event. But if she wants to level up, and she claims she does, she needs a new narrative. Soon. And this is it. *Hollywood princess marries Prince Charming in a white wedding filled with stars!*" Diana spread her hands out as if she'd just strung those words in twinkling lights. "That's a story we can sell somewhere besides Broadway. Which at the end of the day is just a couple city blocks filled with people who can't get good jobs in TV."

"But her Prince Charming's a douchebag."

Diana nodded politely. "A douchebag with no acting ambitions who didn't complain about a single clause in the prenup. And he'll also look amazing on her arm as she walks the red carpets that will take her where she needs to go, which is all the cameras care about. So as long as *we* contain his lack of discretion…" When she saw she hadn't convinced him, she took a step closer. "Marriage is a complicated business when you're a star. You need someone next to you who shines, but not brighter than you. He's not dim, but he's not bright. He gives off a sort of dull, appealing glow, and that's what she needs."

Roman suddenly wondered if this attitude toward marriage was why Diana had gone through six husbands. Maybe they'd all run for the hills after conversations like this one.

"Trust me. In the end, this is what Rachel wants."

He swallowed, speechless.

"She's playing a very difficult game, Roman. Luckily, she has me to help her win." When Diana took his limp hand in hers, her grip was frighteningly firm. "And so do you, remember? I mean, look at the money we had to spend to land you all those followers. If anyone could have scored that many eyeballs the natural way, it should have been you, right? I mean, you're stunning. The straight men who come to work on this house can't even stop ogling you. And yet…" She cupped his cheek in one hand. "The truth about celebrity, darling, is that if you're going to get there and stay there, someone has to pull the levers on your behalf. And then, one day, if you're lucky, you're powerful enough to pull them yourself. But Rachel's not there yet, I'm afraid." She patted his cheek, cool gaze lingering on his face. "And neither are you, sugar."

At first, it didn't compute, what she was saying. What she was *doing*. She'd never done it before. Until now, it had all been encouragement and gifts and big plans she had for his career. Now she was threatening him.

Did she turn to go because she was ashamed she'd done it or because she wanted her parting words to linger and sink in? Suddenly it felt like he didn't know her well enough to be sure.

"Don't forget about your dinner." She pulled the door closed behind her.

Roman, breathless, stared into space.

6

Ethan's come-down ritual after a stressful day's work was a favorite movie and a glass of Chardonnay.

Thanks to Roman Walker, tonight he'd need two glasses and an extra-long flick.

Heat, Michael Mann's classic crime saga starring Robert DeNiro and Al Pacino, would fit the bill perfectly. It was close to three hours long and featured a minimalist electronic soundtrack that always transported him back to the late nineties, when he was an innocent twink bopping it to Moby remixes at his first small-town gay bars in Columbia, South Carolina, a safe distance from his parents' stately home in Charleston. Before New York, before his parents gave him the boot. Before he was ever paid for sex.

He was more rattled than he wanted to be and had spent most of the night since Roman's departure from the hotel assuring himself things wouldn't escalate. Couldn't escalate. If the sharp-tongued *fitfluencer* decided to kick things up a notch, it would be his word against Ethan's. Unless he'd been secretly recorded, and where in God's name would Roman Walker have hidden a wire? His shoes?

Within no time, the movie and the wine were working their intended magic.

He'd first seen it at an art house screening in Paris during a particularly harsh winter, transfixed by its stunning visual style and simple storyline. Panoramic shots of LA's circuit boards of glittering streets beneath clear and starry skies, lonely, beautiful people pursuing ruthless ambitions through a vast, sun-bleached landscape that bled money. He'd identified with almost every character in it. So what if they were all cops and robbers? They were trying to find value and meaning in a world where you couldn't count on anything or anyone. It reminded Ethan of his first days of escorting. Days when every client call brought his heart to his throat. When he was acutely conscious of the switchblade in his back pocket at all times, but the cash at the end was another little steppingstone toward culinary school.

He'd rewarded himself for landing the job at Sapphire Cove with a deep, L-shaped sofa comfortable enough to get a good night's sleep on, and he was in danger of nodding off on it when the film's titular scene jerked him awake.

Robert DeNiro, criminal mastermind, was lecturing his protégé Val Kilmer on his marriage problems as the morning sun sparkled on the Pacific Ocean outside the windows of his unfurnished Malibu beach house. DeNiro was telling Kilmer how men like them shouldn't get involved in anything they couldn't drop at a moment's notice when they felt the heat around the corner.

For the first time, the familiar dialogue sent an ice pick through his gut.

His new place was nice, but it was a sublet in a condo complex where he could probably afford to buy, a fact that had shocked Connor Harcourt when Ethan had mentioned it one day. The hotel had given him a four-year contract, but he'd spent most of his signing bonus on a brand-new BMW 4 series convertible in metallic tanzanite blue. And with the exception of Donnie, his closest friends weren't local. In short, Ethan was doing exactly what he'd done in most of the places he'd lived—throwing himself into his work, putting down the shallowest of roots in case his past came back to turn up the earth underfoot.

There'd been a few brief awkward encounters with former clients over the years, the last one when he worked at the Four Seasons in London. An investment banker he almost didn't recognize until the man gave him a strained smile and toast when they saw each other across a tasting party. It had been jarring, being suddenly distracted from a conversation with his boss by memories of how his old client had loved having his earlobes nibbled and laughed hysterically when he came. But that's all it had been.

His past had never confronted him the way Roman Walker had, even though he'd always been braced for exactly that.

People could survive with secrets. But could they thrive with them? If there was a part of your past you didn't want discovered, ambition made you a target.

Head pastry chef. Reality show judge. These were the things that had placed him in Roman Walker's line of sight.

When the phone resting on his stomach rang, he jumped. A call from the hotel's switchboard operator at this hour was never a good sign. "Someone named Ronnie Burton wanted to be put through to you. When I said you weren't on the property, he asked for your cell. Like that's something *I'm* going to give out. I took down his number and said I'd pass a message along. You want it?"

Scribbling as she read it, Ethan thanked her and hung up. It wasn't exactly a Machiavellian move on Mr. Walker's part, placing calls to the hotel using his old name. But it smacked of some kind of game. Ethan had no plans to play. "Didn't you legally change your name, young man?"

The voice that answered back was outside and fighting to be heard over gusts of wind. "I didn't do that part to mess with you. I just didn't want it getting back to Diana that I'd called the hotel at midnight."

"Fair enough. Out for a stroll?" he asked.

"There's a trail across from her house. I needed to get out," Roman said.

"Billings. I know it. It's across from her house and about seven blocks uphill."

"Yeah, well, I'm Restless Roman. That was my mom's nickname for me. I mean, it was Restless Ronnie back then. But it still fits, I guess. Whatever. I was just calling to say you won."

"What were we playing again?" he asked.

"You were right. I'm her fucking whore. I'm sorry, *sex person.* Whatever."

"I think the term you're looking for is sex worker." He reached over and turned on the lamp beside the sofa. He'd muted the movie, but he hadn't paused it, so he tapped the remote. "Did something actually happen?"

"Oh, *actually* happen? Like, what? You don't believe me? Like you think maybe you just put the thought in my head and ruined one of the most important relationships in my life?"

"The fear did cross my mind, yes."

The admission seemed to calm the young man on the other end of the call.

Footsteps crunched soil that sounded rocky and hardpacked.

The wind was getting stronger.

Roman Walker was cresting open trail. At midnight. When he was upset. How many reckless choices was this kid going to make in one night? Ethan hoped he wasn't intoxicated.

He rose from the sofa, turning on more lights as he headed into the kitchen.

"Well, I guess I appreciate you saying that," Roman finally answered, not sounding remotely grateful, "but I'd appreciate it more if you hadn't turned out to be so fucking right."

"Roman, it's really late and I—"

"Oh, I'm so sorry I bothered you as my whole life falls apart. Again."

"I'm not complaining about the call. You're hiking a trail after dark that has nine switchbacks and hundred-foot drops off the side. I'm happy to keep talking, but why don't you turn around first and—"

"Whatever. I've hiked this trail a million times, Gramps."

Clearing his throat in response to this callback to BeachBoy24, Ethan asked, "At night?" There was no answer. "Do you have a flashlight, *baby boy*?"

"I'm just going to the first viewpoint. Relax."

"I'm perfectly relaxed. I'm at home with a movie and a glass of wine. Perhaps you could try relaxation as well. It would be a delightful change of pace, don't you think?" Dr Pepper would be too much caffeine at this hour, so he pulled a can of sparkling grapefruit water from the fridge.

"You're pretty cool, you know that?" Roman asked. "I don't mean like hip and popular. I mean, like, ice cold."

"I am considerably older than you, as you've seen fit to remind me frequently in a very short time. Maybe it's just my ancient wisdom shining through."

"Whatever," Roman said. "You're just gloating 'cause you're about to get what you want."

"Peace and quiet and a general elevation of our national political discourse?"

"Maybe later. No, I threatened your job. Then my job got threatened a few hours later. Exactly like you said. Remember? You're not a whore *yet. Yet yet yet yet yet.*"

"I don't recall saying it several times in a row like a Halloween store witch, but I do remember the moment."

Roman grunted.

"I also don't recall *wanting* your job to be threatened."

Roman grunted again, and a windy quiet settled.

"Let me guess. She put the moves on you and made it clear your job was on the line if you said no."

"Worse," Roman answered. "She wants to pimp me out to her future son-in-law behind my best friend's back, so he stops cheating on her with strangers."

Ethan slumped against the refrigerator door. "That is quite a directive. I take it you refused?"

"I haven't really given my answer yet," Roman muttered. Then quickly, and as if to distract from what he'd just revealed, he added, "Maybe I'm just hungry. I keep trying to have dinner and the world keeps doing new, horrible things."

"You didn't fill up on cake at Sapphire Cove?"

Silence from the other end.

"Come on. It's a little funny."

"Later, maybe."

"Later you're going to eat, or later you'll laugh at my joke?"

Roman Walker's answer was an unearthly wail.

Ethan jumped, knocking one shoulder into the edge of the fridge. At first, he thought the guy was venting a night's worth of frustration and rage with a sudden primal scream. But then came the words "*No, no, no, no, no, no*" as Roman's voice got further and further away from the phone.

Then the connection went dead.

He called Roman's name several times, then tried calling him back twice, three times. Each time, voicemail answered.

He was already peeling out of his apartment's garage when he remembered the wine. Normally he'd never drive this soon after even one glass, but Roman's terrified screams were still ringing in his ears.

They sounded like the screams of a falling man.

7

The trailhead was at the dead end of a twisting hillside street packed with multistory houses perched high above PCH, some of them commanding expansive views of the ocean below. Ethan parked in its empty dirt lot, rushed to his trunk, and pulled out the Maglite he'd added to his earthquake kit.

Next to the familiar signs warning of fire danger and potential wildlife encounters, the only barrier was an easily scaled ranch gate, more decorative than obstructive.

Warm winds blew west off the desert, gaining strength as they ripped down the ocean-facing hillsides. By the time he'd hoofed it to the turnoff for the first viewpoint, he'd worked up a light sweat. Holding the flashlight at his waist, spraying the trail ahead with as much diffused light as he could, he looked for footprints. But the dirt on this section of the trail was too hard packed to reveal any.

He'd thought about calling an ambulance on the way over, but if Roman had suffered an emotional breakdown and not a physical one, a battalion of EMTs barreling down on him and asking a hundred questions might not help his mental state.

He called Roman's name once, twice.

Only the wind answered.

He knew the first viewpoint had a duo of picnic tables and benches and a stunning view of the ocean far below. But the clump of shadow waiting for him there didn't make any sense. Moonlit ocean stretched to the horizon beyond.

"Roman!"

"Don't!" There was hysteria in his voice.

The closer Ethan got to the picnic area, the more he could make out what lay ahead.

Roman Walker was sitting on top of one of the benches, arms wrapped tightly around knees he'd pulled to his chest, rocking back and forth with the familiar two-step of panic. Or shock.

There was a small square of light off to one side of the bench. Roman's phone. He'd dropped it. Or thrown it. Ethan's money was on *dropped* given the cries he'd heard before the call was cut short.

"Roman, are you all right?"

"Don't, Ethan! There might be more!"

"More what?"

Then his flashlight beamed landed on a serpentine path through the looser dirt close to the picnic table and bench. A fresh path that could only have been made by one creature on earth.

Ethan wasn't afraid of snakes, but that didn't mean he planned on dancing in the dark with them.

"Do you see it?" Roman croaked.

"Are you okay? Did you get bit?"

"You can see it?"

"It's gone now, but I can see the trail it left."

"There could be more!"

Ethan stood his ground, slowly scanning the area around the bench with his flashlight. Dirt, rocks, and one winding snake's trail leading into the nearby brush. That was it.

"I can't," Roman gasped, and for the first time Ethan could hear the guy was sobbing. "I can't with snakes, Ethan. I *can't*."

After a terrible night, he'd somehow wandered straight into one of his worst phobias, and now he was in danger of coming apart.

Next to the bench now, Ethan reached out and placed one hand on Roman's bent knee. The guy jerked then went still. Relatively still. He was shuddering down to his bones.

"Why don't you tell me what happened so we can make sure you're okay? How's that sound?"

"It might come back. You need to check. You need to keep checking."

"It's not coming back. You probably scared it worse than it scared you."

"I can assure you that is *impossible!*" Roman wailed.

"Roman, snakes don't stalk people. They don't hunt in packs. They're not wolves. Now what happened? Did you step on it?"

"I think so. It jerked under my foot, and I heard a ra... a ra..."

"It rattled?" Ethan asked as gently as he could.

Nodding madly in confirmation, Roman screwed his eyes shut. *Shit*, Ethan thought. Rattles were the last stop before a strike, which meant Roman and his reptilian friend had been closer to a rumble than he'd first thought. Worse, Roman's memory of what came after—including a bite requiring immediate medical attention—might be warped by panic. "All right," Ethan said, trying to sound calm. "Here's what I'm going to do. I'm going to examine your legs and your ankles and make sure you—"

"Get up on the bench."

"It's probably better if I—"

"No, get up on the bench. It might come back!"

"Fine." Once he'd joined him on the splintery slats, Roman's breaths slowed. A little. When Ethan stretched out one of his legs and then the other, the guy didn't resist. He tugged up the cuffs of his jeans, pushed his socks down to examine the skin on his ankles and calves. He even examined the fabric of his jeans and his leather loafers to see if there were bite marks that hadn't met skin. Everything looked clean.

"You're good."

Roman shook his head. "I'm not good. I am very, very *not* good. And I am not getting off this bench until the sun rises."

"Dawn is around five hours from now. You sure you want to commit to that?"

"Yep. I'll be able to see everything then, and I'll walk home. And I'm never going hiking again without a flamethrower."

Ethan tried not to laugh. "So you can start the next big wildfire? That doesn't sound like a plan, sir."

"Fine, what's a snake's natural predator?"

"A hawk, I believe."

Roman drew his knees closer to his chest and hugged them more tightly. "Then I'm never going hiking again without my pet hawk."

"And what shall you name your pet hawk?" he asked.

"Gertrude."

"For a *hawk*, really? Was Mildred taken?"

"I don't know. You're asking me annoying questions, and it's the first name I thought of. The point is, I'm not getting off this bench."

"Okay, here's what you're going to do. You're—"

"I am *not* walking down the trail, Ethan Blake. Don't you even try. I'm not walking down the trail until the sun rises. They feed at night. They could be everywhere. I should have remembered. This is why I never hike at night. This is why I never—"

"Roman, stop it. I'm not asking you to walk down the trail. I'm asking you to listen to me and follow my instructions, okay? You're having a panic attack and that means your thoughts are of no use to you right now. They've turned against you, so stop looking to them for help. Your mind is multiplying the scary experience you had times two hundred, and you're seeing things that aren't there. If you want to get back inside your skin, you need to change your *actions*. And you're going to do that by breathing in through your nose for a count of four, then you're going to hold it in your chest for seven and you're going to breathe out for eight. Can you do that?"

Roman nodded.

"Good," Ethan said. "Here we go."

Instead of erupting with another phobic rant, the guy followed along. Suddenly the two of them were breathing in unison. The only sounds other than their long, slow inhales and exhales were the wind gusts buffeting their clothes and the occasional echoing bleep of a car horn far down on PCH. And then, after a while, the gentle sound of the surf which seemed to make itself gradually known, like a reward for their methodical attempt at calm.

No serpents slipping and sliding through the dirt around them, no terrifying rattles.

After five cycles, Roman slowly raised his head from between his knees and said, "I got bit."

"You didn't. I checked."

"No, when I was seventeen." He sounded calmer now. "When I was a kid, I loved the outdoors. I used to hike and run and bike and all sorts of stuff. Then one day I was climbing these rocks and I didn't look up before I reached, and I heard the rattle, and it got me."

"Yikes," Ethan whispered.

"It didn't release its venom, which is apparently a thing. But it scared the shit out of me."

"I bet. So did you stay in the gym after that?"

"Hell, no. Nothing can keep me inside all the time. But I got into paragliding. Snakes couldn't get me up there. And the view's a lot better, so fuck them."

Ethan laughed.

"Also..." Roman trailed off suddenly, playing with a tiny loose thread on the knee of his jeans. But his hands weren't shaking, and that made Ethan smile in the dark.

Each word was coming out of him sounding calmer than the last, so Ethan thought it was essential to keep him talking. "What?" Ethan asked.

"It's stupid. I just..."

"Come now. You already know my biggest secret."

Roman looked up, like he was seeing him for the first time since he'd stepped up onto the picnic bench with him. "I thought I was being punished. I used to mess around with boys out there and I... Like I said, stupid."

"You thought God sent the snake to punish you for kissing boys in the desert?"

"I did a lot more than kiss boys out there."

"Drugs?"

"No, I did more to the *boys*."

"Oh, I see. So why did God send the snake tonight?"

Now Roman picked nervously at the fabric cuff of one of his jacket's sleeves. "To punish me for what I tried to do to you at Sapphire Cove."

"Seems extreme."

He could feel Roman searching his face through the darkness. Could the guy see him better than he could see Roman?

"You really think so?" Roman finally asked.

"I can't pretend to speak for this version of God you believe in. But I can speak for myself and say I have no desire to see you hurt, Roman Walker. By anyone. Including some poor snake that just wants to eat a mouse and go to sleep for a month."

"You really are cool as ice, Ethan Blake."

"Getting older is about learning what's not worth reacting to."

"Thanks, Gramps."

"Watch it, kid."

Roman laughed. "Where do you live?"

"Irvine," he said.

"That's far."

"It's just over the hill."

"It's a big hill. It's more like a bunch of mountains."

"I've driven the Alps."

It was still too dark to read Roman's expression closely, but he could feel the guy's eyes studying him. "You drove all that way because the call dropped?"

"I drove all that way because I heard you screaming and I thought you'd fallen. I could have just called some paramedics, but you'd have a bunch of EMTs trying not to laugh at you right now."

"Appreciate that. But I'm still not getting off this bench until the sun rises."

"Last time I checked, you still hadn't had dinner."

"Good. I'll drop a few pounds."

"Lovely, then your followers will be able to pleasure themselves to the sight of your spleen. Seriously, have you had anything to eat all day?"

Roman grunted. "A protein bar and an Inferno."

"Meth in a can, fabulous. My Lord, you were a panic attack waiting to happen. We need to get some food in you and fast."

"Where? It's after midnight in Orange County. This isn't exactly Manhattan, sir."

"It's been a long time since I've lived in New York, *monsieur*. And there's plenty to eat at my house."

"I can't eat a bunch of sugar. My diet's really strict."

"Tonight your diet is *I need nourishment and quickly because I'm out of my mind.* And I know how to make something besides pastry, thank you very much. I graduated from the Culinary Institute of America. It's not a Sunday afternoon doughnut-making workshop at your local Williams Sonoma."

"Wow. Shading Williams Sonoma? Cooking people are intense."

"Would you like to eat or not?"

It looked like Roman was kissing one of his bent knees. "I'm starving," he whispered into the denim.

"We should go then."

Ethan raised the flashlight in one hand, put one foot slowly to the earth and then the other. Following the beam's fierce halo, he walked in circles around the bench, letting Roman see that there were no signs of reptiles, letting him observe the flashlight's power to cleanse fears from shadows.

"Looks like we're good," Ethan finally said.

"It's a long way back to your car, though," Roman muttered.

"Okay, fine, then." Ethan extended the flashlight to him. He hesitated a minute before taking it. "You do the flashlight. I'll do the walking."

With that, Ethan turned and backed up toward the bench. He stopped when he felt his butt bump wood. When the silence grew awkward, he said, "Hop on."

"A piggyback ride?" Roman asked. "Seriously?"

"Shall we call your boss and order a helicopter? Seems fraught, all things considered."

Ethan stood his ground, hearing the rustling sounds of Roman moving behind him. He waited for the kid to laugh, for the sound of his feet hitting the dirt. Or maybe for a comment accusing him of being an old perv. Instead, one of Roman's long muscular legs curled snakelike around his waist. It was followed by a powerful arm that slid across Ethan's chest.

Well, then, Ethan thought.

As he embraced Ethan fully from behind him, Roman Walker's chin came to rest on his shoulder. "Muscle weighs more than fat," he whispered, his hot breath sending gooseflesh down the side of Ethan's neck.

"Something I tell myself every time I get on the scale."

"You sure about this, old man?"

He was very much not sure about this. For more reasons than one. But there was no turning back now. "Of course I'm sure," he said.

Roman used his arms to hoist himself further up onto Ethan's back.

When Ethan started forward, every muscle in his body seemed to tense at once.

But he was halfway down the trail when he realized the intoxicating bath of Roman's expensive cologne, the forbidden nearness of him, and the firm and confident way Roman held to him from behind were all making the effort seem less strenuous than it was. Which meant his back would probably be killing him in the morning.

For now, he felt stronger than he'd been in a while.

8

Veal piccata would be quick, easy, and delicious, and packed with enough carbs to take at least some of the edge off Roman's wild moods. Even better, Ethan hadn't put the cuts in the freezer when the grocery delivery had arrived the day before, so there'd be nothing to thaw. He'd have to cheat with the sides and use microwave spinach, always his last choice. But Roman's hunger and low blood sugar justified shortcuts and speed.

Whenever he cooked at home, he liked a little background music, usually light classical. Mozart or Bach. But tonight, he was hosting a guest, so as he checked cabinets and drawers to make sure he had everything he needed within reach, he asked Roman Walker for his preference.

"You an opera fan?" Roman said, poking at the latest mail stack on the kitchen counter with a little too much familiarity for Ethan's taste.

"Not a devoted one." Ethan removed a butcher-wrapped pack of veal scallopini from the fridge. "Is that what you'd like?"

"My mom was an opera fan," the young man answered, which wasn't an answer. "Used to blast me out of the house with it. Her favorite was… Who's that old dude from the old movies? The big guy, Mario something."

Ethan rested a hand on Roman's shoulder. "How about we sit?"

Roman seemed startled by Ethan's tone, then looked down at the mail he'd been rifling through. "Sorry, I wasn't trying to—"

"Restless Roman, I know. Just have a seat and I'll get you

something to drink."

Roman waggled his eyebrows at the open Chardonnay bottle as he walked past it. "Wine looks good."

"On an empty stomach, I don't think so. Park it, mister."

"Thanks, Dad."

Under Ethan's pointed look, the guy lowered his eyes and started for the breakfast table.

"Sorry, that was kind of creepy, I guess."

"How about a Dr Pepper?" Ethan asked.

Roman spun so fast his shoes squeaked on the floor. "Wait, what? *I* like Dr Pepper," Roman barked angrily.

"And you're apparently the only one who's allowed to?" Ethan asked quietly.

"You like Dr Pepper?" Roman said accusingly.

"No, I keep it in the fridge for Santa. Of course I like it. Why do you think I'd have a case?"

"Well, it's like a niche drink. It's not very common."

"That's not true. It's actually quite common and quite good. And I love it and have it for a treat every now and then."

Glowering at the table, Roman sank down into one of the chairs. "I just think it's weird that we both like Dr Pepper."

"With all due respect, weird is a pretty stiff competition this evening, and I'm not sure that lands at the top." Ethan moved toward the fridge. "Now, should I offer you something you *don't* like? Some standing water out of the sink, perhaps?"

"I'll take a Dr Pepper," Roman muttered.

Ethan thought about refusing on the grounds that further caffeine consumption might cause Roman to tear his arm off if he enjoyed dinner. But he surrendered and handed the young man a frosty purple can. "Mario Lanza," he finally said. "That's probably the opera singer you're thinking of. He was very famous and did a lot of movies in the forties and fifties."

"Right. And there was one where he went to Mexico and got into all this trouble with women."

"*Serenade.* It's actually based on an old James M. Cain novel that had all sorts of gay stuff in it they took out for the movie."

Roman sipped. "Assholes," he muttered.

"I don't know. The book was written in the thirties by a straight man, so the representation wasn't all that great, to be frank. They might have done us a service. I think the gay character decides he was just confused in the end. Love of a good woman and all that."

"But in the movie there's that big song he sings. I've heard it a bunch of places." Roman sat up erect, spreading his arms out. He mimed his best cartoonish imitation of an opera singer's face and emitted a warbling version of the tune in question, only without any lyrics and a strained parody of its melody.

"'Nessun Dorma,'" Ethan answered, laughing.

"What's so funny? You don't like my opera?"

"Sounds like your talents lie in other areas."

Roman shot him the bird, but he was smiling. This smile, Ethan could tell, was real. Big and goofy and devoid of self-consciousness and poise.

"It's originally from an opera called *Turandot*." Ethan unwrapped the veal. "I saw a production in Florence years ago."

"Oh, well. Smell you, fancy pants. Driving the Alps, operas in Florence. Sapphire Cove's a step down for you, it sounds like."

"*Au contraire.* It's the gig I've always wanted, and I love my coworkers."

The secret to Ethan's veal piccata was the sage and garlic powder he added to the flour, and luckily, he had plenty of both. For the sauce, he could use some of the wine he'd just denied Roman. And one of his nonstick pans was clean, which meant he could ensure he had plenty of remnants to enrich the sauce with.

Within a few seconds, he was in the zone.

"It was funny," Roman said after a while. "She never gave a shit about opera when we lived in New York. She never gave a shit about being *Italian* when we lived in New York. But when we moved in with Grandma Nina, everything changed. It was like she took all that stuff back. Which was kind of crazy 'cause New York's a way more fun place to be a proud Italian than Victorville, but after a year or two, she put up a bunch of posters of Rome and Florence and stuff and started up the opera thing."

"Is that why you changed your name to Roman?" Ethan asked.

He nodded and fell silent. "Anyway, opera was her favorite," he added quickly. "She was so buttoned down most of the time, but get her alone in the house and it was like there was all this music inside her trying to get out."

"Could she sing?" Ethan asked, dumping flour into the mixing bowl.

"No, but in her heart, she could. I think." He hesitated before adding, "She wasn't the warmest person."

Ethan waited for Roman to elaborate, wondering if he'd hesitated because he was ashamed to speak critically of the dead or if he blamed Ethan's long-ago actions for the woman's enduring chill.

As the oil heated in the pan, Ethan shot several looks in his direction, taking the guy's temperature as well. Roman studied his interlaced fingers. He was the most relaxed Ethan had seen him. But there was a soft tug at his features. Not a strain so much as a weight. Maybe he thought he'd wandered too close to the topic of his dad's cheating. Or maybe there was another painful drumbeat going inside of him—grief for his mom. Ethan was willing to bet it was the latter; he was also willing to bet it explained a lot of his recent actions. For the past few hours, at least.

Either way, it wasn't his place to drive the guy further into either subject. He went for the lemons, slicing each one cleanly in half. "So should I put on some opera or…?"

"Whatever you want," Roman muttered.

"Maybe we can just talk then." He dredged the veal through the seasoned flour, listening to the oil sizzle and pop next to him.

Roman looked up. "How long did you see him?"

He'd been braced for this line of questioning; it was a risk he'd accepted by offering to take the son of an old client in for an evening. A very late evening. He'd always obeyed a code stricter than a lawyer or a therapist when it came to discussions of his clients, even though he hadn't seen one in decades. But everything about Roman Walker was a special case.

"Two years."

Roman's eyes widened. "Three times a month for two years?"

"No, there'd be gaps. Sometimes a couple months. But he would always pick back up again."

"And he never said a word about either of us?"

"Never. He was always pretending to be somebody else. He never went by the same name. We didn't have any conversations that were…*real*. They were all scripted."

"He'd literally send you a script?"

Ethan pulled out two place settings and began setting up the first one in front of Roman. "No, he'd send me prompts, and I'd have to improvise. Have you ever taken any acting or improv classes?"

Roman grimaced and shook his head. "I pride myself on being the one trainer in California who doesn't want to be a movie star, thank you very much. The only acting I do is pretending to like squats."

The oil was hot enough now. He added the breaded veal. "I didn't want to act either. I took them to be a better escort."

"For my dad?"

"Him and others. I was good to my regulars. Once I hit my stride, I was all about regulars."

They fell silent again as the oil sputtered and the veal browned, and Ethan worried he'd given Roman more information than he could bear. But the guy seemed relaxed and still. "Thanks," Roman finally said.

"For what?"

"Answering these questions."

"If it helps."

This new silence felt easier, drained of strain. Once he'd sliced some onions for the spinach, he prepared the frozen package for the microwave, then added the wine to the pan. Then it was time to add the veal to the little lake of Chardonnay. After that, the capers. Last came the lemon. He squeezed the halves into the simmering sauce, late in the game so the juice wouldn't heat up too much and turn bitter. Delicious smells filled the kitchen, and suddenly Roman sat up in his chair, as erect and eager as a dog sensing the imminent return of its beloved owner.

By the time Ethan set a plate of food in front of him, there was a hungry glisten in the man's eyes, and he was clearing his throat as if he wanted no obstructions between his mouth and stomach aside from the unavoidable ones.

It was a stunning-looking batch, if Ethan did say so himself. He took a seat at the opposite end of his breakfast table, watching Roman chew his first bites. Just as he'd hoped, the guy's eyes rolled back into his head, and he let out a soft groan.

Then Roman noticed him watching and froze mid chew. He swallowed. "You gonna eat?" he asked.

Ethan smiled. "In a second. This is my favorite part."

"Watching someone eat?"

Ethan nodded. "The first few bites. If I've done my job well."

Looking self-conscious and nothing like the guy he'd been in the penthouse suite, Roman cut off another bite, added some spinach to the fork and chewed. "I guess it's like you said back at the hotel."

"How's that?" Ethan asked.

"You like making people feel good." When Ethan nodded, Roman swallowed. "Was it the same with…uh…*escorting*?"

Time for that plate, he thought, rising to fix himself some food. Interesting that he was less comfortable talking about his own relationship to his old job than he was his fake relationship with Roman's father. "It was. Very much so."

"I bet some of it was gross, though."

"Gross?"

He took a seat, cut himself a big bite and chewed.

Roman chewed as well. "You know…Unattractive men, women."

"Attractive's subjective, and I didn't get a lot of women. They were in a few group settings I worked, maybe a married couple every now and then. But I didn't have any consistent female clients. The truth is, if a woman just wants sex and doesn't care who it's with, she can whistle it up in pretty much any bar on earth. And if she wants something more, an escort's not going to do it."

"That's kind of binary, don't you think?"

"It was my experience. What can I say? I didn't have a rule. They just never called."

"You must have had some rules though, right? Like no kissing."

Ethan shook his head. "That's *Pretty Woman* nonsense. Sometimes a nice, deep kiss was a great way to shut up a really annoying client."

Roman smiled and wiped his mouth. "You're deflecting."

"From what?"

"Come on. Some of it had to be gross."

"Why? Why did it have to be gross, Roman?"

Roman glowered at his food, but it was clear the nourishment had taken some of the edge off him, even as they strayed close to a very dangerous topic. "I tried it once. Sort of."

"Escorting?"

Roman nodded at his plate, quickly forked another bite into his mouth, and chewed with too much force. "I'd just moved to LA and things were rough. I was getting all this attention on social media, so I dropped out of school. Figured I'd put a bunch of private clients together and be training Mark Wahlberg in no time. Woo-hoo! Instead I had two guys for a year—one always canceled just outside the cancelation window, and the other kept offering me more if I let him…

do stuff. He said it would just be a massage with a happy ending. But I knew it wasn't going to stop there. He was a forceful guy. A lawyer for one of the TV studios."

"They're the worst. So did you do it?"

Roman shook his head. "I freaked out on the front stoop of his house the night of our first *enhanced* session. I ran off and never called him again. So I lost his regular sessions too. After that it was a lot of catering gigs and temp jobs until I could get hired at a gym."

"That means it wasn't for you."

"But it was for you?"

Ethan saw a slide show of the nights when he'd enjoyed it. Feeling tight bodied and indestructible as he marched through the lobbies of fine New York hotels, pockets full of fresh cash, dressed in designer labels bought for him by the client he'd just left with a smile on his face. Nights when he felt beautiful and untethered and free, like taking all the shame out of sex meant there was no situation he couldn't sleep his way out of.

He saw Zach Loudon, his old New York roommate from the six-person crash pad he'd landed in on his desperate arrival in New York. When Ethan had worked up the nerve to ask the long-limbed, blond Adonis how he always managed to have a new cell phone and come home most nights bearing Dean & Deluca takeout when the rest of them were flat broke, a twinkle had come into the guy's crystal blue eyes, and he'd offered to show him. Showing him meant mentoring him, and mentoring him meant Zach doing things to Ethan's body that he'd never had done before, things his clients loved, things that made his eyes roll back into his head and had him gasping Zach's name.

After that came the cautions and the rules.

Never, under any circumstances, accept a beverage a client has prepared for you. Not even bottled water. No telling what they might have spiked it with and where you'd end up by the time you came to.

Bookend your calls with a check-in text or a voicemail to a friend in the know. Leave them the address of your destination too, just in case.

Make friends at the hotels you visit more than once. Maybe even offer them the occasional favor, if you can bear it. Then they're in on the game before they realize it.

Never, under any circumstances, threaten someone with blackmail if they refuse to pay. You don't know who they are or how easily they can kill. A thoughtless threat against the wrong client is a great way to end up in pieces in the East River.

But Zach had taught him about things other than dangers—how to relax a client, get them to lower their guard, shed the layers of arrogance and boasting clients used to gird their egos as they paid for sex. Layers that made them both annoying to deal with but also hesitant to tell you what really got them off. Because that information—the fantasy or kink they were afraid to ask for from anyone else—was how you turned them into a repeat client who walked away grateful and loyal. "It's their million-dollar answer," Zach had told him "Once you've got it, you can spin them into gold."

After those first few weeks of training, Zach took him out on his first call. The whole thing had felt both delicious and forbidden because the businessman they'd met at the Mandarin Oriental on Columbus Circle was one of those sweet, older guys who got gooey and grateful in the presence of young, beautiful men. And he was as delightfully turned on by watching the two of them together as he was by the things they'd done to him to finish him off. "One of the easy ones," Zach had whispered in the elevator afterward. "Good place for you to start," he'd added with a wink.

And yeah, there'd been bad nights and creepy calls, mostly guys who tried to force drugs on him he refused to take. "Great way to end up in a shipping container bound for Eastern Europe," Zach always said of the working boys who thought clients existed to feed their vices. But nothing held a candle to the handsome ones, the ones who thought they were entitled to a discount because of their fit bodies and good looks. They were the ones quickest to anger and entitlement, the ones who'd tried to get physical with him as they refused to pay what had been agreed to. For many of those years, Ethan believed the most dangerous thing in an escort's life was a client who wasn't clear on what they'd bought. Then, one night, like a cab jumping the curb, came little Ronnie Burton and his mom.

He was overwhelmed by how quickly these memories had come back. How powerful they were. They'd roared out of a part of himself he'd kept under lock and key for years, but Roman Walker had managed to kick the door open in one crazed night.

"Ethan?"

His silence had the guy across from him looking concerned.

"I was good at it," Ethan answered. "It's that simple. Or it was."

"'Cause you could get it up for all those people."

"No. Because I knew what the job was. And it wasn't to get it up. Not always."

"What was it then?"

"It was about their pleasure, not mine. With some of them, whether or not I got it up was irrelevant."

"You didn't ever freak out like I did?" Roman asked.

"In the beginning it was scary, but then I realized it was just sex. I mean, I had friends who were taking the train in the middle of the night into neighborhoods they'd never set foot in to get a blow job from a stranger who might have turned out to be Jeffrey Dahmer. What I was doing wasn't any more dangerous than that. In fact, I got more advance information out of my clients than my friends ever bothered to get from their one offs. I learned how to always know exactly what I was walking into."

"I don't know, though. I mean, the money might make them think they have a right to do more to you than they should."

"That's why you never go out on a call without a clear understanding in advance of what services will be rendered and how much you're charging."

"Wow. So you were a real professional then."

"Also, a switchblade helps. I only had to pull it once or twice in the beginning."

"Uh huh."

"And I took some Thai boxing classes, but I never really had to use those."

"Uh *huh*."

Ethan chewed and swallowed. "What's the tone about, Roman?"

"I'm just saying. It's not that safe."

"Nothing's safe. I was an adult who made an adult choice. But you made the right choice not going into that house that night. Nobody should be doing it who doesn't want to be. After a while, I figured out some tricks for making the difficult ones easier to deal with."

"Like what?" Roman asked.

"Trade secrets." Ethan winked and sipped his sparkling water.

A silence fell.

Roman broke it. "I can't have sex with someone I don't like. You know, like, *like* like."

"Like like? Or like like like?"

Roman smiled and huffed with laughter. "Stop it. You know what I mean. And it's worse than not being able to get it up. It's, like, total system shutdown. I just can't. And everyone thinks I'm this big player because of the way I look, but I'm not even on the apps or anything."

Ethan raised his eyebrows and set his fork down with a dramatic clank. "Oh, really, BeachBoy24?"

Roman spread his hands in a gesture of surrender. "That was an exception, and I killed him as soon as I got the meeting with you."

"Good. I wouldn't want him to insult any more men who can't spend five hours a day at the gym. Who was that in Beach Boy's pictures, by the way?"

"Some magazine model. I tried not to pick anyone too famous. I do a lot of Photoshop on my own posts, so I know how to make stuff look like it's not a scan."

"I see," Ethan grumbled.

"Don't worry. BeachBoy24 has been officially drowned."

It wasn't an apology, but it was close.

"Do you forgive me?" Roman asked.

The abruptness of the question startled Ethan silent. The vulnerability in the tone was so total, so pure, Ethan could only gaze into it for what felt like several minutes but was probably only a few dazed seconds. He was tempted to dismiss it as a mood swing in someone young and mercurial. But it seemed like something more, deeper. A man who was hurting and searching for connection and family in all the wrong ways.

"Do you forgive *me*?" Ethan was surprised by the speed and force of his response.

Roman seemed surprised too.

They'd returned to the most sensitive subject between them, and there was no anger in his expression. After a single night that wasn't over yet, Ethan had already learned well what anger looked like in Roman Walker's eyes.

"I asked first," Roman said.

"I forgave you before you left the hotel."

Roman nodded, seeming relieved, and cut off another bite of veal.

"And me?" Ethan asked.

"You were just doing your job," he answered, then quickly took the bite he'd prepared. "I mean…"

He fell silent, and Ethan knew if he tried to press, the guy might lock down entirely. It was clear the words he was planning to say next were a struggle. He was hanging his head and playing with his food.

"When we were chatting. Before. You know, when I was…BeachBoy24 or Cody or whatever, I could already tell you weren't who I thought you were going to be. I mean, when I told you things about my life, you actually responded. Like you were really listening. Like you were a good person."

Ethan bit back his urge to point out the details he'd been responding to had been completely fabricated. At this point, that went without saying. Instead, he nodded and said, "When did your mom pass?"

"Six months ago."

"Wow. Recent."

"I guess."

Half a year out from the death of the most important person in his life and Roman Walker wanted to be done with bad feelings about it. Not a good sign. In Ethan's experience, when you ran from grief, you ended up running on grief.

Roman nodded and rubbed his hands over his face. For a second, Ethan thought the guy might cry, but when he lifted his head from his palms, his face was blank. "What am I going to do about Rachel?"

Yep, Ethan thought, *running from grief on powerful legs.* "What's the worst-case scenario if you tell her?"

"Uh, hell on earth basically. I lose my home, my income. I have to go back to LA, find a new job. Diana's spending all this money on my promotions. That'll be over. I'm just starting to get ad revenue, but her people manage all the platforms for me, so who knows what they'll do. Maybe they'll lock me out of my accounts if she's mad enough."

"Could you get a job at Apex again?"

Roman furrowed his brow and looked up at him. "How'd you know I worked at Apex?"

"Research."

Roman nodded with a half smile, as if he was pleased by Ethan's bit of Google-stalking. Really it had been Jonas who'd Google-stalked the kid, and not for reasons of admiration, but no sense in sharing that with Roman now.

"Apex is competitive as hell," Roman continued. "It's the best gym in LA, and every trainer who wants to be an actor is dying to work there 'cause you're with industry people all day. I interviewed, like, five times before I got past go."

"Not to pry, but did your mom leave you anything?"

The guy turned to ice before his eyes. "Her house," he answered stiffly. "And some cash."

In the tense silence that followed, Roman started playing with the few strands of spinach left on his plate.

"Did you sell it?" Ethan asked.

He shook his head, clearing his throat. It took Ethan a second to read the expression on his face when he lifted his head again—shame. "She put everything she had in one of those trust things," he muttered.

"A revocable trust, yeah. Well, that's good. It avoids probate."

"Yeah, but, um... I signed the trust over to Diana."

Ethan set his fork down with too much force. "Oh, Roman," he groaned before he could stop himself.

He grimaced and gently ground one clenched fist against his forehead. "I know, I know. It was stupid, but she said she'd manage it for me and that she'd plow it all back into my career."

"Is she?"

"She's renovating the house and then she wants to sell it when the market's up. Please don't judge me. I know it was stupid. My mom had just died, and I wasn't thinking straight. I just didn't want to deal with any of it. And she was giving me a place to live, and I thought I owed her."

"Clearly she was planning to cash that check later."

"I know. I'm an idiot."

"You're not an idiot. Don't be so unkind to yourself. But you need someone you can talk to before you make these decisions, Roman. A third party. Somebody neutral."

Roman lifted one eyebrow. "You volunteering?"

"I want you to send me all the paperwork you have from this deal you made for the trust. I'm going to show it to a lawyer friend of mine. My treat. Let's do that before you talk to Rachel about anything."

He nodded and swallowed, eyes wide, the authority in Ethan's tone centering him. That, and the meal probably.

"Maybe I just cut my losses and go? Like, just move out and never look back. Start over."

"And not say anything to Rachel?" Ethan asked.

Roman nodded.

Ethan shook his head. "That's never going to happen. Nobody who feels the way you do about what happened to your mom is going to let his best friend walk into the same situation."

Roman sighed harder. "You're right."

"But let me see if you can get your inheritance back first."

Roman pushed his empty plate back from the edge of the table. "That's a really nice thing to do for someone who tried to get you fired tonight."

"We go back further than that, remember?"

"Do I ever." He slouched, resting his hands on his full stomach. "That was really good. Thank you."

"Dessert?"

"I'm stuffed, thanks."

But Roman didn't get up and didn't seem to be in a rush to leave.

"Maybe I shouldn't give a shit," he said after a while.

"About what?" Ethan asked.

"My life."

"All right, let's back up a step there, mister."

Roman shook his head. "No, no. I'm not thinking about…*hurting* myself. That's not it. I mean this fabulous Laguna Beach life I've been living in the Castle by the Sea. Maybe it *should* fall apart. Maybe it's crap. And the social media stuff? It's so stupid most of the time. If I lip-synch to one more song on TikTok, my lips are going to fall off. And then I spend hours twisting myself into a damn pretzel to get one shot that looks hot and natural. Then I've got to stand there and tap out some douchey caption that makes me sound like a half-naked Buddhist or something." He mimed air quotes and made a clownish expression. "*Beach vibes giving me inner peace. Bless.*" He held up a peace sign and tilted his head to one side like his brains were draining out one ear.

Ethan couldn't contain his laughter.

"I mean, what are beach vibes anyway?" Roman added. "What are *vibes*? Are they clouds or waves or some kind of gas? They sound like they might be dangerous if you don't have a helmet or a mask on or something."

Ethan barked with laughter now, and Roman's bright and genuine smile told him he was enjoying the response.

When their eyes met, Ethan felt a catch in his throat, a flutter in his chest he usually associated with too much caffeine.

Roman Walker was a young person who wasn't completely lost in the delusions of youth, and that made him dangerously attractive. The sudden surge of desire within Ethan felt more all-consuming than any flare of lust he'd experienced in the penthouse suite earlier that night, and he hoped Roman couldn't see evidence of it.

"I'm a mess," Roman finally said. "I'm worse than that. I'm a friggin' cliché. Pretty on the outside but fucked up on the inside. My moods are all over the place. I mean, sometimes I get so angry over nothing—"

"Roman."

"—and I grit my teeth so hard I'm afraid they're going to crack and—"

"Roman." He said the guy's name firmer. Enough to silence him this time.

"What?" Roman asked softly, with a little tremor of fear in his voice.

"Your mother died," Ethan said softly. The guy's jaw quivered. "Your mother died and it's hard and it hurts." Roman blinked and swallowed. "And it sounds like you fell in with the Peytons right around then, and all of the gifts and the luxury and the fame might have covered up some of these feelings. But it doesn't sound like you've been *having* those feelings, and you're going to need to be able to fall apart now and then somewhere that's safe."

"Yeah, where's that?" The tremor in his voice was stronger.

"Here."

Roman tried to smile, but it ended up forcing a tear down his right cheek. "You inviting me to move in?"

"I'm inviting you over for dinner. On a regular basis. Where you can unwind and be yourself."

"Dinner and falling apart. Sounds hot."

"I only serve hot meals. That's a promise."

Roman looked to the table, nodding.

And then it hit him. Ethan had felt it himself over the years, the anvil strike of grief.

The tears that followed were stronger than the ones that had struck Roman in the penthouse suite earlier that night, but Ethan was pretty sure their source was the same—grief for a mother who'd found her true self in the desert and done everything she could for her only boy, a mother whose heart sang with opera even as she kept herself buttoned up and task oriented. He'd heard somewhere it was better not to throw your arms around someone as they sobbed. That it would block the venting of emotions that needed to be set free. But the advice seemed suited for some support group or therapeutic setting, not his kitchen at almost two in the morning.

Slowly, Ethan got to his feet.

"She was mad at me," Roman managed between wrenching sobs. "The child support payments, she'd saved them all up... For-for college, and then I dr-dropped out after two years and... She was mad at me."

Standing over him now, Ethan placed a hand on his hunched upper back. "Did she stop talking to you?" he asked softly. *Like mine did,* he kept to himself.

Roman shook his head.

"Then she loved you. Always and forever. People who love us get mad at us sometimes. People who don't love us have no feelings about us at all."

"But I wish... I wish I'd stayed in school so she could know how much it me-meant...to me that she worked so hard for me. But I thought I was hot shit! I was gonna be-be some big fi-fitness st-star and buy-buy her a bigger house and then—"

"Hey," Ethan said softly.

It happened in an instant. Ethan wasn't quite sure who'd initiated it, just that in the blink of an eye, Roman Walker was in his arms.

For a mad, breathless second, Ethan thought the guy might try to kiss him. Which would be wrong, so wrong. Which would make him feel like he was taking advantage of someone young and vulnerable and grief stricken. But Roman Walker held to him instead, head pressed to his chest as sobs wrenched from him, sobs so strong it sounded like he'd been holding them in for months.

Slowly, Ethan steered them toward the sofa. Roman was so out of his body with grief, Ethan could have guided him anywhere. As soon as they sank down into the cushions together, he started to go over sideways, but he held on to one of Ethan's wrists, and that said he wanted Ethan to go over with him.

They were spooning now on Ethan's deep, cushy sofa, and it made Ethan's head spin and his breaths whistle in his nose, a sound Roman probably couldn't hear over his own essential tears.

With his one free arm, Ethan reached up for the end table next to their heads. A few grasps later, his fingers found the remote. The movie was still frozen where he'd paused it earlier that night, a perfect two-shot of DeNiro and Kilmer drinking from their coffee cups before plate glass windows filled with sparkling ocean. He paged out of it and over to his music app. Roman didn't notice.

It was a risk, what he was about to do. It might tip the young man over the edge into a place that was despairing instead of cathartic. But Roman Walker had plenty of grief he needed to set free. More importantly, Ethan was betting on the fact that Roman's earlier talk of Mario Lanza and opera classics had been signs of a latent desire to plunge more fully into memories of the mother he'd loved and the music she'd loved.

And so, with the tap of a button, Ethan filled his apartment with the soaring sounds of "Nessun Dorma." The guy shook with several more strong sobs, then he clutched Ethan's hand more tightly to his, which told Ethan that his mother's favorite song was exactly what Roman Walker needed.

9

In Ethan's fitful dreams, they made love. But his dreams were always wild, cartoonish things he never mistook for waking reality. In this latest round, the flashes of Roman's naked body looked like some plasticized cartoon, and occasionally Roman's face became Zach Loudon's, all warm encouraging smiles but frighteningly out of place. One minute, the living room was flooded with sunlight, then dark and shadow filled. In the next, all the lights would be turned on and so would the TV. And Robert DeNiro and Val Kilmer were giving him a gruff lecture on the mistake he was making, tasting the forbidden flesh of a former client's son. Then it wasn't his living room at all, but a New York hotel room he didn't want to identify.

What woke him finally was the feeling of Roman slipping out from his embrace, followed by the sound of his socked feet padding down the hall. A few blinks before Roman slipped into the bathroom confirmed they were both fully clothed and had been for the entire night.

Outside, morning birds chirped. His apartment faced west, so the morning sun wasn't too blinding, but he hadn't closed the curtains over the walls of glass looking out onto his balcony, and now he'd have to bury his face in the sofa pillows to get back to sleep.

More than Ethan's arms felt empty. He was bracing for the hurried sounds of Roman's departure. A shameful retreat with the dawn that said he thought this night of sofa snuggling had been as inappropriate as the content of Ethan's lusty dreams.

As Roman moved about the bathroom, Ethan debated sitting up, greeting Roman's return with casual chitchat that would turn his speedy exit into a polite and gracious one.

But Ethan couldn't move. Roman's delicious, rich cologne bathed the sofa pillows, and there was no pulling himself away from the scent. In the midst of this thrall, Roman slowly returned to the living room, as if trying not to wake the master of the house.

Eyes closed, feigning sleep, Ethan braced himself for the sounds of the guy hesitating at the end of the sofa, sinking into the chair nearby to tug on the designer tennis shoes Ethan had removed for him last night as he'd wept.

Then he felt Roman's weight fully sink into the cushions next to him, felt the guy slowly spoon himself back into Ethan's body, gently raising Ethan's upturned arm so he could tuck himself under it again. The young man gently pulled Ethan's hand closer to his chest like one might the edge of a comforting blanket. And the breath slowly returned to Ethan's lungs.

The ache in his gut was a warning sign. If he didn't head it off, his cock would soon be a steel rod against Roman's ass. He told his body to give itself over to the comfort and rest, the relief of Roman's return. Silently signaling his desire to the man next to him through a subtle press or a brazen rub, trying to see if the man shared it, these felt like acts of theft. Attempts to distract from the wild storm of feelings that had been unleashed inside him by a night of chaste and clothed snuggling.

In the end, he succeeded. The tension in his gut loosened. Thoughts seized control of blood flow. For now. And after a short while, sleep returned. This time it was deep, and Roman's return supplied the counterweight he needed to keep from flying off into a frenzied dreamland.

When he woke again, there was more sunlight in the room. And he could hear the shower running, a sound that suggested there'd be no rushed departure. Maybe they'd have breakfast. This pleased him more than he wanted it to.

And then he tried to move.

The cry that tore from him was so loud he heard Roman shut off the shower in response. "Ethan?" he called from the bathroom.

Footsteps, the shower door swinging open.

"Yeah, I..." Ethan called back, but his attempt to keep the pain from his voice was a choked, groaning failure. "My back."

Just as he'd feared on the trail the night before, the piggyback ride he'd given Roman was now exacting its terrible toll.

The returning footsteps were hurried, and suddenly he was smelling his own woodsy body wash coming off Roman Walker in waves. Eyes closed against the pain, Ethan had rolled over onto his back. Now he was afraid to move. His first slight motions resulted in knife stabs across his lower back.

"All right," Roman said, "I want you to try to roll toward me onto one side and then we're going to sit you up sideways if it doesn't kill you."

"Not killing me sounds like a good plan." Ethan nodded and rolled up onto one side. This time there were spasms, but no stabs. That was good. Roman pulled gently on his legs and slowly brought them to the floor. When Ethan grunted at the first fiery jolt, Roman paused, waited, then continued once things had calmed. Finally, the side of Ethan's right foot was resting against the floor, his left foot resting limply atop of it like he was a puppet whose strings had yet to be pulled taut.

"Okay," Roman said, "I'm going to sit you up sideways. Use your feet for balance, but don't put a bunch of pressure on them."

Ethan nodded and felt Roman's hands gripping his shoulders. He kept his eyes shut for fear of how much pain and fear—and weakness—Roman would see in them if he opened them. He breathed deeply, a whistle through clenched teeth, and then suddenly he was rising sideways. It had been a wise move, resulting in a few spasms, but no more deep and terrible stabs.

He breathed a sigh of relief, opened his eyes, and found himself staring at Roman Walker's perfectly outlined cock and balls. They were several inches from his face, tucked inside a pair of Ethan's white briefs. A glance up revealed all the smooth, sculpted muscle the guy had tried to tempt him with the night before, and a complete absence of guile in the young man's expression. He looked only concerned for Ethan's health.

"Good?" Roman asked, eyes wide and eager.

"Roman."

"Yeah?"

"Clothes, please."

Roman looked down at his own body as if he'd forgotten it. He grimaced. "Oh, yeah. Sorry. Just don't move 'till I'm back."

"Not going to be a problem."

Roman left the room. A relief.

A few seconds later, he returned. The only item of clothing he'd added was a tank top he'd swiped from Ethan's room. He sank down to a crouch in front of the sofa, gripped Ethan's shoulders. "So is sitting up making it—"

"Roman."

"Yeah?"

"At some point when my back isn't on fire, we'll discuss what constitutes an article of clothing."

Roman looked down at his excuse for an outfit, grimacing just like he'd done the first time. "I'm sorry. You just... You're in pain and I was freaking out and I wanted to get back and I—"

"Later. Just tell me what to do here, Mr. Trainer."

"I can get better pressure if you're on the floor. A lot of times lower back pain is a knot pressing down on something important and so it feels like a worse injury than it is. But the lower back and the legs are intimately connected, so I need to stretch out your IT bands too. Do you need to be at work any time soon?"

Even through his discomfort, he marveled at the speed with which Roman had transitioned into professional trainer mode. Amateur gym bunnies didn't use phrases like *intimately connected* to describe the relationship between body parts, and he'd moved right into assessing factors that would impinge on Ethan's recovery period.

"I'm supposed to go in this afternoon to check on some things, but I worked late so I've got junior chefs on the case until then. It's not a big Sunday for us."

"Good. Floor." Before Ethan could protest, Roman slid both of his arms through Ethan's armpits and hoisted his entire weight off the sofa with a surprising burst of strength. "This is probably from a night's sleep on the sofa," Roman added as Ethan's butt settled onto the spot where hardwood met Oriental rug.

"And the piggyback ride."

"Sorry." Muscles flexing in his briefs, Roman bent over and pulled the coffee table further away from the sofa so they'd have room to work without moving Ethan a second time.

"Don't be," Ethan said, wondering if he was talking about the piggyback ride or the way Roman was currently displaying his backside—plump and round and stretching the cotton of his briefs like it was made of marble underneath. That he could be this suddenly transfixed by the sight of it, when his own ability to move without pain was in question, made Ethan feel like a hopeless lech. "I knew the risks," he managed.

Roman turned to him with a nervous smile. "Let's start on your back."

It took Ethan what felt like a full minute to sink to the floor and roll over onto his back.

"All right, I'm going to start working with your legs, and there's going to be a reaction from your back, which is normal, but I want you to tell me if it really hurts."

The next thing Ethan knew, Roman had bent his right leg at the knee, turning the calf to one side so that it was perpendicular to Ethan's chest, then he pressed his chest and hands down on the entire leg to apply pressure. Pressure that spread along the inside of his thigh and down into Ethan's ass. There was a frightening tug in his lower back in response, but after a minute of scary tension, he felt a gradual loosening begin.

"Good?" Roman said, his face inches from Ethan's. Ethan kept his eyes closed, afraid the nearness of the man's lips would have the same effect on him as his flexing ass of a moment before.

He grunted and nodded, and Roman responded by grinding one clenched fist into the outside of Ethan's bent thigh, driving into his IT band hard enough to cause a painful amount of pressure, then dragging that pressure slowly up the length of Ethan's leg. It was the kind of pain that suggested an easing, a *healing*, was close at hand. It was the kind of pain you could learn to crave.

Roman finished off by twisting the lower part of Ethan's bent leg until it was parallel with his body and then bringing his chest down onto Ethan's knee to stretch out the glute on that side. Then it was on to the other leg. Which resisted harder. "Little imbalance here," Roman said softly. "Perfectly natural, though. We've all got one." There was warmth in his tone, warmth and professionalism, and together they made Ethan smile before he could stop himself.

"What?" Roman asked.

"You're good at this."

"Better be. It's my job," Roman said in close to a whisper.

This Roman, he thought, the one who worked with muscles and joints and *intimately connected* parts of the body, had more confidence and focus than the one who'd fallen apart at his table the night before. There were two Romans, it seemed. *No, that's bullshit,* he told himself. *They're all part of the same Roman. You've just seen every side of him in a very short amount of time.*

Silence fell, silence accompanied by a stirring in Ethan's gut. He was about to start up with some silent, lust-slaying mantras when Roman said, "Face down, please."

Relieved, Ethan slowly rolled over. If a boner burst through his mental controls, now he'd be able to hide it against the rug. There were no stabs this time when he moved, just little jerking spasms that suggested the muscles there were smoldering but no longer ablaze. Roman's work on his legs might have addressed the source of the pain, but Ethan wasn't about to say so.

Weight pressed down on him from behind. Was Roman about to massage his ass? Then, with a jolt, he realized the guy was sitting astride him. The weight was Roman's bulge—still clad in Ethan's briefs. The next thing he knew, his shirt was being pushed up over his lower back, and Roman's hands, still warm from the shower, were kneading the flesh there.

"Is this okay?" Roman asked quietly.

"You're the professional."

"How's it feel?"

Hotter than any sex act I've ever experienced in my long life of sex acts, Ethan thought. "I think you're getting it," he said.

"The leg work probably did it. I'm not feeling a bunch of crazy tension here."

Ethan grunted in the affirmative, then fell silent.

And the silence deepened.

And still Roman's hands worked. Ethan's mind searched for any sign that the kneading and the pressure were turning into something hungrier, less professional. Any lingering designed to arouse rather than to relieve. A slip of the fingers that felt like a caress.

After a while, he started to wonder if Roman had realized what he'd just realized. That there was no evident tension left in Ethan's lower back and still the man was working on it diligently and thoroughly.

Apparently, he didn't want to stop.

"And there it is," Ethan finally whispered.

"There what is?" Roman asked softly.

"All that weight you're feeling down there, I figured that's why BeachBoy24 gave me the boot."

"I told you. BeachBoy24 was a part I played. You should understand."

Roman's hands kept working. Ethan was achingly, painfully hard against the rug.

"So Roman Walker is less judgmental, huh?" Ethan asked, even as he told himself not to.

"Roman Walker likes men. The more man, the better."

Ethan laughed gently into the rug. "Can't tell from his TikToks, I hear."

"Roman Walker looks the way he does 'cause it sells, not 'cause he thinks it's hot."

"Oh, really? How would he look if he didn't have to have a body that sells?"

"Lean, probably. 'Cause I love cardio more than anything else and I have to force myself to do strength training. Even then, my intervals are probably too high intensity for the kind of bulking I try for. So if I just did what I wanted, I'd probably end up looking lean."

He was tempted to give the guy a lecture on how not all human bodies ran on such a clean connection between cause and effect, exertion equals instant weight loss. Tempted to tell the guy he should enjoy this period while he could because eventually his body would change. Bodies, he had learned, both as a sex worker and a man fighting the realities of aging, were endlessly specific and complicated. Roman Walker had genetic advantages and gifts he'd been maximizing as best he could, and more power to him. But as with most gifts, they could expire or wear out thanks to forces beyond your control.

And as with most of Ethan's lectures, this one was an attempt to distract himself from mental discomfort. This time, from the fact that Roman Walker had just expressed a lustful admiration for his lack of a lean, camera-ready torso. The guy who'd rejected Ethan had been a role. This Roman, the one massaging him now, was apparently the real thing.

"A lean guy who likes a lot of man," Ethan finally said.

"Pretty much."

When Ethan felt it, his first thought was to wonder if Roman wanted him to feel it. Roman Walker was aroused, too, only without a way to hide it. Maybe Ethan could have dismissed it as a natural, reflexive response to all the rubbing they'd done in search of pain relief. But this was the same guy who'd lectured him the night before on how he could never get turned on by someone he didn't like. *Total system shutdown,* he'd called it.

What Ethan could feel pressing against him now was the opposite of a total system shutdown.

Then he felt something else.

Roman Walker leaned forward and kissed him gently on the back of his neck.

A light peck, that was all.

A light peck that thundered through Ethan's body from head to toe, rendering him instantly breathless. Making every inch of his skin feel too warm and too tight. It was the surprise and ease of it that had left him instantly feverish, the playful hesitancy. By the time Ethan Blake was out of his twenties, there was nothing he hadn't tried sexually. This accomplishment had left him with a long list of things he never wanted to do again, but his greatest fear was that it had numbed him, dulled both his nerves and his heart, made him immune to the softer, gentler acts of desire. Now he realized it had done the opposite instead. At forty-three, he'd been laid bare by a fleeting act of tenderness; a single peck—especially when it came as a surprise—could be more devastatingly arousing than any crazy sex position, toy, or role-play fantasy.

Roman was sitting up now, bulge pressed against Ethan's ass.

Gently, the man's fingers caressed the spot where he'd just kissed. It was covered in gooseflesh. "Not so cool now, are you, Ethan Blake?"

"Roman..." He couldn't finish the sentence. There were a dozen different tones in his utterance of the guy's name. Fear and self-judgment alongside hunger and desire. As he let silence fill the room, he realized he was leaving it to Roman to decide which tone he'd heard. Roman Walker would decide if Ethan had just issued a plea or a warning. Because Ethan wasn't sure.

"Sorry," he whispered quickly, then swung one leg up and off Ethan's back. "I should probably get dressed. You know, like, *really* dressed."

Roman stood.

Ethan gasped into the rug, wondering if he should reverse this sudden left turn, when the guy's footsteps paused in the nearby doorway. "Can I borrow some more clothes?"

"Of course," Ethan answered, relieved by the idea that a clothes exchange might require another in-person meeting sometime soon.

"I'll be back in a second. No sudden moves."

Finally, as he listened to the sounds of Roman opening drawers in his bedroom, Ethan's ragingly hard cock stopped grinding painfully against the harder floor. When he sat up slowly and reached for the sofa next to him, his back whined a little, but it didn't yell at him. Another few seconds, and he was on his feet, moving into the kitchen, wondering if Roman was as unnerved as he was. A minute or two later, the guy walked into the kitchen, wearing a plain, light blue American Apparel T-shirt and a pair of Ethan's old gym shorts that weren't nearly as tight and revealing as his jeans from the night before.

"What happened to no sudden moves, mister?" he asked.

"I was slow. Where do you need to go? I'll drive you."

"I'll get an Uber. You shouldn't drive until your back's calmed down."

True, he thought, but what Ethan said was, "That's ridiculous. I'll drive you."

"I already called one."

"All right, well get me that paperwork like we said, and we'll get together and discuss my lawyer's response as soon as I have it."

"Great." The breathy, wannabe-seductive tone he'd used the night before was back, and he was gazing at him with puppy-dog eyes.

"And we'll meet in a restaurant next time, to avoid any confusion."

The long, tense silence was filled by ticking appliances and the rush of traffic down the busy street below Ethan's balcony.

"Confusion?" Roman asked, expression going blank.

"It was perfectly understandable, our little moment there. Given our positions. Literally. But in order to keep things appropriate, next time we should have lunch or dinner off campus, as it were."

One eyebrow raised, mouth curling into a half smile, Roman looked much like the fumbling seductor he'd been the night before. "You're afraid to have me in your house again 'cause you got a boner while I rubbed your back?"

"Fear has nothing to do with it. I'm suggesting it's not the best course of action because *you* got a boner when you rubbed my back, young man."

His face fell in an instant. "The kiss was just supposed to be like…you know, a good-bye kiss. You know, like, polite…not weird."

Ethan smiled. "All right, well. Let's let it serve its intended purpose and have this be good-bye, then. Until it's time to meet about what the lawyer says."

"Okay, whatever," Roman muttered as he reached for the doorknob.

"When it's time for you to meet with Rachel, you should do it at Sapphire Cove. I can get you one of the villas, maybe. Someplace private. That way if she completely freaks, you won't be out in public and you won't be on her turf."

When Roman turned in the open doorway, his expression was difficult to read—hazel eyes glazed and distant, upper lip tense. Perhaps he understood the gravity of this offer. For Ethan, it was no small thing, offering Roman protection and security in the very workplace from which the guy had plotted to get him fired. But it was also possible he was too stuck on the bit of sexual rejection Ethan had sent his way to appreciate it.

Ethan was no stranger to young men who based their entire self-worth on how many people wanted to sleep with them. He'd once been one of those young men himself.

"Thank you," Roman said quietly.

"Of course."

Roman opened the door and stepped out onto the open walkway outside. Ethan was still wearing his polite smile when the guy turned back quickly and said, "Also, Ethan?"

"Yes, Roman."

The man pointed to Ethan's crotch. "You're still hard." Then he closed the door as abruptly as he had the penthouse suite's the night before and was gone.

Ethan heard his breath leave him in a long, strained exhale as he gripped the counter on either side of his hips. His plan had been to dart into the bedroom as soon as he could and furiously relieve himself, possibly to the sight of Roman's social media accounts, just to intensify the necessary purge. But that felt like an unacceptable surrender now. Instead, he stayed frozen in the kitchen, gazing into space. He didn't move an inch until he'd deflated inside his briefs.

Cold as ice, he thought, *just as the young man said.*

10

For the second time in less than twenty-four hours, Ethan's voice was following Roman home.

I'm suggesting it's not the best course of action because you *got a boner when you rubbed my back, young man.*

Whatever, dude, he'd wanted to fire back. The whole time he'd stood there in his kitchen lecturing Roman on what was and wasn't *appropriate,* Ethan had a frigging bulge in his jeans. And yeah, pointing it out on the way out the door had felt satisfying. But it didn't make the moment any easier to remember as his sullen Uber driver sped west through the canyon.

Instead, it had him picking apart every move he'd made since waking up that morning.

Had he really thought the kiss on the back of the neck would be friendly, innocent?

Had he started imagining the man holding him down and owning his ass before he saw the gooseflesh spreading across his neck or after? He'd been hard before so… The question sort of answered itself.

Not just hard, filled with the hungry ache that meant he wanted to be filled, pinned down, and owned. And if the man doing the dominating had slightly callused hands and some kind of scruff or facial hair that could brush up against Roman's cheeks, his neck, his ass, the better.

Now he wasn't seeing the rugged, brush-dappled hillsides buzzing past outside. He was seeing Ethan Blake's trim, manicured mustache, crowning lips that looked puckered even at rest, designed for kissing. And seeing those things made him remember the man's comforting embrace. Made him feel it again even as his body was buffeted by warm wind through the half-open car window.

If the man had actually been his dad's secret boyfriend, he wouldn't be feeling any of this.

Or he wouldn't let himself feel any of it.

But the real Ethan—and not Michael, his alter ego—had always lived just outside of his dad's reach. And that special, authentic version of the man was the one who'd held Roman last night as he'd sobbed. This truth had his head spinning, breaking the dam that might have held back the attraction he'd been feeling ever since Ethan had piggybacked him to the car.

That was bullshit.

He'd been feeling the attraction ever since he'd pretended to be BeachBoy24, ever since he'd discovered how damn *kind* the guy was, and it had been messing with his head. He figured this confusion was part of the reason he'd done such a shit job of getting him in bed the night before. During the two weeks he'd spent playing Cody, he'd actually gone to the trouble of looking up some of the words Ethan had used during their chats. Insouciant, for instance. *Showing a casual lack of concern; indifferent.* Roman had always thought it meant cheerful, which was why he'd been so confused when Ethan had texted him—texted *Cody*—that someone in his profession must always be on the lookout for junior chefs who try to pass off insouciance as wisdom.

He was so calm, so wise. So *steady*.

Like a rock Roman could hold on to inside the storm that was his life.

Which was why, with each passing second of the drive, the memory of Ethan standing in his kitchen, boner inside his jeans, cheeks flushed as he lectured Roman about appropriateness and confusion was starting to feel more intoxicating than insulting.

The idea of landing a crack in the man's perfect composure thrilled him now, and for an entirely different reason than the one that had brought him to the penthouse suite.

And maybe a night of rolling around on Ethan's floor together—naked, this time—was exactly what they both deserved. In a way, they'd both been hurt by his dad's secrecy, and so now, years later, they had the right to comfort each other any way they chose.

Or maybe he wanted Ethan's comfort because nobody had comforted him like Ethan before. Since his mom's death, he'd found himself jerking awake once, sometimes twice in the middle of the night. But not the night before. Not in Ethan's arms. His sleep had been deep and dreamless.

Safe. And it wasn't just Ethan's embrace that had quieted his soul. It had been his cooking and his conversation and his absence of judgment. It had been the way he'd appeared out of the dark canyon, bringing light and comfort and warmth to shadows Roman's mind had filled with angry serpents. He'd brought something else with him to, something that felt like—

Not love. Don't use words like love. Not with him.

Roman had never bothered to sit down and write a list of what the man of his dreams would be like. But if he tried now, he was pretty sure it would end up sounding a lot like Ethan Blake.

In hopes of avoiding Diana, he was already planning a quick flight down the Castle's exterior staircase as he punched in the motor court's gate code. But when the wooden gates retreated into the stone walls on either side with a low whine, there was no sign of his boss's rose-gold Maybach on the other side. The Escalade she was always chauffeured in was still there. Diana Peyton, it seemed, had struck out into the world on her own, and thank God.

The kitchen was on the southwest corner of the house's top floor, with a breakfast nook sporting dazzling ocean views and a picture window above the sink offering tree-studded glimpses of the steep public staircase to the beach next door.

Hank was loading the fridge full of sparkling water, some expensive European brand Diana ordered by the caseload and which Roman had approved of because it sported no hidden sugars. The man's unofficial uniform was a pair of black jeans and a white dress shirt—long sleeve or short sleeve depending on the weather. Today it was short. He was spritely for sixty-five. Years of stunt work had managed to keep him in fit condition while sparing him the kind of serious injuries that had taken a lot of his buddies out of the business. If anything revealed his age, it was his insistence on a helmet hairstyle and bushy mustache that made him look like he should be guest starring on a *CHiPs* rerun, a show he'd died on twice as a young man.

"Mr. Walker," he said without turning away from his work. "Someone had a sleepover."

"Where is she?"

Startled by his abruptness, Hank shot him a look. "LA. Back Tuesday night."

Roman tried not to sigh with relief.

"Late night, party animal?"

"Sorry. Just distracted by stuff."

Hank shelved more bottles, but he kept shooting curious looks his way. Maybe because Roman's answer to his question hadn't been an answer.

Could he trust Hank? He'd been at Diana's side for decades. They'd met on a set when Diana was in her prime and Hank was doing the stunt work for a drug dealer character who got blasted out of a third story window before landing in a dumpster below. Today he was the chief of her large personal staff. The minute their boss rolled into her primary home in Pacific Palisades she'd be swept into the arms of her LA-based bodyguards and housekeepers, but they all answered to Hank. Did that mean he was in on the wedding plot?

The Castle by the Sea, once an idyllic refuge, had become a minefield in less than a day's time.

"Why didn't you go with her?" Roman asked.

"Meeting her later. She wants me to drive out to the storage unit in Victorville and bring back some of your stuff. She says your room looks like a mediocre hotel—and I'm quoting now—that I wouldn't make a fired agent stay in. After that, I'm supposed to head up to LA. She's got meetings with the wedding planner tomorrow to look at designs for this enchanted forest thing they're going to do for the wedding."

He pretended to gaze out at the sea so Hank couldn't see his little burst of anxiety. "Scott's not coming back, is he?"

"Nobody said anything to me. Oh, and she wants to train at ten thirty Wednesday morning. Out on the beach, like usual."

Roman nodded, Diana's strategy becoming clear. She was giving him time to digest her offer, while subtly pressuring him to make himself more at home in her home. Her second home. Of several. But come Wednesday morning, she'd expect his decision. Which was good news. Because Rachel flew back tomorrow night.

Boom, boom, done. Good-bye, bougie Laguna life. Hello... He had no idea what.

At the risk of being rude to Hank, Roman whipped out his phone and texted his best friend for the first time since discovering her fiancé was cheating trash.

> **What's up, superstar? Need you for a mtg at Sapphire Cove Tuesday afternoon. You free?**

No response.

"Hey, so, um, what do you want me to pull out of storage?" Hank asked, turning from the fridge.

An idea dawned. It wasn't the solution to his problem, but it was a way to chip away at some of the control he'd foolishly given Diana over his mother's humble estate. "I'll do it," Roman said.

"Do what?"

"I'll drive out to Victorville and get the stuff. You don't need to hoof it all the way out there in Sunday traffic."

"You sure?"

"Yeah, I mean, what are you going to do? Text me a bunch of times asking me which old picture I want? I'll just need the key."

Hank nodded, considering this change of plan.

Then he disappeared around the corner into his cubbyhole of an office. The converted pantry was windowless and full of monitors showing feeds from the house's security cameras. He returned, bearing a tiny brown envelope. "Address is on there, but if you can't read my chicken scratch it's the Extra Space on Yates Road right off the 15."

Roman nodded and took the key, feeling like he'd just pulled off an amazing sleight of hand, which was maybe overstating it.

"Oh, and we don't say anything about this. 'Cause I'm not actually heading up to LA right off. I'm gonna run some errands she didn't give me time for this week, so if she asks, we went to the desert together. Got it?"

Roman extended his hand, and they shook. The more secrecy around this handoff, the better.

"Ten thirty Wednesday morning. Don't forget. She's fired up to burn. Must have had a piece of cake or something the other night."

Yeah, that's not what she's fired up about. Roman kept these words to himself as he slid the little envelope into one of the baggy pockets of Ethan's gym shorts.

Hank shot him a trigger finger and disappeared into his tiny office.

Once he'd sped downstairs to his room, he checked the phone for a response from Rachel but found none. He closed the door, leaned against it and then began scrolling through old emails in search of any paperwork he could find relating to his mother's trust. When he finally hit the thread, he was embarrassed by how unfamiliar it all looked. He downloaded the attachments to his phone, then sent them by text to the number Ethan had called him from the night before. A second later, it felt both cold and rude, beginning their first official text thread with a document dump highlighting Roman's youth and inexperience. And grief.

So he typed out a follow-up message.

Here's the paperwork I could find. Thank you sooooooo much.

His fingers froze as he debated what emoji to follow the text up with. Just then, a text popped up on his screen. From Rachel.

Of course, my love! Tue at SC sounds gr8! Time? Sorry it took me so long to respond. Scott sent me 654 selfies from his hike this morning cause I'm supposed to decide which one goes on the gram. #men

The one where he falls off a cliff, Roman thought but didn't text.

Awesome. I'll get back to you with a time!

She tapped back with a thumbs-up. Then, once he realized the dreaded meeting had been scheduled, and in enough time for him to drop the bomb before he was supposed to see Diana again, Roman's stomach turned to ice, and he found himself struggling for breath.

The next text on his phone came from a number he hadn't paired with a name yet.

Ethan. It had to be.

> **Perfect. I will go through these today and get them to my lawyer friend as soon as possible. I'll get back to you right away and see what she says and what the best course of possible action is. Stay tuned and stand by.**

Roman laughed. A long, articulate text devoid of emoji or even abbreviations. It sounded official, which might have been off-putting, given how vulnerable they'd been with each other the night before. But it was also comprehensive. As if when it came to Roman Walker, Ethan Blake wanted to leave no stone unturned.

How's your back?

> **Better. Thank you.**

Well, that's abrupt, Roman thought.
He sent the emoji before he could stop himself.
The blushing one.
Then he started typing.

We should have sex just once to get it of our

Then his fingers froze and began backspacing against his will, mainly because the next words he'd planned to type were *but not in a getting you fired kind of way.*

What would Rachel say if he told her about all of this?

She might suggest he was trying to compete with his own dad in some weird way.

She might also start screaming at the top of her lungs if he included the detail about how he'd planned to falsely accuse Ethan of assaulting him the night before.

As he suffered the nightmare traffic on the way to Victorville, he told himself he had to do something with this burning urge inside of him. Every second since he'd left Ethan's apartment, he still felt like he was curled up in the man's powerful arms on his sofa. No man had ever made him feel that way before. And that meant he *had* to do something about it, right?

A few hours later, he was moving boxes under the kind of baking desert sun he'd grown used to as a boy, but which after years of living closer to the coast he found oppressive again. He'd known it would be punishing work and dressed accordingly, but his tank top and workout pants were almost soaked through. He could use a shower. Or two.

With Ethan. Maybe I could use his sexy mustache as a loofah.

Romy, honey, he heard Rachel's voice say, *you are ob-sessed!*

He stopped working when a growling Ford F-150 started nosing its way down the alleyway between storage units. It rolled to a stop several feet from the spot where Roman had parked Diana's Bentley Bentayga, with its open cargo door a few feet from the storage unit's gaping entrance.

Andy Rosales stepped from behind the truck's wheel, rosy-cheeked and smelling of Old Spice, his shoulder-length black hair pulled back in a ponytail and still damp from the shower. He was a tank of a man, an old-school body builder turned auto mechanic who thought Roman's holistic approach to fitness was a lot of witchcraft and nonsense. Watching the sheer bulk of him as he approached the open door to the storage unit reminded Roman of all those pleasant nights when he'd come across his mother safely snuggled inside the guy's giant arms on the living room sofa and thought, *Good, she's got someone.* Of the two men she'd dated seriously after divorcing Roman's dad, Andy was the one his mom actually let in. Maybe because he was a gentle giant who listened more than he lectured. He'd entered the picture too late to be the father figure Roman had always craved, but he'd made his mother happy, and that had made Roman happy.

The fact that he'd dropped everything on a Sunday afternoon to respond to Roman's request for help made Roman happy now.

"You sure you've got the room?" Roman asked.

Andy nodded, but he was nosing his way into the storage unit and surveying what was still packed inside. "Yeah, I moved the home gym into the yard from the garage 'cause I was fixing up this old MG roadster. '63. Cherry red convertible. Total beaut. But I sold the thing so I've got space." Andy turned suddenly and gave Roman a once-over. Thanks to knife slashes for eyes beneath bushy, black eyebrows, he always looked suspicious of everything, but in this moment, the curiosity seemed genuine. "Trouble with Boss Lady? She's footing the bill for the unit, right?"

"Top secret, but I might be looking at other options."

"Will they come with a beach house in Laguna, though?"

"Doubt it."

"You want your car back?"

When he'd started working for her full-time, Diana had informed him in no uncertain terms she didn't want him driving his dark green Chevy Spark on errands. At the time, giving him the use of one of her Bentleys had been her way of pampering him. But maybe the thought of one of her employees driving a cheap car embarrassed her.

"Not yet, but maybe soon."

"And your mom's old place? She's gutted the thing, you know. I drive by every now and then. Contractors have been going nonstop."

Roman's stomach soured. "I'll figure it out."

Andy nodded, as if he thought there was more to the story but didn't want to pry. He went to his truck, reached into the space behind the driver's seat, and returned with two cold bottles of water, still dripping from the ice chest.

As they worked, Roman pondered how to phrase the question he was dying to ask. By then, his mother's last boyfriend had loaded a bunch of boxes into the cab of his truck, and Roman had practically filled the four-door Bentley to bursting. Neither one of them, it seemed, had the strength to go through the boxes and deal with the layers of memories within. It was a strange sight, the expensive, impeccably designed luxury car filled with worn cardboard sidewalls. Like they'd stuffed Cinderella's carriage full of old shoes.

Once they'd nearly exhausted themselves, Andy clapped Roman on the back and announced it was time to eat. In Andy Rosales's house, *time to eat* usually meant one thing—giant steaks from his backyard grill.

As Roman and Andy dined in satisfied silence, the afternoon sun lanced Andy's dry, dusty backyard with rosy light. A few years of living at the coast and Roman had forgotten how quiet the desert could get, especially when you were far from the highway. No surf sounds, few birds. Just open space and light and the occasional woosh of a passing car down Andy's street.

He felt more relaxed than he had in days. His mother's possessions, as well as a big chunk of his own, had been moved out of Diana's grip.

"Did my mom ever talk about what happened with my dad?" he finally asked.

"All the time, yeah." Andy licked steak sauce off his fingers, but he watched Roman closely. The topic clearly made him nervous.

"Did she ever say anything to you about the guy he cheated with? Michael?"

Andy shook his head and looked down at his food. "That wasn't his name. He was just some hooker using an alias. His real name's in the file, though."

Just some hooker. The words speared him, and it took him a second to realize what he was feeling.

Defensive. Of Ethan.

"Wait," Roman said, "you've seen the file?"

Andy nodded, shoveling food into his mouth.

"I didn't know she still had it. I thought she threw it away after the divorce."

"Nope," Andy said and swallowed. "She said she used to take it out once a year to remind herself not to be so naïve about men. Didn't exactly melt my heart when she told me that story on our first date, but that came later, I guess. Figure it's in one of those boxes we loaded today. But if you want to do a search for it, we've got to do it another day because I've got drinks with the boys later."

"No," Roman said too quickly, "I don't need to see it. It's fine."

He didn't want to bother with the old version of Ethan.

He liked the new version—the *real* version—far too much.

Thanks to Sunday traffic, what should have been an hour and a half drive back to Laguna turned into a three-hour crawl.

A text from Ethan arrived when he was just north of Corona, and things were moving slowly enough that he felt he could read it without risking a wreck.

> **Meet at boardwalk on Main Beach in Laguna at 8 p.m. for updates and a surprise?**

Roman was grinning from ear to ear as he typed out in all caps **YES!**

No way could he already have an update from the lawyer. It was Sunday.

And the surprise could be so many things.

Roman realized what Ethan really wanted out of him, even if he was too uptight to say it.

A date.

11

Ethan was at his desk, typing up task lists to guide his team while he was visiting Donnie later that week, when a text from his boss arrived asking him to *drop in for a chat.* Even as the words *Uh oh* echoed through his brain, he responded with a thumbs-up.

When he knocked, Logan Murdoch, the hotel's director of security, opened the door and gestured for him to enter. Toweringly tall, the man was handsome in a manner Ethan found severe. Years of service in the Marine Corps had left him capable of instant laser-like focus, which was what he'd fixed Ethan in now. While the large, windowless office behind him was empty save for Connor Harcourt, his presence here might be a bad sign. Or it might mean nothing at all. Perhaps he'd been stealing some at-work personal time with his devoted fiancé and would quickly excuse himself.

No such luck. The blazer-clad giant sank back down onto the office's Chesterfield sofa, studying him with unnerving calm and a placid smile.

"First off, you tell that son of a bitch Donnie Bascombe he needs to send me the Padres schedule if he wants me and Connor to come down soon." Logan grinned.

"Of course," Ethan said with a smile, even as he figured he was being buttered up for a difficult conversation.

"You guys are getting together this week, right?" Logan asked.

"We are, unless that's become a scheduling issue."

Because he'd barely had any transition time between his London gig and Sapphire Cove, he'd negotiated some early vacation days into his contract and was hoping to use the first few on his trip down to San Diego.

"No, no problem," Connor said quickly, then he and Logan exchanged a look. Logan, it seemed, was silently requesting permission to speak again. His fiancé and boss granted it with a small nod, and Logan turned his penetrating attention back to Ethan. "Security heard yelling coming from the penthouse suite during your meeting with Roman Walker, and it didn't sound like you were the one yelling."

"Oh, he's fine. He's just under a lot of stress with the wedding."

"We're not worried about Diana Peyton's trainer," Connor said. "Happy employees make for happy guests. That was my grandfather's motto, and that's how we run Sapphire Cove. If you don't feel safe, you're not happy."

"I'm beyond happy here. Thrilled, actually. But thank you for checking."

"I have to ask, does this guy have some kind of fixation? He specifically requested the penthouse suite, but he came alone. And then he's yelling at you? I mean, you were on that Netflix show, right? The one with the dead people and the cakes."

Logan chuckled. "No, babe, the cakes were just supposed to *look* like—"

"I got it, Mr. Murdoch," Connor whispered.

Logan bowed his head when he realized he'd corrected his boss as if they were at home together.

But Ethan was left relieved by their exchange. As if it had been illuminated by a beam of light from the heavens, he suddenly saw the path to an answer that was just truthful enough. "Roman Walker isn't a stalker, I can assure you." *Sort of,* he thought. "When it comes to this wedding, his boss has some unrealistic expectations. I recognized the situation and promised I'd work with him to make sure he can accommodate her as reasonably as possible while also watching out for his own mental health."

Logan looked satisfied by his answer.

Connor did not. After a tense silence, he said, "I would assume the majority of stress around this wedding would fall on the wedding planner, not the *dietician*."

"Connor, you don't like him," Logan said quietly.

Connor's eyebrows went up. "I don't like that he flirted with two of our security guys to get access to a suite he never should have been let into. Am I going to have to manage Brandon and J.T. by flirting with them now too?"

Sitting up straight, Logan said, "No, because they know good and well any man at this hotel who flirts with you will end up with his voice box in my hand."

"Hot," Connor whispered with a twinkle in his eye, "but we're at work."

"Gentlemen." Ethan cleared his throat. "While you should always feel comfortable being your happily engaged selves in front of me, I can assure you, the situation with Roman Walker is solely that he is young and his relationship with Diana Peyton is very complicated. I'm trying to help him do the best job for her that he can. That's all."

Which in the case of one of her requests, is no job at all, he thought.

"Okay," Connor finally said. "It's a very big event for us, but at no point will Sapphire Cove expect you to place yourself in the line of fire from a personality that volatile."

"He's not that volatile, I can assure you."

Sort of.

One of Connor's eyebrows went up. "Ethan, he yelled out at you during a meeting about *cake samples* and then peeled out of our motor court at seventy-fives miles an hour and was rude to the valets."

"As always, I appreciate your protectiveness, but trust me, I'm doing what I'm doing with Roman of my own volition entirely."

Great, he thought, *now it sounds like I'm fucking him.*

But if that's what Logan and Connor thought, they weren't letting on.

"Let us know if anything changes," Connor said, then he stood and so did Logan, both signals Ethan was being relieved. He rose as well, shook both their extended hands, and departed. In any other circumstance, he would have been moved by management's protectiveness of him. But in this moment, he was essentially conspiring with Roman to knock one of the hotel's biggest events off the calendar, and that made him feel like he was a college kid in South Carolina again, closeted and living a double life.

12

Roman's pre-date grooming ritual, the one that allowed for all penetrative possibilities, usually took him two hours. This time, he added an additional hour, by the end of which he was confident every inch of him tasted good enough to eat. Even to a seasoned chef. Normally, he'd only prepare himself for this level of intimacy with a third date who showed real promise. But Ethan Blake occupied a special category. That's why he occupied Roman's every other thought.

He was smarter and more elegant than the older men who'd asked him out in LA back when he was working at Apex. Mostly investment types and entertainment execs who talked their way through dinner in brusque, emotionless sentences that made clear they were only killing time until the clothes came off. Until Roman made clear he never gave up the goods on night one and the light went out of their eyes and suddenly they were making excuses to cut the night short.

Ethan Blake, on the other hand, spoke in elaborate, detailed sentences that wrapped around you like a comforting embrace—even if Roman had to look up every other word. What mattered was that Ethan spoke like he was actually seeing him, not just imagining what he wanted to do to him later.

And that, ironically, made Roman want to ride him bareback until the sun came up.

Daddy issues, he thought as he styled his hair. His fellow trainers at Apex had given him the diagnosis, based on the fact that the gym patrons he thirsted over were always rawboned with steel gray facial hair. But the brand had felt like an accusation, maybe because it was so obvious. He'd never really had a dad. Not since the age of seven, anyway. And today his hormones fired for men twice his age who radiated stability and confidence. But as the night before made clear, Ethan—the version of him he was coming to know, at least—added other elements to the package. Generosity. Gentleness. Tenderness. And something else he couldn't remember the name of, at first.

Something old world, historical. Medieval, even.

Courtly.

Most of the daddies he'd been out with in LA would have used that morning's backrub as an excuse to mount him on the living room floor. But Ethan had gotten flushed and flustered, before pulling himself together like a British butler from some PBS show with all his talk of *confusion* and *appropriateness.*

To say nothing of his behavior at the hotel.

At the very moment Roman had gone for his throat, Ethan Blake had opened his heart, and every hour since had felt like a wild ride into impossibilities made real.

He left the house in an outfit he considered a cross between sexy and elegant, with none of the porny callbacks to his slutty football player look he'd employed the night before. Dark, tailored slacks with a Gucci belt. A shiny silver cashmere sweater which he planned to remove at the perfect moment, revealing the black dress shirt he wore underneath was actually sleeveless. Maybe he'd duck away and do some quick push-ups before the big reveal. Hopefully they'd have dinner someplace with a spacious, clean, and private men's room.

You are not doing push-ups on a goddamn bathroom floor to impress this man, you thirsty, crazy bitch. But even as he admonished himself, he was pretty sure he'd give it a try. If the floor was clean.

To avoid the perpetual parking nightmare that was Laguna Beach, Roman took an Uber to their meeting place. The sunset crowds had long departed, and the sky over the Pacific was fading from dark blue to black. To the east, the coastal mountains loomed, and the tiny town below was all streetlights and headlights and the occasional twinkle of string lights wrapped around a tree trunk or threaded through its branches.

Sitting by himself on a bench steps from the sand, Ethan scrolled through his phone. His classy outfit made Roman smile and silenced the little bird on his shoulder that kept chirping about how Roman might be reading too much into this meeting.

When he saw Roman approaching, Ethan stood. His navy blue cashmere sweater had a zippered collar. A second collar sprouted from underneath, belonging to a pressed white polo shirt. His designer jeans looked pricey, and his artfully scuffed Docksiders matched his brown belt perfectly. The belt was braided, normally a cause for ridicule in Roman's world, but on a man of Ethan's maturity, it was the perfect touch. There was just enough product in his thick, wavy hair for it to rustle gently in the ocean breeze without losing its tousled shape.

Out of his chef's coat and casual wear, Ethan Blake looked as timeless and elegant as his speech patterns sounded. And he'd come bearing gifts. In one hand was a dusty gold gift bag stuffed with light blue tissue paper.

The unsuspecting tourists who'd been caught out in shorts and T-shirts were complaining loudly about the sudden cold as they surged past Roman on the boardwalk. It was one of those Southern California nights when the temperature had plummeted at sundown.

When Roman threw his arms around him, Ethan completed the hug with three light taps on Roman's upper back that seemed to sound out *Not. A. Date.*

When Roman went to kiss him on the cheek, Ethan ducked his head at the last second and placed the gift bag in Roman's hand.

"I hope this is fun. It was just something that occurred to me." The man sounded as poised and professional as he had when he'd stepped into the penthouse suite the night before. Suddenly, Roman felt an anxiousness that bordered on panic, even as Ethan smiled and gestured for him to take a seat on the bench. "Open it!"

Sinking to the bench, he complied. Buried within the nest of tissue paper was an elegant cardboard gift box bearing the logo of a local gallery he didn't recognize. As Roman balled the paper up, Ethan gently took it from his hands, then he took the empty bag. Setting the box on his lap, Roman carefully pulled off its top half, revealing a creature inside with a wingspan roughly equivalent to his own hands if he'd spread his fingers and interlaced his thumbs.

"Gertrude," Roman whispered.

"I wasn't sure you'd get it. So there's a card in case you'd already forgotten."

Ethan had extracted it from the tissue paper after Roman had almost tossed it by mistake. He tore it open and read.

This is Gertrude, your protector on the trails. Long may she caw. Best, Ethan.

Best? Roman wanted to whine. *Not even an XO?!*

But he now had his very own hawk with a gaping beak, impeccably detailed and painted. "This is very nice."

"Granted, I'm not exactly sure *how* she's going to protect you on the trails. Perhaps we could fashion her to some sort of visor or hat."

Roman hefted her by the base in both hands. "She's kinda heavy for that."

"Yes, well, you're strong. And always looking to get stronger, it seems."

Not hot, Roman thought, *strong. Goddammit.*

"Like I said, it was just something I thought of last minute." Ethan was studying him, a slight furrow to his brow, absolutely nothing that looked like lust in his eyes, and Roman was starting to feel like a little shit for not being more grateful. "Not to give too much of a peek behind the curtain, but I thought it would be much harder to find. Mainly because I forgot how wildlife-driven Laguna's art scene was. If you're ever in the market for a seven-foot-tall plaster of paris giraffe, they've got several here in town."

"You didn't have to do this," Roman said, but it had come out wrong. Like he didn't *want* Ethan to do it.

Because he wanted him to do something else more.

If Ethan heard this note, he ignored it. "So the updates. First off, you're all set at the hotel. I checked and several of the villas aren't booked on Tuesday, so they won't need to be turned over for a guest, and they'll be free most of the day. What time do you want to meet there with Rachel?"

"One p.m. sounds good. It'll give her time to drive down."

"Perfect. Unfortunately, the next update isn't quite so positive."

"The trust," Roman said quietly.

Ethan nodded, studying him, as if giving Roman time to prepare himself for bad news. "You wouldn't be able to remove Diana as trustee unless you took her to probate court. And you'd have to prove she wasn't fulfilling her obligations. Have you seen any evidence she's violating the trust documents as they're written?"

"I don't even know how they're written."

"Okay, well, you should rectify that."

"I know." He wanted to hold the hawk to his chest, but he had to turn it first so its beak wouldn't poke him. "My mother's house is a drop in the bucket compared to what Diana's got. Why would she want to control it like this?"

"To control you."

The simplicity of the statement stung.

"She was planning this six months ago?" Roman asked once he recovered. "Scott and Rachel didn't meet for another month after that."

"Look, I've had a lot of Hollywood clients. In both my professions. The more famous ones, everyone in their life had a very specific role. I mean, beyond just makeup artist or lawyer. When Diana met you, she probably thought she could find a use for your youth and looks eventually. But first she needed something to lord over your head. There's an upside here, though. The entire trust terminates in six months, and you're still the beneficiary. None of that's changed. It all still goes to you in the end."

Roman studied the bird on his lap. "If there's anything left after I piss her off," he grumbled.

"Then you take her to court."

"With the money I don't have anymore. Thanks to her. How's that work?"

"She's a big target. You might find a lawyer who'll take it on a contingency fee."

"What's that?"

"They only get paid if they win. And if you threaten Diana with bad press, she might settle quickly. Hell, she might settle now."

He caressed Gertrude's wings, trying to draw strength from them. "And then I'm the celebrity trainer who turned on his biggest client because he was too dumb to read what he was signing. That should really help my career."

Ethan nodded, but he looked like he was doubting this assertion. "*Or* she ends up becoming the villain who preyed on a grieving young man. And you know how to work social media, which is where these things often play out. It's just a matter of telling the right story."

Roman nodded, but the prospect seemed overwhelming. And his followers were more interested in seeing him work out shirtless than they were in hearing him complain about his business problems.

Happy, hand-holding straight couples moved past them along the boardwalk. For the most part, the surf sounds were drowned out by the passing chatter combined with the rumble of cars behind them, some of the couples probably gearing up for a long drive home as the sunny weekend came to an end.

"I apologize I didn't come bearing different news," Ethan finally said.

"You got in touch with your lawyer on a Sunday?" Roman asked.

"She's an old friend."

"Still, that's kind of amazing that you did that for me."

"A promise is a promise," Ethan said with a smile. "A question, though. Once this all goes down with Rachel, you might need another place to stay for a while. Do you have something lined up?"

"I was thinking of crashing with this guy Andy out in Victorville."

"Someone you're seeing?" Ethan asked without a trace of jealousy or possessiveness.

"Andy Rosales? Oh my God, no. He was my mom's boyfriend. Good guy. He's practically family. I was out there earlier moving some of my stuff out of the storage unit Diana put it in before she started renovating the house. My car's been out there forever. Diana said she'd rather have me driving the Bentley around town. Good impressions and all that."

"Victorville's a bit of a haul."

"With traffic, yeah. I drove it twice today, and I'm beat."

Ethan nodded, sucking in a long breath through his nose. "Well, perhaps you could stay with me for a while."

Roman's heart raced. "On the sofa?"

"I actually have a guest bedroom, but if the sofa's more comfortable…"

"I think what made it comfortable was you."

"I will be staying in my room, as we discussed this morning."

Roman smiled. "We didn't discuss that this morning."

"You know exactly what I mean, young man."

And Roman did, but when Ethan said it in that gruff, commanding voice, Roman wanted to pretend to be confused. On all fours.

"The offer is for a place to stay while you plan your next move. And I'll also throw in meal service while you're there. Preprepared, all things you can heat up. And don't worry, it'll be high protein, low carb. Because as we all know"—Ethan cleared his throat, and his gaze became more intense—"sugar is poison."

Oh, how Roman wanted to believe the man was flirting, but he wasn't. He was reminding Roman of his devious actions the night before.

"Preprepared 'cause you'll be working the whole time?"

"Actually, I won't be there at all for the first few days. I have a vacation coming up."

"Well, that sucks," Roman whined.

Ethan's eyebrows went up, but every other inch of his face remained still. "The offer is for a place to stay, Mr. Walker. Someplace for you to settle for a bit while you plan your next move."

Stop pouting, he told himself, but he was clutching Gertrude to his chest as if he was about to start crying into her feathered head. "All right, well, will you want me out by the time you come back from your little vacay?"

"Not necessarily."

"Oh my God, what does that mean?"

"It means you will need to find another place to live at some point. I'm not inviting you to join the lease."

"I know that. I'm just trying to, you know, think it through."

"Okay, well, see if a little gratitude will focus you."

Roman grabbed Gertrude's head and turned the bird toward Ethan as if it were a ventriloquist dummy. In a deranged, and hopefully, birdlike voice, he screeched. "Is it *appropriate* to ask someone for gratitude?"

"Well, Gertrude," Ethan said, eyes meeting the ceramic bird's tiny ones. "It's far more appropriate to thank someone for a gift. Be it a ceramic bird or access to their home for an undetermined period of days."

Roman's effort not to roll his eyes had him shifting against the bench. "I'm sorry. It's just, sometimes you're like a cross between a butler and that teacher from *Matilda*, and I have trouble keeping up."

"I'll slow down then so as to avoid future Miss Trunchbull references," Ethan said.

An awkward silence settled, punctuated by wind-driven laughter that sounded like it was coming from another world.

"I really do love Gertrude," Roman finally said, daring to look at Ethan again only to find the man's level gaze had never wavered. "And I really do love the idea of not having to drive back and forth to Victorville while I apply for jobs. So thanks."

Ethan nodded, wearing a placid half smile.

"Where are we eating?" Roman asked.

Ethan's smile vanished. "Oh, I'm sorry. I…uh…have dinner plans with a friend."

Roman felt as if he'd fallen off a cliff, hit a jagged set of rocks, and bounced. But what he said was, "Oh, that's fine, 'cause Hank wanted to have dinner anyway." It was a lie. Clutching Gertrude's base with a white-knuckled grip, he looked away from Ethan suddenly as if he'd been distracted by a loud noise.

"Who's Hank?"

"Diana's director of security."

"Is he someone you can trust right now?"

Jealous, Daddy? Roman thought. More like hoped.

"I don't know. That's why we should probably have dinner."

Ethan nodded and rose to his feet. "Keep me posted about Rachel, and I'll make sure everything's taken care of on Tuesday."

When he extended his hand, Roman wanted to scream. Instead, he took it. At the weakness in his grip, Ethan huffed slightly with restrained laughter, as if he could sense what Roman was feeling inside, and it disappointed him.

Scared him, Roman thought. *He's scared because he knows if he gets sweaty with me, he'll lose control, and he probably feels guilty about my dad and so I need to let him off the hook. Because I want him to lose control all over me again and again.*

"Have a good evening, Mr. Walker."

Ethan was several paces away when Roman rose off the bench and said, "We should have sex."

Ethan turned. Even though a passing mother gave Roman a dirty look and tightened her grip on her toddler daughter's tiny hand as they hurried past, Ethan looked unfazed.

"You know," Roman continued, "just to get it out of our system. Especially if I'm going to be staying with you."

"I thought you weren't a casual sex person," he said.

"I'm not," Roman said, heart racing.

"Getting something out of your system sounds pretty casual."

Roman was struggling for a response when Ethan said, "Thank you for the offer, truly, but no. I'll see you Tuesday, Mr. Walker."

Ethan started walking off again.

"I just think it's weird," Roman called after him.

Ethan stopped and turned, this time with more strained patience in his expression. "*What* is weird?"

"That you're all wise and mature and stuff but you can't be authentic and real about how you feel about me."

Ethan took several paces toward him. "And how do I feel about you again?" he asked.

"Well, I think you answered that in your kitchen this morning, right?"

"An erection is not a feeling. It's a biological event caused by a high volume of blood flow to a specific part of the body, often triggered by an excess of physical stimulation. Such as a back rub."

"Wow. You really are Mr. Romance."

"Was last night in the penthouse suite your idea of romance?" Ethan asked. "Also, on the subject of authenticity, let's include your social media presence, where I didn't see a single rainbow flag or LGBTQ hashtag, and every year Pride Month seems to pass you by without notice."

"Marketing is tricky," Roman muttered and then felt terrible because it was a line he'd picked up from Diana when she'd first ordered him to scrub his profiles of anything remotely gay.

"So is romance," Ethan answered.

"And your background makes you a romance expert, huh?"

He regretted the words the minute they were out of his mouth, but Ethan didn't look wounded.

"What it makes me is an expert in what romance *isn't*," he said quietly.

"I'm sorry. I shouldn't have…" But he couldn't finish the sentence.

"I'm not offended," Ethan said. "I'm worried. I'm worried that you don't see what I'm actually trying to do here, which is be something that you might lose once you do what you need to do on Tuesday."

"A job?"

"A friend."

He saw Ethan's meaning instantly. He was trying to step into the place Rachel might leave once Roman told her the truth about her fiancé. Even if she did believe him, their friendship might never recover. And only now could he appreciate how big that loss would be. After getting swept up in the whirlwind of the Peyton family, he'd fallen out of touch with most of his LA friends, couldn't think of anyone he'd be able to text at all hours about everything ranging from nonsense to grief.

And Ethan Blake, even after everything Roman had tried the night before, even given their painful history, was offering to be that person. And now Roman felt ashamed.

"Thank you" was all he could manage, and it sounded inadequate, so he picked his new pet hawk up off the bench and hugged her to his chest. "I love her. She will be my protector always. Thanks to you."

It looked for a second like something inside of Ethan had melted, but he smiled and nodded and crisply said, "I'll see you Tuesday. Text sooner if you need to talk."

Roman nodded, and then he was alone.

An hour later, he was naked.

Naked and posing for a selfie on his bed he was pretty sure would reduce Ethan to a puddle on his kitchen floor.

But when he went to send it, he felt so creepy his finger froze up, and he realized he couldn't.

That was a shame. He wouldn't be able to use it for much else. It was way too hot for Instagram. He prided himself on never running afoul of their censors, which meant he rarely posted ass pics, and certainly not ones that showed this much crack and the outline of his balls pressed to the mattress beneath him. It was one of those classic—if by classic, you meant borderline trashy—over-the-shoulder shots, revealing the naked, muscular expanse of his back right down to the spot where he'd positioned the bedsheets to reveal the twin swells of his ass. He'd used the timer, setting the phone atop the headboard so he could get his face into the frame, then he'd rested his chin on the pillow, gently bit down on his lower lip, and widened his eyes in a manner designed to look eager and innocent.

The end result looked casual, because you couldn't see the ring light he'd hauled out from his closet and positioned off to one side of the bed, or the twenty test shots he'd taken to get everything just right.

And the prep had gotten him so hot he'd come close to jerking off before he snapped a single good shot.

The truth was, casual sex wasn't his thing, but sexting was. Roman had traded naughty shots with scores of guys on social media apps he'd never met, infinitely more than he'd ever hooked up with IRL. Never too naughty. If anything, a leaked nude would help his career, especially if it didn't seem to come from him. But a video of him performing a sex act, even on himself, was a different story. What he loved was the tangle of fantasy and words sexting offered. Most specifically, the words of adoration that often flowed his way.

But everything about this little photo shoot had felt different from the many others.

He'd come to know this picture's intended audience fairly well in a very short amount of time. As he'd prepared, he'd imagined the intent expression on Ethan's face as he studied the shot, the glaze in his brown eyes, the way the tip of his tongue might appear in the corner of his mouth, something he'd done a bunch as he'd cooked for Roman the night before. The thought that Ethan might break down and start pleasuring himself to it—alone, frustrated, and captivated—had made the blood thunder to Roman's cock and balls.

Still, sending it would feel like a violation of what they'd just agreed to.

And the truth was, it hadn't been an agreement.

It had been a condition set down by Ethan whether Roman liked it or not.

Violate it and Ethan Blake might leave his life in the blink of an eye.

He figured it was one of the things Rachel called a *boundary*, usually while complaining that she didn't have any when it came to her mother. And at the very least, it would mean crashing on Andy's sofa come Tuesday.

He rolled over onto his back, horny at a level that seemed to demand a different, more elegant word. A word Ethan Blake might use.

Smitten...

Intoxicated...

Enamored...

There was plenty of saved porn on his phone that would bring him some quick relief.

But if his fingers so much as grazed his phone while he was in this wildly aroused state, he might break down and send the photo after all. That would be bad. The kind of bad he'd only want more of.

Instead, he closed his eyes, and when his hand found his cock, he realized he didn't need porn at all. All he needed to do was imagine he was back in Ethan Blake's arms.

Once he'd satisfied himself, he decided to honor their new friendship by taking the man's advice.

A little while later, he sat down with a printout of his mother's trust document and began to read over it with a highlighter in hand.

13

Late Tuesday morning, Ethan received word that Roman was on the property and waiting for him in the restaurant bar. As he headed toward the lobby, he checked the pocket of his chef's jacket to make sure he still had the keycard for the villa he'd picked out for the man's face-off with Rachel Peyton. Then he stepped outside to the valet stand and retrieved Roman's surprise for the day.

"We really don't have to do this, man," Joey Verdugo said as he followed Ethan through the lobby.

"We do," Ethan answered brightly, then he spotted Roman sitting by himself, glowering down at his clasped hands. The bar top was white marble with spare gold detailing. The young man's outfit matched it almost perfectly. His jeans were so acid washed they were almost bleach colored, and his white dress shirt was baggier than anything he'd seen the guy wear. The outfit made sense. White was the color of peace. Hiding your perfect muscles was advisable when revealing to your best friend that you'd been propositioned by her fiancé. Roman Walker, it seemed, had thought this afternoon through. Which was probably why he looked like he wanted to die.

The bartender on duty poured the martini she'd just finished shaking, then started carrying it toward Roman. Ethan intercepted it the second she placed it on the bar.

"*Please*," Roman whined when he saw Ethan sliding the drink out of his reach.

"Nope. That will not make this better." To the bartender, Ethan said, "I'll settle that with you later." She nodded and departed. "Roman, this is Joey Verdugo, the valet who helped you on Saturday."

"'Sup? My friends call me Joey V." The lanky, goateed guy gave Roman a weak wave and then both men stared at each other like teenagers whose parents were trying to force them to hang out together. Ethan stayed silent. Yes, it was partly a test, and with each passing second of awkward silence, Ethan was afraid Roman was about to fail.

"I'm really sorry I almost ran over your feet, Joey," Roman finally said. "I should've…uh…been paying closer attention."

"That's okay," Joey said, even though Ethan had told him specifically not to use those words. "You seemed super upset so…"

"I was," Roman said, nodding aggressively. "I was super upset."

"Which is still not an excuse to shove a ticket in someone's face and almost run over their feet," Ethan said brightly.

Roman glowered at him. "I'm really sorry, Joey. I'd give you an extra tip, but I'm about to be broke and homeless."

"Herbal donations are always welcome," Joey said, rubbing his thumb and forefinger together like he was rolling a joint.

"Thank you, Joey. That'll be all," Ethan said and gave the guy a firm pat on the back.

"Really?" Roman asked once the valet was out of sight.

"Don't you feel better?" Ethan asked.

"I'd feel better if I had that martini."

"I figured focusing on something other than Rachel for a few minutes before your meeting would ground you somewhat. Also, it's always good to be reminded that the people who work in hotels are human beings with feelings."

"Sure. Can I be one of them? 'Cause I'm about to need a job."

Ethan gripped one of Roman's shoulders and gave it a squeeze he meant to be comforting and parental. "I'll look into it." He leaned in closer, dropping his voice to a whisper. "But I'm not sure it's very likely given you and I are about to knock the biggest event of the year off the calendar."

"That's what I thought," Roman grumbled.

He gently lifted Roman off the barstool by one elbow. The guy started walking so quickly he almost forgot the canvas tote bag resting on the floor. He spun, grabbed it, and they started moving again.

As he led them in the direction of the villas, Ethan said, "That can't be all of your things."

"No. The car's full of suitcases. I loaded it all this morning before Hank woke up. Diana's not coming back till later tonight, and I'm supposed to train her tomorrow morning. Oh my God. Am I allowed to throw up at least? Can we stop so I can throw up?"

"There's a bathroom in the villa if you feel the need, but let's get you settled first."

"I'd be settled if you let me have a martini."

"After. As a reward for a job well done. My treat."

They moved out onto the grassy lawn that separated the conference center from the private villas.

"Yeah, I'm not really sure there's a way to do this job well," Roman muttered.

Ethan stopped and spun to face him. "Okay, let's be very clear about something here. You're putting your career and your home on the line for your best friend so she doesn't sign up for a lifetime of heartbreak. That's courageous and selfless, and there's no doing it perfectly. Just doing it. If Rachel walks away from today with the truth and the power to make a decision about it, you should be nothing but proud of yourself."

Gone were the pout and glower, replaced by what looked like desperate eagerness to believe Ethan's proclamations. After a few seconds, Roman nodded, sucked in a deep breath, and they started forward again.

Nine villas total descended the south-facing slope of the resort's grounds. Their side doors opened onto walkways that traveled downhill between each row. He'd picked 9E, which at the top of the slope had a commanding view of the coastline to the south. Underneath a cathedral ceiling in the sitting room, the coffee and tea service had been set up on the small, round dining table like he'd asked. Today, the plunge pool in the little backyard would probably go unused.

"About as nice as the penthouse suite, but the view's not quite as good. Also, apparently you flirted with two of our security guys to get in there Saturday night?" Ethan asked.

"It wasn't hard. Those guys were hot. They looked like porn stars."

"They were porn stars."

Roman's eyes widened.

"Before Sapphire Cove. It's a long story. What's in the bag?"

Roman pouted, shaking his head. "Nothing. It's stupid." He looked into Ethan's eyes, then he reached inside the bag and hefted out the ceramic hawk Ethan had given him two nights before, setting it on the wet bar next to him. "She's my protector," he said softly, hanging his head. "I can't do this without her."

It was such an adorable display, Ethan's laughter carried him across the room. Suddenly his arms were around Roman as the man wilted into his embrace like his legs had gone boneless.

"I can't do this," Roman whispered into his shoulder.

"You can. And I'll be close in case anything goes wrong."

Just as a dangerous heat started coursing through him, Ethan heard the familiar slip of a keycard entering the slot in the door outside. They broke like cheaters being discovered by a cuckolded spouse. Seconds later, Jonas Jacobs peered through the open door, wearing a solicitous grin. Behind him was a woman Ethan had last seen in an episode of some crime show set in a national park. If he remembered correctly, she'd played a ranger guilty of a murder she'd tried to blame on a bear.

"Romy! Hugs! Immediately!" Rachel Peyton threw her arms wide before she had a chance to take off her sunglasses. For an awkward few seconds, Roman was frozen. But the pull of their friendship proved stronger than the man's fear. The two of them embraced fiercely as Rachel rocked them side to side like a mother squeezing her young child after their return from summer camp. Her love for Roman seemed genuine and warm. Seeing it in action, Ethan felt as nervous about this meeting as Roman had been on the walk there. "If he stole anything," she finally said, "just put it on my card. He's got sticky fingers when it comes to shiny things."

Rachel Peyton wore what looked like a designer, if baggy, running suit, and had pulled her hair back in a ponytail. Ethan had met a lot of young actresses in his life, and she was dressed more modestly than most of them. While she lacked her mother's cover girl beauty, she had cherubic cheeks, intense blue eyes, and a big, expressive mouth that served her chameleon-like acting abilities.

"Rest assured, he hasn't stolen anything," Ethan said.

"That we know of," Jonas muttered, then looked quickly to the floor. Clearly he shared in Connor Harcourt's distrust of the man.

"All right," Ethan said, "well, we'll leave you two alone to—"

"Woah." Rachel removed her sunglasses, revealing a face devoid of makeup. "I thought this was a wedding meeting. Aren't we supposed to talk about something related to the wedding? I don't know, like, candles or something. I mean, where are we with the…you know

...wedding?"

Unsure of how deep Roman's cover story went, Ethan didn't know quite what to say. He was also struck by how remarkably out of touch the young ingenue seemed with her fairytale nuptials-to-be. "We've been in conversation with Roman about some of the details. I think he'd like a little time to go over them with you first before we all dive in."

Roman's deer-in-the-headlights expression suggested he might spill his guts right there in front of all of them. Instead, he swallowed and nodded.

Rachel set her handbag down on the dining table. "Okay, well, whatever works for you guys. But word of warning to all, I am *dramatically* out of the loop. I've been in New York for months doing a play."

"We heard. Congratulations on your Tony, by the way," Jonas said.

"That's very kind of you. I really thought that hologram of Carol Channing they brought back to do a revival of *Moose Murders* had it in the bag."

Ethan was the only one who laughed.

Rachel pointed at him dramatically. "Someone knows his theater references!"

"*Moose Murders* is one of the most notorious flops in Broadway history." To Jonas's quizzical look, he said, "I used to live in New York." *And I had a regular client who was a former Broadway producer who used to love sucking my toes,* he didn't add.

"So I take it you weren't up against a Carol Channing hologram?" Jonas asked.

"Not yet," Rachel said, "but according to one theater critic, I benefitted from it being an off year for drama. So every now and then I have to come up with a new joke like that to cover for the fact that I'll never forget his review for as long as I live even though I'm always the first to claim I don't pay attention to them."

Jonas and Ethan both guffawed.

"*Could we be alone, please?*" Roman's cry wasn't ear-piercing, but it was close.

Before a stunned silence could seize the room, Ethan said, "Of course. Jonas, let's give them time to catch up."

He took his supervisor by the arm and led him out of the villa even as the man stared back over his shoulder as if trying to determine the source of Roman's outburst. Ethan pulled the villa's door shut behind them with a loud *thunk*. They were halfway up the walkway when Jonas whispered, "Are you attempting some sort of Pygmalion dynamic with that young man?"

"I am. What do you think?"

"Keep at it, friend. You have your work cut out for you. Care to tell me why he's so stressed?"

At the top of the walkway, Ethan stopped and turned. "Would you care to address the rumor that you had an affair with a closeted NFL player right out of college and that's why you're so reticent to discuss those years?"

Jonas nodded and smiled. "Yes. The rumor's false. Now tell me, what's going on with that child?"

"That's a shame. I really saw you with a football player."

Jonas rolled his eyes. "Then you do not know me at all, good sir."

Ethan shrugged and started across the lawn toward the main building.

"I'll remember this the next time you're looking for information out of me, Mr. Blake." Jonas hurried to catch up.

"You know how it goes. Weddings are stressful and celebrities are nuts. Put the two together and it's a nightmare in white for the support staff."

Jonas caught up with him when he reached the entry door to the conference center. "Tell that to the wedding planner, who's met me four times and has never so much as raised her voice."

"Yeah, well, she's probably getting paid a good deal more than our friend Roman."

Jonas stepped in front of him. "And he's young," he said with dramatic emphasis. "Too young to handle certain emotional stresses the way you or I might."

"I'm not sleeping with him, Jonas."

"This isn't judgment. It's concern. Two of our security team are in real trouble with the GM over that young man. I don't want to see you end up in the same boat. You and I, we are an endangered species here at Sapphire Cove. We must be protected."

"I'm sorry. What species is that?"

Jonas lifted a warning finger. "Gay men in their forties who read full-length books, who have an appreciation for art and culture. Actual culture. Not the kind you watch for thirty seconds on a phone."

Ethan snapped his fingers. "I trumped you on the theater reference just now, though."

Jonas shook his head, waving both hands in the air in front of him. "Doesn't count. Broadway is a different animal. You're one of the few people here who knows the difference between a Dürer and a Degas, and neither of us listens to roaring club music on the way to work that sounds like Britney chewed up the *Benny Hill* theme song and spit it out at ten times the tempo."

Ethan grimaced with false humility. "I do enjoy a bit of Armin van Buuren now and then."

Jonas cleared his throat. "I'll say this only once. Don't sleep with that boy, Ethan. He's nothing but muscles and mess. And I need you here. Desperately. The other day Connor tried to engage me in a conversation about the *Real Housewives of Beverly Hills*, and I had to breathe deeply and silently recite some mantras so he couldn't see how badly I wanted to cry out for help."

"Roman Walker and I are *not* sleeping together."

Jonas nodded and moved off into the halls of the conference center.

But before he pushed through the doors, he looked back over one shoulder. "Yet," Jonas added.

Realizing he'd just had one of the lines he'd used on Roman used on him, Ethan sucked in a deep breath and stretched out his neck a bit before returning to his office.

14

"So does every room here have a hawk?" Rachel asked.

Roman didn't answer. He was staring through—and not at—the glossy pages of the magazine she'd just handed him. When his best friend noticed his fugue state, her expression turned worried. She gently tugged the copy of *People* from his weak grip and looked down at the photo spread as if there was something unflattering in the images she'd missed.

"What's wrong, sweetie? You look great in these. I thought you'd be thrilled."

The headline read, *Peyton Princess Has Sundrenched Workout with Sexy Trainer During Broadway Break*. The pictures were a few months old, taken during one of her brief visits home during rehearsals. In all of them, they were working out on the sand in front of the Castle by the Sea, but in the close-up shot he had a muscular arm curved around her shoulders as he laughed at one of her jokes. They almost looked like lovers. It wasn't the first time they'd appeared in paparazzi shots together, but still, he was rattled.

"It is kinda weird we didn't even know they were there." Roman's voice had a little shake to it. He grabbed a handful of mixed nuts from the ramekin Ethan had left nearby and chewed. "I mean, whenever they followed us shopping, we knew they were there, right?"

"Mom knew. She set the whole thing up. But seriously, this is good for you. Your name and social media's down in the copy. I mean, you'll get a bump from this, right? And all I had to do was get a sunburn while you forced me to do six thousand crunches."

Rachel smiled. Roman tried to smile back. His face didn't respond.

"Are you okay?" she asked, setting the magazine aside.

"No. No, I'm not, Rache."

She swung her legs to the floor and reached across the distance between them. It was painful—maybe too painful, in this moment—that her primary concern was for him, and that she'd taken one of his hands gently into her own. "What's wrong, sweetie?"

"I don't know how to say this, but...Scott hit on me. Hard."

Her eyebrows went up. "*Hit* on you?" she asked, as if she'd never heard the term.

Roman nodded and swallowed. "I didn't say yes. I threw a glass of water in his face."

"Oh."

Oh? Roman thought. She hadn't let go of his hand or even lightened her grip. Maybe she didn't believe him. But wouldn't her disbelief have made her angry too? Was she in shock?

"Is Scott okay?" she asked gently.

These were the last words he'd expected to hear. "Um, I kind of don't care," Roman whispered.

"I mean, his face. Like, is his face okay because if he's going to make any of his own money, it's not going to be from anything else."

"His face looked...wet. What's going on right now?"

At the very moment he assumed she'd be throwing plates and screaming, she brought her other hand up to caress the outside of Roman's. "Is that all? He hit on you, and you turned him down?"

"No. It's not at all. Your mom... She wanted me to do it."

He figured this news would go off like a bomb. Instead, Rachel rolled her eyes and shook her head and made a small sound like she'd just remembered she had a dentist appointment early the next morning.

"She said he was cheating all over, and she was worried about it ending up in the press, so she wanted him to keep it in the house. With *me*."

Rachel nodded and looked to the floor, but she didn't release his hands or withdraw. "I'm sorry you had to go through that, sweetie. I know things in that house can get...intense."

"Me? What about *you*?"

She gave him a sheepish smile. "Oh, Romy. I kind of wanted you to believe this whole wedding was real because you seemed so excited for me."

Roman felt like he was breathing through a straw, and when he spoke again, it sounded like it. "Wait. It's not real?"

She grimaced. "Not really, no."

"So…you don't care about Scott and you're just marrying him because your mom picked him out for you?"

Still grimacing, Rachel nodded. "Basically."

Was it possible to hold your breath for three whole days? It felt like that's exactly what he'd been doing. Like he could feel his extremities again for the first time. He could feel the upholstery of the chair beneath him. He was no longer reflexively glancing at the nearest exits as if he'd have to race from the villa at any moment. But with the easing of tension came a realization. "Well, why didn't she tell me *that*?"

"Because there's something she's hiding. Something *I'm* hiding. Because she wants me to hide it." Worried any guess might end up being offensive, he waited for her to break the silence. "I'm ace, sweetie."

"You're what?"

"I'm asexual. And not in an *I haven't had a good enough roll in the sack* kind of way. It's my identity. It took me two years in therapy to figure it out, but it's who I am. I'm on the asexuality spectrum, and I'm firmly at the asexual end. That means sexual intercourse, orgasms, mutual nudity, they're not part of my love language. I develop deep romantic feelings for people, men mostly. But those feelings don't result in a desire for physical contact beyond…tenderness, I guess."

Roman cleared his throat. "Do you have deep romantic feelings for Scott?"

"God, no. The only person who has deep romantic feelings for Scott is Scott. He's just right for the role."

"Why wouldn't your mom tell me any of this?"

"'Cause she doesn't know how to sell it. When I told her, she said we could get more juice out of the story if I was lesbian or trans. Because what I am, according to her, is an *absence*. Nobody will get it, and she won't be able to get me any roles or press if everyone assumes I don't want to fuck *any* of my costars. Which is insanely insulting on many levels, but that's what the whole wedding's about, sweetie."

She gave him a second to process this.

"It's kind of crazy that all the publicity machines around actors hinge on the fact that we never trust them to actually act, but that's how it goes, I guess. As soon as the play's over, she wants to get me married as fast as possible so I can level up."

"Do *you* want to level up?"

She sighed and opened her hands as if the answer was obvious, even though the noises she was making made clear it was anything but. "I want to work for as long as I can on something other than direct to streaming horror films. In this business, that means leveling up."

"But when you were in town last, I heard you guys going at it like crazy."

"No, Romy, you heard *Sexy Sorority Surprise*. I was in the bathroom reading with my earbuds. Scott was on the balcony taking selfies."

"A porn film? Oh my God. Your balcony doors were open. That's why it was so loud."

"That was the point. You were supposed to hear it. Mom says you're in the inner circle but you're not in the inner *inner* circle, so we had to make you think it was real."

Roman needed a minute to think—a minute that might last several months.

His best friend had a love language that didn't include sex. A few days before, he would have had trouble wrapping his head around the idea. Then he'd woken up in Ethan's arms and experienced what it was like to feel ravished by a night of snuggling. Tenderness. Touch. These things could be seismic on their own. And for some people, people like Rachel, they could be a sufficient culmination of their romantic feelings toward others. It didn't describe him, but it made sense to him. It was the only thing in this moment that made any sense.

"So," Rachel finally said, "I know that's a lot."

"I packed. I figure this would blow everything up and I'd have to move out."

"Oh my God. I hate that you were that freaked out. Honestly, I was planning to tell you before the wedding. Promise."

"It's fine. I mean, you've been away and…"

"But what, honey?"

"I don't like that they both thought I would do that to you."

"Well, that's on Scott. He probably jumped the gun, and she was trying to do damage control."

"She made it sound like my job was on the line."

He waited for her to tell him this wasn't true. That he'd misheard Diana, interpreted threats where there were none. Instead, Rachel went still and studied him, and the silence between them deepened.

"You should do it, babe," she said brightly—suddenly—as if the idea had just occurred to her and the result would be no more consequential than a walk along the beach.

"Do what?"

She jumped to her feet, a clear sign of discomfort, then she poured them both cups of coffee. "He's kind of your type, right? Big and somewhat older. Also, he's *big* big. I've seen it. By accident. We've had to share a lot of rooms."

So they didn't even sleep in the same bed in their Beverly Hills condo? The deception went that deep. He could see the signs of a fake marriage everywhere now, but they'd been hidden in the frenzied rootlessness of an actor's life.

She handed him his coffee with a smile, then went to retrieve her own.

"You actually want me to hook up with your fiancé?" he finally asked.

Taking a careful sip, she nodded. "I think he's on the spectrum, too, but he's what we call aromantic. He doesn't form romantic attachments to people, just sexual ones. So there's no risk he'd fall in love with you. As hard as that is given how wonderful you are." She returned to the chaise and smiled. It seemed genuine. But she also seemed afraid. Her nervous stage business with the coffee, her sudden difficulty looking him in the eye made it clear—you didn't say no to Diana Peyton without consequences.

But so what? He already had one foot out the door. Hell, his bags were literally packed.

But if he left now, it would be for a different and more tangled reason.

It wasn't about protecting Rachel anymore.

It was about him—his body and who he allowed to touch it and why. Why were those questions so much harder to answer?

"I don't like him," he finally said. "I don't know if I can sleep with someone I don't like."

"Oh, babe." She sat forward. "Are you demi?"

"A what?"

"Demisexual. It's another spot on the spectrum. It's someone who can't get sexually aroused by someone they don't have romantic feelings for."

"I don't know. A lot of this is…new."

"Sorry. I shouldn't be diagnosing people. Or not diagnosing, 'cause that makes it sound like a disease. I shouldn't be *articulating* other people's identities for them. Honestly, this is new to me too. But God, it explained so much. I thought there was something wrong with me. I kept having these *awful* sexual experiences in search of the one moment that would fix me. And no matter how I felt about the person, every time it was like having my skin peeled off. And then one day I had to accept that I was a person who could love deeply, but I don't express it the way I'd been taught to. And it gave me permission to stop treating sexual intercourse like some level of the game I could never reach."

Thinking of all the clients who'd flown Ethan around the world, Roman said, "Yeah, well, most sex doesn't involve love anyway. People just say it does."

"Exactly," she said with a sheepish smile.

"Why can't you have an asexual marriage with someone you really like?"

Rachel sighed. For the first time, she reached for the ramekin and gathered up a handful of nuts too. "Mom says we don't have the time to find that person. She's got me on a schedule."

"And she wants them to look like Scott."

Rachel nodded.

"And agree to the pre-nup."

Rachel nodded again and chewed.

A silence fell.

"Did you really pack?" Rachel asked.

Roman nodded.

"Sweetie, I know it's weird, and I know Mom can be…challenging. But she could do great things for you. I mean, look, she kind of already is." She gestured to the magazine resting on the chaise next to her. "Think about it before you give up on it. Or on her."

"And you? Would I be giving up on you?" The frog in his throat swelled, and suddenly his vision had misted. "'Cause honestly, that was the thing I was worried about losing most."

Suddenly, her arms were around him, and he was swimming in her sweet designer perfume and sniffling like a little boy in a way that he hated and wanted to stop but couldn't.

"Never," she said quietly. "We're Romy and Rachelle, remember?"

"Only without the high school reunion part because high school sucked."

It was their usual refrain, and once he performed his part, she laughed warmly and tightened her embrace. Then, after a long silence that went from feeling comfortable to strained again, she said, "Sometimes the path to doing what we love is lined with things we really don't love."

He couldn't disagree.

"And I know your mom would want you to live at your full potential," she added quietly.

Her words went off like a bomb inside of him, blasting him backward in time.

It hadn't been her intention, he was sure, but he was seeing the despairing look on his mother's face the day he told her he was dropping out of college to try to make a go of it in LA. The fear that he'd spend the rest of his life struggling to pay the rent while being verbally berated by a series of managers and disloyal clients at a series of low-end gyms.

Which is exactly what he'd be signing up for again if he told Diana Peyton no.

Rachel's embrace was warm, but inside Roman felt very cold.

There was nothing more Ethan could do. He'd encouraged Roman to tell the truth, set the meeting in motion, and if the ordeal left Roman devastated, Ethan would have no choice but to offer him a shoulder to cry on. And a guest bedroom. And a week's worth of lean steaks and chicken breasts currently marinating in his fridge. And that was fine. Their shoulders were not the body parts he'd wisely declared off-limits.

He gave himself over to the only thing capable of occupying his thoughts as he anxiously awaited word from villa 9E—design. The first few pencil strokes of a botanical-themed anniversary cake were shaping up nicely when the door to the pastry kitchen flew open, slammed shut, and a breathless Roman was suddenly standing behind him. "I need you to teach me how to be a hooker!" he gasped.

"Roman!" Ethan shot to his feet and moved swiftly to ensure the door was firmly closed.

"No one's out there. Relax."

When he demanded to know how the meeting had gone, the story came tumbling out of Roman in a rush. "So obviously I'm going to do it," Roman announced once he finished the tale.

Ethan needed a moment to catch his breath. "Obviously?"

"Well, why not? I mean, this is good news, right? It's all good news."

"And you think this will become better news if I teach you how to escort?"

Roman held up a finger as if he had a very important point to make, but all he said was, "Trade secrets."

Ethan waited for more. "Excuse me?" he finally said.

"Saturday night, at your apartment. You said you knew some trade secrets to make difficult clients easier to deal with. Well, Scott's pretty damn difficult, so you're going to teach me how to make him less annoying so that I can have sex with him."

"I'm not teaching you how to have sex with anyone."

"I'm not asking you to teach me how to have *sex* with him. I'm asking you to teach me how not to barf when I do."

"The nature of your request is not lost on me. But it's also not very achievable. I can't make you into a whole new person. I *shouldn't* make you a whole new person. Look, I have a different relationship to sexuality than you do. And your relationship to sexuality is perfectly fine and healthy, and you shouldn't change it just to accommodate this *insane* situation."

Roman furrowed his brow. "Are you aromantic?"

"Excuse me?"

Roman waved one hand through the air. "Nothing. It's something Rachel said. Whatever. Look, it's six months. Six months of sleeping with someone who's actually really hot when he keeps his mouth shut and doesn't, like, you know…*do* anything. I can make it work."

Six months, Ethan wanted to point out, was actually quite a long time in most circumstances, but Roman seemed hellbent on his new plan, and Ethan knew if he argued the minor details the man would only become more obstinate. So he went after the big picture instead. "It's not about Scott, Roman. It's about Diana. Say yes to this and who knows what she'll hit you with next."

"Well, once I have my inheritance back, it won't matter."

"And the promotions she's paying for and all of the followers?"

"I don't care about any of that." Roman swallowed, and Ethan could see the roil of painful emotions he was hiding behind his energetic plans. "I care about...my mom."

Ethan waited for him to elaborate, but he didn't. He couldn't, it seemed. Was he talking about the inheritance, or something bigger and more complicated? Saturday night he'd broken down over the thought that he'd disappointed her by dropping out of Cal Poly. The buildup to those sobs had made him look a lot like he looked now.

"Ethan," Roman finally said, "if you really want to help me, you'll give me what I'm asking for, not what you think I should be asking for."

It wasn't *you owe me,* but it was close. Ethan winced and cleared his throat. "We'll have drinks. Tonight. I'll text you the name of the place. It'll have to be late."

"Diana gets back tonight. She might want to talk to—"

"Well, it'll have to be tonight because I leave tomorrow for San Diego. Are you willing to put Diana off until I get back?"

Roman sighed. "What should I wear?"

"A comprehensive outfit. This is going to be a discussion session. That's all."

Roman nodded.

Ethan nodded.

And then they found themselves staring at each other.

"Roman?"

"Yeah?"

"Where's Gertrude?"

"*Shit,*" Roman hissed and then took off.

15

All it took was one visit to Long Beach for Ethan to discover it was a rare and special place where the aesthetics and values of a Midwestern industrial city bled into California's glittering coast, making for an oceanfront sprawl more down to earth than its neighbors. Its gay bars were a pleasant reflection of this humble irony.

In Los Angeles, an hour north, the clubs were packed with a heady mix of celebrities and porn stars, a too-pretty-to-be-real crowd that considered age and experience to be handicaps and not valuable acquisitions. When it came to Orange County, its most popular gay bars were memories. Like many queer men of his generation, he still mourned the loss of the Boom Boom Room in Laguna Beach, a club so well-known its name had been the title of a popular dance floor tune in the mid-nineties. Today it was a seafood restaurant catering to tourists of all orientations.

In Long Beach, the real estate was more affordable, the massive port complex provided scores of working-class jobs, and the gay bars were intimate, neighborhood watering holes where everybody knew your name or seemed eager to learn it. They reminded Ethan of those first few roadside dives in South Carolina he'd worked up the nerve to visit when he was still closeted, places where the rainbow-colored Budweiser signs above the bar and the jukeboxes that played a constant stream of Whitney and Madonna made him feel like he'd finally found home. A real home, far from the Greek Revival mansion in Charleston where he'd been raised by two parents who'd shown him as much tenderness as he'd gotten from the Civil War-era portraits of their ancestors hanging on the walls of the house's antique-stuffed double parlor.

Despite The Queen Mary's name and nautical décor, it was several blocks inland from Long Beach Harbor where the real Queen Mary, a retired ocean liner from the early twentieth century, held court. The booths along the back wall offered relative privacy, even if they were a stone's throw from an always popular pool table. It was Ethan's special spot, somewhere he fled to when he was feeling uncomfortable in his skin, one of the few places where he felt like he could relax and be himself in the presence of other gay men. That's why when he'd texted Roman the address and the guy had responded with **Ugggggh**, he'd been tempted to drive down to the Castle by the Sea and bop him upside his head.

Maybe Roman had just been complaining about the lengthy drive—about forty minutes without traffic. But if he decided to get snotty about the décor and clientele, they were sure to have words.

He reminded himself of his real goal for the evening, which was not, in fact, to teach Roman how to have emotionless sex.

It was to find out what the hell Rachel Peyton had said in that hotel room that convinced the young man he was somehow cut out for this ridiculous job.

He was silently running through his lesson plan again when the bar's front door opened with a creak of old hinges, and every head in the place turned to watch Roman Walker saunter toward Ethan's booth.

As if Ethan had called him out for his preposterously revealing outfit, the young man placed a hand to his chest, feigning indignant surprise. "What? You said a *comprehensive* outfit. This is Saint Laurent, Dolce, and Versace. Seems pretty comprehensive to me." He'd pointed to his skintight tank top as he'd said Saint Laurent, and then his super-short shorts when he'd said Dolce and Versace.

"Versace makes shorts?"

"The shorts are Dolce." He smiled and slid into the booth. "The *underwear's* Versace."

"Those are swim trunks."

"Pays to advertise." Roman smiled.

"To who?"

Roman winked at him.

Ethan sipped his club soda and sighed. "Scott Bryant's the customer here. Is he a fan of Victorian swimming outfits reimagined by gay porn studios?"

"Someone's testy tonight." Roman looked over one shoulder and scanned the crowd, giving seductive smiles and a few winks to the various men ogling him from their frozen, slack-jawed positions around the bar. "And someone's choice in bars is *traaagic*," Roman whispered.

"I'm quite fond of this place, actually."

Hands clasped on the table in front of him, Roman gave him a condescending grin. "'Cause you're the hottest one here."

"Most of the queers in this bar marched for rights you take for granted and buried a friend a week during the eighties. They don't need to win your Instagram underwear contest, BeachBoy24. They've earned their place. Let's get down to business, shall we?"

Roman opened his mouth, either to protest or ask a question, it wasn't clear. Ethan didn't care.

"I gave you a clear direction on how to dress for this meeting, and you didn't take it. Because dolling yourself up like a pretty boy and being sassy to an older man is your fantasy. That's fine. But let me tell you something right now. This gig you're signing up for isn't about your fantasy. It's about Scott's, and your number one job is to find out what that is and fast."

Roman smiled and bit his lower lip. "Oh my God, you have a little Southern accent when you're angry. It's cute."

"I assume you're not going to take any notes?"

Roman tapped on the side of his head as if to imply his memory was unassailable.

"Fine," Ethan said. "There are two types of clients. The ones who want the boyfriend experience—I call them BEs for short—and the ones I call Right Nows. The Right Nows want something very specific. And they usually want it quick. Typically, they're also the least respectful, the least likely to look you in the eye. But that's beside the point. The point is, they make it easy for you. They usually open things up with a very detailed set of instructions, which is good. The problem is, they're not as consistent over time, so they weren't the high-value clients for me."

Ethan tapped a finger straight down on the table and held it there for emphasis. "Boyfriend experience, that's where the money was.

And for a very simple reason. Pretending to be someone's boyfriend takes time, and time, as I'm sure you know, is money. You've got dinners, movies, charity events, sometimes even an overnight. That's serious bank, and it adds up. Play those clients right and suddenly they're flying you to Paris and buying you outfits that cost as much as your rent.

"But here's the problem. BEs, which is the category Scott will most likely fall into, don't really want you to be their boyfriend. The boyfriend they want is a version of you they made up the minute they laid eyes on you. And so you have to listen for what that is. Constantly. They don't want to hear you rattle on about your life story just because you're young and have a hot body. The trick is this. Every time you're talking about yourself, you're really talking about them."

Roman furrowed his brow, but at least he was listening. "How's that work?"

"Simple. Whatever they do for a living, you've considered doing it too. Or you have a cousin who did and he washed out and you're wondering where he went wrong. Do they have an oil painting in their house you can't miss? You want to know more about art. You were even thinking of taking classes. Because your priority is to become a vessel for what they want, while making them *think* it's really you. And once they're comfortable that the real you isn't going to get in the way of their fantasy, that's when they start talking about the real stuff."

"Real stuff? Like what they want to do in bed?"

"Deeper. What they want to do in bed's part of it, but it's just another piece of information. If you want to turn them into a high-value, repeat client, someone who will move *their* schedule around to meet with you instead of the other way around, you're after one thing. I call it the million-dollar answer."

It was actually Zach Loudon, his old friend, mentor, and one-time fuck buddy, who'd called it that, but nobody had heard from Zach in years, so it wasn't like he was going to bust the door down asking for credit.

"What's that?" Roman muttered.

Enunciating slowly and clearly, Ethan said, "It's how they want to be seen by you. It's how they want you to look at them when you're at dinner and when they're trying to fuck your brains out.

Because it's the same look, and if you get it right, you've got them on the hook for as long as you want them." He gave Roman a moment to swallow that. "Don't get me wrong. Finding out their kinks is important. But don't be fooled by the surface of a kink."

Roman grunted. "The *surface* of a kink. What does that mean?"

"Kinks can be deceiving. You've got to look closer to find out what the kink really *means*. The guy who wants to be called Daddy isn't into incest. He wants to be trusted. He wants you to look at him like you believe he'll protect you from anything. The guy who wants to be tied up and blindfolded doesn't want to be treated like trash. He wants to be told he's so damn irresistible you can't bear to let him get away. And the guy who wants you to hurt him, to slap him and spank him right up until you hear the safe word, he wants to control you from the bottom. He wants to turn you into a robot at his command. He might be on all fours, but what he wants is to look into your eyes and see powerful obedience. You can act out a client's kinks, but if you do it grudgingly or like you're distracted, they're not coming back more than twice, maybe three times."

"Well, Scott's not a…traditional client."

"That's correct. He's far worse."

"'Cause he's a douche."

"Because he can go right down the hall and complain to Diana about the service. The fact of the matter, Roman, is you're going to have to deal with something I never did."

"What?"

"A pimp." He let that sit. It looked like it did. Hard. "Because, Roman, what you're about to do isn't what I did. You're being manipulated and controlled by someone who's trying to hold you hostage, and that's the opposite of what I was when I was out there on my own. I was alone, but I was free. Do this and you're neither."

When a server arrived to take his drink order, Roman was still gazing vacantly at a spot just above Ethan's right shoulder, nostrils flaring with strained breaths. He looked to Ethan's club soda, muttered something about a Diet Coke, and swallowed. For a while, neither man spoke. Roman's cocky swagger was gone, and Ethan felt a strange blend of satisfaction and regret.

"So what was my dad's million-dollar answer?" Roman finally asked.

"No dad talk. That's a different conversation for a different night."

"You don't think it's relevant to—"

"No, I don't. I think you're deflecting because you don't like what I'm telling you. You asked for help and my trade secrets, so I'm giving them to you with no sugar coating. Because, as you well remember—"

"Sugar is poison," Roman drawled, eyes hooded with anger. "Yeah, I heard."

Just then, a giant bear of a man eased down into the booth next to Roman, mouth so agape it looked like drool was about to drip from its corners. He slid one meaty arm over Roman's exposed shoulders and leaned in close to his cheek. After sucking in a dramatic, predatory whiff of Roman's neck, he purred, "Sweet boy. Sweet-smelling pretty *boy*. What's your name, hot stuff?"

Roman cleared his throat. "Could you excuse us, please? We're kinda—"

Ethan raised a finger. "Manners, Roman. Let's find out what our new friend here's buying. It might be top shelf. And you have expensive tastes."

Roman swallowed, eyes blazing with anger, jaw tensing. When he suddenly sucked in a quick breath through his nose, Ethan figured the handsy bear was sliding one hand up his exposed leg. "I sure would like to take you for a swim in these, pretty boy. Not sure how long they'd stay on, though."

Miserably, Roman stared down at the table.

"That's good, Tom," Ethan finally said.

The bear straightened, dropping the act. He patted Roman lightly on the back of his bowed head and chuckled. "You guys are into some weird shit. Pay up, Ethan."

He put out his hand, and Ethan passed him a twenty.

"Sorry, fella," the bear told Roman as he slid out of the booth. "I've got a pool game later, and we're putting money down. Your man here always comes through. You boys have fun. Whatever it is you're...doing."

And then the bear was gone, and the two of them were sitting alone in angry silence. Roman's breaths had slowed, but he was still glaring down at the table as if it had tried to bite him.

"Tell me what you're feeling, Roman."

"I thought you were going to make me sleep with him," he muttered.

"I'm not here to make you do anything."

Roman rolled his eyes. "Fine. I thought you were going to *tell* me to sleep with him. As part of my *lesson*."

"And how did that make you feel?"

Roman's answer was in his miserable silence.

"Okay. See? That right there. That revulsion. That coiling up inside you feel when a total stranger puts his hands on you. That's what you're going to have to kill to do what you want to do. Can you do that?"

"Answer my question first."

Ethan sank back into the booth. He took a slug of his club soda to stall, then set the glass back on the table with more force than he'd intended. "I looked at your father like he was the opposite of who he was. I looked at him like he was brave."

They fell silent as the server delivered the Diet Coke. Ethan gestured for the guy to put it on his tab and then they were alone again, sitting in frosty silence.

"I thought you didn't know he was married," Roman finally said.

"I didn't. But I figured he was deep in the closet. Any client who makes up a new life for himself every time he hires me doesn't like the one he's living, but he's too afraid to leave it."

Roman nodded, adjusted himself in the booth. "Yes," he finally said.

"Yes, what?"

"You answered my question, I'm answering yours. Yes, I can kill that...*coiling up* inside feeling. Bring your friend Tom back. I'll suck his dick right here."

Ethan ignored the jab, but he thought this whole thing had gone far enough. "What did Rachel say to you in that hotel room that made you suddenly think this was a good idea?"

Nostrils flaring, lips pursed, Roman glowered at the table before draining his glass in several thirsty sips. "You first," he finally said. "Why'd you quit escorting?"

"You," Ethan answered softly, even as saying the word aloud made him feel like there was a tremor deep inside his gut that might slowly but steadily send cracks running through him from head to toe. "I quit because of you."

Roman looked too stunned to speak.

"I quit because I couldn't stop seeing your face on that street corner. But I was still about fifteen grand short of what I needed to finish culinary school, so I flew back to South Carolina and I confronted the parents who banished me like I had the plague after I refused to renounce my sexuality for the benefit of their church friends. I told them they could either write me a check for the difference or I could set up shop in their backyard. I already had it on good authority that I'd have some pretty steady clients among their church friends."

Roman seemed stunned by the answer. When it was clear Ethan wasn't going to say more, he broke the silence. "What did your parents do?"

"They wrote me a check, and I was on my way." It had been years since he'd told this story to anyone, and he'd only ever told it twice. He wasn't prepared for how hollowed out and exhausted he'd feel once the words left him. Years since he'd ever had to see anyone react the way Roman was reacting now, wincing and making sad eyes over the heartless efficiency of the exchange. It was easier to keep your pain stuffed deep down when you never had to see anyone else react to hearing it for the first time.

"Did you ever talk to them again?" Roman asked softly.

"I believe you said you'd answer my question when I answered yours."

Roman sucked in a deep breath and stared down into his now empty glass. "She didn't mean it but…"

"But what?"

"It was about my mom. She said I should do it because my mom would want me to live at my fullest potential, or whatever. And that's when I realized I just…can't be…"

"Can't be what?"

Tears slipped down his face. "Homeless. Broke. Couch surfing. Again. Everything I saw in her eyes when I told her I was quitting school, when I told her I was throwing everything she'd given me down the drain." He shot to his feet.

"Roman, sit. Please."

"No. Look, this is what I have to do, okay? And I know you don't approve, and I know you think I'll fuck it up or lose my mind or whatever, but I've got no choice, okay? And I'm sorry if asking you to talk to me like this was inappropriate. But it's my life, and I have to make my own decisions."

"I understand, but Roman—"

He was striding toward the door on his powerful legs.

"Roman!"

When the entry door swung shut behind him, Ethan sprang from his feet, but by the time he reached the parking lot, the Bentley's taillights were shrinking into the dark.

He pulled out his phone.

I would never judge you.

He didn't expect a response, but he was staring down at his phone, wondering if he'd been too hard on the guy. And wondering simultaneously if he should have tried harder to stop him.

A guy he'd dated in France a few years back had yelled at him during one of their many fights that he needed to learn the difference between protecting someone and suffocating them. Where did tonight fall on the scale?

You are not dating *that young man, Ethan Blake.* He was tempted to ignore the voice in his head because it sounded like his late mother's. Imperious and dismissive and cold. But the only way to drown it out was to imagine taking Roman into his arms, holding him there, protecting him.

Guiding him to the bed...

Finally, he added.

Let me know when you get home safe. And never feel like you can't call me.

He snagged a Diet Coke in a to-go cup and hit the road.

He was almost home when his phone chimed with a new text

Home. Sorry.

When he reached the driveway for his parking lot, he stopped, knowing he'd lose cell service the second he descended under the building.

> **No matter what happens, your mother, wherever she is, is proud of you. Never forget that. I can hear it in all the stories you tell about her.**

Unlike mine, he thought. When his vision misted and he found himself blinking back tears, he was shocked. He sat frozen behind the wheel before a neighbor's headlights swung into alignment with his car.

As he opened the door to his apartment, he saw he had another text from Roman.

> **You're a good man, Ethan Blake.**

Given their history, the words meant far more coming from Roman Walker than they would anyone else.

He slept more peacefully than he thought he would. Until about three in the morning, when he woke from a dream of Roman Walker snuggling into bed next to him, whispering the words of his last text into his ear, their bodies entwined and grasping beneath the covers.

16

The next morning, Roman found Diana standing in the sand a few paces from the concrete-floored rec room that opened right onto the beach. Her eyes were concealed by highly reflective, cat-eye sunglasses, her platinum hair pulled back in a ponytail she'd threaded through a pink visor branded with the logo for her top-selling face cream.

"How'd you sleep, sugar?" she asked.

"Great," he lied.

By the time Roman had gotten home the night before, she'd already returned from LA and retired to the master suite. She'd made no move to intercept him as he'd hurried to his room and locked the door. Still, he'd laid in bed for hours fearing a knock that never came. Then, right before dawn, he'd given up on sleep for good and gone to the kitchen to fix himself a fortifying breakfast of egg whites and turkey bacon and was back inside his room before the sun fully rose. That's where he'd stayed until session time, running over the words he planned to say to his boss once he could look her in the eye.

"Stair sprints," he announced with as much enthusiasm as he could muster.

She sighed. They were her least favorite exercise, and this sort of exchange usually preceded each round. The house's service stairway was tucked between the Castle and its northern neighbor, three flights of concrete steps that sharply ascended the cliff, with high, spiked security gates at the top and bottom. They'd confine their session to the bottom-most flight. It was easiest to scale, and the one time he'd tried to make her run up the final and steepest one, she'd slapped him across the shoulder and accused him of elder abuse.

He opened the gate with his key and started up toward the first landing. Diana remained at the bottom, stretching out her hips and quads the way he'd taught her.

He pulled his stopwatch out from his tank top, timing her first sprint. Two minutes. Not bad, but not her best. "Minute rest," he told her as she struggled to catch her breath.

She usually spent these little breaks peppering him with polite, breathless questions about how he was spending his free time or giving him updates about his social media campaigns from her marketing team—businesslike attempts to distract him from the timer so she could steal a few extra breaths. Now, she was silent except for her gasps.

On the second sprint, she beat her time by twenty seconds. When he informed her, she didn't seem pleased.

"I'll do it," he said. "With Scott, I mean. But on one condition." She was breathless and hunched over, but he could tell he had her full attention behind her sunglasses. "I want my trust back."

She straightened quickly. "Well, technically, it's your mother's trust, sweetie. You were just the successor trustee."

"And I'd like to be again."

Carefully, she reached up and took her sunglasses off. "Why do that to yourself? You really want a house back that's been torn down to the studs? Let me finish the renovations and earn you a nice little profit."

"It's fine. I'll figure it out. I just want the house back."

She nodded, placed her hands on her hips, and studied him behind her sunglasses. "So you met with Rachel at Sapphire Cove yesterday?"

Every muscle in his body tensed. No way would Rachel have blabbed to her mom about what they'd discussed. Someone else on staff had probably made Diana aware of the meeting, and the timing had clued her in to the subject. His fault for not asking Rachel to keep it a secret in advance.

"What'd you guys talk about?" Diana asked.

"Wedding stuff."

Diana nodded. "I see. I don't mean to be rude, darling, but I need to remind you about the NDA you put your name to when you started working here."

"No need. Rachel's my best friend. I'd never violate her confidence."

Diana didn't move. "And me? What about the one who's been doing all these good things for you while Rachel's been off at theater camp? Am I a friend?" *A pimp, apparently,* he wanted to say. "'Cause I thought we were family. But this isn't sounding very familial, you going behind my back to my daughter and all."

"Really? Don't siblings complain about their moms all the time?" Roman managed a sheepish grin.

Diana didn't crack a smile. "Don't play dumb, sugar. It's the one look you can't pull off." Her anger was quiet and forceful, but she'd never directed anger of any kind at him before and its arrival felt as powerful as a slap.

He told himself to hold his tongue.

He didn't listen. "You know, my mom might not have been the warmest person in the world, but she never threatened to show me the door if I didn't have sex I didn't want to have. So maybe I've just got a different idea of family."

Diana was nodding, but she'd also pursed her lips and tensed her jaw, which Roman had learned was a sign of repressed, roiling anger, and her blue eyes blazed. "We're going to leave the trust the way it is for now. That's all for today. I'll put in some time on the rower. You seem unfocused, and I prefer you at your best." She patted him on the shoulder. "Get some rest."

She descended the steps toward the sunlit sand, leaving him trembling with rage.

When his phone's ring belted from the BMW's speakers, Roman's name flashed in the cupholder next to him.

"I can't..." Roman coughed between tears, tears it sounded like he was trying to muffle. "I can't, Ethan. You're right. It's *her*. The problem's her. She's a monster. I can't...I need to get out of here or I'm going to do something I'll really fuckin' regret."

"Okay, well, don't do that. Just tell me what happened."

"I told her I'd do it if she signed the trust back over to me and she said no."

Of course she did, Ethan thought, hands tensing on the wheel.

"Like she's got a right to it or something, and she never even met the damn woman and now she's got her house and she won't..." A growl devoured the last of the sentence.

"Where are you?"

Roman sniffled, cleared his throat, and spoke in a steadier tone. "Locked in my bathroom like a friggin' teenager."

"Go to my place. There's a key under the third rock out from the front door on the lefthand side. It can be yours for a while."

"Did you already leave?"

"Yeah, but I'll be back in a day or two."

There was a long silence, during which he heard the sounds of Roman packing up what sounded like toiletry items and bath products—dozens of them. "So I didn't lose out on the offer when I changed my mind the first time?" Roman asked.

"You most certainly did not. And food's still included."

A few sniffles later, Roman asked, "So who are you going to see in San Diego?"

"My friend Donnie. He runs a porn studio but he doesn't have any shoots scheduled this week, and he got me the meeting at Sapphire Cove that got me the job, so I owe him a thank you dinner."

"Which porn studio?"

"Are you a porn fan? I figured your no casual sex policy might extend to other media."

"Hardly. I love porn. It keeps douchebags out of my house."

Suppressing a laugh, Ethan answered, "Parker Hunter."

"You don't want company?" Roman asked quietly.

"Roman..."

"I know, I'm sorry. I'm a mess, and I'm being too much."

More zippers, more items being stuffed inside some kind of bag.

"Are you?" Roman asked. "Into porn, I mean."

"A little, I guess. I've been friends with Donnie for years, so I've seen how it gets made. It takes some of the thrill out of it, to be frank."

"I see."

More zipper sounds, more rustling fabric. Roman must have started to pack a larger bag.

"What'd you cook me?" he asked.

"It's all protein and vegetables. Don't worry. The sauces are on the side if you're feeling adventurous."

Roman cleared his throat. "I do love an adventurous sauce now and then."

Ignoring the flirtatiousness in Roman's tone, Ethan said, "Text me when you get to my place just to let me know you got in okay. And make as clean a getaway as you can for now. Don't try to get the last word. It won't be worth it. Make a quick, clean exit. I'll help you figure the rest out later when I'm back."

"Thank you, Ethan."

When the call ended, the traffic suddenly seemed less thick and less stressful, and his hands were tingling pleasantly atop the steering wheel. How had he gone from heavily ruminating over their conversation the night before to feeling like he was made of shimmering light waves?

One call from Roman, that's how.

One moment of being needed by Roman and he felt like he was on top of the world.

He should have expected the wave of nostalgia that washed over him when he was thirty minutes from San Diego, but it took him by surprise, nonetheless. He'd lived in the area fifteen years ago and had only been back a few times since. But San Diego had been his city of dreams, the place where he'd first succeeded at something other than giving men toe-curling orgasms for money. In the shadow cast by his sunny memories of the place, his New York years felt like a strange, and often dark, prologue, full of excitement and risk, but lacking in the hopeful focus of true ambition.

Now as he passed the Del Mar Fairgrounds and over the marshy, sun-sparkling pools of the San Dieguito Lagoon, his heart raced with excitement. A few minutes later, woodsy hills closed in on either side of the freeway and he was zipping by familiar exits for La Jolla, the tiny enclave where he'd worked his first real restaurant job—line cook at a high-end seafood place where most of the bills got paid on Amex black cards and the millionaire customers sometimes sent their dishes back four times in a row. But he'd loved the work, loved the kitchen's rigorous discipline and all-consuming energy, and he'd thrived under the mentorship of the place's head chef, who'd identified and encouraged his passion for pastry before hooking him up with his first job in Europe.

Driving along the expanse of Mission Bay, he found it the same as he had back then, its serpentine shorelines fringed with tall palms beneath a cornflower blue sky. His spirits were so high that if Tom Cruise had come thundering past him on a motorcycle, bellowing about the need for speed, Ethan would have bellowed joyously along with him in unison.

A decade and a half earlier, fate had granted him his first gig post-culinary school in the same city his old friend Zach Loudon had moved to the year before. But unlike Ethan, Zach hadn't left sex work behind entirely; he'd moved behind the camera at Parker Hunter, then a fledgling gay porn studio specializing in amateur scenes with muscle boys who were either gay for pay or pretending to be. The man who'd often referred to himself as a *true courtesan* had whittled his client list down to one or two loyal regulars by then. In short, Ethan's old escorting mentor was doing exactly what Ethan had once feared he'd have to do—slowly aging out of the profession in which he'd once excelled. When Ethan told him he was headed west, Zach had offered him the guest bedroom of his little rental house in Hillcrest, and Ethan had happily accepted. The gay neighborhood felt like a quaint village compared to the roiling streets of Manhattan, the house like a palace compared to the East Village crash pad where they'd once lived with four other roommates.

But Zach hadn't lived alone. Not truly.

One of Parker Hunter's newest models, a fresh-off-the-streets wild child named Donnie Bascombe had been a frequent visitor to Zach's bed. After Ethan moved in, the two men had added him to their sexual mix with ease.

For Ethan, the arrangement was ideal. Casual, but consistent. It gratified him and offered him a level of companionship while also protecting him from the uncertainty of entering the city's gay dating world with his escorting past still close at his heels. Their relaxed throuple, which usually ended up with Zach in between them and on the bottom, made for the perfect transition between his old life and his new, client-free one. Something about the spontaneity—the way they'd go from playing Xbox on the sofa to falling into a slurping daisy chain on the floor of Zach's living room—had matched the heat of his escorting days, but without the constant unknowns.

It helped that Donnie and Zach were both sex workers who knew his history. Helped that after having said good-bye to his final client, after changing all his numbers and email addresses and deleting all his profiles, he didn't have to worry about if or when he should disclose his past to a man he'd seen more than a handful of times. All three of them had been sexual outlaws, free to scratch each other's itches without labels or prying questions or expectations.

Then one day, Zach had vanished, leaving a heartbroken Donnie sobbing in Ethan's arms, and the two of them had transitioned from occasional sex partners to lifelong friends.

While he'd lived hand to mouth back then, today Ethan could easily afford a luxe room at one of the nicer downtown hotels. But he preferred the giant conference compounds along the Embarcadero that were swarmed with cosplaying superhero fans every Comic-Con. The Wyman was his favorite, two half circles of gleaming glass and steel, the curve in each tower designed to maximize guest room views. Just like he'd asked, they'd given him a king on a high floor with a little balcony. When he stepped outside, he could see all the way from the boat-stuffed marina below, across the bay to Coronado Island, and as far as the confident swell of the Point Loma peninsula.

Once he'd unpacked the essentials, he checked in with Sapphire Cove by text and spent the next hour re-prioritizing his team's task list based on their status reports. Then he composed several different drafts of an email to Janene, the lawyer friend he'd consulted with about Roman's trust. Without sharing too many details, he made clear there was a chance his friend was going to take an aggressive stance and try to reinstate himself as successor trustee. What would that look like? And what would it cost Roman for Janene to represent him?

It was more than Roman had asked for, and that was fine.

He hadn't asked for a week's worth of food either, but he'd been plenty happy to hear about it.

When he realized Roman hadn't texted him, he sent him a short message asking if he'd made it to the apartment all right and got a thumbs-up in response. Then it was time to check in with Donnie, who said he was running late at work and asked Ethan to meet him at the studio.

North of the city and just south of Marine Corps Air Station Miramar, Parker Hunter's magic happened inside a drab, windowless, one-story industrial building that had no signage and all the fortifications of a federal prison. Its neighbors were clueless as to the business being conducted within. Gone were the days when the studio's founder, a former Broadway stage manager who'd chain-smoked himself into an early grave, shot his films guerilla-style in the living rooms and backyards of friends' homes. But the front parking lot was more choked with cars than Ethan had ever seen it, a few of them utility trucks.

There was usually an elaborate check-in process that required him to slide his ID under a glass partition to the person working security inside, but Donnie must have been watching out for him. As he drove into the lot, his old friend came bounding toward him with a big, goofy grin on his scruffy face.

Ethan wasn't prepared for the emotions that rose in him once he was in Donnie's arms. They'd talked almost three times a week for most of their adult lives, but this was their first in-person meeting in almost two years, and he found himself squeezing his old friend as hard as Rachel Peyton had squeezed Roman in Villa 9E.

Before he'd moved behind the camera, Donnie's alter ego, Bo Bonin, had enjoyed one of the most auspicious careers in gay porn as a brutish, growling power top who knew how to pitch his dirty talk in that sweet spot between lecherous and abusive. He still crowed about the time a popular porn blog had described him as "gay America's favorite perverted football coach." As for the website that had given him his start, today he was running the place, after years spent turning it from a shabby amateur outfit with questionable business practices into a brand name studio that had once been the punchline of a joke on *Saturday Night Live*, a pop culture reference for unvarnished queer male lust.

"The parking lot's certainly active," Ethan said. "A casting call for your sword and sandal epic?"

"Nah. I'm adding two new sets, actually, and we've got to figure out some wiring stuff first. The electrician was two hours late, but they're clearing out. It's this model interview that came out of nowhere at me. I would have made him come another day but the guy's hot to trot and hot as hell. I'll introduce you. Come on."

The security guard buzzed them through a solid metal door that looked capable of surviving a bomb blast, then they entered a narrow hallway between particle board walls that had been used to carve out a small nest of offices at one corner of the warehouse. After a near collision with the contractors departing the studio, Ethan stood there patiently while Donnie wrapped up with them. Then the guys brushed past Ethan with nods, and he was finally alone with his friend. Sort of.

"I'll need you to hang in the office while I shoot the interview, but let me introduce you guys real quick. He's *smokin'*."

"Thank you, but I've met attractive men before, Sex Monster."

"No doubt. But this one's got flags on the field in the model department. So I'm thinking he might make a better distraction for you during your visit if he's interested." Donnie winked.

"I'm not opposed to a good distraction now and then. It's been a while, actually."

Donnie laughed. "Follow me."

They entered the main studio. It was vast and drafty, thanks to frosty air conditioning. The exterior walls had been reinforced and soundproofed so the sounds of professional moans and groans couldn't be heard from the parking lots or side alleys. Ringed around the center of the space were the sets for various bargain-basement fantasies. A gym floor next to a fake locker room with working showers. A classroom. A generic corporate office. A BDSM dungeon featuring a glistening leather pommel horse, an equipment wall, and a mattress on the floor laced with bondage straps. There was even a barn set piled with actual hay bales.

The only set that wasn't deep in shadow was a college dorm room with matching twin beds in front of a fake window inside a false wall painted bright blue. The wall was also covered in what looked like posters of rock stars until you got up close and saw they were all hand drawn. Donnie had told him once that they were all the work of one of Parker Hunter's superfans, a middle-aged woman who lived in Idaho and ran a fruit canning business on the Internet and sent them long but well-intentioned emails pointing out the continuity errors in their videos.

Sitting on the end of one twin bed was a physically flawless, olive-skinned man stroking one of the biggest cocks Ethan had ever seen. When the potential model raised his head in response to their approach, Ethan saw piercing hazel eyes and lips so kissable it was like they dripped honey.

"Hi, Ethan," Roman said, and then everything got real quiet.

17

"What?" Roman said into the tense silence. "I need a job."

Ethan's feet suddenly felt like they were made of lead. His temples throbbed thanks to matching bolts of tension in either side of his jaw. To calm himself, he made a quick mental list of all the things he wouldn't allow himself to do in this moment—all of which he wanted to do desperately and with force. He wouldn't explode with anger. He wouldn't yank the covers off the twin bed next to Roman's and cloak the young man's naked body with them. He wouldn't carry him out of the studio with as much determination as he'd piggybacked him down the Billings Trail that Saturday.

Do these things, he thought, *and Roman wins*. And this had to be a game. He couldn't seriously be on the verge of auditioning for porn.

"Well," Donnie said, "someone's ready to go." In the harsh industrial light pouring down from above, the sight of the young man's gorgeous brown nipples, the same ones he'd coated in icing a few nights before, made Ethan flinch and look away as if he'd stared into a fierce flame. "Wouldn't have brought my friend in if I'd known you'd stripped down. Anyway, just a quick intro, then he'll step out so we can get to work. Ethan, this is Ro—"

Donnie fell silent as Ethan turned and headed for the door.

A few seconds later, Ethan took a seat behind the cluttered desk in his friend's office and was scrolling through emails on his phone. He might have seemed calm and composed to someone sitting across from him—save for the fact that his breaths were whistling in his nose.

There was a light knock before Donnie poked his head in. "So you know this guy?"

Ethan answered with a nod. His anger was so total he didn't trust himself to speak.

Even though the office was his, his friend took a cautious step inside, then closed the door gently behind him as if he were the intruder. "You want to tell me what's going on here?"

With too much force, Ethan set the phone down on Donnie's desk, trying—and failing—to blink away the sight of Roman Walker's engorged, veiny, lube-slick cock, which had seemed enticing and obscene.

Had he fantasized about seeing it one day?

Perhaps. Maybe.

Okay, fine, yes. But as the culmination of some more elaborate fantasy in which they came to know each—really know each other—over time.

A lot of time.

Enough time for Roman to see him as something more than a mentor and a temporary refuge from his upended life. Enough time for Roman to grow up a little.

But it had been just that—a fantasy. A fantasy that had seemed so farfetched and so far off that he'd never have to contend with its implications should it become real.

And Roman's attempt to make it real felt like a violation.

Focus, Blake, he told himself. *You're a grown man, and a grown man should never be undone by the spontaneous nudity of a wild child.* "What did you mean when you said he had flags on the field in the model department?" Ethan asked quietly.

"He wouldn't send nudes, but he wanted to shoot a test, like, right away. Usually means a guy's not serious and he's trying to rush it before he loses his nerve. And since this whole thing seems like it was maybe about *you*, I'm sensing that's the case."

"He's a grown man. He can do whatever he wants."

"Okay, but this is my studio and so I'm going to do what I want. And this guy isn't my priority, you are. So are we cool if I shoot this? 'Cause I won't lie, with his following it could be huge for us. If he's serious. But if you've got even the slightest issue with it—"

"I don't. Go ahead."

Donnie nodded slowly, like he didn't believe him. "All right, well I haven't given him the talk yet, and you know forty percent of them bail when I do so...we'll see."

Ethan was familiar with *the talk*. He'd overheard some version of it for years. Donnie, a former performer, always went out of his way to make sure new models knew what they were getting into—all the things no one had told him when he'd first started in the biz fifteen years before. Porn wasn't sex, it was the *performance* of sex, and that meant shoots were uncomfortable and long and required you to fake arousal under a variety of challenging circumstances. Also, the pay was lousy unless you supplemented it with some other form of sex work. Once, it had been escorting. Now it was OnlyFans, a demanding content beast most guys weren't up to satisfying in a way that might earn them a living. And then, of course, the most important part—in the Internet age, porn never went away, and you shouldn't do it unless you were prepared for your grandmother to find out.

"It's fine," Ethan said. "You and I are fine. Don't worry. I'm not letting this little...*game* ruin my visit."

"So this is a game, huh?"

"Yes," Ethan said, "and I'm getting tired of it. But I'll give you the whole story later. Let's not let this kid get into our heads."

Holding the edge of the open door, Donnie made no move to leave. "*Kid*, huh? You sure as hell don't look at him like he's a kid."

"Please. Everyone looks at Roman Walker like they want him to take his clothes off."

"Maybe. But that's not how *you* look at him, Blake."

With a lift of both eyebrows, Donnie was gone before Ethan could ask him what he meant.

Then he was alone with a bank of security monitors off to one side of the desk that showed views of the entrance and the office hallway. Was there a camera inside the studio? His hand started reaching for the mouse before he forced it to the arm of Donnie's desk chair.

For the next few minutes he read *The New York Times* on his phone as if his life depended on it, but he was only absorbing every few lines as his pulse raced. Every creak in the walls, every rush of a car outside, made him sit up. After about twenty minutes, there was a light knock on the door, and Donnie poked his head in again.

"Total bust," he said quietly. "His wood left with you, apparently. I finally called it."

In an effort to hide his relief, Ethan nodded at the desk.

"He's kinda nerved out. You want to go talk to him?"

The relief that washed over Ethan was so total, he had only a moment to enjoy it before he was ashamed of its depth. "He's upset because his little mind game didn't work. I'm perfectly content to stay right here until he leaves. Tell him we can talk when I'm home."

"Okay, Daddy." Grinning, Donnie sat down on the sofa across from the desk. "Guess it was a bad idea for me to invite him to have dinner with us on the boat then."

"Why am I friends with you?" Ethan growled.

"What? You wouldn't tell me what's going on. This was the only way to find out. Hey. It's cool if I hook up with him, though, right? Since you're being Mr. Gruff Daddy about all his sexy naked mind games or whatever."

Grinning like a jack-o'-lantern, Donnie was taunting him, he was sure, but when Ethan tried to swallow, it turned into a cough.

"There you go. *Now* you're telling me what's going on. You're just doing it with your angry eyes like you always do."

"It's your visit and your thank you dinner. If you'd like him to join, that's absolutely fine."

Donnie stood and slapped his thighs. "Not only do I want him along, I want you guys to talk through whatever the hell this is first. Remember. The *Golden Boy*'s a stress-free zone."

"Well, you've made a terrible mistake then. Because Roman Walker is nothing but stress."

"Just the way you like 'em."

Fighting the desire to give voice to every word of profanity he'd ever heard, Ethan got to his feet and gave his best friend a polite smile. "Tell him to meet me in the marina parking lot by your slip in an hour."

"He's showering. You sure you don't want to—"

"One hour."

And then Ethan was out the door.

By the time he reached the Shelter Island Marina, late afternoon had turned the sky overhead a dusty rose. To the west, the Point Loma peninsula rose in a wooded, rooftop-studded swell that would soon obscure the sunset. To the east, and a good ways beyond the rounded hangars of the North Island Naval Air Station, downtown San Diego's skyscrapers tossed the sunlight back at them in little blinding coins. Gathering his thoughts, trying to pull the coherent threads from his confusing tangle of anger and frustration, Ethan paced the lot close to his parked car until he saw the gleaming Bentley pull into the lot.

Roman's sunglasses hid his eyes as he approached. There was a tense, angry set to his jaw, but his walk was a shuffle without any of his usual strut.

"Have fun?" Ethan asked.

Roman shook his head. "No, not really. Guess I'm not cut out for it."

Ethan nodded. A tense silence fell, interrupted by the caws of wheeling seagulls overhead.

"Donnie says you're really mad."

"I am."

Roman huffed and sneered. "Why?"

"*Why?* Okay, well, take your pick. There's the fact that you wasted my good friend's time and used his legitimate business as some sort of tool in whatever this game was. There's the fact that you set up a situation where I'd be forced to see you naked against my will. Then there's the fact that a trip that was supposed to be about thanking my good friend for helping me get the job of my dreams is now about you and whatever stalkerish mind game you're playing now. Should I keep going?"

Roman shook his head at the pavement, but a silence settled. Finally, he broke it and his voice sounded winded and weak. "When you told me you were coming down here, I saw you in a Jacuzzi making boy soup with a bunch of porn hotties and I thought that's what I needed to be to get you to see me as somebody other than little Ronnie Burton."

"If you're worried about me seeing some other version of you, you should worry about the one I saw on Saturday night at the hotel. Because that's what today felt like."

Roman threw his hands wide. "You're just not going to say anything about the fact that I have feelings for you?"

"If someone would like me to recognize their feelings for me, they should also try respecting me."

"Is that why you keep rejecting me? Because I don't—"

"*Rejecting* you?" Ethan barked. "Roman, you have a key to my house. I was up at the crack of dawn making you a refrigerator full of food. I risked my job to set up that meeting with you and Rachel, not knowing how it would go. Do you have any idea what it meant to let you stay in my place when I'm not around? After Saturday? I sat there for hours this morning wondering if I should lock up my personal papers just in case you got a little taste for revenge again."

"I would never do that," he whispered. "Not after this week."

"A week in which you have acted like everything I've done for you means nothing, all because I won't treat you with the same slobbering, blind sexual attention as the strangers who follow you online."

"That's not what I want from you."

"No, you want validation and distraction instead of actual help. And forgive me if that seems as one-sided as what I used to give your father."

Roman bowed his head as if he'd been slapped. Ethan didn't regret the words. But maybe they could have used a bit more varnish. The young man held his ground, jaw quivering, eyes hidden behind his sunglasses.

"I'm sorry. I'm sorry if today crossed a boundary or whatever."

"Thank you," Ethan said quietly. "Because it did."

Because deep down, he thought, *whether I wanted to admit it or not, I wanted to see you naked someday, but not in that studio, not under those hot lights. And now it feels like that special moment has been stolen from me forever.*

For a while, neither of them spoke, and with each passing second, Ethan wasn't sure if he was afraid Roman was about to leave or hoping for the young man's quick exit.

But after a while, Roman lifted his chin and spoke again. His voice was ragged but steady. "And I'm sorry that I'm not as smart as you are and that I don't have the words to say how you make me feel. Because the truth is no man has ever made me feel the way you do, Ethan. And maybe that's just 'cause I'm young and inexperienced or whatever. But I could feel it when we were texting last week, when I was lying to you about who I was, and it fucked with my head because I didn't know the real story and I thought I was seeing how my dad fell for you. And I could relate, to be blunt. And it's why I was so crazy by the time I got to the hotel.

"Then we met for real, and there was this...strength in you. This quiet. And it quieted me too for the first time in I don't know how long. I couldn't believe it when you came walking out of the dark on the trail that night. At first I thought I was imagining it. You, there. Opening your heart to me after I went for your throat."

Run, Ethan thought. But it was his mother's ghostly voice who said it, his mother who'd once lectured him on how two men could never truly love each other. Pleasure each other in sinful ways, but not love each other. *Run. He's too young, too fragile. Maybe he believes all this now, but he'll change his mind tomorrow, and you'll be humiliated and alone. Better to just be alone. So run.*

But Roman wasn't finished. "There's always been a storm inside of me for as long as I can remember, but I feel like no matter how big it gets it would never blow a man like you off course. You're so strong. You're so steady. All I want to do every time I'm with you is sink into your arms. And I feel like if I'm with you, I won't just get better. I'll *be* better. Because when you talk to me, you see me. You see *me* and not the things that I have to put on or take off to get attention. And it scares me and it makes me excited. And I guess it makes me desperate and crazy too. And I'm sorry if I haven't figured out the right way to throw myself at you, but you should know the only reason I'm doing it is because I never wanted to leave your arms on Sunday morning."

"Roman..." But he couldn't finish the sentence. Everything inside of him wanted to lean into Roman's words the same way Roman wanted to lean into his embrace. Inside of him was a war between decades' worth of defenses and precautions and decades' worth of longing for a man who would surrender to his protection and his care the way Roman had just described.

Send him home, he thought. *Send him away. He's right. He is a storm, and he'll drag you under.*

"Roman, I appreciate that you might feel this way *now*, when you're facing all these challenges, but—"

"Oh, God," Roman whined, face in his hands. "You *appreciate* it? Oh, God. I should have kept my mouth shut."

Suddenly, there was a loud war whoop close by, and they both jumped. Donnie's SUV idled a few yards away as the man leaned out the driver's side window. "Howdy, boys. We better hurry if I'm going to take us out past the harbor mouth so we can watch the sunset." He made a wavelike motion with one hand. "So wrap it up and jerk each other off or whatever you guys need to do to get the bugs out of your asses."

"Mix a few more metaphors while you're at it, Sex Monster," Ethan barked, grateful he was able to blink back the tears without wiping at his face.

"Bite me, Tolstoy." Donnie grinned and turned for his parking spot. "On second thought, bite *him*. He looks like he wants it."

Then Ethan was left with Roman staring at him expectantly. "Do you want me to go?"

Yes, Ethan thought.

"No," Ethan finally said. "You shouldn't drive when you're this upset."

Yeah, that's it, Gramps, he thought. Roman deflated, as if he'd finished a race only to be granted a medal made of aluminum foil.

"Let's get on the boat," Ethan added. "Come on, now."

Only once he was headed down the dock toward Donnie's slip did it occur to him that he'd just addressed the man who'd poured his heart out to him as if he were a small dog. And he was following Ethan like one. His heart was hammering. He wondered if he'd just made the biggest mistake of his life, not sending Roman away, not nipping off his genuine advance in the bud. Not giving them both time to see if this surge of emotion inside the man was feelings or just another storm that would blow over a soon as Ethan was out of sight.

The *Golden Boy* was a forty-five-foot sun deck trawler, three decks tall and designed for long, slow cruises and overnight stays. It was also Donnie's home and had been for years.

Standing behind Roman as Donnie helped him aboard with one hand, Ethan placed one palm against the young man's lower back to steady him, which sent heat shooting from his wrist to his shoulder. And all he could think during the next few minutes of touring the boat was *Oh, dear God. What have I done? What am I doing?*

The boat felt bigger than Ethan remembered, maybe because he wasn't staying on it this visit and hadn't been forced to cram his suitcase into the cramped forward berth. Some of the woodwork inside looked freshly varnished. He was always surprised by how orderly it was. When they'd first met, Donnie had known how to survive on the streets, and his first living spaces had all looked like tornado touchdowns. It was Ethan who'd gone with him to the grocery store and helped him stock the products that ensured a sanitary kitchen. Who'd taken him to the bank and showed him how to open an account. Who'd taught him how to cook something other than instant mac and cheese. Since then, reducing his life down to the size of the *Golden Boy* had taught his old friend how to be tidy.

"Wow," Roman said as he studied the spacious seating area right off the galley. "I thought you said porn didn't pay."

"Honestly, this baby costs less than a house around these parts," Donnie called back. "And I didn't exactly buy it myself."

"What he means is he inherited the *Golden Boy* along with Parker Hunter," Ethan said.

"What *he* means is I'm a lucky son of a bitch," Donnie corrected.

"Not luck," Ethan corrected him. "Eddie loved you like a son, and you were good to him."

Roman studied him.

"Eddie ran the studio when Donnie first started working for them," Ethan explained. "Eventually he let Donnie take over when his health started going downhill. He left him the boat in his will."

Donnie nodded, grinning. "Dude smoked like they were about to ban the things any second. Anyway, biggest prize I ever got in this life, and I never had to sleep with him for it. Probably 'cause he was a total voyeur and got off on watching me get with his other models, but whatever. A boat's a boat."

"And a house, apparently." Roman fell suddenly silent.

Ethan moved a few steps toward him to see why.

On a display shelf atop a row of locked cabinets, a framed photograph had stolen Roman's attention—a picture of Ethan, Donnie, and Zach in their younger days, after a hike down to Black's Beach so they could spend the day cavorting with other nude sunbathers. Right before sunset, they'd set the timer on the camera and wedged it in the sand a few feet from their towel before piling their bodies on top of each other like they were rolled-up rugs. Ethan was on top, so his was the only bare ass you could see, but all three of them had been naked as the day they were born.

"You guys were hotties," Roman said.

"Were?" Donnie hissed through clenched teeth. "Ouch. This guy's tough."

"Not what I meant," Roman said quietly as he took the picture down off the shelf. "Who's that on the bottom?"

Zach's half smile was muted. Shoulder-length, cornsilk hair spilled out from under his green and yellow Parker Hunter baseball cap. While Ethan and Donnie both looked ecstatic to be playing out in the sun together in the buff, their bottom layer seemed as subdued and pleasantly unreadable as always.

"That's Zach," Donnie finally said after an awkward silence, moving to the picture. "First guy who broke my heart."

"Oh, I'm sorry."

Donnie gently took the photo from Roman's hands, reached up, and tousled his hair. "Don't be. It grew back stronger." His smile looked forced as he put the picture back on the shelf. "All right, boys. To the high seas we go." Donnie popped open the galley fridge and handed them both a frosty bottle of Corona. "Don't worry. The captain never imbibes at the helm. But he does keep the good stuff flowing just in case the passengers have opinions about his captaining. Which Ethan usually does. 'Cause he's, like, eighty-five percent opinions."

"Lies," Ethan responded. "My opinions are about your cooking, and I keep those to myself."

On the fly bridge, Ethan and Roman settled onto opposite ends of the built-in sofa right behind the helm chair as the engines beneath them rumbled to life.

As soon as the Golden Boy entered the choppy bay, the temperature dropped, and the winds started to do a number on the canopy overhead.

Ethan told himself to stay still, to keep his head turned in the direction they were headed. But he didn't listen. He looked back and saw Roman sitting at the sofa's far end.

"Hey," Ethan said before he could stop himself.

Roman removed his sunglasses. The canopy offered decent shade. "Hey," he said back.

His mother's ghostly voice still scolded him, but the words that had rushed from Roman in the parking lot made for a louder chorus in his head. Ethan patted the bench seat next to him and said, "Come here, stormy."

Without hesitation and chewing his bottom lip with excitement, Roman slid across the seat and wilted into Ethan's side. The touch of him, the warmth of him, made Ethan feel like he was floating high above the water rather than resting on a bunch of pleather and wood. It was as powerful, as total, a feeling as the one he'd felt on Sunday morning.

If it was a mistake, he might as well enjoy every second of it before it drowned him.

18

Ahead of the *Golden Boy*, a giant Navy missile cruiser was rounding Point Loma, heading out to sea. Donnie chose to cut across its wake, a move that took them well south of the peninsula's rugged end, a wise course since kelp beds filled the waters just offshore.

Ethan could make out the squat Point Loma Lighthouse perched atop the cliffs hundreds of feet overhead. Somewhere behind it but out of view was a statue of Juan Rodriguez Cabrillo, allegedly the first European to ever touch West Coast soil with his own two hands. The first time they'd visited the monument years ago, Donnie had jumped up onto the statue's base and pretended to hump its stone leg.

Then the Pacific opened before them and the missile cruiser, which had seemed to tower over the harbor moments before, now seemed smaller and less significant as it headed north up the coast.

Once they were clear of the harbor's mouth, Donnie killed the engines. The boat gently rose and fell. In an instant, the three of them had been handed over to the gentle currents of the sea.

The quiet that descended over them stilled Ethan's soul. The sunset, which would have been obscured by Point Loma even from the height of his room at the Wyman, was on full display here, the orange ball turning deep pink as it set the ocean waters ablaze.

"Shit, man. How is this my life?" Donnie asked. "I used to dream about this kind of thing when I was covered in crap in some oil field in North Dakota. Now here I am. God bless America. And porn."

He felt the power of Donnie's gratitude pulling at him. If you'd told him on the day his parents had banished him from the family that someday he'd be floating on a sea of blue and gold with a man as beautiful as Roman in his arms, he wouldn't have believed you.

"From oil fields to porn?" Roman asked. "How's that happen?"

Donnie turned the helm chair to face them, one foot braced against the edge of the sofa seat. "Well, first your dad finds you behind the barn messing around with another boy and literally—and I do mean *literally*—beats you with a Bible. Then you haul off and break his nose and suddenly everyone in the family agrees sixteen's old enough for you to be living on your own. Then it's a lotta hitchhiking, lotta turning tricks I thought I might not live through. But thank God for those old porn clips on the net, 'cause they really made California look like a great place to live. Gave me something to shoot for."

He grinned, and Roman laughed. The full story was harder and had even more sharp edges, but Donnie hated dumping it all on people. The fact that he'd shared this much with Roman meant he was trying to welcome the guy into the fold, encourage whatever he'd seen developing between him and Ethan.

"What about you, influencer?" Donnie asked. "What brought you out west?"

Ethan tensed.

"My dad cheated so my mom divorced him," Roman said. "We ended up in Victorville when I was a boy."

If Ethan hadn't felt let off the hook before, something about the simple, unadorned honesty of Roman's response allowed him to feel that way now.

"In California, that makes you a local," Donnie said.

"Yeah, but there are a lot of different Californias."

Donnie nodded. "Smart kid," he said to Ethan.

"Yeah, maybe don't call someone a *kid* after you filmed them jerking off," Roman said.

"Sure," Donnie said, "we can call that jerking off."

When the sun dipped below the horizon, Ethan noticed the storm clouds far out to sea. "Rain?" he asked. "In Southern California? Is that allowed?"

"It's not supposed to blow in until the crack of dawn. All right, boys." Donnie returned to the helm chair and started the trawler's engine. "Show's over! I've gotta *eat*."

A short while later, the boat was docked, and they'd gathered on the sun deck to watch Donnie grill tilapia and vegetable kabobs. By the time Roman had shared the whole sordid story of his history with the Peyton family, the sky overhead was dark and star flecked. For a long moment after Roman stopped talking, Donnie just shook his head. "Hollywood people, man. When I was still escorting, I got hired by these Mormon boys who'd just smoked a bunch of PCP for the first time. They were nothing compared to the movie stars."

Ethan said, "I've been in touch with a lawyer friend of mine. We're going to figure out the trust thing."

Roman sank down onto Ethan's lap, curving an arm around his back that sent gooseflesh up Ethan's neck. "I thought your lawyer said I was screwed."

"I emailed her again today." Ethan slid a hand gently over Roman's thigh. "Said we were going to get aggressive and come up with a new plan."

"I can't afford that," he whispered.

"My treat," Ethan said.

"All right, you two," Donnie barked. "No bussy play on the sun deck, please."

"God, Donnie. Really?" Ethan moaned.

"Oh, shut up, Blake. I swear, the damn lingo out there's more complicated than ever. I mean, I hooked up with this guy a few weeks ago who was wearing high-top sneakers he spray-painted bright pink and attached little Hermes wings to—you know, the kind who's got a voice like a cross between Fran Drescher and an Ewok. Cute as hell, nice and open on the backside. Everything's working, and he's mewling like a kitten. So I think, all right, I'm going all in. I'm calling it a pussy. Suddenly he's got a knife at my throat and he's threatening my family."

Roman exploded with laughter.

"Did this really happen to you?" Ethan asked.

"Maybe not the knife part. But he did turn into, like, that hooded, venom-spitting thing from *Jurassic Park*. I thought he'd be into it. I mean, shit, the whole term's a metaphor. It's not like systemic women have an actual cat down there."

"Cisgendered, Donnie. Not systemic," Ethan said.

Once Roman stopped laughing, he asked, "So, are you single?"

"Perpetually. But don't worry. I'm no threat to you and your new man here," Donnie answered. "Blake and I tried that shit a long time ago. We've got the sexual chemistry of me and a Kardashian."

They'd been enjoyable enough, their few post-Zach couplings. But he'd done them mostly to console Donnie, and eventually the guy figured out that Ethan took to bottoming the way he'd once taken to P.E. classes, as something to be endured with gritted teeth. But they'd been enjoyable in a narrow and specific way, a specific channel on the radio of human desire. And he'd tuned himself to many of those channels throughout his adult life. Sex that raced like a fun adventure between friends. Sex that throbbed in the shadows of anonymity, where the players shifted by the minute and no names were exchanged. Sex that swelled into an emotional, all-consuming symphony. Sex that thundered with anger and animosity and frustration. And, of course, the low and once constant drumbeat of sex as a professional obligation. But when he looked at Roman now, he thought whatever they might do to each other's bodies could blow out the speakers and melt the radio.

Once he'd scooped the fish filets and kabobs onto paper plates he'd stacked next to the grill, Donnie gestured for them to take their seats as he served.

"Who's the Kardashian in that equation?" Ethan asked.

"You are, Khloe."

Ethan looked for something to throw, but that would have meant letting go of Roman, who was shaking his head as he said, "That's not why I asked about your love life, but okay."

Once they were all seated around the table, Donnie said, "I don't really date, to be honest. I make…guest appearances."

"What about the one who broke your heart?" Roman asked quietly. "What happened to him?"

A watery silence fell. Donnie sucked in a deep breath as he tucked the edge of his napkin into his jeans. "Nobody knows," he finally said. "One day he just left us a bunch of good-bye notes and walked out. Weird notes, too. Buddhist shit or something."

Ethan waited for Donnie to add the detail that he'd spent a year trying to track the guy down, despite Ethan's insistence that he should let him go. Despite their mutual realization that when it came time to find out where Zach had gone, they both realized they only had scant—and mostly unverifiable—details about where he'd come from in the first place.

Ethan still cursed himself for not reading the signs earlier. If he had it to do over again, he would have taken Donnie aside the first time he saw the guy look at Zach with love in his eyes, would have explained to him there were some things Zach Loudon would never be for anyone, and a true boyfriend was one of them. Zach was a sexual chameleon who gave a little something special to everyone, while being fully present for no one. But Ethan held his tongue, and so when Zach vanished, Donnie had been devastated for months.

Now Donnie jerked his head in Ethan's direction and said, "Blake's got a theory, though."

As he absently cut a bite of fish, Roman turned his attention to Ethan.

Ethan cleared his throat. There'd been a time in their lives when the topic of Zach could reduce Donnie to tears. When he'd clap back against Ethan's theories about Zach's disappearance with a raised voice and a reddened face. They were past that now, Ethan was sure, but how far? Measuring his next words carefully, he gave Roman his attention.

"Everything you and I talked about last night. Million-dollar answers. Strategies for dealing with clients. That was all Zach. He was my escorting mentor, and he raised all that stuff to an art form. Even with us. I mean, I don't think he *meant* to treat us like clients. He just got so into the job there was no other way for him. He was always trying to be what everybody else wanted him to be. One day I think he just got sick of it, but he was in it so deep the only way to start over was to cut all ties."

Donnie was staring down at his plate and cutting fish with a little too much force.

"Sound fair?" he asked Donnie.

Donnie looked up suddenly, then took a few seconds to answer. "Don't ask me. I was young and blinded by love. I'm down with the moral, though."

"What's the moral?" Roman asked.

Donnie took too long to swallow a small bite. "In the end, you can't be with anyone if you're not being yourself."

A silence settled. Donnie took a long slug of his beer.

"I'm sorry," Roman said. "I didn't mean to—"

Donnie shook his head. "Nah, it's fine. Look, here's the thing. I mean, here's why it really hurt. My family was shit, like I told you. I laugh about it now, but it's a miracle I survived those fuckers. I thought what we had with Zach was my first *real* family. A good family. And then he vanished, and for a while I thought, there went my last chance.

"But I was wrong. Ethan became like a brother, and then Eddie at Parker Hunter became my porn dad. Which is not most people's idea of a dad, but just, whatever, roll with me on this one. I'm not most people. And the boys at the studio became a family. I don't know… I guess the point is, guys like us, we gotta make our own families, and sometimes we don't do it until we leave home. But once we do, we're never orphans and we're never alone." Donnie stared at Roman as he chewed. "I'm sorry about what you're going through, and I'm sorry about what happened to your mom. But if you treat my brother Ethan right, you got a family right here."

Roman's eyes glistened. "Thank you," he whispered.

"But I'm *never* putting you on camera, so don't try that shit again."

"Deal," Roman said, then shoveled food into his mouth. "One question, though."

"Shoot," Donnie said.

"What does it mean to treat Ethan right?" Roman asked. A silence fell. He'd been looking at Donnie when he asked the question, but now his eyes were on Ethan.

"What do you think it means?" Donnie asked.

"I think…"

But Roman seemed to lose his grip on his words, and when he looked down at the table, Ethan felt a protective, anxious urge to interject and let him off the hook.

But the guy spoke again, determined to continue. "I think when your life is about how you look, your body, you want to know that people…some people, at least, see what you *do*. Hear what you *say*. Because in the end, that's who you really are, right? I mean, that's who we all are. What we look like changes, but we'll always be what we *do*. How we, you know, act and stuff. And I think Ethan needs to know that that part of him is kind of amazing. I mean, screw that. He doesn't just need to know. He deserves to know, 'cause I don't think it's something he heard from the people who raised him."

That tremor he'd felt the night before, a small shake in the center of his chest that felt like it could crack him from head to toe, was back. And before he knew it, he'd reached under the table and taken one of Roman's hands in his.

"Out of the mouths of babes, right?" Donnie finally said.

"Sorry," Roman whispered.

"Don't be," Ethan answered with enough firm command in his

voice to lift Roman's head and bring the man's gaze to his.

Later, after Donnie had chatted them off the boat and they were both walking toward their parked cars, Ethan felt the kind of electric tension in his chest he hadn't felt since first hooking up with other men in college—anticipation and raw hunger and a knife's edge of fear.

When they reached the Bentley, Roman turned to him, eyes wide and full of expectation as he asked, "So should I go back to Orange County or…"

Roman froze when he saw the look in Ethan's eyes, sighing when Ethan brought one hand to the side of his face. It felt more forbidden than a kiss, gently caressing Roman's cheek.

Finally, Roman turned his head slightly to one side so he could kiss the side of Ethan's hand.

That did it.

When their mouths met, Roman's kiss was as hungry and unguarded as the speech he'd given Ethan earlier. But it was the feel of the man's hand gripping the back of his neck, his caressing—then grasping—fingers that threatened to do Ethan in, that turned his rising moan into a growl.

It had been years since he'd enjoyed a kiss that felt full and complete by itself, and not just the sloppy prelude to a quick disrobing. He felt as if he were kissing all the Romans at once. The Roman who cried, the Roman who grieved, the Roman whose eyes twinkled when he was excited, and yes, also the Roman who'd bared himself in the hot lights earlier that day. They were all one man, one man with whom his breaths were now joined.

And when they broke, Ethan found himself gripping the sides of his face, savoring the sight of the young man's slick and swollen lips.

"I could consume you, you know that?" Ethan whispered. "I could do things to your body that no man's ever done before. That doesn't scare you?"

"The only thing that scares me is that you'll be too afraid to try," Roman whispered back.

19

It was sweet torture, driving in separate cars back to the hotel.

In the lobby, their steps quickened until it felt like they were jogging for the privacy of the elevators.

As soon as the doors closed behind them, they fell into each other again, Roman dropping the bag he'd brought in from the Bentley with a loud *thwack*. One hand seized the back of Ethan's head as they kissed. It was one of the young man's signature, hungry moves, Ethan was learning, and it had the effect of melting Ethan's spine.

He told himself to wait, but as the elevator ascended, he yanked Roman's shirt up over his flawless chest, revealing the nipples the man had teasingly dabbed with icing nights before. He gave in to the temptation he'd repressed then, suckling them both, one after the other, alternating between hard sucks and wild flickers of his tongue, finding out which one made the young man grit his teeth and growl—the answer was both. As he held the back of Ethan's head with both hands now, his hips bucked, upper back pressing flat against the mirrored wall. It thrilled Ethan to discover that even during that twisted game, Roman had baited the parts of himself that were alive with nerves, centers of pleasure. That even as he'd plotted Ethan's destruction, his desire for Ethan had lit up his skin and warped his quest for revenge.

Then it was a race down the subtly curving hallway and into the dark room.

Their room, now.

He'd planned for a quick frenzy of disrobing, but Roman pulled him to the bed before either of them could undress.

Suddenly they were lying together, side by side, mouths locked as Roman clawed Ethan's cock from his jeans, moaning approvingly over the hardness, stroking quickly and firmly and without hesitation. Ethan did the same to Roman, rendering their pose full of lustful contradictions. The two of them almost fully dressed, cocks exposed, unable to tear each other away from the other's mouth, kissing hungrily as they stroked madly—the pose of experimenting young men powered with the voracious kisses of seasoned lovers.

Roman's cock was thunderously hard and throbbing with the vigor of a man in his twenties, a man in peak physical condition, with a desire that couldn't be faked. And it was his heat and thickness and pulsing blood that gave even more truth to Roman's earlier emotional confession of desire. The realization enflamed Ethan's already radiant desire. The fantasies of all the things they'd do together in this room were making him dizzy when suddenly Roman cried his name—high, sharp, and full of warning. Ethan realized—too late—that the throbbing in Roman's cock wasn't just evidence of his good health.

Roman erupted.

Hips bucking, mouth flying open against Ethan's. No choice but to commit to it, Ethan realized, to finish him off, empty him of the desire that had boiled to the surface so quickly it could barely be contained. But there was so much of it, and Ethan's groans turned to appreciative laughter as his hand was slicked with Roman's seed. And he was grateful for the room's darkness and shadows, grateful Roman's cock wasn't garishly lit the way it had been in the studio. That it was wet heat and hardness in his hand—more feeling than object.

As he gasped for breath, Roman brought their noses together. "Sorry," he finally said. "Didn't mean to… I mean, thought I could hold out longer but…"

"Usually one only apologizes in these circumstances when one can't finish at all."

Roman unleashed a breathy, nearly silent laugh. "I should take care of you now."

"Actually, this is probably for the best," Ethan said. "You see, there's a certain hazard to being intimate with a man in his forties."

"Oh, don't worry." Roman grinned. "I love razor burn on my ass."

Laughing, Ethan kissed his forehead. "No, it's that a reliable erection after dinner is like a…"

Roman kissed Ethan on the cheek, then brought his lips to his ear. "A perfect dessert?" he whispered.

"More like a pig with wings," Ethan grumbled.

"Ah. Gotcha. Well, maybe my youthful energy will compensate."

"Or we could just conserve *my* energy and I could release it full force at the right time. Trust me, it'll be better if we wait. Besides…" Ethan put more force behind this kiss. "There's one thing I'd very much like to do with you."

"What's that?"

"If memory serves, it's quite pleasurable to wake up with you in my arms."

Roman moaned gently and leaned into his embrace. As time passed, he wondered if they'd fall asleep this way. "All good, I guess," Roman suddenly said, "but at some point you're going to need to wreck my bussy."

"My stars! Your generation is so forward!"

"Don't you sex shame me, old man. You were *literally* a prostitute."

"Well, I do appreciate you sharing your naming preference. As Donnie made clear, the lingo can be quite confusing to those of us who aren't in our twenties."

"Also, just to get the awkward stuff out of the way, I'm negative and on PREP, so if you want to raw dog me dirty, I'll be happy to beg for it on all fours."

"Lands!" Ethan said, then mimed adjusting a fake tie. "While that description applies to me as well, I'm a bit old school, which means I always travel with protection, so perhaps a progression in that regard."

He rested his head against Ethan's shoulder. "Whatever works, Gramps."

"Let's not. Gramps is not going to be a thing."

"Sure. Hey, but you do want it like that, though, right?" Roman sat up suddenly and looked into his eyes. "Not Gramps. I mean, you *are* a top, right? I figure any man as grumpy and difficult and controlling as you has to be a top."

"Oh, well. Not sure if I've ever heard it put quite like that before."

"Sorry. I'm not trying to stereotype. I mean, I get a lot of it myself. I'm six four and covered in muscles so a lot of guys want me to pound them into the carpet, and it's just really not my thing."

Ethan waggled his eyebrows. "I'm sure your gargantuan member plays no role in their requests."

"You really think it's that big?"

"Come, now. Don't be coy. You weren't flashing it at the studio today because you thought we'd have trouble finding it."

"Okay, let's not relive that mess. It was totally cringe," Roman said quietly. "Just please confirm. And don't use big words and talk like you're on *Bridgerton*. We're sexually compatible, right? My heart and my bussy are on the line here."

Ethan brought the tips of their noses together. "I am going to fuck you until you forget your name. Sound good?"

Roman's lips parted, and their kiss was shallow but determined this time. "You still want to wait?" Roman whispered.

"Good things come in boys who wait."

Sputtering with laughter, he caressed the sides of Ethan's face, then gave him a light kiss on the lips. "All right, go back to your *Bridgerton* routine. It's clearly your thing. I'll handle the cheap porn talk."

Another kiss, and then Ethan gently slid away toward his side of the bed. In a British accent made convincing by the years he'd spent working in the UK, he said, "I shall get you a rag to clean yourself with and then I shall promenade down the hall and fetch us some ice so as to make libations. I brought a bottle of my favorite scotch. Would you care for a spot, my dear Duke of Bicepia?"

Roman's smile looked forced. "Sure."

Another kiss, and then they parted.

Ethan headed down the subtly curving hallway with the ice bucket in hand. When he returned, canned laughter filled the room. Roman was in bed watching television, temptingly shirtless, the pillowy white covers pulled up to just below those nipples they'd made a meal out of in the elevator.

After pouring them both a glass, Ethan moved to the sliding deck door and opened it. Cool ocean air filled the room like a caress. He could smell something familiar in it, something that reminded him of his youth in the South—the damp threat of rain. Below, the harbor and bay twinkled, but far out to sea, two little flashes of lightning lit up the deeper dark beyond Point Loma. That he and Roman were safe and cozy in this room, floating above it all, put a skip in his step as he ducked into the bathroom.

He showered in a rush so he could slide into bed with Roman as quickly as possible without smelling like the sea. Once they were together under the covers, they toasted.

Roman swallowed, then made a concerted effort to stare dead ahead at *The Golden Girls* rerun. When he barked with laughter at one of Betty White's lines, he ended up coughing several times. Once he'd caught his breath, he met Ethan's stare, eyes watering.

"How's the scotch, young man?"

"Killer," he croaked, reaching for the glass on the nightstand without looking back at it. When he sipped it this time, his brow furrowed. He tried to swallow again. It looked like his Adam's apple had gained a few pounds.

"You're a connoisseur, I take it?" Ethan asked.

"Never had it before." He cleared his throat. His nostrils flared twice in a row.

"Your thoughts?"

"Well, one time when I was four I put a tree branch in my mouth for a few seconds before my mom caught me. It's kind of like that, only with Tabasco sauce. And I guess you get drunk eventually, so that's cool."

Ethan exploded with laughter. "Why are you pretending to like it then?"

He grimaced. "I wanted to seem sophisticated. Like you."

Their lips met, and they snuggled into each other.

"I don't need you to pretend to like things you don't like."

"Good." Ethan heard a loud thud on the nightstand. "'Cause it tastes like ass. The bad kind."

Ethan drifted off to the sound of television laughter.

When he woke next, the lights were out and the bed next to him empty. Despite the dark, he felt like he was in a sound bath, gravel hitting tin everywhere. He rolled to one side. The sliding door was still open, and outside on the balcony, Roman stood with his back to him, still in only his briefs, arms resting against the balcony rail.

Rain. It had been so long since he'd heard it—especially this much of it—the sound had seemed foreign at first. But it was the sight of Roman's muscular back, the swells of his ass inside his tight white underwear, the casual way he'd crossed one ankle over another, that drew Ethan from the covers like a tiger emerging from its den.

The rain masked the sound of his approach, so when he wrapped his arms around Roman from behind, the man let out a soft, surprised sigh then stood up straight so their bodies could press together. Ethan planted gentle kisses along the nape of his thick, muscular neck, then down one shoulder.

"How'd you sleep?" Roman asked.

"Has it been that long?"

"Six hours."

"Deeply. How'd *you* sleep?"

"Pretty well, but I, uh, had to get up a little while ago and get ready for something."

Nothing stirred Ethan's desire quite like a bottom telling him he'd prepared himself to be ravished. Conquered. Filled.

"I hope," Roman added in a whisper, then he pressed his underwear-clad ass back against Ethan's thickening cock. "And so do you, it looks like."

Another kiss, this one matched with grinding pressure down below. When they broke, they were staring into each other's eyes as the rain hammered the building, filling the gap between towers in a sparkling veil. "I want to be what you want," Roman whispered. "But is it going to creep you out if I ask for your million-dollar answer?"

Nobody had ever posed that question to him before, maybe because he'd never discussed Zach Loudon's escorting advice with a man he'd been intimate with. Ethan brought one hand to the waistband of Roman's briefs and slid several fingers inside the waistband. "It starts here," he whispered. "It starts with me owning every inch of this. Filling every inch of this."

Roman cooed. "I'm sure I can take every inch you've got."

"Yes, well, sometimes I like to go beyond that." With both hands, he slid Roman's briefs down over his hips. "Sometimes I like to fill it with other things. Things that will *challenge* you so I can watch what the effort does to the rest of you. But you're all about endurance, aren't you, Mr. Walker? You love pushing your body to the limit." He sank down a bit so he could push Roman's briefs the rest of the way down his thighs, then tugged them off his ankles before rising to savor the sight of Roman's naked flesh pressed back against his as cold, wet air rushed to embrace their naked skin.

"I do," Roman said. "I pride myself on being able to push my body to the limit. But my toy collection's packed up down in the car. Should I go get it?"

"While the fact that you're in possession of one is quite promising, there's no need at the given time. In my experience, of which I have a great deal, I find that when you can't rely on size, you can rely on something else."

"What's that?"

"Temperature," Ethan whispered into his ear, then gave the lobe a little nip.

He moved back inside and retrieved the ice bucket from the room's desk, whisking it around with his wrist a little as he returned, letting Roman hear the whispering swirl of the melting cubes. Still holding to the rail in front of him, Ethan's gorgeous target looked back over one shoulder and managed a simple "Oh."

After setting the bucket next to him on the balcony floor, Ethan sank to his knees, giving himself a moment to savor the spectacular sight before him and the delicious feel of his hunger for it rising in him.

Slowly, he spread the cheeks of Roman Walker's ass and began to do what he'd fantasized about doing ever since the man had pranced across his apartment in nothing but his underwear. He started with a single, slow lick right across Roman's hot core. The response was a sharp intake of breath loud enough to be heard over the pounding rain. Then came the sight Ethan had been hoping for. Not tension or a recoil. Instead, Roman went swaybacked, chest getting closer to the rail as he moved his deliciously hairless ass closer toward Ethan's hungry mouth, a move that said, *More, please.*

Ethan complied. Long, slow, lingering licks, meant to stimulate as many nerves as he could while also sending the message that he was utterly at home here, rooted to Roman's musky crack by primal hunger. The key to good oral sex, he'd learned long ago, was confidence, the ability to give your partner the sense that you felt leisurely at home amidst their most intimate crevices. And so he made sure to keep his grip on Roman's cheeks steady and firm and nuzzled his crack as much as he slathered it. He became so lost in his work he sank from his knees to a seated position on the concrete, cock rising into the cold air. He couldn't have cared less about the chill and the wet floor. His world had become Roman's tastes and smells, the inviting smoothness of his skin, and the stuttering music of his gasps and moans, audible over the pounding rain.

Slowly, Roman raised one leg off to the side and rested his heel atop the balcony rail, opening himself further to Ethan's wet and hungry exploration, cock hard and bobbing slightly.

When Ethan added stroking fingers to his tongue's work, Roman's groans gained a note of desperation.

Occasionally, he glanced up at the marvel of the man's outstretched leg, let his hands wander to the thigh muscles there. Savored the sight of his throbbing cock, the pre-cum slickened head. Then, once he'd left almost every inch of Roman's ass slick with his spit, Ethan reached back for the ice bucket and removed a nearly melted cube. The key to what he planned to do next was to remove all sharp edges, but the time they'd spent asleep had done that for him.

He brought the ice to the top of Roman's crack. Roman let out a surprised cry, followed by hissing breaths as Ethan traced the melting cube between Roman's cheeks, circled his entrance—once, twice, three times—before he shoved the rest of the cube inside Roman's welcoming hole with a gentle nudge.

"*Hollleeeee,*" Roman managed before jerking forward, chest now pressed against the rail, head poking out into the rain as he gasped for breath.

Quickly, Ethan replaced the freezing aftermath of the ice cube with the warmth of his tongue. Freezing cold inside, wet warmth on the outside. The combination was meant to drive Roman wild.

And it did.

The leg Roman had kept rooted to the balcony's floor was tremoring with desire.

Struggling for breath, Roman asked, "How many are you going to make me take?"

Ethan answered with a focused, flickering assault on his hole.

"Before?" he asked once he could bear to pull himself away. He was already reaching back for another ice cube.

"Before you fuck me."

This time, Ethan traced the melting cube in small circles around Roman's hot hole before popping it inside with more force than the last one. The sound that came from him sounded like a cross between a growl and a moan, and for a few seconds, Ethan held the man's cheeks, letting him savor the ache of cold inside of him. Then, slowly, he granted him the blunting effect of his hot and hungry tongue, kneading him as he worked.

"Seven," Ethan finally said.

"I don't know if I can."

"Then I don't know if you want this cock badly enough," Ethan growled.

"I do, though," Roman whimpered. "I do want it badly enough."

"Then prove it."

This time Ethan took two cubes from the bucket, starting them in different locations. One at the top of Roman's crack, the other at the bottom. He brought them past each other in opposite directions, once, twice, letting them melt further, then he slid them inside of Roman one after the other and immediately rewarded his hole with his tongue. *Four down, three to go.* He turned the next cube into another torture session, letting Roman endure the cold for what felt like an eternity, then adding the next one right after. Again, he rewarded him with slathering licks. After the last cube, he went in again, this time all flickering focused on the center of Roman's desire.

Finally, he stood, reached out, and brought Roman's outstretched leg off the rail as he pulled the man to him with one arm clamped around his hard chest.

"Is this what you want?" Ethan growled into his ear. "You want an older man to take control?"

"God, yes," Roman gasped.

"Is that *your* million-dollar answer?"

"Every fuckin' penny."

Ethan steered them into the darkness of their hotel room. There was a special thrill that came from shoving Roman back first to the mattress given his size and strength. It made Roman's submission feel more powerful and willing. In no time, Ethan had the condom on and the lube poured and was heading back to the bed.

The sight that greeted him left him breathless.

Roman had brought his legs up off the floor and pulled his thighs apart with his hands, exposing his spit-slick ass to Ethan's approach, and he was gazing up at Ethan with wild-eyed intensity—a combination of aggression and submission that made Ethan's hunger for him thunder.

Probing Roman's entrance with lube-slick fingers, Ethan said, "Is this what you wanted when you danced around my apartment in your underwear?"

Roman nodded fiercely.

"You like teasing older men? Like knowing how bad they want you?"

Gasping, Roman nodded eagerly.

"Did it get you off to see me fight it?"

The balcony light streaming in through the open door revealed a hard and hungry glint in his hazel eyes. "It's not teasing if you want it. So stop fighting and *take* it."

There was a brief moment of resistance, and then Roman yielded and gave way and Ethan was sliding into him.

"Oh," Roman cooed as Ethan began to rock and slide. "Oh, wow... It bends up and it...hits. Wow."

Ethan answered by gradually increasing the tempo of his thrusts.

"If you keep... I mean, what you're doing... That's not... I won't last long, Ethan."

"Good."

"But what about—"

Ethan grabbed Roman's chin in one hand and squeezed. "Shut your goddamn mouth so I can fuck the cum out of you."

As Ethan's thrusts found a steady, determined rhythm, Roman went silent, lips pursing, eyes turning to slits, pleasure-filled moans gurgling in his throat. His nostrils flared as he struggled for breath.

All the while, Ethan pistoned. Determined, focused, reaching for the bottle of lube as Roman's groans grew more frenzied, he slathered some on Roman's cock and stroked in time to the fuck. It was working perfectly, his signature rhythm. Jackhammer thrusts resulted in peaks and valleys that forced a top to take a breath right at the moment their bottom might explode. Instead, Ethan fucked slow and steady and without missing a single beat—a marathon of pleasure meant to push his bottom inch by inch by inch toward the edge of bliss. And with Roman, it was working.

"Mine," Ethan said, and his own lust was eroding the confidence with which he'd spoken earlier. "This ass is mine now, Roman. You know what that means?"

"It means you're going to make me come."

"It means the next time you shake it at me, I'll shove you up against the wall and take it. I don't care where we are. I don't care what you're wearing."

The telltale grip and spasm, the sudden electric silence—Ethan knew it was coming.

Roman's beautiful eyes shot open, pleasure blasting away the veils between Ethan's and Roman's souls. The wail that came from him sounded almost pleading. Astonished. Roman sounded astonished to be jetting cum while Ethan stroked him confidently, sliding in and out without missing a single second. His eruption was as strong and healthy and vibrant as the rest of him, and in an instant Ethan's hand was slick.

"Are you close?" Roman asked once he'd emptied.

"I was close as soon as I tasted you."

"Mark me." Roman sounded dazed. He brought one hand to his own right nipple, tugged it slightly, then did the same to his left.

Holy shit, Ethan thought. He pulled out, shed the condom, and used Roman's cum to slick his own cock even further. The man squeezed his legs together so Ethan could rest his knees on the mattress on either side of his waist. Gazing down at his eyes, Ethan stroked. The closer he drew to bliss, the more he sank back onto his haunches, aiming for the target Roman had identified.

"Mark me," Roman whispered again. "Mark me, *Daddy*."

It was as if Roman had reached inside of him and pressed a button.

Erupting, Ethan lost sense of up and down—the single filthy final word, and all of its taboo complexities, tearing through him from his feet to his scalp, leaving only shimmering heat in its wake.

For a few seconds, he thought he might have ended up on the carpet. But when he managed to catch his breath, he found himself staring down at Roman, who was beaming at the icing of cum Ethan had given his bare chest.

Slowly, Roman slid his fingers through the seed covering his right nipple, then, hazel eyes twinkling as he stared up at Ethan, he brought a dollop of it to his mouth and sucked it off his fingertip, just like he'd done the cake icing in the penthouse suite. The debauched little display sent a shudder of pleasure through Ethan at the very moment he thought he'd been emptied of all bliss. Then he was melting onto Roman's hard body. When they kissed, Ethan suckled the man's lips briefly in search of his own taste. There was none, and that meant Roman had swallowed him entirely.

And then there was only the sound of the rain, loud enough to drown out the sound of their gasping breaths.

"You were right," Roman finally said between gasps. "I'm glad we waited."

Once he'd caught his breath, Ethan lifted his face from the sheets next to Roman's shoulder and gazed into the man's eyes. "How did you know that would do me in?"

"What? Daddy?"

Ethan nodded.

Roman grinned. "I could tell last night when you gave me that lecture about kinks. The one about how guys who want to be called Daddy aren't into incest. It's about trust. There was a light in your eyes when you said it, and I was like, that's totally him. But I knew you'd probably never ask for it given our…complicated history, so I wanted to give it to you." Roman reached up with one hand and brushed Ethan's sweat-matted hair off his forehead. "Just like I want to give you everything else."

Ethan was still struggling for breath.

"Not used to having guys unlock your naughty million-dollar answers, are you?"

"No," Ethan whispered.

After a gentle kiss on the lips, the man beneath him whispered, "Well, get ready because there's plenty more where that came from."

I am done for, Ethan thought as their mouths touched. *I am absolutely, totally, and blissfully done for.*

20

The deadbolt clicking into place roused him from a dreamless sleep. It was five minutes after eight, but Ethan felt compensated for the early wake-up by the sight of the gorgeous, freshly showered young man charging into his hotel room with a beaming smile. Roman held a grease-stained white paper bag emanating a sweet aroma.

"You know," Ethan said between yawns, "I keep hoping to wake up with you in my arms only to regain consciousness in an empty bed."

"That's 'cause I keep planning fun stuff. Besides, I'm Restless Roman. What do you expect?" After freeing the Danishes from their moist wrappings of wax paper, he kicked his shoes off, then scooted across the covers toward Ethan on his knees, a treat in each hand. When he raised a pastry to Ethan's lips, the look Ethan gave the thing caused him to draw it away quickly. "Okay, fine. They're from the deli in the lobby. I didn't have time to whip something up in the kitchen."

"Not complaining, just examining."

"Bet you'd scarf it down in a hot second if I put it on my ass."

"Correct," Ethan answered with a wicked grin.

"I'll save one for later then."

Roman airplaned the Danish toward his open mouth. "Thank you," he said once he'd swallowed.

After a bite of his own, Roman chewed manically, then swallowed quickly, all signs he was bursting with something he wanted to say. Finally, he sputtered, "You're going to be totally excited for my big, amazing plan for the day!"

"We just made a plan. Ass up, mister." He waggled his eyebrows, then swiped up a glob of lemon filling from one corner of his mouth with his tongue.

"That's for *tonight*, Daddy. My bigger, better, and totally amazing plan is for the daylight hours." Roman set what he hadn't devoured on the nightstand, planted his fists against the mattress on either side of Ethan's chest, and brought their noses together. "We're going paragliding!"

Ethan swallowed.

"You know what paragliding is, right?"

Ethan hoped the proximity of their faces didn't make it easier for Roman to see he was fighting the urge to barf Danish onto his stomach. "Of course," Ethan said calmly. "It's the thing you learned how to do after your snake encounter when you were a teenager. Are you sure the weather's right for it?"

Roman leapt off the bed and tore open the drapes. Hoping for thunderheads and lightning bolts, Ethan instead found himself raising an arm to shield his eyes from the fiercely sunny day outside. "They have a glider port over in La Jolla."

"I know," Ethan said with forced cheer. "I worked in La Jolla for years. I used to see them sailing off the cliffs all the time." And whenever he did, he'd turn to the person next to him and say something along the lines of, *You couldn't pay me a trillion dollars to get up there with those fucking lunatics.*

Roman threw himself onto the foot of the bed and bounced up and down to vent his excitement. "We're going to do it, right? Can we do it? Please. Please. *Please.*"

"Of course." Ethan cleared his throat. "I would be honored to take you paragliding. How long since you've done it?"

"No, no. *We're* going to do it! I got certified as a pilot when I was eighteen."

Every muscle in Ethan's body tensed. "A pilot is required? Fascinating."

"It's a tandem chair, and we both sit in it." Roman's eyes lit up. "I've been on the phone with the glider port all morning, getting them copies of my certifications, and it sounds like we're good to go." He threw his arms around him, a good thing since it allowed Ethan to look at the ceiling and silently pray. Part of him thought he should fess up and admit his fear of heights. But was that something a strong, confident, older man would say? Was that something that should come out of the mouth of the man who'd plowed Roman into bliss hours before and wanted eagerly to do so again? The man Roman had held on to on the deck of the *Golden Boy* as if he were a rock in stormy seas?

Roman broke their hug. "I was lying here all morning thinking about what I could do for you, you know."

"Oh, you did plenty last night."

"I know, but beyond bussy. I mean, I know it's not as amazing as you talking to your lawyer about the trust. But it's so *fun*, and you're going to have such a good time."

Ethan wasn't sure what it felt like when your heart melted, but he was pretty sure this was it, and ironically, he was feeling it mostly in the sides of his neck. He pulled Roman in for a big, Danish-flavored kiss. Then he was alone in the shower, practicing various expressions he could say on repeat between now and their date with certain death to make him sound confident and excited. Mostly military expressions he'd picked up from Donnie, whose every other model had a Marine Corps background. *Boo-rah. Let's do this. Get some.* Etc.

"Are you feeling okay?" Roman asked when he emerged from the bathroom.

"I'm excellent. Why do you ask?"

"It sounded like you were coughing."

He tugged on a polo shirt. "Oh, no. I'm great. Let's *do* this! Boo-rah!" Once he had his arm through the sleeve, he pumped a fist in the air.

"*A* for energy, but you're going to need something warmer. The winds can be intense, and once we get up to about four hundred feet, the temperature really drops."

Nodding enthusiastically as the words *four hundred feet* ripped through him like a pinball, Ethan said, "Good thinking. Clearly I'm in excellent hands."

He knew his way to the glider port because it was close to where he, Donnie, and Zach used to hike down to Black's Beach. On the way there, he'd asked Roman to talk about every flight he'd ever taken, thinking it would make for a good distraction. It worked. At first. But by the time they reached the parking lot, Roman's descriptions of sailing off desert cliffs, near collisions with ornery hawks, riding thermals that seemed to surge out of nowhere had grown so vivid and constant that Ethan's palms were greasing the steering wheel. Ethan saw the open grassy field perched right at the edge of the cliff's three-hundred-foot drop to the sea. It was strewn with little parachutes spread out across the grass and dotted with helmeted flyers preparing to take the leap.

"Oh my God, look how perfect the weather is!" Roman said. "It's like the rain cleaned everything and now there's nothing but wind."

"Indeed." Ethan parked and Roman leapt from the passenger seat and raced for a nearby trailer plastered with various wooden signs. Warnings, mostly.

Telling himself he should keep his eyes on Roman, Ethan did his best to put one foot in front of the other as he watched a paraglider and their accompanying pilot literally run toward the edge of the cliff, the parachute lifting behind them so weakly he was sure they'd plummet to their death in an instant. Suddenly, the wind caught and they went sailing as Ethan's heart roared.

He focused on the stunning view. A coastline made up mostly of bluffs extended north and then a little way's west. He could see all the way to the smokestacks of the desalinization plant in Carlsbad and farther up the coast to the sudden jagged mountains of Camp Pendleton that marked the boundary between San Diego and Orange County. The only clouds were high white cotton puffs sailing briskly across the cornflower blue. For miles and miles, the ocean sparkled. And if he kept his gaze up and not down, everything was big open skies filled with nothing but promise.

Look up and not down. The words settled into him, almost as if they'd been spoken by someone else—the encouraging parents he'd never had or the deep, intuitive voice some folks called God.

Inside the trailer, Roman excitedly talked over procedure with the attendant, who handed him two helmets, but he kept looking back over one shoulder at Ethan with delight in his eyes.

Roman didn't just want to fly, he wanted to fly with Ethan. This knowledge filled him with a warmth that drowned out his anxiety, a feeling more powerful than his terrible fear of heights. Roman, in all his wild, restless enthusiasm, wanted to share something with Ethan that brought him joy, and that fact alone brought Ethan joy before they'd even left the ground.

When Roman emerged onto the trailer's porch, helmets in hand, he said, "Are you sure?"

"Absolutely," Ethan said firmly, but this time he didn't have to work very hard to keep the fear from his voice.

He wasn't sure they would survive. Wasn't even sure he might not lose the contents of his stomach. What he was sure of was that he wanted to do whatever he could to fill Roman with more of this intoxicating enthusiasm.

The next thing he knew, they were standing a few yards from the cliff's edge while his pilot-to-be strapped him into the chair, which was really more like a double harness. He could barely feel his feet, and he was nodding a lot to hide the fact that he was having trouble breathing and wasn't hearing much of what Roman said.

"Cold?" Roman asked before snapping a buckle closed.

"Perfectly comfortable," Ethan lied.

"Really? 'Cause your hand's shaking."

"I'll heat up once we get going, I'm sure." *Once I piss myself,* Ethan thought.

Then the two of them were fully strapped in. Roman's warm body pressed against his back was a soothing balm for his paralyzing terror.

Turning him to face their destination, the cliff's edge and the shining sea beyond, Roman said, "Now, don't worry. That fifteen-minute training class I took online was super comprehensive."

Ethan dug his feet into the dirt. "Fifteen minutes?"

Roman cackled. "I'm kidding. It was a bunch of training sessions. I know what I'm doing. Ready? On three."

If he waited that long he'd chicken out, so he started running right away, and by the time Roman got to two, they'd left the edge and Ethan was howling as his feet cycled through open air.

Every fiber of his being was braced for a terrifying plummet through the void below. When it didn't happen, his desperate yell turned into a high, barking laugh. The force that filled the parachute behind them, lifting them above the cliff's edge at the last possible second with a confident yank, felt otherworldly, divine.

They were floating. Then they were flying. Sailing. *Soaring.*

It felt suddenly like they could touch the sky. The air that had looked so empty and dangerous before revealed itself to be full of texture. Levels and currents they rode in the gentlest and smoothest of ways. An invisible miracle made possible by the right wind, the right equipment.

The right man.

After a few minutes, he realized he'd been laughing hysterically since they'd first taken flight. Roman was laughing, too, and there was pure, unbridled joy in the sound. Joy to which Ethan could well become deliriously addicted. When they both ran out of breath, the peaceful quiet embraced them, save for the occasional ruffle of the wind in the parachute overhead. Thanks to Roman's steering, they'd turned south and were traveling along the top of the cliff, occasionally swerving to the right until beach and white surf appeared hundreds of feet below their dangling feet.

They swooped to the left, inland, over a colossal Italianate mansion that sat perched on the edge of the cliff like some emperor's summer palace. He realized he was breaking his vow not to look down. When he lifted his gaze, he saw the expanse of the coast sweeping south. Familiar to him from years before, but never from this angle, this awe-inspiring height. There was the mansion-studded rise of Mount Soledad, the little cluster of buildings at its base that made up La Jolla's Village on the shore.

A man who'd been in his life for only days had given him a new perspective on a place that had been familiar to him for years, and that seemed as miraculous as the power with which the wind had given them flight. When Roman started to turn them around, the slow revolution added some nervousness to Ethan's joy. But his coordinated pulls on the dual handles were smooth and confident.

"How you doing up there?" Roman asked.

"Amazing."

"What?"

"This is amazing," Ethan said louder. "*You're* amazing."

With no way to turn in the seat, he couldn't clutch Roman's face. Couldn't bring their lips together the way he wanted to, but he felt Roman press them as close together as he could.

"Maybe you could learn to pilot someday and then you could sit behind me and steer."

"You're doing a fine job."

"Yeah, but if we switched places, we could fuck up here."

Ethan laughed. "The things I need to do to your body require more privacy than that."

Roman sighed. "A boy can dream."

"I'll give you plenty to dream about. On solid ground."

Roman managed to bring his lips to Ethan's ear. "You already are."

In another few minutes, they came in for a landing. The second Roman freed him from the buckles, the minute he could turn to him, Ethan kissed him wildly. The deflating parachute gave them cover from potential onlookers.

I did it, Ethan thought. *I did it for* him.

After they returned to the hotel, they took the ferry across the bay to Coronado Island. They spent the early afternoon exploring its most famous resident, a sprawling, red-roofed Victorian hotel that offered wide sidewalks along the beach.

Out of all of San Diego's beachfront jewels, Coronado had never captured Ethan's heart the way La Jolla had, but he'd saved the latter for that evening. Maybe a walking tour of the village's quaint streets after the sunset dinner reservation he'd made at the restaurant where he'd worked years before.

They'd vowed to spend the late afternoon getting ready back at their hotel, but getting ready resulted in a sudsy joint shower and what felt like hours of Ethan on his knees, milking and savoring Roman's spectacular cock, bringing him a gasping release with his hand as their sputtering lips met through the spray, sneaking a forbidden taste of the man's seed that made his eyes light up.

That evening, as their Uber navigated the quaint web of streets in La Jolla's oceanfront village, Ethan saw familiar stores he'd wandered before work and on his breaks years before. The old Saks Fifth Avenue was gone, but Warwick's Books was still there, its double front windows lined with the latest hardcover releases. Then at the end of Girard Avenue, right before the dip it made toward La Jolla's park-lined oceanfront, La Valencia Hotel rose like an unofficial city hall. Atop its pink tower, its gold-tiled dome reflected the light of the west-leaning sun. Just up the street, housed inside the top floor of a glass-and-steel ocean-facing office complex and sporting jaw-dropping views of the sea, was Jillian's, the restaurant where he'd landed his first kitchen job.

He'd made the reservation in his name, but he wasn't sure if he'd be recognized or if anyone still worked there from the old days. He was taking note of the renovations in the front hallway—lots of chrome and darkly tinted plate glass where once there'd been blond wood and old nautical paintings—when he heard a high-pitched squeal and saw a familiar face rushing toward him from the host stand. Fifteen years older but still bright eyed and cherub cheeked and prone to blushing, Sarah Aubrey, once a shy and diminutive UCSD freshman unsure about her restaurant industry ambitions, was now an assistant manager, as indicated by the jeweled seahorse pin on her lapel, a replica of the restaurant's logo. She threw her arms around him.

"Of course you're still here," Ethan said as he fell into her perfumed embrace. Roman, smiling, took a step back to give him some space.

"Oh, what's that supposed to mean, mister? You're not the only one with a passport."

"No, it means they'd never let you go. You're too sweet."

"Charming as always." Sarah hugged him harder, then she pulled away, regarding Roman. "And I see you've brought the most attractive man on the planet. Oh, sorry. He's not your nephew, is he?"

At this, Roman exploded with laughter. Ethan felt himself flush, but he was enjoying the fact that Sarah had to fight to keep her tongue in her mouth as she shook Roman's hand. In skintight designer jeans and a sleeveless turtleneck that revealed his sculpted arms, he was quite a sight. Ethan, on the other hand, had donned a tweed blazer and chinos.

"So who's still here?" Ethan asked Sarah as she led them to their table. It was one of the best, right next to the wall of plate glass and a stunning sunset view.

She handed them their giant, leather-encased menus. "Oh, you know. You kitchen folks burn out too fast to stay in one place for too long. It's the front of house people like me who stay fresh as daisies." She made flower petal fingers on either side of her face before launching into a brief history of almost everyone they'd worked with back in the day. It was a similar story to the one told at many restaurants where he'd worked over the years—the owners had grown less invested over time before trying to hand off the place to the next generation, which in the life of a restaurant could either spell a miracle or a disaster. In this case, it sounded like Jillian's heirs were doing a bang-up job. Then Sarah vanished but returned a second later with a complimentary bottle of Puligny-Montrachet, Ethan's favorite Chardonnay.

Once they were alone, he and Roman toasted.

"So if I say this place is nicer than the Queen Mary, are you going to slap me around and give me a lecture about gay rights?" Roman asked.

"Only if you'd like." Ethan sipped, watching closely as Roman's glass froze an inch from his lips.

Roman caught his look. "Oh, you think it's going to go like the scotch?"

"Possibly." Ethan smiled.

"Well, scotch is gross, but wine is just kind of dumb."

Ethan made an expression of mock horror. "I'm sorry. Did you say *dumb*?"

"You know, people just get kind of ridiculous about it. Like they're all"—he swirled his glass and scrunched up his nose in his impression of a snob—"this one is quite woodsy, with base notes of lettuce and suntan oil."

"Take a sip."

Roman complied. When he swallowed, his eyes lit up. "Wow. This is really good."

"See? It's important to try new things."

"Like paragliding. Although, I don't know, you were pretty chill about the whole thing. I should probably come up with something that pushes you out of your comfort zone a little."

Ethan sipped his wine. "I was terrified, Roman."

Clearly startled, Roman set his wine glass down, eyes wide. "You were?"

"Absolutely. I have a total fear of heights. I thought my heart was going to explode out of my chest the minute you mentioned it."

Roman sighed and threw up his hands. "Well, why didn't you say anything?" he whined. "I didn't want to force you to do something that freaked you out."

"You didn't force me," Ethan said gently. "And I didn't say anything because I wanted to do it. For you."

Jaw slack, Roman cocked his head to one side as if Ethan had presented a complex mathematical theorem. "I don't understand..."

"It was clearly something you wanted to share with me, and that meant a great deal to *me*. I guess your joy proved infectious, and so it became more important than my fear. Oh, dear. Are you crying?"

Roman nodded and wiped at his eyes with the back of one hand. "It's, like, maybe the nicest thing anyone's ever said to me. Also, maybe I'm drunk? I don't know."

"I doubt that, baby. You've had one sip."

Still sniffling, he lowered his hands from his face, revealing a twinkling in his eyes beneath the glisten of tears. "Baby," he whispered with a spreading smile. "So I have a pet name now?"

Ethan felt himself flush. "It just came naturally, so I guess so." He took a sip of wine. "Baby," he added once he swallowed.

It felt as if they'd just crossed some threshold.

Maybe this was how it was supposed to happen. Maybe you were supposed to meet someone fast and furious and without expecting it. Maybe at first, the right one always seemed like a terrible choice. It was a stark contrast to the methodical, bullet-pointed-based dating system he'd used with men ever since he'd quit escorting—a process that had always struck him as cold, perhaps a form of overcompensation for having been a libertine for so many years.

The menu had changed some since he'd left, but not much, so he was able to do a fairly good job of recommending dishes to Roman. And by the time they were halfway through their entrees, they were working on a second bottle of Chardonnay. Occasionally their bursts of laughter drew startled glances from some of the other diners. And as the candles inside the restaurant seemed to glow brighter, Ethan realized the sunset to which he'd timed their reservation had passed without their notice. That's how intensely they'd been focused on each other throughout the meal.

Then, once the dishes were clear, Roman went quiet and still, staring at Ethan as he held his half-empty wine glass close to one cheek.

"What is it?"

"Something's bothering me," he finally said.

"By all means, let's discuss." He braced for a question about Roman's dad.

Roman swallowed and set his glass down. "Did you ever talk to your parents again? I mean, after they wrote you that check."

Not a question about his parents, Ethan realized, *a question about mine.* With a jolt, he realized he would have preferred the former. "Afraid not," he answered.

"Are they still around?"

"No," Ethan said. "They both passed."

Eyes on his empty plate, Roman nodded grimly, as if this was the news he'd been fearing most.

"I just hate to think that I ruined your relationship with them because—I mean, you quit escorting because of me and that's when you went to see them for the last time and so it's like—"

"You didn't." It came out more brusque than he'd intended. Did the startled flash in Roman's eyes mean he was offended or surprised to be so quickly let off the hook? "Seriously. You don't have to take that on board. It's not your fault."

Roman nodded, but he was waiting for more.

Wanting more.

He'd opened a door, and with every second Ethan didn't elaborate, he could hear the creak of its hinges as it swung closed again. He told himself this was good, this was right. This was self-restraint. He was protecting their perfect, romantic evening from depressing talk of the life he'd left behind in South Carolina. But Roman had gone from looking curious to embarrassed, as if he thought he'd overstepped. And was that a fair thing to let him think after all he'd shared with Ethan about his own life?

"I'm sorry," Roman said, but he sounded tentative, as if he wasn't sure if he should be apologizing.

And what Ethan wanted to say was, *Don't be,* but the door he'd heard creak a second before was now firmly closed, and he was staring at Roman in awkward silence. Fear spreading cold in his gut, he wondered if this would be the hardest part about being intimate with someone. These little split-second moments that required honesty and candor and revealing more of himself than he'd ever revealed to a client. He wondered suddenly if that was how he'd fail at this. By going silent, covering up his feelings with a fixed expression. Letting the person who asked to know him better feel fidgety and awkward and like they'd crossed a line or made a mistake. Because they'd cared.

"Should we get dessert?" Roman finally asked.

"I thought we could walk around the village before it gets too dark." He was proud of how steady he sounded.

By the time he'd paid the check and they'd said their good-byes to Sarah, the silence between them had grown tense. He held the restaurant's front door for Roman, but when they reached the sidewalk outside, Roman shoved his hands into his pockets and was looking everywhere but at Ethan as they strolled. He was also shivering. Ethan took off his blazer and tucked it around Roman's shoulders. Head bowed, eyes averted, Roman pulled his hands from his pockets and slid his arms through the sleeves. But his smile was sheepish, his eyes downcast. "Such a gentleman," he said, as if he were reminding himself of this fact in the wake of Ethan's coldness.

They walked alongside La Valencia's sloping base, down the dip at the end of Girard Avenue. Before them, a broad stretch of lawn dotted with tall, slender palm trees made for a grassy, open park right at the water's edge. Between the lawn and the rocky shore was a serpentine sidewalk with a white painted wooden fence you weren't supposed to scale, but many tourists did so they could walk the tops of the rocks on the other side.

Waves pummeled the jagged shore. He could hear a barking seal in the distance. But all he could feel was the painful story of his life before New York rattling the cage inside of him, demanding to be freed.

As Roman stared out to sea, hands resting on the fence in front of him, it was impossible to tell if he was enamored by the view or put off by Ethan's shut down.

"It's like this," Ethan began, as if no time had passed between Roman's question and the present moment. When Roman looked to him quickly, intently, and without puzzlement, he realized those moments had played for Roman in much the same way. "They hated me, Roman."

"Your parents?"

Ethan nodded. "I know it sounds dramatic and extreme, and I don't want to be one of those people who blames his parents for everything. But the fact of the matter is they could tell right away I was gay. I must have been four or five. My mannerisms tipped them off, and it was like something inside of them died and never came back.

"I was too young to realize what was happening. And so I spent most of my life believing their coldness and their contempt was normal. I never challenged it and I never rebelled because to be perfectly honest, we were rich, and I thought that would be enough. So long as I worked at hiding whatever it was about me they didn't like. So long as I showed up and played the part I was supposed to play. So long as I forced unsuspecting women into relationships that were as ungratifying for them as they were for me. So long as I never made a scene, never spoke up, I wouldn't be thrown away.

"I never thought to ask for love or acceptance. Not being cast out seemed like the only goal. And if I played the game well, met social obligations, expressed the right opinions to their friends, then I'd be rewarded with financial support. But their strategy for containing me was simple. They taught me that my first instinct was always wrong. If I didn't want to make a fool of myself, I should discuss everything with them first. It was their way of containing what they knew they couldn't change."

"Your sexuality," Roman asked as he moved a step closer.

Ethan nodded. "It was all coded language. To teachers and their friends, they described me as…easily confused, prone to distractions. All these constant references to my deep inadequacies just under the surface. But the truth was I was a good student. I was polite. I never stepped out of line. But the criticism was relentless. It was constant and it was cold.

"I was promised a job at my father's firm if I managed to do even halfway decent in law school. But my passions? My ambitions? Not allowed. The one time I said anything about being a chef, my father called it faggoty nonsense. Those were his words exactly. They knew that if I did anything authentic to my personality, to who I truly was, eventually it would bring my sexuality to the surface. When I look back now, I was just staying for the trappings and the perks. The nice house, the family name, the invitations. I was more addicted to those things than I wanted to admit."

Slowly, Roman twined their fingers together atop the fence. He was breathing deeply but rapidly, as if the story Ethan was telling was a tale as suspenseful as a Marvel film.

"But then, one night, the summer before college, I allowed some friends of mine to convince me to go to this gay bar about four hours away. The minute I stepped through the front door, something opened inside of me that I knew I could never shut.

"I didn't come out. I even lied to the people there and said I was just supporting some friends. Then I got blind drunk and made out with another guy in a bathroom for an hour and ran off before he could get my name. Then I started hooking up in secret. Nothing serious, nothing that could get me in trouble. No entanglements. It was all about AOL chat rooms back then, and I made the most of them. I thought the forbidden thrill of it all would compensate for the lack of everything else. Then one day I got a call from my parents summoning me home immediately for some sort of emergency meeting."

"What did they do?" Roman asked, only inches away from him now.

"When I got there, they were waiting for me in the living room. A guy I'd been chatting with online, a guy I'd decided not to hook up with, had figured out who I was and sent our entire chat session to my parents to get back at me. Including the nudes I'd shared with him. It was all laid out right there. There was no denying it.

"I had two choices, they said. I could go to a reparative therapy camp recommended by their pastor, or I could never set foot in their home again. They would also stop paying my tuition to Davidson, cancel the payments on my car, and instruct everyone in the family to have no further contact with me. And since they were the richest members of the family, it was very likely everyone would agree. They weren't angry as they said it. They were…resigned. As if we'd arrived at something grim but inevitable, and they were making the best of a terrible burden."

Roman's jaw was slack. "What did you say?"

"I asked them how long I had to decide. They said five hours. Then my mother looked me in the eyes and explained to me that what she was doing was the loving thing because it was impossible for two men to truly love each other. She conceded that they could have sex, sure. Provide each other with *sinful pleasure*, as she called it. But they could never truly open their hearts to each other the way a man and a woman could because that wasn't God's design. And by forcing me to make this choice, she was sparing me a lifetime of delusion and loss and emptiness and disappointment. It was bigotry, plain and simple, but she made it all sound so…sophisticated. So well thought out.

"So I told them to give me a little while to make up my mind, then I walked the neighborhood for hours. And I sobbed. I sobbed because their masks had dropped and finally I'd seen the cold, bigoted, disapproving parents I'd been living with for years. Given how ready they'd been for the conversation, I realized this had been it, the whole time. The thing they'd loathed about me. And it had all ended with my mother, who showed the world as much tenderness as a kitchen knife, lecturing me on the true nature of love while my future hung in the balance. It was almost more than I could take."

"So you went to New York," Roman whispered.

"No." Ethan shook his head. They'd reached the hardest part of the story, and it felt like there was an apple lodged in his throat. "I was going to go along with it. I went back to the house to tell them. Yes, I'd go to their crazy clinic so long as they didn't yank the rug out from under me. But I was late. Five minutes late and they'd already boxed up everything from my old room and put it out on the front walk. And I realized what it was really about. What it had always been about with them."

"What?" Roman asked.

"The neighbors. They wanted the neighbors to see them throwing me out in case any gossip spilled about my predilections. *That's* when I went to New York."

Roman looked stunned.

"But it haunted me for years, how close I came to killing myself for them. And for what? Their coldness? Their money? Their empty, hypocritical lectures? Not every family heals. Donnie's right. Sometimes we have to make our own. Some exist so they can throw us out and set us on the right path. But I guess what I really want you to know, what I need you to know, is that my relationship with them was long dead before I went to them and got that check, so you shouldn't blame yourself. You can't blame yourself."

"I'm so sorry, Ethan."

"It's haunted me ever since, the things my mother said. About how two men can only give each other pleasure and not love."

"Eventually you found out she was full of shit though, right?" Roman was inches from him now, a pleading look in his eyes. "Eventually you found out she was wrong."

Ethan turned and looked into his eyes. "Today, Roman. I found out today at the glider port when you looked at me and I realized you wanted to share something that gave you joy. That's when I realized my mother was wrong. When you taught me how to touch the sky."

Was it possible to put down a weight you didn't know you were carrying?

The kiss Roman gave him suggested it was. That's how he felt as they rode back to the hotel, as they settled into bed together, as they stroked each other to sleep, as brisk winds through the open deck door cooled their entwined bodies.

When he felt a gentle kiss against the back of his neck, saw morning sun through slitted eyes, he thought he was dreaming at first. Then Roman let out a little sniffle and laid a hand briefly against his shoulder. Half asleep, he wondered if he was getting a cold thanks to the sleeveless turtleneck he'd worn the night before. When he heard a door shut, he assumed Roman was going to the bathroom and fell into a pleasant series of dreams.

Restless Roman, he thought with a lazy smile.

Later—he wasn't sure how much, at first—his eyes opened to a sun-filled room. The bed next to him was empty. And cool. No sounds came from the bathroom. He rolled over, saw the drape fluttering in the breeze through the open deck door. Then he noticed something else.

An absence.

Roman's bag was gone.

He swung his legs to the floor, telling himself Roman could have tidied up and moved it to the floor of the closet. But it wasn't there or anywhere else in the room. And when he stepped into the bathroom, he saw the guy's toiletries were gone as well. Saw, with a growing sense of terror, that all traces of him had been removed.

There had to be an obvious explanation. Another big, exciting plan for their day.

When he picked up his phone off the nightstand, he saw a text message from Roman. Surely that would explain everything. It read:

> **Bye whore. Now you'll know how my mother felt.**

21

Ethan had only been hit twice in his life—a roundhouse punch during a bar brawl his freshman year of college that had landed him on his back and left him seeing stars, and an accidental elbow strike to the jaw during a sparring match in a Thai boxing class when he lived in New York.

This pain was worse.

His throbbing face was suddenly too tight for his skull. The carpeted floor felt uneven, like a fault line was spreading between his feet.

In a daze, he tapped out the only text he could think of—three question marks in a row.

His response turned green. A quick scroll revealed their previous texts were all blue, including Roman's hateful one, which had come through at 9:15 a.m.

What did that mean? Had he been blocked?

With trembling fingers, he did his best to research, saw that being blocked was one of several possibilities. But the ghosts of his parents were already scolding him from their gilded perches in their antique-stuffed front parlor. *You fool,* they crowed. *Don't you see? You've been played.*

He called. It went to voicemail after one ring. An automated message.

Had it been the same message on Saturday? He'd phoned Roman a dozen times the night of his trailhead scream, but each time he'd hung up when voicemail answered and so he couldn't remember the content of the greeting. Was it this anonymous, robotic woman or had it once been Roman's actual voice?

"Call me, please. I don't understand what's going on. Is this text for real? I just..." What more could he say than that? "Just please call me. I hope you're okay."

Yeah, sure, he thought once he'd hung up. *I hope you're okay as you throw rocks in my face the morning after I bared my soul.*

He wished suddenly he had a number for Andy Rosales, the guy Roman was keeping his stuff with out in Victorville. But the more he thought about calling the man out of the blue, the crazier it seemed. Reaching out to the last boyfriend of the woman who'd probably blamed him for the demise of her marriage until her dying day? What good would that do when it looked for all intents and purposes like this entire thing had been a... *Don't go there yet,* he scolded himself. Without showering first, he threw on some clothes and sped down to the lobby.

The valet told him the Bentley four-door and the young man driving it had left sometime around 9:30. Ethan had slept until 10:00, believing himself to be free of schedules and burdens and poised to enjoy his last day of vacation with the man who'd allowed him to touch the sky.

Now he felt like a lazy drunk who'd missed the most important work meeting of his career.

As he shuffled back to the elevators, he had to swallow over and over again just so he could breathe. Once he'd closed the door behind him, he cursed the suddenly empty and abandoned room, still redolent with Roman's cologne, still filled with fresh memories of the hours they'd just spent devouring each other, owning each other.

Hours being played.

There was no avoiding it now. The truth was staring him in his flushed, pulsing face.

Saturday night, he realized now, had been the start of Roman's plot, not the end.

Suddenly everything on the room's desk was flying, and that's when Ethan realized he'd swept the surface clean with one arm. His laptop's collision with the far wall dented the top of the screen, which had been open during the swipe. His wallet, his keys, and his phone were spread across the carpet like tossed doubloons. The rage that had risen in him was so total and complete he shook down to his bones. And he knew what it covered.

Humiliation.

Big, grown-up Ethan, *Daddy* Ethan, had been played. Seduced, tricked, abandoned, and smeared.

And the words that echoed through his head were the same ones that had accompanied his darkest and most destructive thoughts for years.

Your mother was right. It's not for you. It's for the brides and grooms whose wedding cakes you've crafted, whose perfect memories you've captured in special, custom desserts. It's for the guests who glide past you in the lobbies and ballrooms you've graced with your creations over the years. It's their *world, a world of romance and true love and happily ever afters, and you're the guest in it, not them. You are love's servant, not its recipient. That joy belongs to the men who weren't whores.*

He could reason with this voice when he had his wits about him, when he was in the zone and loving his life. But not now, not when he'd opened his heart only to have it all end in this.

Another Ethan showered and packed up his things.

Another Ethan got his car back from the valet.

Another Ethan wound his way through downtown San Diego's grid of one-way streets until he made his way to the freeway. It was the Ethan who'd sold most of his possessions to pull together bus fare to New York because he'd known his parents would report his car stolen if he tried to take it. It was the Ethan who'd slept on benches after days of looking for a place to live in the big, cold, heartless city that would supposedly grant all his wishes if he just stuck it out long enough.

It was the Ethan who'd taught himself to delay despair until some small victory delayed it even further.

But whatever this version of Ethan was—some crazy hybrid of the past and the present—he kept his phone in his cupholder, looking down at it every few minutes, waiting for Roman to respond. By the time he pulled into the parking lot at his building, the only texts he'd gotten were from Donnie, asking if he wanted to stop by for lunch on his way out of town. He couldn't bring himself to answer.

As soon as he crossed the threshold of his apartment, he went to work throwing out the meals he'd made for Roman, tearing open the Tupperware containers and forking the contents into the sink, the trash, the sink, the trash. There was no rhyme or reason. His mad rush to stomp out all suggestions of the man had left him crazed. He was jamming an entire marinated steak into the garbage disposal with a fork when he realized he'd lost his mind. He never threw away untouched food. He always donated it to shelters. And that's what he'd do with the rest of it.

If he could sit...

If he could just breathe...

He was trying to do both when his phone lit up with a text. It was Donnie.

> **Woah man. This should make yr lives interesting. wut does Roman say???**

The main body of the text was a link to a news story on a gossip site with the headline *NFL hunk and Peyton fiancé caught in hot bi 3way with CW star and girlfriend.*

The image attached was a grainy screen cap from what was obviously a sex tape. Two slightly blurry male faces pressed together in a sloppy kiss above a grinning woman who must have been the one holding the phone out to one side to capture the image. One of the men was clearly Scott Bryant.

He read the article. No surprises. It was all in the headline. Just as Diana Peyton had feared, Scott had been reckless—drunk and reckless, if the censored clips of the video he was able to watch were any indicator—and now he'd brought scandal down on the wedding.

And now Roman was gone.

Shock and rage turned to a dull confusion. But now, instead of galvanized by anger, he was paralyzed.

A call came through on his phone. Someone was ringing him from the box downstairs.

He went to the built-in screen inside his front door and hit the button to give him a view of who was waiting for him.

Not Roman. A petite woman in huge sunglasses, the hood of her sweater pulled up over her baseball cap. But he'd seen that large, expressive mouth before—a few days earlier at Sapphire Cove and several times before on various television shows.

A second later, Rachel Peyton was stepping through his front door.

"He's not here," Ethan said, hating the thin and reedy sound of his voice.

"I know." She removed her sunglasses. Her eyes looked bloodshot and tired. "So there's a story that's about to—"

"It broke," he said and handed her his phone.

Shaking her head, she scrolled and read. After a tense silence, she handed the phone back to him. "Well, crap. I was hoping to beat it here, but whatever. I'm supposed to do a jilted woman walk past the paparazzi at some point. Guess I'll do it when I go home. They'll all be camped outside the Castle then." He'd closed the door behind her, and for a moment they stood awkwardly staring at each other. "I hope this is okay. He told me where you lived."

"When?"

"Tuesday, when I was at the hotel. We talked about you a bunch." She smiled as if this were a compliment.

Her easy nature suggested she wasn't aware of what had gone down that morning, but she seemed poised to add details to the larger events of the day, so he gestured for her to take a seat at one of the barstools along his kitchen island. To get as much information out of her as he could, he needed to play it cool. Keep the day's terrible marriage of anger and hurt veiled. "So I take it the wedding's off?" he asked, rinsing out Tupperware containers he'd already emptied.

"Not really," she said. "It's being recast. With my trainer. He didn't tell you because he's probably afraid of her."

His hands went still. "Roman?"

Rachel nodded.

"You're going to marry *Roman* in a month?"

She nodded.

"Where is he now?"

"On my mother's plane. They're headed overseas somewhere to hide out from the media and regroup. I'm supposed to meet them in a few days for our big *20/20* interview. That's when we announce to the world that Scott and I have been in trouble for a while but we didn't want to make our separation public, and during that time Romy and I got even closer and fell in love and that's why *we* are now getting married at Sapphire Cove in a month."

Did the green texts mean he'd turned his phone off because he was somewhere over the Atlantic? Or the Pacific?

"It's not too big of a stretch," she continued. "I mean, we've been in a bunch of magazines together. Shopping, training on the beach. Or at least that's how it'll look now."

"Why not just cancel?"

Rachel looked away, but he figured she was measuring her next words, not studying his apartment. "It's very important to my mother that this wedding proceed," she finally muttered, as if she was quoting words that turned her stomach.

"I can see that, but why?"

She laughed silently. Elbows propped on the counter, she rubbed her face with both hands. "*Vanity Fair*," she finally said.

He waited for her to continue. She didn't.

"The magazine?"

She nodded.

"What about it?"

"They're going to profile her. For the first time. Because of this wedding. Most of her career they've dismissed her like a B-list nobody. Now they're assigning a reporter to her the night of the wedding, and it's going to be part of a career retrospective."

Ethan took the slowest, deepest breath he could. "And that's a reason I'm supposed to understand?"

Rachel rubbed her forehead. "Not necessarily. It's just how my mother works."

"And you're going along with it."

Rachel lifted her chin defiantly. "Last time I checked, she's the only mother I've got."

"And you want to be famous."

"Okay, I'm sure this morning with Romy was kind of awkward—"

Ethan sputtered. "Awkward. That's one way of putting it."

At the bitterness in his laughter, she flinched. He looked away from her quickly, busying himself with a rag and the one vaguely dirty corner of his counter.

"Look," she said quietly. "I came because I know my mom probably told him not to say anything to you about what was really going on and so he probably jetted out this morning with some weird excuse. I wanted you to know this wedding isn't real. You guys can still pursue whatever it is that's happening between you two."

Tired of distracting himself with meaningless tasks, Ethan tossed the rag aside and turned to face his houseguest. He picked up his phone. "How much do you know about my history with Roman?" he asked her.

"*History*? You guys met, like, a few days ago. I mean, I know he's got it bad for you. We talked about you for like an hour on Tuesday. But all he kept saying was that you were never going to give him a shot because he was too young. Then when he texted that you guys were in San Diego, I was so happy 'cause I know how crazy he is about you. I mean, that's why I'm here, because I didn't want this fake wedding to get in the way of whatever's starting with you guys."

Ethan took several breaths to consider what he was about to do next. Yes, he was doubting everything he'd come to believe about Roman, but Rachel had just revealed to him that the celebrity wedding of the year was a sham, and she'd done it to protect what she thought was her best friend's budding relationship. Maybe she could be trusted.

"Eighteen years ago I worked as an escort in New York. Roman's father was one of my clients. His mother found out, and she brought Roman into the city one night to confront us, and he saw us kissing. He was seven."

She was an excellent actress, but he was fairly sure the astonishment he was seeing now couldn't be faked.

"Why are you having the wedding at Sapphire Cove, Rachel?"

She shook her head. "I don't... I think it was either going to be there or Montage because they're both big and nice and close to the Castle."

"And which one did Roman suggest?"

After a tense silence, she whispered, "Sapphire Cove."

Ethan nodded and began scrolling to his text thread with Roman as he continued. "I was a guest judge on a reality show. He recognized me. He wanted you to have the wedding there so that he and I could be reunited. And on Saturday, he scheduled a tasting in the penthouse suite where he tried to take his clothes off and get me in bed. When I didn't bite, he confronted me about our past and admitted that his plan had been to make a false accusation against me to get me fired."

Rachel shook her head, but her breaths were high and sharp. "But he didn't do it, right? I mean, none of that happened. You guys are...you guys are..."

He placed Roman's good-bye text on the counter in front of her. "*This* is the explanation I woke up to this morning. This was his good-bye."

As if the phone might be hot to the touch, Rachel pulled it toward her carefully. And when she read the words on screen, her breaths went silent. "No," she finally whispered, "I don't believe this. I don't believe he wrote this. I mean, why did your text go to green?"

"He's forty thousand feet in the air with your mother. His phone's probably off."

"They weren't wheels up by ten a.m."

"You know this for sure? You saw him this morning before they left?"

Rachel was still shaking her head, but more slowly now, her eyes full of doubt and alarm. "No. She wanted me in LA to make sure Scott didn't steal anything from the condo after he got the boot. We've known about the story for two days now, but she thought she could make some deal to keep it quiet. Yesterday it all fell through, and Scott was…"

"Fired," Ethan said for her. "Your fiancé was fired."

She nodded slowly, eyes drifting shut, as if the coldness of the term drove home the craziness of the situation in a way that gave her a headache.

He drew a deep, steadying breath. "Rachel, with all due respect, I appreciate your good intentions, but you'll have to forgive me if I don't accept your version of events. Because the one thing I've learned about your family this week is that no one in it, Roman Walker included, ever tells anyone the truth."

When her eyes flashed with anger, he thought she might storm out. In his experience, the children of privilege were never very adept at swallowing hard truths about themselves. But while she'd cooled toward him, it seemed, she made no move to leave.

"It doesn't make any sense, Ethan," she finally said. "He'd just risked his entire future to tell me what he thought was the truth about my fiancé. If it was just some act and he was going to pull this after a few days, why tell me about *you* at all?"

"You'll have to ask him. And until he tells me otherwise, I have no choice but to take his text at face value. And just as a sidenote here, I left my bigoted family in the dust when I was twenty so I could live as who I really am. A relationship in the shadows of a straight marriage everyone's talking about on TV? Not my first choice, Rachel. But I appreciate the consolation prize, and I realize for some people, career trumps all."

As she got to her feet, Rachel looked down at the screen of Ethan's phone. "I get that you're upset. But he didn't write this. I'm telling you. He didn't write it." It sounded like she was trying to convince herself.

"I respect the depth of your friendship. I do. But it was a wasted visit, Rachel. It doesn't seem like there's anything between me and Roman for you to protect."

She exhaled sharply. Apparently Roman wasn't the only one who thought him occasionally cold as ice.

When her hand reached his doorknob, she looked back and said, "Goes without saying, but I'd appreciate it if you didn't go to the press about any of this." She smiled broadly.

"That goes both ways. Mutually assured destruction, and all that."

She nodded, and then she was gone.

And for the first time that day, he couldn't be alone with his thoughts.

Donnie answered after the second ring. The day's events came pouring out of Ethan in a rush, but he didn't sound nearly as wrecked as he had that morning when he'd left the voicemail for Roman. His conversation with Rachel started to feel like a dress rehearsal for this one.

"That's bullshit," Donnie said once he was finished.

"Which part?"

"He didn't send that text."

"Why is everyone giving him the benefit of the doubt?" Ethan asked.

"Why aren't *you*?"

"It's from his phone, Donnie."

"But why would he send it?"

"It was a long con. Saturday was just the beginning. He wanted me to…"

"What? Wanted you to what?"

Even though he'd thought the words a dozen times that morning, giving voice to them felt like expelling hot gravel from his throat. "He wanted me to open my heart to him. Okay?" he blurted out. "Because it would be the perfect moment to kick the wind out of me. Christ, don't make me say it. It's already awful enough… I mean, I told him everything last night, Donnie. *Everything*. About my parents and how we parted and how I never saw them again. I made a fool of myself with him…" His voice choked up before he could get control of himself. He screwed his eyes shut because the threat of tears made him feel like even more of an idiot.

When he opened them, he was leaning forward over the sink, gripping the edge of the counter, struggling to catch his breath.

"All right, listen," Donnie said. "I know you think I'm just your big sex monster friend who never left the business, but I gotta say a few things, and you need to hear them. So do you promise you'll let me finish?"

"Yes."

"It was a job, okay? What we did was a job, and we're not broken and we're not tainted. And we're allowed to want people and they're allowed to want us. And showing someone who you really are, someone you care about, is not making a fool of yourself. It's your right. It's everyone's right. So if you spent five minutes last night not being mister calm and in control like you always are, well, then good. But the minute you stop believing you deserve to be punished for something, you'll stop believing the worst of him. And then you'll be able to see what today's really about."

Donnie's words acted like a soothing balm across flaming skin.

"All right, Sex Socrates, tell me what today's really about then," Ethan finally said.

"Something really weird happened at that hotel this morning before you woke up, and you don't know what it is. And Rachel doesn't either, it sounds like."

Desperate to believe Donnie's words, Ethan turned from the sink, forcing himself to stare into his sun-filled glass box of an apartment. *Something really weird.* It sounded pretty accurate.

"And another thing," Donnie added. "Faking it is my business, Blake, and that guy couldn't fake what he was feeling for you this week. Hell, he couldn't fake being turned on in my studio for more than ten seconds."

"Fine, then maybe he got upset about the past all over again. Or he woke up and regretted everything. I don't know."

"That's just it, Blake. You don't know. Listen, I got contractors breathing down my neck, but I'm going to call you later, okay?"

"Sure." They were about to hang up when Ethan said, "Donnie. Thank you."

"You *carried* me when Zach left. He broke my heart, and you carried me. I'll carry you through this, whatever it turns out to be. We're family, and we always will be."

When he hung up, feeling comforted and encouraged, he felt a strange tickle on the back of his neck and reached up to rub the skin. Nothing was there, and that's when he realized the sensation wasn't physical—it was a memory. A memory of a detail about that morning he'd forgotten.

A kiss, he realized.

Roman had kissed him early that morning. He'd figured the man had been on his way to the bathroom, but maybe he'd been on his way out the door. Had it been a taunt, a way to drive the knife in before his text arrived?

How did that work? Ethan had been half asleep and had barely stirred. It had been the kind of kiss you gave someone so that *you* could remember it, not them.

He wasn't scheduled to go into work until the next day, but he wasn't willing to sit at home, staring at the walls and checking his phone every ten seconds. And with Roman somewhere high above an ocean, what would he be expecting anyway? He texted his team members who were on site and scheduled debriefs for later in the day.

An hour later, he was back at Sapphire Cove, the change of scenery and pace making his time in San Diego feel like it was a distant fever dream. But of course, the hotel was abuzz with talk of the Scott Bryant tape and whether or not it would kill the Peyton wedding. He had emails from both Connor and Logan asking him if he'd heard anything from Roman. In the strictest of legal terms, his response was truthful. *I have not heard anything from Roman at this time about the wedding.*

The absence of a query from Jonas, however, was odd. As events director, the wedding was under his purview, and a cancellation would be his complicated, headache-inducing matter to handle. He should have been the most eager for an update.

Chloe cornered him, on fire for information, and he gave her the same response he'd given the GM and director of security, then mollified her with an hour of one-sided conversation where she downloaded about the squabbles she and her wife were having about their home renovation. After that, he threw himself into cake design on two different upcoming projects. By the time he looked up at his phone, it was eight o'clock, and most of the day was gone.

Good, he thought.

Then he noticed he had a visitor.

Jonas Jacobs was standing behind him, expression unreadable. "You're working late. On your vacation."

"Design is my favorite part of the process. I tend to lose myself in it."

Jonas grunted and gave him a coy, half smile. "Follow me, please."

Ethan complied.

Well, this is it, he thought, expecting to be led into a conference room with Connor, Logan, and possibly several managers of the bank trust that owned the hotel. To learn Donnie was wrong and Rachel was wrong and that Roman had smeared him to management in an attempt to get him fired. Maybe with a lie, maybe with the truth about Ethan's past. But then they were moving through the conference center and out the door toward the villas. It was dark out, and the sky was clear and star-flecked, the cool winds rustling the palm fronds overhead.

"So I understand you didn't follow my advice," Jonas said.

Ethan sighed. "What's going on, Jonas?"

"We're meeting your friend Donnie. We have some information to share with you."

"I see," Ethan said, even though he didn't and thought it best to keep his confusion quiet.

When they stepped through the door to one of the villas, Donnie rose quickly to his feet from the cream-colored chaise lounge next to the balcony doors. The honey-colored light inside made the scene seem ironically romantic.

"I didn't realize you two knew each other," Ethan said.

Jonas opened his laptop and set it on the coffee table. "Indeed. Donnie actually worked with us during the big crisis we had a few years ago."

Nodding and smiling, Donnie added, "And I've tried to get in his pants ever since, but he always shuts me down. I'm a little down-market for him. Jonas is a fancy guy."

Jonas was also ignoring this ribbing and opening up windows on his computer.

"He went to *Georgetown*," Donnie added in a dramatic whisper.

"Correct. I'm a fancy guy with friends at the Wyman in San Diego. And I was able to get you this footage of your *friend* Roman Walker on the surveillance cameras this morning." With several efficient keystrokes, Jonas opened three different QuickTime files, then he stepped away from the computer to give Ethan and Donnie room to crowd in. "Play the lobby one first."

The camera angle was a wide shot that included the long row of automatic entry doors and the walls of plate glass on either side as well. To the right of the screen were the reception desks, and in the near distance, a corridor that led to the twenty-four-hour deli and the larger restaurant beyond. The sight of Roman walking in the direction of the camera, a skip in his step, holding a white paper bag just like the one he'd brought the Danishes in the morning before, seemed like some intrusive memory of a past life that had died early that morning.

"Are you sure this is today?" Ethan asked.

But it was a silly question. When Jonas tapped the bottom of the open window, Ethan saw it was both date and time stamped.

Just then, a hulking figure moved through the automatic doors with such speed and direction it was clear the man had been watching Roman from the other side of the glass. He wore chinos and a short sleeve khaki-colored shirt and sported a bushy mustache and muttonchop sideburns. In the instant before the man took him firmly by one arm, Roman looked at him with muted surprise, like he recognized the guy but wasn't alarmed to see him. They started walking together toward the camera as the man held Roman's left arm with a threatening amount of force. Whatever words he was quietly saying as they both self-consciously faced forward turned Roman's expression to one of shock and outrage.

Roman froze, spun, attempted to pull out of the man's grip. Mustache Man responded by turning them to face each other. He didn't seem angry. He seemed determined, controlled—like someone resigned to do the best of an unpleasant job. Roman bowed his head and shook it. Fighting tears.

"Who the hell is that guy?" Ethan finally asked.

"He pops up behind Diana Peyton in a bunch of her red-carpet photos," Donnie answered. "Probably her bodyguard or something."

On screen, Roman raised his head as Mustache Man gripped him by his shoulders. Heart in his throat, Ethan watched Roman look back in the direction of the elevators, eyes wide.

Crying.

Crying as he looked in the direction of the room he'd shared with Ethan for two nights. Then he sagged with something that looked like defeat, and when the man extended one hand, Roman reached into his pocket, removed his phone, and handed it over.

Ethan's first deep breath in hours thundered through his lungs and brought oxygen to parts of his body that had felt starved all morning.

Because the time of the exchange was right there on the screen. 8:30 a.m.

Roman had handed over his phone forty-five minutes before the text had been sent.

"Show the hallway one," Donnie said.

Jonas complied.

This view was of the gently curving guest corridor outside their room. When Roman appeared, with Diana's bodyguard still holding his arm, Ethan's heart dropped. Seeing both men in the same pose in another part of the hotel drove home the extent to which Roman had been overpowered, threatened. When they came to a stop outside the door to Ethan's room, Roman gave his abductor a miserable look before stepping inside. Then Mustache Man put his arm out to keep the door from closing all the way so that he could eavesdrop and watch.

He felt the gentle kiss Roman had given him that morning, remembered the low sniffle he'd blamed on a possible cold. Not a cold. Tears. And a kiss was all he could give because someone had been waiting for him right outside.

A minute or so later, Roman emerged from the room with his bag, watching the carpet as he walked. When Mustache Man reached out for his shoulder, Roman jerked away from him as if he'd been scalded, then raised a hand warning the guy not to come any closer.

"See," Donnie said, "sometimes I know things."

Ethan reached out and gripped his friend's shoulder. But he didn't want to get too emotional in front of Jonas. How much of the story did his coworker know? The man in question was standing off to the side now, watching them impassively, hands folded primly over his crotch.

"Don't worry," he said, "this stays between us. I have a lot of experience with secrecy."

Was he referring to his knack for never spilling any details about how he'd spent the first part of his adulthood, or was he referring to how he'd actually spent those years? Speaking of past professions...

"And how much have you been told?" Ethan asked, but he was looking at Donnie.

"Just enough," Donnie said. "If he wants to know the rest, he's going to have to give me the goodies."

"That's never happening, Sex Monster," Jonas said calmly.

"How does he know your nickname?" Ethan asked.

Donnie shrugged. "I love that nickname. I spread it around. So is this your way of thanking me? Because now feels like it should be the thank you part."

"Shouldn't I be the one to get thanked?" Jonas asked. "I'm actually the one who called the Wyman."

"Yeah, but I called *you* for help." Donnie pointed a finger at him. "And you always talk to me like I'm eight, so that's kind of a big sacrifice."

Ethan raised one hand. "Do Connor and Logan know about any of this?"

"Hell, no. That's why I called Jonas," Donnie said.

"Yes, but you and Logan go back almost as far as we do, and I don't—"

Donnie put his hands out. "I'm not telling Murdoch. Don't worry. Neither is Jonas. Right, Jonas?"

But what Jonas said was, "If I always talk to you like you're eight, why do you insist on hitting on me so brazenly?"

Ethan gripped Donnie by both shoulders and looked him in the eye. "Thank you. I still don't know what this all means, but thank you."

But Donnie was looking past him at Jonas. "Maybe I've got a thing for guys who think they're better than me."

Ethan let go of Donnie's shoulders and turned to Jonas. "Would you like me to step out so you two can work out this tension alone? It's a lovely villa."

Jonas raised one eyebrow. "That depends. Will I have to sign a model release?"

"Oh, that's it!" Donnie barked. "You took some sexphobic class at Georgetown and you're anti-porn because you put all kinds of feminist ideology on porn that doesn't have any women in it!"

"No, I just think you hit on me excessively because you know you don't have a shot, and given how many men probably throw themselves at you because of your prior career, it drives you somewhat insane." Jonas smiled.

Donnie took a step past Ethan toward Jonas and said, "All right, look, Pocket Square, I can—"

"Mother of Christ!" Ethan exploded. "Both of you shut up! I'm the one having a horrible day. *I'm* entitled to be a drama queen for once." As they fell silent, both men nodded gravely as if Ethan had spoken a profound truth. "Jonas, thank you. Truly. I will buy you dinner."

"You're a chef," he answered. "Make me dinner. And you're welcome to review the footage again, but it stays on my laptop, and we don't distribute it. That's the agreement I made with my friend in San Diego."

"Of course," Ethan said. "And not to ask a gift horse to cough up even more, but I don't suppose you have a direct line to Rachel Peyton?"

Jonas shook his head. "We've been dealing entirely with the wedding planner. I don't even think I have her email. But I'll check. If it's a really good dinner."

"The best," Ethan said with a wink. "Donnie, with me."

As Ethan took his arm, Donnie wailed, "I'm, like, saving your relationship here. How am I in trouble?"

"You're not, but if you would like us not to talk to you like you're eight, stop *whining* about being in *trouble*." Outside, Ethan steered them down a few steps of the walkway that ran downhill between two rows of terraced villas. "Did you tell Jonas the entire story of how Roman and I—"

"Holy crap, no," Donnie whispered.

"And Logan?"

"I told you. I didn't tell him anything about this."

"I know, but over the years, did you ever mention friends who used to escort?"

Donnie cocked his head to one side and sighed dramatically. "No, no, and *no.* I barely talk to Logan about how *I* used to escort. It freaks him out. He's pretty traditional for a guy who plowed every twink in Orange County five times before he met the love of his life."

"Be sure to include that in your wedding toast." Ethan's phone chimed. He pulled it from his pocket. "And thank you. I appreciate your discretion as always." But when he saw the text on his screen, he froze.

"Is it him?" Donnie asked, peering forward to read it.

"No. It's the hotel operator. Rachel called."

Donnie's eyes widened.

Several hours later, they were winding their way through dark, serpentine suburban streets in Donnie's SUV, not too far from Ethan's complex. Their destination was a parking lot off Laguna Niguel Lake, a compact reservoir in the hills just above Irvine. It was almost one in the morning, and Rachel had informed them the number she'd given them was for a burner phone.

"This is some cloak and dagger shit, man," Donnie said. "Makes me wish I brought my gun."

"Let's try to remain Orange County about this, Donnie. Perhaps a raised voice. Maybe a passing threat of litigation."

The lot was empty, and Donnie took care to park outside the halos of the nearest sodium vapor lights. The reservoir was bordered by low, dusty hills with almost no trees, beyond which the uniform rooftops of surrounding subdivisions were visible in security-light cast silhouettes.

Rachel had asked to meet at a picnic table and benches on the shore. At that very spot, two shadows awaited them, one about Rachel's height and with a baseball cap on its head, the other taller, larger, and bulkier and running one hand through his hair over and over again. Not Roman. Ethan figured they must have used some secret passageway to get out of the Castle, given the media that was now camped outside on either side of PCH.

"The idea here is to let her do the talking," Ethan said in a low voice. "It worked pretty well with her earlier."

But when they were paces from the bench, the taller, bulkier shadow turned. As his eyes adjusted to the darkness, Ethan made out a familiar mustache, the same one he'd seen earlier on the security footage from the Wyman, and suddenly he'd clenched his fists at his sides and could feel his jaw working.

"Who the hell's *he*?" the bodyguard barked.

"Who the fuck are you, Mustache?" Donnie shouted back. "I'm whoever I want to be. This isn't your drug deal."

"That's not how we're starting, boys," Rachel said in a firm voice.

A silence fell, and Ethan saw the admonishing finger she'd raised was actually pointed at the large man next to her. "Hank, do you have something to say to Ethan?"

It sounded like the man was cursing under his breath. "The direction, initially, was to find out where Roman took the Bentley. It's got anti-theft tracking. When I found it, she wanted to know what he was up to, so I sent her pictures of you guys in San Diego."

"Her being Diana?" Ethan asked.

Hank nodded. "She recognized you."

"That's becoming a refrain. From what, exactly?" Ethan asked.

"She has a file. Roman's *mom* had a file and now Diana's got it. It's old. It's about you and his dad. A PI put it together, like, I don't know, a lot of years ago, when Roman was a little kid. His mom was keeping it in one of the AC vents at the house in Victorville. When they started the remodel, the contractors found it and brought it to her. Then the shit hit the fan with Scott's sex tape, and the direction changed."

Hank studied the dirt at his feet.

"Keep going," Rachel said.

"Shit," Hank whispered, then he raised his head. "The direction was to tell Roman that if he didn't come back to the Castle immediately, and if he didn't agree to go along with the new marriage plan, she was going to send the file to Sapphire Cove. And anywhere else you might apply for a job. For the rest of your life."

Ethan heard Donnie's sharp exhalation next to him as if from a great distance. All he could feel was that sudden, last-minute yank of the wind catching the parachute behind him and Roman the day before. He was hearing the ruffling sounds it had made as they'd sailed out over the sunlit sea.

"He got real upset," Hank continued, "because he said there was a time in your life when someone tried to get back at you by sending a bunch of personal stuff to your parents and that it really hurt and if it happened to you again you'd... Anyway, he got real upset."

Ethan's head was spinning like it had that morning, and he fought the urge to reach out for Donnie's support to stay standing. A deep breath helped, but it made for a loud sigh that filled the shadows, alerting everyone around him that this news had rocked him sideways.

He didn't leave to break my heart, Ethan thought. *He left to protect it.*

"Anyway," Hank continued, "I didn't realize how serious you'd gotten. I wasn't prepared for him to break down like that."

Donnie said, "Blackmail tends to have that effect on people."

Hank shook his head and raised his hands as if the whole thing was awful but entirely beyond his control.

"Keep going," Rachel said.

Hank sucked in a breath as if whatever he had to say next would be the worst revelation of all. "Look, she's lying to the kid, okay? I was supposed to tell him that if he pulls off this big announcement interview in two weeks, she'll let him talk to you. See you, even. But it's not going to happen, all right? She just switched grooms. She's not going to risk another headline before the wedding."

"Who wrote it?" Ethan asked. "You or her?"

The question brought a sudden silence down on them all.

"Who wrote the text?"

After an interminable silence, Hank said, "Her orders were to make it a clean break. She left the wording up to me."

"Jesus Christ, dude," Donnie whispered.

"All right, look," Hank barked. "None of us would be here if you hadn't decided to engage in a little human trafficking back when you were young and hot. And I just want to add that—"

Then suddenly Hank had gone abruptly silent and Rachel had let out a high, sharp cry. And that's when Ethan realized he'd closed the distance between him and Roman's abductor and his fist had connected cleanly with the man's jaw, sending him stumbling backward into the edge of the picnic table. He skittered sideways then his ass landed on the bench hard enough to creak the wood.

"That's for making Roman cry," Ethan growled.

There were a few seconds of dazed silence.

"So much for keeping things Orange County," Donnie mumbled, but it sounded like there was admiration in his voice.

Hank heaved with pained breaths, rubbing his jaw. "You're just going to let him do that, Rachel?" Hank asked between coughs.

"Yes," Rachel answered.

Donnie's hand came to rest firmly on Ethan's shoulder, no doubt to avert a fight he thought was about to break out. Ethan held his ground, but not his tongue.

"Human trafficking?" Ethan shouted. "Really, asshole? You and your rich boss kidnapped someone this morning. You strong-armed his phone away and you used blackmail to put him on a plane to the other side of the world, and you have the nerve to lecture me about what I did with my body and other consenting adults eighteen years ago when I was a grown man?"

Nobody said anything for a while. Donnie rubbed the space between Ethan's shoulder blades, but his own breaths suggested he was almost as angry as Ethan was.

"Look," Hank finally croaked. "I'm not saying I support any of this. I mean, it hasn't been easy with her these last few years. She's not exactly aging gracefully, okay? On the inside, anyway. She's being forgotten, and it's making her kinda nuts."

Donnie cackled. "Well, *we'll* always remember her, that's for damn sure."

Rachel said, "Go wait in the car please, Hank."

"I can't leave you out here with these—"

"Please go wait in the car." Her tone was that of a wise and confident princess who was uninterested in further discussion on the matter.

The three of them listened silently as Hank's retreating footsteps crunched dirt and twigs. Once he was gone, Donnie said, "How much of a threat is this really? I mean, Logan's got three of my old models working security in his department."

"Porn's different," Ethan said. "It's legal. And it was a unique situation, Donnie. They were desperate for staff, so the bank looked the other way."

"And they've been looking the other way ever since," Donnie said. "J.T, Brandon, Scott—they're all still there. And their old vids are all online for anyone to see. I mean, I don't think Connor and Logan would fire you."

"The problem wouldn't be them. It would be the bank that manages the trust that owns the hotel. If Connor and Logan don't react, she could send it to the press and then it's a PR issue and the bank's raising objections. Then guests raise objections. It starts with a few wedding couples asking to work with a junior chef instead of me, then maybe it turns into a whole conference because they do some kind of activism that makes them opposed to sex work."

"And then after a while it dies down because everyone forgets," Donnie said.

"Maybe," Ethan said.

Rachel had her back to them now, arms crossed over her chest, staring out at the lake water glistening in the moonlight. "When Mom was twelve," she said softly, "her mom drove her to her agent's house and left her there. Forever. Never came back. He was a grown man, in his forties. But most of his clients lived with him, and most of them were kids. It never would be allowed today, but it was a different time. The kids were always at each other's throats. That was his strategy, you see. Teach them how to compete. Teach them at a young age that in this business everyone's out for themselves."

Ethan tried to hide his impatience. "Clearly, we all have our pasts, Rachel. I'm not really interested in—"

"I'm not trying to make you feel sorry for her, Ethan. Just let me finish, please."

Ethan gestured for her to continue.

"There was this one girl, about my mom's age. They got to be friends, but then one day they were up for the same role, and the girl had previously made the mistake of telling my mom she was allergic to sesame seeds. So the night before her audition, my mom volunteered for kitchen duty." Rachel didn't need to fill in the rest. "Something's missing in my mother. I think because she had to kill it all those years ago after her mom abandoned her. Like she went so deep inside herself that she's the only thing she can see. But the point I'm trying to make is that if Connor and Logan don't react to the file, she will keep going until she finds someone who does. An actor quits when they're dead. That's, like, her motto."

"Very spiritual," Donnie grumbled.

No one said anything for what felt like an eternity.

Rachel finally broke the silence. "I thought about becoming a doctor, when I was in high school."

"Why didn't you?" Ethan asked.

"A voice in my head said the only way my mother would see me was if I went into the same business. Then she could see my career as an extension of her own. And it's worked for this long. I feel like I've had as much of her in my life as I possibly could. But now we're here and I feel responsible."

"Rachel," Ethan finally said. Whatever she heard in his tone made her turn to face them. "I don't want to seem ungrateful because I needed to hear all of this, very much, but there's another way to end this."

She shook her head. "No, there isn't. I threatened to come out as asexual an hour ago and she made the same threat. To you."

There was another silence during which Donnie's hand came to rest on his shoulder again. "Looks like you've got more people looking out for you than you thought."

"You spoke to them?" Ethan asked.

Rachel nodded. "I spoke to her after they landed. She wouldn't let me talk to him. She said he was too upset and he needed to calm down."

"Still upset? After an eleven-hour flight?"

He was guessing about the flight time, and so he threw out the average travel time between the West Coast and Europe, especially after the refueling stops needed for a smaller private plane. But she didn't rush to fill in the blank about where her mother had taken Roman.

"Where are they, Rachel?" he asked her.

"I'm not going to tell you that, Ethan. If you try some hero shit and jump a wall or something, it will end very badly for both of you. Some of her craziest fans are overseas, and her security when she travels is hard-fucking-core. And I've never seen her this invested in something. Hank's right. She thinks this wedding is her swan song. She hasn't gotten offered a good role in a decade, and this whole thing is her chance to shine. Maybe her last."

"What makes you think I'd pull some hero shit, as you put it?"

"Ask Hank. He could use some ice for his jaw."

"Yeah, but," Donnie interjected, "you'd better tell Roman that Ethan punched your Mustache Man 'cause eventually they're going to have real good sex over it, 'cause that was fucking hot, dude."

"That's enough, Sex Monster," Ethan whispered.

"Seriously, though," Donnie responded. "I didn't know you had it in you. I figured you'd just flambé him or something."

Ethan wanted to laugh, but he couldn't manage it.

"I'm headed there this week," Rachel said. "Write him a letter, something he can tear up. I'll give you his response. 'Cause something tells me she's going to keep him under armed guard until the wedding. Literally."

"Deal," Ethan said.

"All right," Donnie said, stepping between them, "let's walk the lady back to her car. Something tells me her security detail isn't working at full strength tonight."

22

"It felt like a miracle, honestly," Roman said.

He was proud of how he'd said *honestly*. Like it was an afterthought. Three dots appeared before it in the script, so he figured that was the right read.

Perched on the edge of the sofa across from his, the boss he couldn't get free of watched his every move with penetrating intensity. Behind her, Melanie, Diana's birdlike and perpetually anxious publicist had stopped pacing and texting long enough to watch his performance. She'd flown in the day before. Now, her toothy smile encouraged him to continue.

Roman cleared his throat. "I mean, one day, you turn and you look at the person who's been next to you the whole time, and all of a sudden you see something you've never seen before. You see—"

"No!" With a loud clank, Diana slammed her coffee cup into its saucer. "No, no, sugar. Some*one*! You see *someone* you've never seen before. That's the point. You're supposed to be telling us how you fell in love with your best friend. You're making it sound like she sprouted a wart on her chin."

"I'm sorry."

"Don't be sorry. Just bring your A-game. Come on. I know you've got it in you. This interview is *key*. For all of us."

This whole nightmare would be easier, he thought, if she'd be nastier to him. But in the days since they'd boarded the plane, she'd oozed gentle condescension, ignoring the angry looks he'd sometimes given her during moments of weakness. Again and again she'd described the new marriage plot as the best thing for everyone involved. Especially Roman, who she claimed would become an overnight celebrity the minute the *20/20* interview aired. And during all her long, pep rally-style speeches about a wedding that involved no love or authentic feeling, he'd kept his mouth shut. Because he was sure that if he stepped out of line, Ethan would be marched into some big scary office at Sapphire Cove and forced to answer for the contents of a file his mother had kept secret for years.

And, of course, Diana hadn't mentioned that threat once. She'd let Hank do her dirty work in that regard.

"I'm sorry," he said now, "I'm just really tired."

"More coffee then," Diana said, gesturing for Melanie to hop to. "Would you like more coffee?"

"I'd like to talk to Ethan."

Dammit. He'd been holding the words in for days now. No wonder they'd slipped out. Still, he should have kept his mouth shut. But he wasn't lying about how tired he was. They'd been rehearsing for hours, but maybe it was still jet lag. He'd never been out of the country before, so he couldn't be sure. Stress alone had kept him up the first two nights after their arrival. By night three, he'd collapsed and managed a good eight hours of sleep. Now he was on something close to a regular schedule.

If anything about this situation could be called *regular*.

The anxiety of captivity was wearing him down, but his prison was stunning.

Allegedly they were in Provence, but he'd have to take their word for it. They'd landed after dark before a hired car had sped them through miles of twinkling, rolling hills. Since then, he hadn't been allowed to leave the property. The villa was as spare and modern as the Castle by the Sea was fussy and elegant. The walls were all plain, rugged sandstone, and severe metal sculptures—some of them vaguely religious—hung from concealed hooks. The blocky furniture was upholstered in creams and taupe. Off to his left, a wall of French doors stood open to the sundrenched, manicured garden outside.

Diana rubbed the bridge of her nose between her thumb and forefinger. "I believe you and Hank went over this. If the interview sticks, we'll see what we can set up with you and your friend."

"He's not just my friend, Diana."

If he ever speaks to me again after the way I left him in San Diego, he thought.

"Well, he's a terrible choice for anything else, darling. So let's not add a stressful conversation onto an already stressful process. What do you say? Can we get back to work?"

Suitcase wheels clattered on the flagstones outside. When Roman saw Rachel, his professional composure threatened to shatter. Fighting tears, he shot to his feet, closing the distance between them before he threw his arms around her. Instantly, her mouth was at his ear. "I've got a message from Ethan," she whispered. Then she pulled away as if she hadn't spoken and turned to her mother.

"All right, now we can really get things underway." Diana stood and gave her daughter a weak half hug. When they parted, she added, "I hope you rested on the plane."

When Rachel released the handle of her suitcase, the publicist fetched it with the speed of a valet. "Some." Rachel removed her sunglasses. "It looks like Roman could use a break."

"What he could use is more rehearsal," Diana grumbled, refilling her coffee cup from a silver carafe. "You've got your script?"

"Printed it out before I left." Rachel swung her shoulder bag in front of her, pulling the pages in question from the side pouch. "I'll take him outside and we can run lines."

Diana studied her daughter skeptically, then Roman in turn. "Five minutes," she said, "then we're back in here and back to work. The ABC crew arrives in twenty-four hours."

Rachel took him by the arm. The next thing he knew, they were moving through the frenzied lattices of shadow offered by the regiment of ancient olive trees outside. Their backs were to the villa. Ahead of them, a dark-bottomed pool shimmered, surrounded by square planters exploding with lavender. "He gave me this." Across her chest, she passed him her copy of the script. "I slipped it in there between pages four and five. You've got a minute or two to read it. Once you make up your mind, give me back the whole thing so I can chuck it."

Make up his mind? What did that mean? A scraping sound nearby made him jump. It had come from the direction of the pool. There, one of the security team, a towering hulk of a man with a cue ball head and a menacing scar on one cheek, spotted them and slowed.

"But Romy," she whispered, looking in the direction of the guard, "don't cry and don't go back in there and confront her about any of this."

Hands shaking, he stopped and opened the script.

"What's that?" Diana barked. She was standing just outside one of the French doors behind them.

"The script, Mom. What do you think?"

Diana eyed them warily before heading back inside.

It was Ethan's penmanship, the same sturdy cursive with which he'd written the note that had accompanied Roman's pet hawk. Then the words seemed to wrap around him, and the gentle buzz of insects, the swimming pool's steady gurgle, and the distant call of a bird all seemed far away suddenly.

My Dearest Roman,

The man who showed me how to touch the sky. You have opened my heart in a way that has made clear to me how firmly it was closed before this week.

No one has ever stood up for me the way you're standing up for me now.

No one has ever protected me like this.

No matter what happens, I will always in some sense, in some part of my soul, feel what you are doing for me now, the same way I'll always feel your warmth and your joy as we flew together above the cliffs and the sea.

But you must know the risks of what you're doing.

You must know that Diana cannot be trusted to keep the terms of even this awful agreement. The morning you left, she ordered Hank to send me a text from your phone making it sound as if you'd deliberately seduced me and then left me to get revenge for your father.

If she doesn't get what she wants out of this, there's no telling what she will do to you next.

I can barely sleep knowing you are under her control like this. Rachel and I have spoken at length. If you want to leave wherever she's taken you, if you want to abandon this sham wedding, you have my blessing.

I don't care what the consequences are to me or my career. I won't have you held hostage and abused like this because of my past and my choices.

Whatever happens, I will figure out what comes next.

For both of us. But I will not, under any circumstances, make you pay an ever-increasing price to this woman.

If you want out of there, if you don't want to go through with this, Rachel has agreed to defy her mother and bring you home. And if she does, I will be here waiting for you as if we'd never parted, as if we woke up together in that hotel room in San Diego with the memory of our magical night together in La Jolla still fresh in our minds.

Love,
Ethan

"What did I say?" Rachel hissed when she saw Roman's tears.

"I'm trying," he whispered.

"Guys!" Diana barked. "We have work to do. Come on!"

"We'll be right in," Rachel called back.

Diana threw up her hands and started venting her frustrations to Melanie in a voice he couldn't hear.

"So what do you say?" Rachel whispered. "You ready to start World War III, and damn the consequences?"

Roman couldn't look up from Ethan's beautiful, steady penmanship. "He doesn't know what he's saying. Are you going to talk to him? I mean, there's no landline and she won't let me have a phone."

"I'll try calling him tonight when everyone's asleep. Maybe they won't watch me like they're watching you."

Roman took a deep breath. "Tell him this is all my fault and it's mine to fix. Tell him if I'd never tried to come for him, none of this would have happened, and I've got no choice but to make it right."

Rachel swallowed and shook her head. "You know she's not going to let you see him before the wedding, right? You know she was lying, right?"

"I do now," Roman whispered, "but I've got no choice. I'm done being some crazy kid. I've got to see this through. For him."

Now it was Rachel fighting tears. "Oh, Romy. You sweet, stupid, beautiful boy."

Diana's voice shattered the moment. "Guys, enough of this! Come inside and—"

"Mom, please!"

Diana jerked as if she'd been slapped. A stunned silence seemed to settle over the entire property. Nature itself was reacting to the monumental event of Rachel clapping back at her mother for the first time. Roman watched as Diana marshaled the performance of an injured party—hand floating up to her chest as she shook her head in dumb shock, turning and stumbling back inside as if the wind had been knocked out of her.

Once she'd managed a deep breath, Rachel said, "Clearly I was ready to fight for you, Romy."

He pulled her close and kissed her on the forehead. "Come on. It'll be fun. Like a game. Pretend marriage, or whatever. Like dress-up."

"You a big fan of dress-up?"

"Not really, no," he said as he started them back toward the French doors. "According to Ethan, I have trouble wearing anything."

When he handed the script back to her, the pain of letting go of Ethan's loving words felt like a stab in the gut.

At 7:00 p.m., exactly a week after Roman had been flown out of the country, Rachel's number lit up the screen of Ethan's phone as he was driving home from Sapphire Cove on Laguna Canyon Road. He pulled into the parking lot of a lumber yard, knowing whatever response Roman gave to his letter might seize control of his emotions.

In a whispered rush that made it sound like she was being watched, she gave him Roman's response to his letter. And suddenly he was resting his head against the top of the steering wheel.

"Can I talk to him?" he finally asked.

"She's got a guard outside his room."

"So what happens next?"

"We do the interview tomorrow, it airs the day after that, then I'm on a plane back to New York to close out my run."

"And Roman?"

"He stays here until the wedding. With her. They're flying home twenty-four hours before and then going to the Castle. And then to the hotel, obviously, when it's time."

"So no rehearsal dinner?" he asked.

"The cover story's going to be that with all of the scandal swirling, the other events are going to be private and for the family. We're doing the rehearsal on the beach by the Castle with a shit ton of security. The *paps* will get tipped off so they can be stationed nearby. She'll claim we had a private dinner in the house after, but that's doubtful since everyone wants to kill her. The wedding will be the big show, just like she wanted."

"Tell him that I'll have a special dessert waiting for him when he gets to the hotel," Ethan said. "Tell him *I'll* be waiting for him."

"I will, but listen, I gotta go."

When they hung up, it took him several minutes before he felt capable of driving the rest of the way home.

After hours of bickering, all of which Roman could overhear from his makeup chair in the adjacent room, the camera crew and Melanie—under Diana's instructions—settled on a location for the first interview—a spot close to the pool with plenty of lavender-filled planters and the vine-shrouded, tiled-roof guest house in the background.

When he first took a seat next to Rachel, he was relieved to find the garden wasn't as hot as he'd feared. But after only a minute or two into the interviewer's invasive questions, he was sporting a layer of sweat under the drab, boring outfit they'd chosen for him—an eggplant-colored dress shirt and dark slacks.

He recognized the reporter who'd been sent to cover them, but he wasn't sure he'd ever seen her report on a story that didn't involve murder. Maybe that was why her tone was more serious than he expected. After interrogating Rachel on the pain and misery she must have suffered due to Scott's betrayal as if they were discussing a missing child, she resorted to arch skepticism over how quickly the romance between Roman and Rachel had blossomed. He figured she was on the hunt for any tidbit suggesting Rachel might have strayed as well. But Rachel played her part perfectly, always circling back to the talking points they'd both rehearsed.

Diana's silhouette was visible just behind the camera, arms crossed, tense as a coiled snake. But the glare of the hot lights concealed her expression, which Roman found a relief.

"All right," the reporter finally said, "it can't be easy starting a romance in the midst of all this...*intrigue*. So tell me, what's the happiest memory you two have shared together?"

Roman's heart raced with a new feeling, something other than nervousness. Something that took him back to Ethan's warm embrace in that San Diego hotel room as the scent of oncoming rain blew in through the open deck door.

He spoke before he could tell himself to stop.

"I think it was when we touched the sky."

The reporter's eyes met his. "I'm sorry, *the sky?*" she asked, smiling.

He shook his head. "I'm a certified paraglider pilot. It's something that's always made me really happy in my life. Something I've always wanted to share with the people that I really care about." He looked right at the camera lens. "The people I love."

Slowly, Diana lowered her arms to her sides as she took a step toward the camera, her face still lost to glare. But their interviewer looked charmed. He continued. "It seems like love, true love, is about sharing all your life and not one part of it. I mean, there's, like, wanting to share your body. Then there's wanting to share where you live. And then there's wanting to share your joy. That's what I did at the glider port in La Jolla a little while ago. That's probably my happiest memory ever. Teaching someone how to touch the sky."

Rachel reached across the distance between them, gripped his hand, and brought it to her knee. He couldn't tell if she was comforting him or warning him.

Then suddenly the interview was over.

As the crew broke down, Melanie removed his body mic. "Nice little improv you did there," she whispered. "That was sweet."

But as he strolled past her, Diana said quickly, "Upstairs once you're unhooked."

As soon as he stepped inside the house, a guard fell into step behind him, tailing him all the way to the staircase. Once the open door to his cell-like bedroom came into view, he saw Diana standing right inside the threshold, hands on her hips, blue eyes blazing. When he stepped into the room, she pushed the door shut behind him. "That was unwise."

"I don't know what you're talking about. Everyone said it was—"

"That was a story about you and that whore, wasn't it?"

Roman answered by looking at the hardwood floor between them.

"Great. That's just great, Roman. Now anyone who saw you two together in La Jolla could come forward and question everything about this interview. All of that work down the drain." She started for the door.

"Well, maybe if you'd let me talk to him I—"

Diana's eyes blazed with an anger he'd never seen in them before. "I said you could talk to him once we saw how the interview was received. But now that's all in doubt, thanks to your childish little stunt."

"I'm sorry," he muttered.

"You're not sorry, Roman. You're ungrateful."

He raised his eyes from the floor. "You're right," he said, even as he told himself to shut up. "I'm not sorry. It wasn't a stunt. It was a message, and he deserved to hear it after the way you made me leave him in San Diego."

He burned with a desire to confront her about the text message she'd ordered Hank to send Ethan, but Rachel was his source for that one, and he didn't want to get her in trouble.

"That man belongs nowhere near you, and someday you'll thank me for all this."

"Oh, I have something to thank you for already." *Don't, Romy,* he heard his best friend saying in his head. "You know, I used to judge my mom for not always hugging me and giving me nice presents and saying sweet things to me all the time. Then I met you and I realized someone can do all those things and still be a terrible person. So, thanks, Diana. Thanks for giving me my *real* mom back."

Diana's face turned to stone. For a second, he thought she might slap him. He also thought that the mask had finally dropped and he was seeing the natural expression of the woman who'd lived underneath all the smiles and pet names. And it scared him.

"And what would your *real* mother think about your new boyfriend?" she asked.

Roman was shamed silent.

"That's what I thought." She turned for the door. "Fingers crossed the interview comes off. Otherwise it's going to be a very long month for us all."

<hr>

Donnie drove up the night of Rachel and Roman's widely hyped *20/20* interview so Ethan wouldn't have to watch alone. To make up for the thank you dinner he'd never treated Donnie to in San Diego, Ethan knocked himself out in the kitchen. Beef Wellington, Donnie's favorite. By the time his apartment filled with the show's blaring theme music, they'd stuffed themselves like pigs. But they'd both left enough room for a beer as they settled down onto the sofa to watch.

Only those who knew Roman would have been able to tell how uncomfortable he was. To the rest of the world, his reticence and poise and reserve—such a far cry from his restless and joyful spirit—would have seemed like rehearsed maturity. All Ethan wanted to do was step through the screen and put his arms around him.

Then, suddenly, Roman was describing to an audience of millions the moment they'd shared above the La Jolla cliffs, no names or gender pronouns included. Ethan set the beer aside, brought his hands to his mouth, and sat forward. *The people I love...* The words closed the vast distance between them in an instant, as if suddenly it was just him and Roman, speaking to each other across the thousands of miles and millions of dollars being used to keep them apart.

"I take it that's something you guys did?" Donnie asked.

Ethan nodded.

Donnie nodded, but his jaw was quivering. "Sounds like he just used the L word on you, dude."

"You're crying?" Ethan asked.

"Bite me," Donnie croaked.

"Don't go soft on me, Sex Monster."

Donnie shot him the bird, then downed a slug of beer. As Ethan glanced to one side, he saw his best friend reach up and flick a tear from his cheek with the side of one fist.

The last portion of the interview was devoted to Diana, who was—of course—interviewed on her own and in a better location and with better lighting. She talked about how her betrayals at the hands of various men over the years—*Sure, Jan,* Ethan thought—had endowed her with reservoirs of wisdom she could share with her daughter during this trying time. File footage of department store displays featuring her various, top-selling products—all branded with her image—were used as B roll.

A few minutes after the interview ended, his phone rang.

It was Rachel. "I take it you got his message."

"I did. Where are you?"

"New York. I landed an hour ago. Listen, there's something I need you to know." He could hear her fidgeting with something that sounded like a pen or a small piece of jewelry. "Does the name Andy Rosales mean anything to you?" she asked.

"Yeah, Andy was his mom's last boyfriend. He's out in Victorville. Roman's storing a bunch of his stuff with him. Why?"

"I got a text from Hank when I landed."

"Hank the kidnapper?"

"He's trying to atone by giving me a tip. And the tip is that my mother got a tip after I left France. Andy Rosales has an interview scheduled with an LA news station tomorrow. He's going to tell them the last he heard from Roman he was trying to wind things down with my mom and now he can't get in touch with him, and he suspects something really fishy with this wedding."

"Like the truth."

Rachel took a bite of something crunchy, then quickly swallowed. "This Andy guy's got a record, Ethan. If he gives that interview, my mom's going to make mincemeat out of him in the press. Think Meghan Markle's dad times a hundred."

Ethan drained the last of his beer in several long swallows he never wanted to end. Unfortunately, they did. He had to clear his throat a few times before he could speak again. "Does your mother have anything else to do other than threaten to destroy people's lives?"

"She's got a PI on retainer. I don't want to think about how she's used him over the years. We need to stop Andy from giving that interview. Roman obviously cares about this man, and if my mom reacts, it'll hurt Roman even worse."

"Why won't your mom let Roman call Andy and give him some cover story to keep him quiet?"

"Because he's on probation after his *touch the sky* moment in the interview. She's not going to put him on the phone with anyone if she doesn't have to."

Ethan sighed. He could sense what she was asking of him. But the implications for Ethan were perhaps bigger than Rachel could understand in this moment.

Asking him to sit down with the boyfriend of the woman who'd probably blamed him for the death of her marriage.

But he owed it to Roman.

And he owed it to Roman's mother too.

"I'll try to get out there first thing in the morning and talk him out of it," he said. She read him the address, and he wrote it down with a pen.

"Good. Listen, I'm beat, so I'm going to…"

As he hung up, he could feel Donnie staring at him. He gave him a rundown of the call, and when he was done, Donnie took a long slug of beer. "Meeting the family. Wow. This is serious." He waggled his eyebrows.

"Yeah, that's one way of putting it," Ethan growled.

23

Ethan left Donnie sawing logs in his guest bedroom and made it to Victorville around dawn.

A fierce rising sun was cresting the limitless horizon to the east, its spreading orange light casting the surrounding landscape into sharp relief. In it, Ethan saw fleeting glimpses of young Roman exploring the vast dry expanses, visions that filled him with a longing for the man so acute he almost grabbed his chest.

He waited until 8:00 a.m., then he pressed the button on Andy Rosales's Ring cam. The one-story ranch style house needed a paint job, but most of its neighbors were trailers so it was the nicest place on the block by default. When he heard footsteps creaking floorboards inside, he took a step back. The man who opened the door looked like he could have stopped a tank with one hand raised in front of him, but he was dressed in a fuzzy bath robe and slippers that made him look like a big stuffed animal. His sleep-matted black hair was tied back in a loose ponytail, his face a mask of shock.

Not shock, Ethan realized. Recognition.

"Mr. Rosales, my name's Ethan Blake. I'm here about Roman."

The man slouched against the side of the door. "Why are *you* here about *Ronnie*?"

"I take it you recognize me."

"You're older, but yeah, I've seen your picture."

Ethan nodded. "I'm in touch with some of the people Roman's staying with, and I wanted you to know that he's okay. He might be—"

"He's not okay." Andy took a step out onto the porch. "I watched that interview. He's *not* okay. That wasn't him. I don't know what that woman's doing, but she's making him do something he doesn't want to do. Ronnie's never been interested in girls. Now he's marrying one? Come on!"

"You're right. But I *do* know how she's making him do it, so if I could come in…"

Turning his back, he gestured for Ethan to follow him inside. The entire place had the feel of a mancave, but its clutter was organized in neat piles, and the front room's furniture, while sporting a crazed rainbow of mismatched colors, looked comfortable and worn. On shelves right inside the front door, Ethan stopped cold at one of the framed pictures.

Lucy Russo—an older version of her with much shorter hair—smiling out at him from a black lacquer frame, a younger Andy leaning in close to her, one giant arm curved around her shoulders. Behind them, a neon-splashed bowling lane extended into the near distance. Her eyes were brown, but they had Roman's size and emotional depth. Then came several pictures of Roman as a teenager and a man close to the age he was now.

"Coffee?" Andy asked as he poured himself a cup.

"That would be great, thank you."

Andy nodded and poured. "I might take some whiskey in mine, if you don't mind. 'Cause you here at the crack of dawn, in the middle of all this? That's some fucked-up shit, if you'll excuse my language."

"So you've seen the file, I take it."

"How'd you know there was a file?" Andy handed him a steaming mug, then indicated for him to take a seat at a breakfast table piled with well-kept back issues of automotive magazines and a few copies of *Fish & Game*.

"Roman told me about it." He took a seat, but Andy stayed standing.

"Curiouser and curiouser." Andy returned to the counter, bit off what looked like half of a Pop-Tart, and chewed. "I told her to throw the damn thing away, but she said she liked to go through it at least once a year. It reminded her not to be so damn naïve. About men, about the world." Andy studied him. "She really loved him, you know. Thomas. Your *client*. He broke her heart."

Ethan managed a small sip of coffee, even though he'd felt like he'd been slapped. "I know this is weird," he said, "but I've got a very strange story to tell you. So perhaps I can give you the headline now in case you don't want to listen to the rest."

Andy gestured for him to continue.

"Diana Peyton knows you have a criminal record. If you give that interview today, she's going to use it to destroy you in the press."

In an instant, the man who'd been poised to judge had been brought down to Ethan's level.

He gazed out the window as he ate the rest of one Pop-Tart. Then he devoured the second one in several big bites quickened by a new anxiety.

"I did stupid shit with cars when I was a kid." He swallowed his last bite. "*Other people's* cars," he added. "Whatever. I did my time. I mean, I work with at-risk youth now, for Christ's sake."

"We all have a past," Ethan said quietly. "What do you do today? For a living, I mean."

The man sighed heavily. "I work on people's cars."

"Damn," Ethan said. "That would be like if I went into marriage counseling."

When Andy's eyes flashed to his, Ethan expected to see anger there. Instead, the guy's chest shook with laughter. "That's pretty damn funny," he said once he caught his breath. "You're funny."

"Thank you."

Andy tightened the fuzzy belt of his bathrobe and took a seat across from Ethan. "Tell your strange story. I want to hear every word."

By the time Ethan was done, Andy's jaw had gone slack, and his hands were resting weakly against the base of his coffee mug. After what felt like an eternally long silence, he said, "The glider port story. The one about La Jolla. That was you he was talking about, wasn't it?"

Ethan nodded.

"Only real part of that whole interview."

"Cancel yours, Andy. If you do it, you'll get hurt, and Roman doesn't want that for you, I'm sure."

He sighed and rested his hip against the kitchen counter. "So he's just going to go through with it and do the wedding and it'll be over? I mean that'll be the last thing this psycho lady ever wants from him?"

Ethan wanted to answer confidently in the affirmative, but he couldn't. He'd been tortured by the same thought ever since Roman had announced his plan to sleep with Scott Bryant.

"They're gonna have to have real wedding documents, right? He'll be signing stuff. He'll be a member of her freakin' family. If they don't do all that, someone's going to find out it's not real."

"I expect it will be a real wedding on paper."

Andy shook his head and drank his coffee. "I knew that woman was trouble, but I didn't want to say anything. That's how I was able to be in his life, you know. I didn't try too hard to be his dad. It was too late by the time I showed up. He was a teenager, so you know, I did the older buddy thing. I didn't boss him around. And I didn't need to. He was a good kid, emotional at times, but he's always been a good kid."

Ethan nodded.

"You love him?" Andy asked.

He felt Lucy Russo's eyes on his back and wondered which touches in the house she'd left behind. She hadn't lived here, but she'd probably considered it a second home and spent many nights under its roof. When he spoke, he realized he was addressing her as much as Andy.

"There's a spot on my sofa that still smells like his cologne. If I sit down on it, I can't get up for at least an hour, and I spend most of that time hearing his laugh and seeing the light in his eyes when he smiles."

Andy nodded, sipped coffee, nodded some more. "And clearly he wants you," the man finally said. "Otherwise he wouldn't be doing any of this. And you want him. So maybe I keep my mouth shut and mind my own business."

In the silence that followed, a question started to bubble up inside of Ethan that made his chest feel tight and hot, tensing his hand around the coffee mug's handle. He must have been wincing at the tension he was feeling because Andy was studying him closely all of a sudden. "What?" the man asked.

Ethan shook his head, trying to shed the question like a dog sheds rain. But he couldn't. "If she were alive today, do you think she could ever wrap her head around this? Me and Roman. Together. After everything."

"She was tough," Andy said. "It would have taken time, but... maybe."

Or maybe Andy was being generous with him. When Andy started to speak again, Ethan was startled.

"Ronnie was about fifteen when she found some stuff on the computer that made it pretty clear he was into dudes. And she figured enough time had passed that she should try to find his dad, see if he had any advice. She figured he'd finally come out of the closet, you know. That he was living his best life, and maybe he'd be able to tell her how she could support their son. But boy, was she wrong."

"Wrong how?" Ethan asked.

"He wasn't living with a man somewhere. He'd married another woman, but he'd met this one at church camp where they'd *de-gayed* him or something. At least that's what he said. He had some technical, religious term for it. But the point was, he wanted her to send Ronnie there too. He said he could save him. And boy, did she flip her lid. She told him that if he went anywhere near Ronnie she'd call the cops on him because he didn't have any kind of custody. She said no way was she going to let his shame get into their boy's head after everything she'd done."

"What *she* did?" Ethan asked. "What did she do? She didn't cheat on anybody."

Andy sighed and sipped his coffee. "It was about taking Ronnie into the city that night. She never forgave herself. She was trying to humiliate Thomas, but she said she never stopped to think about how it would affect her kid. And then fast forward, he's fifteen, it turns out he's got the whole gay thing in common with his old man, and she's sitting there wondering if what she did that night is going to make him feel worse about who he is."

"Did they ever talk again?" Ethan asked.

"Two years later. I told Ron I was taking his mom on a little vacation, but we went to see him. 'Cause he was dying. He wrote to her out of the blue. Told her he didn't have much time left and he wanted to see them both. But she wouldn't bring Ronnie, and I don't blame her. She was afraid it was a trap, that if she showed up with him, some of Thomas's crazy ex-gay friends would pop out of the woodwork and try to throw him in a van or something. So I went with her."

"You saw him?"

Andy nodded. "Yeah, I mean, I shook his hand, but mostly Lucy sat with him. He was in hospice by then. Shame was he'd met someone."

"Someone?"

"A guy. He'd left that nutjob group and actually started living with a man. He'd come to terms with who he was and then, boom. Pancreatic cancer. He finds out he's barely got any time left. He told

Lucy he understood why she didn't bring Ron. The trip was good for her. In the end, Thomas did her a solid. She was a different woman after that. Like it took her that long to accept that the whole thing wasn't her fault. That it hadn't been 'cause she wasn't pretty enough or loveable enough or sweet enough."

"And Roman doesn't know any of this?" Ethan asked.

Andy shook his head. "But please, let me be the one to tell him when he comes home. *If* he ever comes home. To answer your question, even before all that, she would have walked through fire for her boy. And so if you're the one he wants, she would have found a way to accept it. I'm not saying it woulda been quick or easy, but she would have found a way. You want to know what woulda really helped?"

"Yes," Ethan answered, wondering if he'd ever been as eager for an answer in his entire life.

"If you got him away from that damn woman and out of this damn mess," Andy said.

Ethan felt a focus and clarity he hadn't felt in days.

"On it," Ethan finally said.

24

The first few days after Roman's arrival, Diana's publicist had taken a dozen photos of him lounging around the house, then another batch of him and Rachel walking the gardens together as a hand-holding, happy couple. He figured they were posting them to his social media accounts during the run-up to the wedding. A smart move on their part, since he might have refused to pose for any after the blowup following his interview.

But it left Roman with blessed little to do during the final weeks of his captivity.

He worked up a sweat in the villa's state-of-the-art gym, occasionally convinced the security guards to accompany him off the property so he could go for a hike himself, and relieved himself each night to fantasies that he was back in Ethan's arms as they rode ocean swells or slept peacefully high above San Diego Harbor.

In the hours left over, he did something he'd never done before—he kept a journal.

It wasn't a daily chronicle of his life in Provence. Instead, he filled it with various versions of an exercise one of his fellow trainers at Apex had taught him years before. Gratitude lists, she'd called them. Lists of all the things in your life, ranging from the tiny to the grand, that you were grateful for—the beauty of a sunset you'd witnessed the night before, the fact that both your legs were in good working order, the taste of a warm croissant in the morning. Only the lists he made this time all had the same focus—his mother.

He detailed all the gifts, both large and small, she'd given him over the years—from the way she'd picked him up from school every day, never one minute late, to the used car she'd found for him at a steal once he got his license. The lists made his vision of his own past expand and grow warmer.

And if Diana got her hands on the damn thing and dared to flip through its pages, she'd simply be reminded of how much he'd come to despise her.

But as they neared the end of their stay, his chief captor spent less and less time at the villa. Shopping trips to various European cities. Jetting off to Paris to get fitted for her dress for the wedding. He caught a glimpse of the design, a strapless gold ball gown that puddled like drapes and came with a matching wrap. Intended, no doubt, to upstage her daughter and remind everyone who the real star was.

Halfway over the Atlantic, he was drifting off while watching a movie on one of the private plane's built-in screens—she'd still denied him the use of personal devices—when he heard his mother's voice speaking to him from someplace between dreams and memory.

You know, Ron. You're going to have a wedding of your own someday. The memory came back to him clear and vivid for the first time in years, no doubt stirred up by all the writing he'd done.

Freshman year of college he'd made his first rich friend since leaving Scarsdale as a child, a girl from San Francisco who lived in his dorm at Cal Poly and happened to be the daughter of tech billionaires. She'd asked him to be her platonic plus one for another rich friend's wedding at the Flood Mansion in Pacific Heights. He'd never been to San Francisco or a fancy wedding, and his mom reacted as if he'd gotten an engraved invitation from the queen of England. She'd excitedly ordered him to make the four-hour drive home so she could outfit him with a good rental. Then, when they arrived at the store, she'd surprised him with the news that she was going to buy him a tuxedo instead.

Never the most physically affectionate, once they'd found the right one and the tailor had marked it for alterations and loaded it up with pins, she'd primped him endlessly, adjusting the jacket and cummerbund with little bursts of fussy pride. Petting him like a puppy. He didn't mind. Lucy Russo was always happiest when fully engaged in a task. Focus and exertion relaxed her. The source of his restless nature, no doubt.

"You know, Ron," she'd said to him, her big brown eyes beaming up at him as he stood atop the fitting platform. "You're going to have a wedding of your own someday."

The topic sent prickles of tension racing up his neck.

He'd come out to her awkwardly and abruptly around the end of high school, mainly because she wouldn't stop asking if he and Nicki Garcia were more than friends since they spent so much time together. Finally, he'd blurted out that he couldn't be interested in Nicki that way because Nicki wasn't a boy. He'd been living in fear that his gayness put him in a terrible league with the dad who'd derailed their lives. Blurting it out the way he'd done had only made him feel worse. So what if his mother had simply nodded and said, "Well, all I want is for you to be happy, Ron. You know that."

He'd thanked her and made a hasty exit, but since then, the conversation had felt perpetually unfinished. He'd shared nothing with her about the few guys he'd dated—more like hooked up with—at college. So when the subject of weddings came up in the tuxedo store that day, his throat had gone quickly dry. "Yeah, I'm not sure I want to spend it in a monkey suit like this, Ma."

"Monkey suit? Come on, now. You look handsome as a prince in this thing. Although, you keep at it with the weights and you'll be bulging out all over the place like the Incredible Hulk. We might have to take it out or something."

He'd laughed, and she'd started fastening the bowtie around his neck. "Seriously, though," she'd said, "what kind of wedding do you want?"

"Nothing this fancy. Something outside, probably."

"Outside," she'd whispered, shaking her head. "Huge shock."

"I'll have an umbrella for you, though. 'Cause I know how you are about the sun."

"How about a tent? Most people go for a tent."

"Deal," he'd said.

She'd nodded and stepped back to admire the complete ensemble.

"I mean, you'll be there, right? For real?" he'd asked. There'd been a catch in his voice as he'd said it. It had felt like he'd stepped out to the edge of a cliff without a parachute. "Even if I marry a guy."

When her eyes had shot to his, he'd feared she'd storm out. Instead, she'd taken a step toward him and placed her hand on his cheek. "I want you to have whatever wedding you want, to whoever you want. And I'll be there with bells on no matter who it is. Unless he's a freakin' serial killer or something." When she'd kissed him on the cheek, it had felt suddenly like his messy little coming out scene had resolved itself. Then, quickly, she'd added, "Although, honestly, I don't think you're ever going to stay still long enough to get hitched, Restless Ronnie."

He'd laughed.

Forty thousand feet over Greenland, he laughed again. Then he remembered he was destined for a wedding he didn't want, and his laughter died.

They chased the sunset across the Atlantic, then most of North America, and by the time they touched down at John Wayne Airport, there was still pale light in the sky. On the tarmac, two different SUVs greeted them, the excuse being that Diana's dress, which had been hanging in the back of the plane for the entire flight, needed to lie flat across the backseat. But he was grateful for the separation.

He arrived at the Castle after she did. He refused to let the driver carry his bag, as if any assistance from someone paid by Diana might taint him.

Then he was alone. Alone and only miles away from Ethan, which somehow felt worse than being separated from him by an ocean. With the distance between them shrunk down to almost nothing, it was clear the only thing separating them was Diana.

The next day, it was Rachel who knocked on his door around 11:00 a.m. The wedding's first act would be a stroll on the beach with Diana and the *Vanity Fair* reporter writing her profile. When they went upstairs, the interview subject was alone in the sitting room. In the kitchen, Hank—to whom he couldn't bring himself to say a word even as the man repeatedly shot him guilty looks—and one of Diana's LA housekeepers who'd been brought down for the weekend, fussed over a coffee and tea service.

She saw him and stood, then moved to him and gripped him by both shoulders. Quietly, she said, "I trust that you'll give everything that comes next a hundred percent."

"Of course," Roman whispered.

She nodded, and then it was time to get to work.

He'd never been much of an actor. Never tried to be. But this time he dug deep, deeper than he'd dug for the interview, maybe because there was less of a script to guide him. Their role during the beach stroll was to be background for the weekend's true diva. And this gave him and Rachel little breaks to wander off on their own, where she talked to him about how he'd spent his time in France. When he asked her how Ethan was doing, her eyes glazed over, and he felt his heart skip a beat.

Eyes averted, she said, "We've figured out a way for you guys to be in touch, but it's risky, so just follow our lead, okay?"

The next evening, the rehearsal on the beach went off without a hitch. Of course, all the groomsmen worked for Diana's security team, and Rachel's maids of honor were distant cousins flown in from all over the country, most of whom she barely knew and all of whom had come looking for a handout. Arm in arm, he and Rachel made the rounds at the awkward cocktail party that substituted for a rehearsal dinner, and then, mercifully, Diana gave him a silent nod, indicating he was allowed to retire to his room.

Shortly thereafter, Rachel left for Sapphire Cove.

The customary separation of bride and groom the night before the wedding had commenced.

He didn't sleep a wink.

The closer he got to Ethan, the more the torture of not being able to talk to him, hold him, *love* him, became unbearable. And by the time they were headed to Sapphire Cove at 2:00 p.m. on the day of the wedding, he was in danger of gnawing his fingernails to the quick. As the SUV mounted the winding road that led to the resort's promontory, he heard his mother's voice again.

I want you to have whatever wedding you want, and I'll be there with bells on.

Silently, he said to her. *If you're watching, Ma, sit this one out, 'cause it ain't the real thing.*

They took a sharp left turn before the motor court, just enough time to glimpse the red carpet rolled out before a step-and-repeat covered in logos for Diana's product lines.

They entered through a loading door, then a startlingly tall hotel security agent, whose name tag read *Logan*, was escorting them through service corridors. Additional blazered security agents walked ahead of and behind them. They were whisked to the top floor by a service elevator that opened onto a housekeeping closet, then they were moving swiftly down a quiet and familiar carpeted hallway lined with guest room doors. He should have known where they were headed, but somehow seeing the words emblazoned on the double doors slugged him in the gut. He would be getting ready in the same place he and Ethan had first laid eyes on each other after eighteen years—the penthouse suite.

When Logan opened the doors, Roman's eyes went immediately to the silver-domed tray resting on the center of the dining table. His breath caught.

Logan said, "A gift from our executive pastry chef. Something special he does for all wedding couples."

Roman smiled and nodded, but inside he was melting.

When he lifted the tray, he found himself gazing down at the dessert in question along with a handwritten menu card describing its contents—in Ethan's handwriting. It was just like he'd said in this very room the night they'd been reunited—a special dessert meant to capture one of the happiest memories shared by the bride and groom. Only this memory was theirs—his and Ethan's.

Point Loma

Champagne jelly and accents of caviar—the Pacific
White chocolate and pandan—the coast
Kombu seaweed—the Shelter Island Marina

Out of medallions of white chocolate, Ethan had fashioned the San Diego coastline. Roman recognized its shape from when he'd done map searches for directions to the Torrey Pines Glider Port. At the top were the bluffs from which they'd launched. Then, just south, the round inward bend of the La Jolla Cove. The cove's southern shore came next, where they'd dined together at Jillian's before walking down to the surf line.

To his astonishment, Ethan had made a white chocolate shoreline that went all the way down to the finger of Point Loma. Just behind and to the right of it, the Shelter Island Marina, where Donnie docked his boat, was indicated by little cross hatches of seaweed. All told, the dessert was about half the length of Roman's arm. The detail was incredible and meticulous. He shouldn't have expected anything less from Ethan.

"He said to tell you white chocolate and caviar are actually surprisingly good together," Logan said. "Have a taste. Please."

Logan pulled out a chair, and Roman sat down in it. From the place setting nearby, he took a fork, and carefully, as if its tines were gathering up the most precious items in the world, brought a bite to his mouth that included a little of everything that had been used to create the confection. He hated to destroy it, but he knew the taste was what Ethan would want him to savor most.

When the flavors hit his mouth, his eyes closed, and he was in Ethan's arms aboard the *Golden Boy* as the ocean rose and fell gently beneath him and the sun glittered off the water and the limits of the everyday world felt abandoned on shore. A perfect memory. A happy memory.

See this part, Ma. I hope you're seeing this part. Because no matter our history, this man is the real deal.

"Shall I take your compliments to the chef?" Logan asked.

"Please," Roman answered quietly. "Tell him it's everything I hoped it would be."

"Congratulations, Mr. Walker," Logan said, then he left the room.

He'd been so entranced by the dessert he'd almost missed the can of Dr Pepper sitting next to it.

Suddenly, Hank was leaning in behind him. Before he'd realized what he'd done, Roman had reached up and grabbed the man's wrist, prepared to break it if the man so much as touched Ethan's gift. "I was just going to tell you," Hank said quietly, "there's more on the back. But I guess I deserve that."

When Roman released his wrist, Hank backed away, then quietly left, no doubt so he could stand guard outside the doors. Roman tried to make sense of the man's parting words, then he looked to the menu card he'd set aside and turned it over. There, on the bottom, in the tiniest version of Ethan's handwriting he'd ever seen were the words, *STRAP YOURSELF IN. WE'RE ABOUT TO TOUCH THE SKY.*

Was this what Rachel had meant by putting them in touch?

Would Ethan knock on the door in the next minute or find a way to crawl up the balcony? It seemed risky, given Diana and her accompanying journalist could come calling at any minute.

He searched the room—its cabinets, the top shelves of its walk-in closet—for any other message but turned up nothing.

The phones had been removed, so there was no calling in. And when the knock came a little while later, it was his tuxedo, escorted by members of Diana's LA security team he barely knew, all of whom had taken on the role of groomsmen and were now crowding into the suite to change. The only privacy he had left was in the spacious, marble-lined bathroom. There he took his time changing into the designer tux they'd fitted him for back in France. It probably cost ten times more than the one his mother had bought him years before, but when he finally put it on, it felt as sticky and uncomfortable as a wet suit.

Strap yourself in. We're about to touch the sky.

What did it mean? They were minutes from wedding time and no further word.

When he emerged from the bathroom fully dressed, he found his pretend groomsmen lounging around the suite, gazing glumly into their cell phones, with all the comradery of men recently thrown into a jail cell together. Then Hank stood, responding to a text on his phone. "Time to head down," he said.

It was a similar walk to the one that had brought them up to the suite earlier. Only when they reached the first floor, he heard a clamor just beyond the walls that rivaled the gathering crowd in an arena.

His heart raced with anxiety.

When the double doors before them were opened, he saw they were poised to cross a carpeted corridor and then enter the ballroom opposite. Silent signals were exchanged between Hank and the security guard manning the ballroom doors, and from inside, what sounded like a full orchestra began to play some classical tune he didn't recognize.

By the time he and Hank crossed the threshold of the ballroom together, it felt like his feet weren't touching the floor.

The ballroom's interior was so transformed that at first he didn't even notice the sea of faces staring back at him. At the end of each row of chairs, spindly, twinkling trees soared upward toward the ceiling, their inverted deltas of branches forming a single glittering canopy above the heads of all the attendees. Inside were more twinkling lights wrapped inside some kind of golden-hued taffeta-like fabric. Concealed above it were the ballroom's chandeliers, but it looked like they were aglow and giving the entire canopy a celestial backlight.

The altar ahead was a soaring wall of white roses. From overhead, a thick circle of wisteria garlands dangled, outlining where he and Rachel were supposed to say their vows like some floral recreation of the teleportation deck on *Star Trek*. Most of the faces he could see wore some version of an admiring smile. Many were familiar to him, but not because he'd ever met them before. They were actors and celebrities, a politician or two he'd seen on the news. The guest list was a who's who of famous people he'd never met.

In both back corners of the ballroom, camera crews had been set up on little stages made of scaffolding. And there, seated in the front row in a strapless gold ballgown he'd only glimpsed, sat Diana, watching him with hawklike precision to make sure he didn't miss a step. He smiled at her as he passed; she smiled in return. The minister was an old costar of hers from *Santa Monica,* once a prime-time stud, now a snowy-haired grandfather type who played serial killers on Lifetime.

Once he reached the altar, Roman turned, watching the rest of his faux wedding party process down the aisle in couples. Then, after a short pause, the wedding march began to play, and everyone rose to their feet. He felt his skin prickle on the back of his neck.

Diana was glaring at him.

His mind had wandered, and he'd gone numb. Obviously both things had revealed themselves in his expression. It was time to play his part.

And there was only one way to do it.

He imagined Ethan walking down the aisle toward him in a matching tuxedo, giving him that patient, comforting look that always made Roman go wobbly inside. Within a few seconds he'd managed to muster something that felt like semi-convincing tears.

Beneath her bridal veil, Rachel's smile was perfect but plastic. When she joined him at the altar, it felt like they were both trapped. His stomach lurched. For the first time since returning to Sapphire Cove, he wanted to run.

They turned to face each other.

"Please be seated," the minister said.

The attendees sank back down into their Chiavari chairs.

Then suddenly Rachel was holding both of his hands tenderly. "Showtime, Romy," she whispered.

And then everything went dark.

25

At first, Roman thought he'd passed out. But the low murmur that went through the crowd in response to the sudden blackout convinced him he was conscious. It was followed by voices.

Two loud, clear voices. Coming from everywhere and nowhere at once.

One of them was Rachel. But not the version of her holding his hands, standing barely a foot from him. This version had been recorded.

"...No, listen, Mom. Seriously, if I came out instead, you could do just as many interviews about it and get just as much press."

"No one will get it, Rachel. This isn't Twitter. They're not going to understand this bullshit about love languages and not wanting sex. It just doesn't make any sense to people. It's not something I can sell!"

Out of nowhere, a spotlight's halo slammed into Diana in the front row, so fiercely bright the attendees sitting beside and right behind her raised their hands to shield their eyes. The wedding hadn't suffered some massive technical failure. It had been hijacked. And Diana was now the star.

"*We'll* make *it make sense, Mom. That's the point. It's an opportunity for us. And the media will be all over it. Trust me. If we—*"

"*The* opportunity *here is for you to get married to someone everyone wants to* look at *and* sleep with. *Because marriage is a story people know and love. Not this* asexuality *craziness you keep trying to* push on me."

"I'm not pushing it on you, Mom. It's who I am!"

"Oh, for Christ's sake, Rachel. If you want one ounce of the career I've had, just learn your lines and hit your mark, all right?"

"So that you can get all the good press."

"Whatever! The only reason I ever slept with your father is 'cause he was a producer."

Diana was paralyzed, blinded, searching, it seemed, for her daughter through the spotlight's glare. Struggling, it seemed, to accept the fact that her only child had secretly recorded her. When it was clear the recording was at an end, she shot to her feet and opened her mouth, but just then, the spotlight swung away from her and toward the back of the room.

To Ethan.

He was dressed in his chef's uniform. In one hand, he held a wireless microphone.

"Good evening. My name is Ethan Blake." His powerful voice filled the vast ballroom, but he had to pause lest he be drowned out by the sound of three hundred people quickly turning in their chairs at once. Even as all eyes in the room were on him with suspicion and alarm, he looked calm and steady, the confidence coming off him and wafting down the aisle, enfolding Roman in its embrace. "And I'm here to tell you that the two people standing at the altar tonight are not up there because they love each other or because they want to be. They're up there because Diana Peyton is forcing them to be."

Slowly, the lights had started to come up again in the ballroom, revealing a sea of stunned faces and slack jaws. "*Hank!*" he heard Diana whisper fiercely off to one side.

Roman looked to Hank, standing next to the stage in the best man's position. He and the rest of Diana's team should have been moving down the aisle to wrestle Ethan to the ground. But they hadn't budged.

"*Hank!*" Diana hissed again. The man didn't move.

"They're up there at the altar because Diana Peyton is using me and my past against them."

Stunned, Roman realized what Ethan was about to do and he started moving toward the steps. "No, no, Ethan. Don't, Ethan, she'll—"

Rachel grabbed him by the elbow. "Let him do it, Romy," she

whispered. "Let him do this for you." But her whisper carried throughout the ballroom. Someone had turned up their body mics.

Ethan continued toward the altar, all eyes on him. "They're up there to protect me. To protect my job. And so fifteen minutes ago, I tendered my resignation from Sapphire Cove so that I could tell all of you the truth about this wedding."

"Ethan, *don't!*" Roman wailed.

"Listen to Roman, Ethan," Diana growled.

Instead, Ethan walked to the edge of the front row, microphone to his mouth, glaring at Diana with an intensity that brought the room's full focus to him. The uncompromising intensity of his stare and the few feet of distance between them froze Diana and brought an electrified silence to the entire ballroom.

"Between the ages of twenty and twenty-five, I was a sex worker in New York City, an escort. My clients paid me to have sex with them and more. Diana Peyton got her hands on information proving this, and she used it to blackmail Roman Walker and her daughter into this marriage so she could use the wedding for her own publicity purposes."

As she realized how little he'd omitted from this account, Diana sank back down into her Chivari chair as if she'd been pressed into it by a giant hand.

"And she was able to do it because Roman and I are in love," Ethan continued, "and he wants nothing more than to protect me from a boss who extorted him and kidnapped him to make this night happen. And so I'm doing what I have to do to show Roman that I love him as much as he loves me, so it can't be used against him anymore." Ethan turned toward the altar. "Roman Walker, the man Diana Peyton has used as a tool and a prop, has protected me, stood up for me, unlike anyone else I've ever known, and this has made him one of the bravest and most beautiful men I will ever know. And he's done more for me in the last month than anyone else I've ever met. But I won't let this go any further."

"These are lies!" Diana screamed. "These are *filthy* lies!"

"They're not." Rachel's voice boomed through the room—a stage actor's ability to project backed up by a body mic buried in the folds of her wedding gown. Diana spun toward the altar.

"They're not lies," Rachel said. "It's the truth. Every word of it."

Diana looked devastated by her daughter's betrayal, and her

confirmation was apparently what the crowd needed to fully believe Ethan's confessions.

"You should be ashamed of yourself. And if this is what the final act looks like, I don't want an *ounce* of your career."

Diana spun to face the crowd, studying their shocked and disapproving looks. She shook her head as if she was judging the crowd in return. "He's a whore!" she screamed. "He was a *goddamn whore!*"

There was a brief, stunned silence before Rachel broke it. "Not sure someone who only slept with my dad to get a role should be that judgy on that topic, but whatever, Mom."

A new sound filled the room.

Laughter.

Rachel had stolen the show.

After a series of shocks, Roman still wasn't prepared for what came next.

Diana took off. By the time she reached the nearest set of doors, one of the camera crews had decamped from their stage at the back of the room and was blocking her exit. The second crew got tangled up with it, and suddenly Diana, fighting against the glare of their camera lights, was swinging her arms, batting her way through them. "Get away from me!" she screamed before she managed to burst through.

He caught one glimpse of her turning down the hallway as the cameras chased.

"Get away from me!" she screamed again, loud and shrill enough to make many of the attendees wince. Then, the lower part of her gown gathered in both hands, she ran.

In the stunned silence that followed, Roman looked down and saw a familiar woman crouched next to the altar, trying to get Rachel's attention. She wore a pants suit, and her wiry gray hair was pinned back on her head with a jeweled barrette. In one hand, she held a scribble-covered notepad. The *Vanity Fair* reporter who'd been at the rehearsal the night before. "Hi, uh, Rachel, real quick. This is all real, right? Like this isn't some hoax or something?"

"All real," she answered, then she reached up, yanked off her veil, and tossed it aside.

But now all Roman could see was Ethan. Ethan approaching the altar just like he'd imagined him doing moments before as Rachel had walked down the aisle. Suddenly they were standing face to face.

"Told you to strap yourself in." Ethan kissed him gently on the lips.

"I can't believe you did it," Roman whispered, tears coming.

"You cry a lot, Roman Walker." Ethan smiled and whisked tears from Roman's cheeks with his fingers.

"You make me cry. For all the right reasons."

Rachel leaned in. "Um, guys, just so you know, they can still hear everything you're saying on Roman's body mic." The crowd was watching them intently.

"So are you guys going to get hitched instead?" A new voice asked this question, and when Roman turned, he saw Hank staring up at them. Hank, who'd told him about the secret message written on the back of the menu card earlier. Hank, who'd refused to order the team to wrestle Ethan to the floor. Like Rachel, he'd been in on this plot all along.

"Wow." Ethan gulped and looked from Rachel to Hank. "I mean, there was a lot of planning that went into this, but nobody really thought about what would happen with the actual, you know, wedding. I mean..." He looked to Roman, trying to read his eagerness to tie the knot right there on the spot. "Eventually, maybe. I mean. Just not sure the mood right now is—"

"This isn't my kind of wedding anyway," Roman finally said.

"Let me guess," Ethan whispered, taking him in his arms. "Outside? With the wind in your hair?"

"And yours," Roman whispered. "But there's one part we can do now."

He pulled Ethan in for the kiss he'd dreamed of giving him for a month.

There were some shocked gasps, but mostly what followed was a building swell of applause and several hundred versions of *What in God's name is happening?*

When they broke, Ethan dug into Roman's jacket and disconnected his body mic. He felt a tug and saw Rachel had pulled it from his hand. To Roman, he whispered, "We're about to have a hundred reporters all over us, so now's the part where we touch the sky. Take my hand, baby."

Roman obeyed, and suddenly they were rushing down the aisle together.

"Play some kind of wedding thing!" Rachel shouted behind them.

The orchestra responded by taking up the wedding march. Because nobody in attendance knew quite what else to do, large sections of the crowd rose to their feet and applauded.

"Wait," Roman shouted to Ethan as they ran. "We didn't just get married for real, right?"

"No. Everyone's just very confused," Ethan answered. "Keep going!"

As they did, Roman realized the hotel's security team had cleared a path before them, but when they entered the carpeted corridor, he saw one of the camera crews that had chased Diana out of the hotel had returned. It was racing toward them, camera lights a shocking wall of white. Then he and Ethan were racing through the bowels of the hotel, past offices and storage rooms and electrical closets. The next thing he knew, they were outside, running through a tunnel-like corridor past a security booth that he figured was the hotel's employee entrance.

A familiar SUV squealed to the curb. Ethan practically hoisted him into the backseat, and suddenly they were blissfully tangled in each other's arms as it sped away from the curb. When he looked up, he saw another camera crew racing down the hillside toward the employee entrance. But they were shrinking through the back window and entirely on foot.

"All right, you guys haven't seen each other in forever, so feel free to get as freaky as you want back there." Donnie was driving. "I promise not to look. But please, no bussy action 'till I get you home."

They fell into a kiss that made Roman feel like he was floating up and out of his body, but somehow still in Ethan's arms, as they left the nightmare of the past month far below.

The minute they stumbled together into his apartment, Ethan began tearing the studs from the front of Roman's tuxedo shirt, groping through the fresh openings for his smooth, muscular skin. Kissing him like shared oxygen would make them both immortal.

Roman, he thought, *home, mine again. Mine always.*

He felt like he was laying claim to another man for the first time, maybe because Roman was the first man he'd ever saved.

As they fell against the side of the island in his kitchen, Roman breathed deep, nostrils flaring, eyes twinkling. Chewing his bottom lip, he steadied his hands enough to undo the buttons on Ethan's chef's jacket, then fell to his knees and started unbuttoning Ethan's pants.

Ethan yanked him to his feet, bringing their mouths together again. "My bed," he said. "Finally in my bed."

They hit the mattress, and as Ethan tried to take control, Roman got the one up on him and flipped him onto his back, freeing his cock, devouring it in a wet frenzy. He'd been almost instantly, throbbingly hard when his shaft met open air. Now he was dangerously close to an eruption. Roman sensed it, tasted it, it seemed, and pulled off. He sprang to his feet, tore his pants off, then his briefs. There were a few studs left in the top of his shirt, and his bowtie was still in place, but he went for the nightstand drawer in a hungry rush.

"Lower," Ethan said.

Roman pulled open the little door below and found the bottle of lube. Eyes locked on Ethan's, he poured a thin stream of it across Ethan's jerking cock, spreading it with several firm strokes. Then, a hungry smile on his face, he swung one leg over Ethan's body, positioning himself for swift entry.

Ethan watched in amazement as Roman sat back on his haunches, hand behind him, guiding Ethan in, just skin and heat and lube. Watched the telltale dance of hungry surrender play across Roman's face, the flash of surprise, the furrowed brow and parted gasping lips, followed by the sharp intake of breath as he sat back on the fullness of him. Then he looked to Ethan, eyes glassy with lust, smile growing again, as he began to rock, to ride.

Ethan loved that Roman's bowtie was still in place, his tuxedo shirt reduced to two sweaty dangling flaps, like prison manacles broken and defiled. The parody of Diana Peyton's sham wedding blown to bits as every raw inch of him slid inside the first man for whom he'd been willing to risk it all.

Holding to Ethan's shoulders with both hands, Roman accelerated his thrusts, a wild light in his eyes, building speed and strength until it felt like Ethan was the one being topped by Roman's thrusting muscular power coupled with his willingness and hunger. They fucked like they had no time at all, when the truth was, now they had nothing but time and each other. Time to reclaim all that had almost been stolen from them.

"Roman…" He was close, and he'd filled his tone with warning.

"Flood me," Roman said. The words themselves were pure porn star, but the tone was pleading and eager.

"Roman…"

"Breed me, Ethan. Make me yours."

That was all it took. He yowled as his hips went molten and his balls jerked. He couldn't remember the last time he'd unleashed himself in another man like this. Couldn't remember the last time a man had laid him flat and taken control and drained him of all fear and fight. Because no other man ever had. Only Roman. Roman, who shuddered now at the feel of Ethan's seed filling him, whose cock jerked in response, who only needed to stroke himself once or twice before he was jetting all over the T-shirt Ethan hadn't had time or the willingness to tear off.

Their mouths met, but their attempt at a kiss turned into shared breathlessness.

It took them a while to part. For Roman to slide forward and then off him. When he fell to the comforter next to him, Ethan tenderly unfastened his bowtie, then removed the few remaining studs from his shirt until Roman was gloriously naked beside him, one arm and leg looped over Ethan's body.

"What did you do, Ethan?" he asked softly, stroking Ethan's hair back from his forehead, but his voice was full of wonder. "What did you do?"

"Set you free."

"How long have you been planning this?"

"Rachel told me Andy was going to go the press and say he hadn't heard from you and Diana was going to try to destroy him. I went to talk to him."

"You met Andy?" He sounded as thrilled as he did surprised.

"That's when I realized I had to do this for you and for your mom. Because Andy knew the same thing I did. This was never going to end with her. Once you'd legally joined her family, she'd see you like she owned you. But there was another reason."

"Yeah?" Roman asked.

"This was the only way we could be together without secrets."

"You can't be with anyone if you're not being yourself, right?" Roman caressed the side of Ethan's face.

"And another thing," Ethan whispered. "Andy said this is what your mother would have wanted me to do, and so I did it."

A kiss this time that seemed to last forever, followed by the delicious feel that Roman's hard body was melting into his.

And so they lay together. Unhurried, unrushed. Free.

When Ethan heard the helicopter outside, he prayed it would pass over his building with a dull roar. It didn't. Somewhere in the sky nearby, it hovered.

"I hope my mom didn't watch us bang just now," Roman said.

Ethan jerked. "Wait, *what*?"

"Nothing. I was just talking to her in my head earlier, 'cause she always wanted me to have the wedding I wanted and in my head I said, *Don't watch tonight, Ma, 'cause this ain't the real deal.* Then I got your dessert and I said, *Watch this part, Ma. 'Cause whatever our history, this man is the real deal.*"

Their mouths met in a leisurely kiss. Outside, a new sound had joined the helicopter's buzz. Low voices in hurried conversation. It sounded like they were coming from the sidewalk below his balcony. He expected them to pass by. They didn't. They gathered and grew louder.

"What are you going to do for work?" Roman asked.

"We'll see. It'll be the beginning of an exciting new chapter." He caressed the side of Roman's face. "I found a place in San Diego. It's a little bit bigger, but it's actually cheaper. And since you're going to need a place to live, I thought maybe you could come with me. I mean, the lease is month to month but..."

"An exciting new chapter," Roman whispered, "together?"

"Correct," Ethan said and kissed him gently on the lips.

"I'd go anywhere with you, Ethan Blake. But..." Roman smiled, slid from the bed and picked his underwear up off the floor.

Ethan wasn't quite sure where he was heading until he looked back over his shoulder and smiled, then he pulled the drapes apart. Sure enough, a news helicopter hovered overhead, angled right at Ethan's building. Reflecting off the balcony's glass wall were the camera light flares of news crews gathered below.

"What are we going to do about them?" Roman asked.

"Who cares? We've got nothing to hide anymore."

Roman nodded, then he slid the deck door open and pranced out onto the balcony, swinging his hips proudly. More camera lights flicked on. Roman raised one arm and waved at them like a passenger on a departing cruise ship. "Hey there!" he yelled. "Just thought you guys would like to know we just had sex. And we're probably going to have a lot more because we're totally in love. Good night!"

Some of the reporters where shouting questions as Roman pulled the sliding door shut with a squeal, followed it with the drapes, then threw himself back onto the bed and into Ethan's arms.

26

The next day, Ethan regretted having been so cavalier about the media. While it was true he and Roman had nothing left to hide, they'd also turned the celebrity wedding of the year into an altogether different and more dramatic story, which made it impossible to get from point A to point B without a hundred cameras being shoved in their faces.

After an aborted attempt to reach Ethan's new apartment in San Diego, the two of them sought refuge where cars full of reporters couldn't follow—at sea, aboard the *Golden Boy*, which Donnie, who'd wisely kept his license plate covered up the night before, piloted all the way to Catalina Island as Ethan checked the skies for helicopters and drones.

One day anchored off the dry, grassy mountain of land turned to three, thanks to the little skiff Donnie used to get supplies from the island's shops while Ethan and Roman stayed hidden on board. For the most part, they kept the *Golden Boy* away from the more popular harbor, spending the daylight hours cruising the more remote southern shore. At night, Donnie scrolled the headlines and read them updates.

Diana had fled the country the night of the wedding. But not to France, apparently. The security company she'd hired there had released an ass-covering public statement claiming they didn't have the slightest idea Roman Walker had been held under duress at her villa in Provence, and they were ceasing all business operations with her immediately. Two different department stores dropped her product lines, a development which shocked Ethan silent when Donnie read it aloud. He'd expected the woman to suffer some level of blowback, but nothing that extreme.

In the court of public opinion, the former sex worker had faced off against the once-beloved diva, and the sex worker was winning.

Maybe a contempt for blackmail was universal.

No doubt, they had Rachel to thank.

She'd stayed behind to face the cameras, even going so far as to hold an impromptu press conference in Sapphire Cove's motor court while baffled guests streamed out the doors past her, some wondering aloud on camera whether they would still be getting free food and drink even though the wedding had effectively been canceled. In the days that followed, and with the even temperament of a seasoned politician, Rachel gave interviews on everything from the nuances of her asexual identity to the specifics of why she'd personally decided to defy her mother after years of obedience. "She went too far, and she did it with someone I care about, someone I hope to always call a friend," she said more than once.

After three days of watery isolation, Donnie's work obligations could no longer be avoided, and they had no choice but to head back to the mainland.

As they sailed the open sea for the second time that week, Roman in his arms, the ocean winds blowing across them both, Ethan felt confident he could face whatever was to come. His life felt as upended as when he'd left Charleston for New York. With one big and wonderful difference—Roman. This time he wasn't alone. And he had some money in the bank.

Instead of his usual slip at Shelter Island, Donnie had taken the added precaution of renting one at Mission Bay, a little way north. Waiting for them at the dock was a surprise Ethan had arranged for Roman—Andy Rosales, who hopped aboard the boat and enfolded Roman in a powerful bear hug that lifted the guy's feet off the deck.

A short while later, Ethan made them all lunch as they drifted just outside the entrance to La Jolla Cove, the glider port and its little insect cloud of paragliders within view just to the north. As Ethan cooked, Andy shared with Roman everything about the attempts his mom had made to bring his father back into his life, and then to protect him from the man, which, as Ethan had expected, left Roman crying softly in his arms.

For the next few days, the boat was all theirs during business hours, so they wiled away the hours filling the forward berth with their sweaty passion. Making up for lost time. Then, around day six, the freedom of the open sea started to feel like a kind of confinement for them both. Especially Restless Roman—the man who lived to hike and run and bike and fly. Donnie's reports each day from the studio didn't include any mentions of reporters or strange, lurking vehicles. It was time to take a risk. Make some attempt to return to real life.

But this time when they docked, the men walking toward their slip were a surprise to him and Roman both. Even though they were about an hour and a half south of their place of business, Connor Harcourt and Logan Murdoch were dressed in work attire—dress shirts and blazers bearing the hotel's gold emblem.

"May we come aboard, Captain?" Connor asked.

Ethan nodded and extended his hand, and a few moments later, the four of them were standing inside the galley kitchen and out of the sun.

"How are things, Mr. Blake?" Connor asked.

"The way they need to be."

Connor nodded. "Did you have another position lined up before you sent me your resignation?"

"Once we're a bit more settled, I plan to reach out to former colleagues, past contacts. Explain my situation in light of my public disclosures. If their opinion of me has changed, better that I know."

Connor nodded, then he looked to Logan, who had been looking mostly at the floor since they'd come aboard. "You involved my fiancé in your escape plan without involving me. That's made for an interesting moment in our engagement."

"Plausible deniability, babe," Logan said softly.

"I apologize for that," Ethan said. "But I figured there was no way to do what I needed to do unless I had a plan to stop Diana's security team once I started down the aisle."

"But you didn't need to," Connor said. "I heard one of her own defected. Hank, or something. He gave an interview and said he lined up jobs for half the other guys in case she fired them on the spot. And then they quit anyway."

"I also involved Chloe and my team so they could take over everything seamlessly. I trust that's happened?"

Connor raised an eyebrow. "I'm not sure *seamless* is a word I'd use to describe any of this."

"I understand, but I hope they're not in trouble. My goal was to do right by the hotel, given the circumstances."

Connor nodded and waved Ethan's concerns away with one hand. "Your team did fine. They'll be fine. Don't worry. The hotel's survived worse. I mean, honestly, it was a great ad for the Dolphin Ballroom. The place looked amazing in all the footage, and we've been getting tons of bookings so…" Connor smiled, and then an easier silence settled. "Did you think I'd judge you? Is that why you didn't come to me? I could have helped you figure out a way to weather it."

"I appreciate that. But I didn't need to weather it. I needed to set Roman free. My secrecy was her power. My only choice was to take it away."

Nodding at the floor, Connor was clearly struggling with whatever he had to say next. "I was really hoping to drive down today and tell you I didn't accept your resignation. But I met with the bank and…"

When Connor looked him in the eyes, Ethan saw the shine of tears in them.

"I couldn't get you your job back, Ethan."

"I didn't want to put you in that position."

"I tried, though. Boy, did I try." He swallowed, managing to hold his tears at bay. "But I couldn't make them see it the way I do."

"How do you see it?" Ethan asked. He wasn't in the habit of asking anyone for their opinion of his sex work, and so the question left him anxious.

"Like this whole thing is just another way to punish a queer man for coloring outside the lines," Connor finally answered. "It was an ugly meeting, to be frank. They made threats they'd never made before. So did I. In the end, I'm not sure my strategy of accusing most of the men in the room of having hired a sex worker at some point in their lives was my best choice. But it made for a great exit line. Their reasoning was that it wasn't the substance of your past, it was the manner in which you revealed it. Perhaps there's some truth to that.

"But *my* truth is that I don't really give a shit. And the bank's actual truth is that the trust manager we've worked with for years left a few months ago, and the new guy's trying to cut pennies from quarters. I can't get anything out of him for improvements, and we've been fighting tooth and nail for months. I've started a search for someone to buy out the bank's interest in the trust, but that'll take months at least. Probably years. Too long to get you your job back any time soon."

Had Ethan nourished some small hope that Connor would try to save his job? Perhaps, given the man's history with blackmail and scandal. Whatever the size of that hope, now was the time to let it flicker out. And the four of them were quiet for a while.

Ethan felt it was his turn to speak and that a simple thank you wouldn't suffice. "Connor, I hope it doesn't diminish my time with you and Sapphire Cove to say this. But maybe it'll make you feel better to know that I'm happier than I've ever been." He took Roman's hand. "I'm all the versions of myself in one. I'll never have to look over my shoulder again, and I'm with a man who makes me feel like I can touch the sky." He slid his arms around Roman's shoulders and pulled him close. "There's having your dreams come true and then there's getting things you didn't know to dream. That's how I feel."

Connor's smile seemed genuine. "I must say, Mr. Walker, my opinion of you is much improved."

"Good," Roman said. "'Cause I've been working on improving."

"One other thing, though," Ethan said. Connor nodded. "Let Logan off the hook."

Connor sputtered his lips and waved a hand through the air. "Please. He went two whole days without his morning blow job. He'll be fine."

"Babe," Logan groaned.

"Also, we have a very effective way of him working off debts," Connor continued.

Logan winced, and his broad shoulders rose and fell with a deep, strained breath. "Babe, *please*."

Connor grinned. "I make him do housework naked. I love it. I mean, you wouldn't think I would because I'm a total power bottom, but when he's got a sponge in hand, something about my big bulky boyfriend down on his knees really works for me." Connor waggled his eyebrows. When he saw Logan's grave expression, he added, "What? I can talk about all this stuff with him now because he doesn't work for us anymore."

Logan nodded, nostrils flaring, still blushing.

"I appreciate you delivering this news in person," Ethan said.

"We're not done," Logan said. "There's a car waiting outside. Come on."

And with a nod of his head, Logan seemed to take command of the situation.

It was a clear, sunny day, and the streets of La Jolla's Village were filled with elegantly dressed women toting armloads of shopping bags. The Village was largely free of high rises, and the picturesque storefronts along Girard were housed inside quaint, one-story buildings with sloping rooflines. Jonas waited outside one as if standing guard, and when a Sapphire Cove branded Suburban pulled to the curb, he stepped forward and opened the front passenger side door for his boss.

"Good afternoon, Mr. Harcourt," he said cheerily.

"Greetings, traitor," Connor responded with a smile, then he started for the papered-over glass doors of the storefront behind him.

When Ethan stepped from the back, he took Jonas by the elbow. "It hasn't been too rough, has it?" he asked.

"A little ribbing," Jonas said. "He'll get over it. Nobody was fired, so we're fine. Mostly he's furious with the bank."

Relieved, Ethan helped Roman down from the backseat, and Logan squeezed out behind them. Then they were all walking into the cool, air-conditioned space beyond the papered-over windows. It was immaculate and empty. Custom display shelves covered both walls. And through a back door, he glimpsed an expansive, restaurant-style kitchen. Out of which came Rachel and Donnie, who stopped and smiled when they saw him.

"Boys!" Rachel cried before throwing her arms around them both in turn. They'd spoken to her several times over the past few days as she'd untangled control of Roman's social media accounts from her mother's team. But it wasn't like Roman was about to post any time soon. Diana still had his phone somewhere in her possession, and Rachel didn't seem to have it with her. Ethan thought that was for the best. For now. The phone could be used to locate him. Let Diana fend off the resulting press attention if she couldn't bear to part with the thing.

When they parted, an awkward silence descended. Ethan realized all eyes were on him. He looked to Roman for an explanation, but he shook his head, clearly as stumped as Ethan was.

"What is this place?" Ethan finally asked.

"It's yours," Rachel answered. "I'm offering them a year's rent upfront. That's how I outbid some old witch whose husband invented antivirus software or something. She wanted to open a jewelry store in this place, and I was like, 'No, I don't think so, ma'am.' This location is primo. So it's mine if I want it. If you guys want it." She gestured to Connor and Logan. "And right here, I've lined up your first account."

Connor nodded. "Sapphire Cove would be more than honored to sign a one-year contract for...whatever it is you manage to produce here. Preferably something sweet."

"Two years," Donnie interjected.

Connor shot him a look. "Fine. Two years."

"Three," Donnie added.

Logan said, "Stick to porn and leave the agenting to the grown-ups, Donnie."

"Fine. Four," Donnie said.

Logan shook his head. "Not how that works."

"Wait a minute," Ethan said. "What's going on? What do you think this place is going to be?"

"Yours!" Donnie barked, moving toward him. "Come on, dude. Wake up and ride the guilt train for as long as you can. This is going to be your bakery, your store. And it's in La Jolla." Donnie patted him on the chest with one palm. "So it's going to be as fancy as you think you are."

Ethan's eyes found Rachel's. "One year's rent in La Jolla is a lot of money."

"Please," she answered. "It's the least I can do. I should have raised a red flag the minute she tried to pimp Romy out to Scott. You have no idea the responsibility I feel here. So like Donnie said, ride the guilt train. You've earned it."

Roman went to her and put his arms around her.

Ethan hated what he had to say next, but there was no way around it. "Is it just your money that's going to pay the rent here?"

Rachel and Roman parted. She held Ethan's gaze as her expression lost its tender smile. "A little of both, to be honest. But it's nothing like an investment. She wrote me a check upfront for her portion."

"And she had no terms at all?"

Rachel waggled one hand in the air as she scanned the empty space around them. "I might have promised not to fund a case against her for extortion. Even though a considerable portion of the Internet thinks I should do exactly that." Rachel wandered over to the counter where a register might go, running her finger along its edge. "She called me three days after. She was out of her mind, so I took the call. I expected her to threaten me, but instead she pulled a whole mental health thing. I wouldn't call her contrite, but she's not fighting.

"She's going to a therapist. A real one, not just one who doles out prescriptions by request. So if there's even the smallest chance she's going to finally work on some of her issues, I'm going to stand by her while she does it. She's paying a heavy price for what happened, and she should. But if she can call me asking for help after I exposed her to the world, then I'm the last thing to go. Like I said, she's the only mother I've got, and right now, I'm all she's got. So if that doesn't work for you, I get it. But if you let me make this right, I promise I'll never put either of you in her path again."

She'd followed through on every promise she'd made as part of their plan to thwart the wedding. Despite the anger he still felt in his heart toward Diana Peyton, her daughter's conviction to stand by her, to give her the chance to change, seemed admirable. And he had no reason not to trust her. No reason, it seemed, not to consider Rachel a part of his family.

And then there was Roman, gazing at him with those big, beautiful hazel eyes that always broadcast his heart to the world.

"*Sucre vérité,*" Ethan finally said.

"What's that?" Roman asked.

"It means sweet truth, and it reminds me of you," Ethan said. "And that's what we're going to call this place." Then he pulled Roman in for a big kiss as everyone applauded lightly.

And, of course, when he pulled back, Roman had tears in his eyes.

"Why are you crying, baby?"

"'Cause it's like they're your family now."

Ethan kissed him gently on the lips. "Our family," he corrected him.

Epilogue

Three Months Later

When they stepped out onto the canopied terrace of their suite at the Hassler Hotel, Roman gripped Ethan's hand and said one word under his breath. "Rome."

As if the name itself was so resonant with meaning, it needed no further detail.

"Rome," he said again, as if he were tasting something sweet and rich. He pulled Ethan to him. "We're in Rome," he whispered against Ethan's lips before they kissed.

And Ethan felt a surge of pride for having kicked in extra for the hotel room and its stunning view. Perched atop the Spanish Steps, the Hassler offered sweeping views of the Eternal City's sea of domes and cupolas, now turning gold-edged in the light of dusk. Denis Michel, the designer label that had lobbied vigorously for Roman to be the centerpiece of their latest men's formal wear campaign, had paid their airfare—and after Ethan's steady agenting, coughed up a model fee big enough for Roman to take over half the rent on their new apartment without tapping into the cash he'd made off the sale of his mother's house after the return of her trust. The bakery wouldn't be open for another few months, so they were able to pad the trip with some time spent exploring the city.

Two days of city walks and jet-lag naps later, they were standing in a fenced-off area of the Colosseum, hemmed in by bright lights and a row of folding director's chairs as Roman, clad in a series of elegant, brightly-colored tuxedos that looked almost like a gay pride version of the one Ethan had torn from his beautiful body the night of the wedding, struck a series of poses that ranged from the elegant to the tiger-like.

Photo shoots, Ethan learned as he played the role of dutiful boyfriend, were shockingly tedious affairs, and everyone on the crew was impressed with Roman's patience and professionalism.

After the Colosseum came a day of shooting at Trevi Fountain, followed by the Spanish Steps, just below their hotel. Then their time was their own again, the city theirs to explore.

There was only one event left on their schedule.

And only Ethan knew about it.

But Roman had his suspicions, and at dusk one night as they lay entwined on one of the cushioned loungers on their suite's balcony, Roman asked, "Want to tell me why you told me to bring my own tux?"

"Nope."

"Or why you brought one too?"

"Tomorrow night we're headed to the opera," Ethan said and enjoyed the sight of Roman's jaw going slack and his eyes going wide. "*Turnadot.* Your mother's favorite."

"The opera," Roman said, his voice thick.

"You're gonna cry," Ethan said.

"I'm not. Shut up."

"You're crying. I knew you'd cry if I told you."

Roman sank back down onto Ethan's chest. "I'm *gently* crying."

"And that's just fine. I love that you're my big muscle-bound boyfriend with a soft, gooey center."

"I'm not a pastry, Ethan."

"Maybe not, but you're good enough to eat."

Which he did a fair amount of later that night and the following day.

As they walked with crowds of operagoers toward the stark façade of the Teatro dell'Opera di Roma, Ethan's heart was in his throat. Inside, the theater was several stories of gold gilt and red velvet, with four rows of boxes ascending toward the domed, frescoed ceiling. He'd reserved them a box on the second level. With one hand on the small of his back, he gently ushered Roman ahead of him into their box, heart hammering as Roman pulled back the red velvet curtain.

When Roman froze with a small gasp, that's when Ethan realized it had all gone to plan.

He watched Roman bend down and pick up the small velvet box that had been resting atop a rose laid across one of the chairs. Ethan vowed to emblazon this image in his memory, to hold it close for all time—Roman, wide eyes glistening as he picked up the ring box, one of the world's most beautiful opera houses stretching out behind him.

Then he turned. Behind Ethan, Rachel, Andy, and Donnie, who'd arrived the day before in secret, stepped through the curtain and into their little box.

Blinking back tears, Roman stood up straight.

And that's when Ethan sank to one knee, gently taking the ring box from Roman's palm and opening it.

"Restless Roman, you will forever run circles in my heart. I'd tell you that you were everything I dreamed I'd find one day, but I didn't know to dream of someone as wild and beautiful and wonderful as you. Throughout our lives, we have meant different things to each other. But from this day forward, I want to play only one role in your life. The man who protects you, nourishes you, and loves you."

"I get to cry now, right?" Roman croaked.

"If the answer's yes, then of course, baby."

"Yes," he said, nodding as the tears came. "Yes, Ethan Blake. I will marry you."

"Now's the part where you kiss him, Romy," Rachel whispered.

As more heads turned to take in the scene in their box and the familiar pose of a proposal was recognized, a little ripple of cheers broke out. And they kissed for the first time as fiancés.

A short while later, they were sitting hand in hand as Lucy Russo's favorite aria, the one that had once sustained her heart, rose to the rafters and beyond. And as the music soared, Ethan, hand in hand with Roman, felt like he'd touched the sky once more.

Discover More Christopher Rice

Sapphire Sunset, Sapphire Cove, Book 1
By Christopher Rice writing as C. Travis Rice

For the first time *New York Times* bestselling author Christopher Rice writes as C. Travis Rice. Under his new pen name, Rice offers tales of passion, intrigue, and steamy romance between men. The first novel, SAPPHIRE SUNSET, transports you to a beautiful luxury resort on the sparkling Southern California coast where strong-willed heroes release the shame that blocks their heart's desires.

Logan Murdoch is a fighter, a survivor, and a provider. When he leaves a distinguished career in the Marine Corps to work security at a luxury beachfront resort, he's got one objective: pay his father's mounting medical bills. That means Connor Harcourt, the irresistibly handsome scion of the wealthy family that owns Sapphire Cove, is strictly off-limits, despite his sassy swagger and beautiful blue eyes. Logan's life is all about sacrifices; Connor is privilege personified. But temptation is a beast that demands to be fed, and a furtive kiss ignites instant passion, forcing Logan to slam the brakes. Hard.

Haunted by their frustrated attraction, the two men find themselves hurled back together when a headline-making scandal threatens to ruin the resort they both love. This time, there's no easy escape from the magnetic pull of their white hot desire. Will saving Sapphire Cove help forge the union they crave, or will it drive them apart once more?

Sapphire Spring, Sapphire Cove, Book 2
By Christopher Rice writing as C. Travis Rice

Under his new pen name, C. Travis Rice, *New York Times* bestselling author Christopher Rice offers tales of passion, intrigue, and steamy romance between men. The second novel, SAPPHIRE SPRING, once again transports you to a beautiful luxury resort on the sparkling Southern California coast where strong-willed heroes release the shame that blocks their heart's desires.

Naser Kazemi has never met a problem a good spending plan couldn't fix. But working as the chief accountant for his best friend's resort isn't turning out to be the dream job he'd hoped for. It doesn't help that his fashion designer sister is planning an event that just might bring Sapphire Cove crashing down all around them. When the wild party unexpectedly reunites him with Mason Worther, the gorgeous former jock who made his high school experience a living hell, things go from bad to seductive.

The former golden boy's adult life is a mess, and he knows it's time to reform his hard partying ways. But for Mason, cleaning up his act means cleaning up his prior misdeeds. And he plans to start with Naser, by submitting to whatever the man demands of him to make things right. The offer ignites an all-consuming passion both men have denied for years. But can they confront their painful past without losing each other in the process?

Dance of Desire
By Christopher Rice

When Amber Watson walks in on her husband in the throes of extramarital passion with one of his employees, her comfortable, passion-free life is shattered in an instant. Worse, the fate of the successful country music bar that bears her family's name suddenly hangs in the balance. Her soon to be ex-husband is one of the bar's official owners; his mistress, one of its employees. Will her divorce destroy her late father's legacy?

Not if Amber's adopted brother Caleb has anything to do with it. The wandering cowboy has picked the perfect time for a homecoming. Better yet, he's determined to use his brains and his fists to put Amber's ex in his place and keep the family business intact. But Caleb's long absence has done nothing to dim the forbidden desire between him and the woman the State of Texas considers to be his sister.

Years ago, when they were just teenagers, Caleb and Amber shared a passionate first kiss beside a moonlit lake. But that same night, tragedy claimed the life of Caleb's parents and the handsome young man went from being a family friend to Amber's adopted brother. Has enough time passed for the two of them to throw off the roles Amber's father picked for them all those years ago? Will their desire for each other save the family business or put it in greater danger?

DANCE OF DESIRE is the first contemporary romance from award-winning, *New York Times* bestselling author Christopher Rice, told with the author's trademark humor and heart. It also introduces readers to a quirky and beautiful town in the Texas Hill Country called Chapel Springs.

READER ADVISORY. DANCE OF DESIRE contains fantasies of dubious consent, acted on by consenting adults. Readers with sensitivities to those issues should be advised.

Desire & Ice
by Christopher Rice

Danny Patterson isn't a teenager anymore. He's the newest and youngest sheriff's deputy in Surrender, Montana. A chance encounter with his former schoolteacher on the eve of the biggest snowstorm to hit Surrender in years shows him that some schoolboy crushes never fade. Sometimes they mature into grown-up desire.

It's been years since Eliza Brightwell set foot in Surrender. So why is she back now? And why does she seem like she's running from something? To solve this mystery, Danny disobeys a direct order from Sheriff Cooper MacKenzie and sets out into a fierce blizzard, where his courage and his desire might be the only things capable of saving Eliza from a dark force out of her own past.

The Flame
By Christopher Rice

IT ONLY TAKES A MOMENT...
Cassidy Burke has the best of both worlds, a driven and successful

husband and a wild, impulsive best friend. But after a decadent Mardi Gras party, Cassidy finds both men pulling away from her. Did the three of them awaken secret desires during a split-second of alcohol-fueled passion? Or is Mardi Gras a time when rules are meant to be broken without consequence?

Only one thing is for certain—the chill that's descended over her marriage, and her most important friendship, will soon turn into a deep freeze if she doesn't do something. And soon.

LIGHT THIS FLAME AT THE SCENE OF YOUR GREATEST PASSION AND ALL YOUR DESIRES WILL BE YOURS.

The invitation stares out at her from the window of a French Quarter boutique. The store's owner claims to have no knowledge of the strange candle. But Cassidy can't resist its intoxicating scent or the challenge written across its label in elegant cursive. With the strike of a match and one tiny flame, she will call forth a supernatural being with the ultimate power—the power to unchain the heart, the power to remove the fear that stands between a person and their truest desires.

The Surrender Gate
A Desire Exchange Novel
By Christopher Rice

Emily Blaine's life is about to change. Arthur Benoit, the kindly multimillionaire who has acted as her surrogate father for years, has just told her he's leaving her his entire estate, and he only has a few months to live. Soon Emily will go from being a restaurant manager with a useless English degree to the one of the richest and most powerful women in New Orleans. There's just one price. Arthur has written a letter to his estranged son Ryan he hopes will mend the rift between them, and he wants Emily to deliver the letter before it's too late. But finding Ryan won't be easy. He's been missing for years. He was recently linked to a mysterious organization called The Desire Exchange. But is The Desire Exchange just an urban legend? Or are the rumors true? Is it truly a secret club where the wealthy can live out their most private sexual fantasies?

It's a task Emily can't undertake alone. But there's only one man qualified to help her, her gorgeous and confident best friend, Jonathan Claiborne. She's suspected Jonathan of working as a high-priced escort for months now, and she's willing to bet that while giving pleasure to some of the most powerful men in New Orleans, Jonathan has uncovered some possible leads to The Desire Exchange—and to Ryan Benoit. But Emily's attempt to uncover Jonathan's secret life lands the two of them in hot water. Literally. In order to escape the clutches of one of Jonathan's most powerful and dangerous clients, they're forced to act on long buried desires—for each other.

When Emily's mission turns into an undercover operation, Jonathan insists on going with her. He also insists they continue to explore their impossible, reckless passion for each other. Enter Marcus Dylan, the hard-charging ex-Navy SEAL Arthur has hired to keep Emily safe. But Marcus has been hired for another reason. He, too, has a burning passion for Emily, a passion that might keep Emily from being distracted and confused by a best friend who claims he might be able to go straight just for her. But Marcus is as rough and controlling as Jonathan is sensual and reckless. As Emily searches for a place where the rich turn their fantasies into reality, she will be forced to decide which one of her own long-ignored fantasies should become her reality. But as Emily, Jonathan, and Marcus draw closer to The Desire Exchange itself, they find their destination isn't just shrouded in mystery, but in magic as well.

Kiss the Flame
A Desire Exchange Novella
By Christopher Rice

Are some risks worth taking?
Laney Foley is the first woman from her hard working family to attend college. That's why she can't act on her powerful attraction to one of the gorgeous teaching assistants in her Introduction to Art History course. Getting involved with a man who has control over her final grade is just too risky. But ever since he first laid eyes on her,

Michael Brouchard seems to think about little else but the two of them together. And it's become harder for Laney to ignore his intelligence and his charm.

During a walk through the French Quarter, an intoxicating scent that reminds Laney of her not-so-secret admirer draws her into an elegant scented candle shop. The shop's charming and mysterious owner seems to have stepped out of another time, and he offers Laney a gift that could break down the walls of her fear in a way that can only be described as magic. But will she accept it?

Light this flame at the scene of your greatest passion and all your desires will be yours...

Lilliane Williams is a radiant, a supernatural being with the power to make your deepest sexual fantasy take shape around you with just a gentle press of her lips to yours. But her gifts came at a price. Decades ago, she set foot inside what she thought was an ordinary scented candle shop in the French Quarter. When she resisted the magical gift offered to her inside, Lilliane was endowed with eternal youth and startling supernatural powers, but the ability to experience and receive romantic love was removed from her forever. When Lilliane meets a young woman who seems poised to make the same mistake she did years before, she becomes determined to stop her, but that will mean revealing her truth to a stranger. Will Lilliane's story provide Laney with the courage she needs to open her heart to the kind of true love only magic can reveal?

About Christopher Rice writing as C. Travis Rice

C. Travis Rice is the pen name New York Times bestselling novelist Christopher Rice devotes to steamy tales of passion, intrigue and romance between men. He has published multiple bestselling books in multiple genres and been the recipient of a Lambda Literary Award. He is an executive producer on the AMC Studios adaptations of the novels The Vampire Chronicles and The Lives of the Mayfair Witches by his late mother Anne Rice. Together with his best friend and producing partner, New York Times bestselling novelist, Eric Shaw Quinn, he runs the production company Dinner Partners. Among other projects, they produce the podcast and video network, TDPS, which you can find at www.TheDinnerPartyShow.com. Learn more about C. Travis Rice and Christopher Rice at:

www.christopherricebooks.com.

Sign up for the Blue Box Press/1001 Dark Nights Newsletter
and be entered to win a Tiffany Lock necklace.

There's a contest every quarter!

Go to www.TheBlueBoxPress.com to subscribe.

As a bonus, all subscribers can download
FIVE FREE exclusive books!

Discover 1001 Dark Nights Collection Ten

DRAGON LOVER by Donna Grant
A Dragon Kings Novella

KEEPING YOU by Aurora Rose Reynolds
An Until Him/Her Novella

HAPPILY EVER NEVER by Carrie Ann Ryan
A Montgomery Ink Legacy Novella

DESTINED FOR ME by Corinne Michaels
A Come Back for Me/Say You'll Stay Crossover

MADAM ALANA by Audrey Carlan
A Marriage Auction Novella

DIRTY FILTHY BILLIONAIRE by Laurelin Paige
A Dirty Universe Novella

HIDE AND SEEK by Laura Kaye
A Blasphemy Novella

TANGLED WITH YOU by J. Kenner
A Stark Security Novella

TEMPTED by Lexi Blake
A Masters and Mercenaries Novella

THE DANDELION DIARY by Devney Perry
A Maysen Jar Novella

CHERRY LANE by Kristen Proby
A Huckleberry Bay Novella

THE GRAVE ROBBER by Darynda Jones
A Charley Davidson Novella

CRY OF THE BANSHEE by Heather Graham
A Krewe of Hunters Novella

DARKEST NEED by Rachel Van Dyken
A Dark Ones Novella

CHRISTMAS IN CAPE MAY by Jennifer Probst
A Sunshine Sisters Novella

A VAMPIRE'S MATE by Rebecca Zanetti
A Dark Protectors/Rebels Novella

WHERE IT BEGINS by Helena Hunting
A Pucked Novella

Also from Blue Box Press

THE MARRIAGE AUCTION by Audrey Carlan
Season One, Volume One
Season One, Volume Two
Season One, Volume Three
Season One, Volume Four

THE JEWELER OF STOLEN DREAMS by M.J. Rose

SAPPHIRE STORM by Christopher Rice writing as C. Travis Rice
A Sapphire Cove Novel

ATLAS: THE STORY OF PA SALT by Lucinda Riley and Harry Whittaker

LOVE ON THE BYLINE by Xio Axelrod
A Plays and Players Novel

A SOUL OF ASH AND BLOOD by Jennifer L. Armentrout
A Blood and Ash Novel

FIGHTING THE PULL by Kristen Ashley
A River Rain Novel

VISIONS OF FLESH AND BLOOD by Jennifer L. Armentrout and
Rayvn Salvador
A Blood and Ash/Flesh and Fire Compendium

A FIRE IN THE FLESH by Jennifer L. Armentrout
A Flesh and Fire Novel

On Behalf of Blue Box Press,
Liz Berry, M.J. Rose, and Jillian Stein would like to thank ~

Steve Berry
Doug Scofield
Benjamin Stein
Kim Guidroz
Tanaka Kangara
Asha Hossain
Chris Graham
Chelle Olson
Kasi Alexander
Jessica Saunders
Stacey Tardif
Dylan Stockton
Kate Boggs
Richard Blake
and Simon Lipskar

CPSIA information can be obtained
at www.ICGtesting.com
Printed in the USA
LVHW030446130423
744167LV00001B/135

9 781957 568256